I DREAM OF IBERIA

THE HEIR OF ATARGATIS
BOOK TWO

A.G. WHITT

For Ryan,
Whose knowledge of gems, rocks, and fossils brought the stones of
Atargatis to life.

PROLOGUE

*P*rofessor Liam Brennan absentmindedly rapped his fingers on his desk. The exasperatingly loud clock that the college refused to let him remove due its historical significance ticked away on the wall of his office, driving him to the brink of insanity. Of course he had returned to Dublin, but now that he was here, he felt a lingering sense of regret for his lack of presence on the voyage taking place across the country.

But that was foolish. He knew he had made the right choice in turning away. In fact, he felt more than mildly embarrassed that it took a lad he barely knew reminding him to be a man to get him to see sense. To think that he had even considered risking never seeing his wife or child again for the sake of chasing myths...it sent a shiver of shame down his spine.

Still, there was the adventurer's spirit within him–the one that often battled with the academic persona he outwardly portrayed–telling him he had missed out on the opportunity of a lifetime. He looked wistfully around the room at all of the artifacts procured from his adventures across the globe, thinking that even a simple pebble from the phantom island of Hy-Brasil would have been enough to complete his collection.

And *when*–if ever–would he hear of their success or demise? Would he have to go back to Galway and track down Aidan McCarthy in his signature dingy pub? Or would he simply turn on the news one day to find that two brothers, Seamus and Aidan from Belfast, had been swept out to sea and never seen again?

His thoughts were interrupted by a loud knock on the door that made him jump.

"Professor, do you have a moment for me?"

Given the time in the evening, he should have known it would be *her*. It was an hour that most students wouldn't consider appropriate for visiting their professors. But of course, she wasn't like most students. She batted her long, dark eyelashes at him in her usual mischievous way that presumably worked on everyone else as she entered his office without waiting for permission. She had undoubtedly come to ask for an extension on her *Comparing The Ideals of The Middle Ages and Renaissance* essay, or to make extremely inappropriate comments designed to make him sweat. She relished Liam's discomfort, and she was the bane of his existence.

"Sure, Carly, what is it?" he said, sighing and rubbing his nose with exasperation. He had dropped the pretense of patience for her long ago, but his careless attitude only seemed to encourage her.

She did not take a seat, but rather pranced around his office with her ballerina's grace, gently running her fingers across his possessions in a manner of presumed authority that made his blood boil.

"The essay..." she began.

"Let me guess, you need an extension."

She glanced up at him with deep brown eyes that looked like they belonged to the face of a newborn puppy rather than the countenance of a devious young adult. The trait was extremely misleading, and surely assisted in trapping many others in her web. But not him. Liam found her insincerity revolting.

"I've been working so hard," Carly said, unblinking. "I just need one more day."

He wanted to say no, to tell her that she was a lazy, dreadfully over privileged child whose aristocratic daddy had bought her way into one of the most prestigious universities in the world. He wanted to tell her that she had no business being in the same *universe* as her classmates, let alone lecture halls.

But he couldn't say that, because as much as he hated to admit it, she frightened him.

The truth—and that's all that *should* matter—was that not a single one of the indecent interactions that occurred between himself and Carly Connor were any fault of his own, and he would defend his honor regarding that statement until the day he died. Not only did the sheer existence of the girl repulse him, but he loved his wife Bridget and their precious son Angus dearly. He had never—and *would* never—do anything to jeopardize his family.

No, Liam Brennan was afraid of Carly Connor because one of his oldest friends and mentors in higher education, Raj Atarga, had warned him long ago about students just like her.

"YOU NEED to be careful around your students," Raj said, wagging his finger at him over the coffee table. "As a young professor, all eyes will be on you. Everyone expects you to fuck up, and the temptation will be there. Trust me, I would know."

They were sitting out on the back patio of Raj's house in South Florida, and he was giving one of his fatherly lectures that Liam hadn't asked for after having told him the good news—he had received his first offer for a teaching job. It was a teaching assistant position at a small local college outside of

Cork, but still. It was something. It was the first big step in his career.

He vaguely remembered Raj alluding to an unsavory situation with a student from his past, but if Liam hadn't held his mentor in such high regard, he might have rolled his eyes. In Liam's opinion, Raj had been far too harsh with himself when speaking of her, whatever her name had been.

"But Raj, nothing ever happened between you two," Liam said. "And besides, she was of age. So even if it had, it wouldn't have been the end of the world."

He glanced up at his friend again and saw the distinct shadow of shame cross his face that told him his assumptions regarding Raj's past may have been wrong.

"I made a mistake that I'll regret every day for the rest of my life," Raj said quietly, dropping his voice so there was no chance of his teenage daughter overhearing their conversation. Jasmine was reading on the couch just inside the sliding glass door, entirely oblivious to her father's misdeeds. "I should never have done it, but she was a pretty girl, and I was a lonely idiot."

Liam slumped in his chair, taken aback.

"So you *did* sleep with her?" he whispered, trying his best not to allow the esteemed opinion he held of the man across from him to be warped by this discovery. But it was difficult. He couldn't believe it.

"Once," Raj replied curtly, nodding his head as his eyes misted over in regretful recollection. "And I'll never forgive myself for it. Especially considering what ensued afterward."

"Well, as I said before, she was an adult," Liam replied, trying to justify the transgression aloud. "And of course you were lonely. You've never been married, or even had a girlfriend in the time I've known you."

"Oh, thanks for the reminder, man," Raj said sarcastically, pouring a glass of port for both of them. "Do you come visit just to insult me?"

"No, it's because I need a place to stay when I come to the states," Liam quipped, taking a deep sip of the aubergine liquid that truthfully was a bit too sweet for him. Port had never been to his liking, even when he had gone to school right next to the Duoro Valley, the rolling hills from which the delicate beverage originated. "And hotels in Miami are ungodly expensive."

Raj let out a hollow laugh, but he wasn't finished with his sermon.

"Make no mistake, it wasn't in any way acceptable," he said severely. "And I had no one to blame but myself for the nightmare she became after I did it."

Liam cocked his head. "What did she do?"

"It started off as mild stalking on campus…dropping into my office late at night, leaving notes, all that stuff," Raj replied. "But it evolved into something much worse, and obviously I couldn't do anything about it. One of the most unbelievable things she did was photoshop a picture of us together and put it on my desk before class. It actually looked real, even back in those days. Can you *imagine* if someone on staff had seen that?"

"Yikes," Liam replied, his own stomach turning at the thought. "So what happened? She graduated and left you alone?"

Raj grimaced.

"Ah, I'm so glad you asked, young Liam," he said, the air of wisdom exuding from him in the way it always did when he prepared to bestow a lesson upon his young mentee. "Her delusions about our fake relationship combined with my fear of discovery for being a piece of shit quite literally drove me out of the country."

Liam's jaw dropped. He hadn't been expecting that. "*That's* why you took the post at The University of Porto? Because of *her*?"

"Yes," Raj replied bitterly. "I was convinced she was going to ruin my life. She nearly did, several times. I got tired of the paranoia."

"So you picked up and moved to Portugal?"

"Yes," he said simply. "I kept thinking of Jasmine, and what it would do to her if she ever heard something like that about her father. It would destroy her."

Liam nodded, glancing at the girl in the living room who he knew thought the world of her dad. And then his final bit of curiosity got the better of him.

"What was her name? The student?"

Raj rolled the port around in his mouth as revulsion colored his face. Liam thought he might even spit it out.

"Camila."

PART I

AVENGER

CHAPTER 1

THE HEIR AWAKENS

NOHOVAL COVE, COUNTY CORK

*H*e was an incredibly selfless lover when it came to using his mouth. Each time—and there had been many, even in the short period we'd been together—his head dropped below my waist, he became a dutiful servant in the pursuit of satisfying me. Of course I never wanted to envision how much *practice* it had taken him to master the art of it, but I appreciated the novelty of it, nonetheless. There were so few men who understood why it was considered a delicacy on the menu of the female experience.

I was rising and falling like the waves on the shore where we rested, undisturbed in the privacy of our isolated oasis.

"*Seamus*," I said his name in the same voice of overwhelmed resignation that I had now grown accustomed to sighing as if I had said it all my life.

He looked up at me, emerald eyes twinkling.

"Are ye pleased, *a stór?*" he asked, slipping two fingers inside of me while I temporarily mourned the loss of his tongue.

He knew how much I loved it when he called me various Irish Gaelic terms of endearment, particularly considering his rich, nearly old-world Northern Ireland accent. Now knowing his mother's origins as a mystical selkie, a mermaid-like creature of the sea that could have been significantly older than she appeared, I wondered if it were her influence that still made his *"you's"* sound like *"ye"* and prompted his usage of *"aye"* so often. As he pleased me over and over, I didn't really care where it came from, to be honest. I just liked it.

"Yes," I replied.

His dark red hair caught the sunlight with a glimmer of auburn as his freckled cheeks rose into a smile of autumn leaves. With his ruggedly handsome embodiment of the most beautiful features of the Irish people, he was so inexplicably attractive to me.

He continued his methodical practice, finding the nerves in my body that threatened to shatter me at any moment. I let my head fall back onto the rough sand, deeply breathing in the salty air as he serviced me. I felt, especially at times like these, extremely fortunate that the curse of being an Amalgam–a mermaid unable to transform back into the human version of themselves–had evaded me despite having been marked by one when I was just a child. That's what they did, after all. Marked innocent, human victims with the mermaid curse that would eventually drag them back into the sea forever.

Even if I had only avoided the curse because I was actually the descendent of Atargatis, the original mermaid goddess of ancient Mesopotamia, and therefore thrust into a world of underwater conflict in which I was obligated to participate...I was still exceedingly grateful that Seamus and I could both change back and forth at will. My tail's transition to legs took several minutes longer than a regular selkie's—including the one who was between mine now—but it was worth the wait.

The familiar wave of ecstasy that Seamus brought upon me

each time he made love to me was approaching, and I didn't resist. I allowed myself to be pulled underwater with the current, succumbing to the limp helplessness that sent the addictive heat radiating through my body.

I sighed.

He smirked and rose to meet me, placing a hand on the large rock beside my head. He was, of course, more than ready for me, and although I thought I could die happily where I was, I still wanted him again. I reached up and pulled him down toward me, kissing him tenderly and tasting myself in his mouth.

"*Christ*," he swore under his breath as he pressed himself inside me.

This time I smirked as the uncontrollable chemistry that existed between us ensued, with Seamus giving himself to me while he whispered Irish curse words into my ear that sent shivers of pleasure down my spine. Before I had ever been with him romantically, I had speculated about his nature as a lover in my dreams, and I had been right. When he made love to me, he liked to make me *his.* I let him do it now as he braced himself against the rock with one arm, the other holding my waist flush to the shore.

After another few thrusts of impassioned force, he bent down to kiss me gently, reminding me of his love. I shuddered as he slowly dragged his lips down my throat, sending me to the surface again. I had never had a lover like him—someone who knew what I wanted at all times, even if the desires were hidden in the darkest corners of my mind. Because we had fallen in love with one another so suddenly and deeply, it was intoxicating.

But there was a tiny voice in my head that told me I shouldn't enjoy it as much as I did. My almost-fiancé from my human life, Matt, had been dead now for over a year, and I wondered when the guilt I felt for being with someone else would subside. Especially now, considering I had learned the boating accident that had taken both Matt and my father's lives on the morning I was supposed to get engaged may not have been an accident at all.

Camila, the nefarious Amalgam who claimed it was her right to seek the stones of Atargatis in order to harness the power of the seas, along with Cearbhall–the leader of the Hy-Brasil Irish Amalgam clan–had made it clear only days ago that my late father, Raj, had been a victim of their choosing. How they knew him, I had no idea. I would find out, as soon as I could get a moment alone with the evil woman who I now knew was responsible for ruining my life.

But another factor behind my guilt was the fact that I *didn't* think my life wasn't ruined, despite having lost the two most important people in my world. Matt's death and my subsequent depressive episode had led me to go on the trip to Ireland with my friends where I met Seamus, who I knew now was my soulmate. This new, supernatural existence we shared was just one of many ways that we were bonded. He had gone to the literal ends of the earth to find me after my disappearance, acting on the whim that he, too, thought the Irish selkie blood ran through his veins.

And finally…I had discovered that my mother who had abandoned me as a child had, in fact, only done so out of obligation regarding the mermaid curse. My Irish mother, Aine, was also a selkie. When she had a child with my Syrian father, Raj, who was a descendent of Atargatis, it ignited the ancient bloodline of the mermaid goddess once more. Somehow–and I didn't fully understand it yet–my mother had been imprisoned by the Amalgams in Cyprus for the entirety of my life, and now she had escaped. Now she was looking for me, and I for her.

* * *

SOME TIME LATER, Seamus ran his fingers through my black hair and kissed me on the shoulder before standing decisively.

"We should go, aye?"

We had quickly departed the Skellig Islands when my newly discovered cousin, Aisling, informed us of my mother's escape. Thanks to Seamus bringing one of the stones of Atargatis from Professor Brennan's office, I had a brief vision of my mother in a place reminiscent of my childhood home with my father—Porto, Portugal. I was somehow able to communicate with my loved ones through the stones, and I hoped the citrine that hung around Seamus' neck would lead us to Aine as it had led him to me.

Aisling had hurriedly told us that The Green Window we'd need for the fastest passage to Porto was just as temperamental as the mermaid portal of the seas back in Bangor Bay–it was not always open. But unlike the mysterious whirlpool in Belfast, this one was relatively predictable. The Window was in the sea just south of Cork, and would be open only when the moon was visible.

We knew the closest we could get to wait for our passage without risking being seen was Nohoval Cove, a picturesque inlet near Cork, just east of Kinsale. The sun was setting, momentarily relieving the pain that my connection to the goddess of the moon (among many other things Atargatis was known for) caused me. I had discovered that while my bloodline to her meant I *could* land-walk unlike most Amalgams, it was extremely painful for me to be in the direct sunlight when I had legs. For that reason, Seamus and I had chosen to pass the time in the shady parts of the inlet.

We'd been here for two days, patiently waiting for the sky to clear and reveal the moon. We could likely have already made the full swim to Porto without the underwater highway network within that time frame, but…I hadn't minded how we passed the time.

The final rays of sun hit me as I stood, sending a sharp surge of discomfort down my leg again. I winced, hoping Seamus didn't notice, but he did.

"Jasmine," he said seriously. "I don't want ye to keep hurting yourself. Ye promised you'd tell me if it was painful."

"I'm fine," I said quickly. "The alternative is much worse, anyway."

The alternative being we didn't go on land and we didn't get to have one another. He had carried me up to the top of Skellig Michael when I was nearly shaking in pain from the sun, helping me find relief in the shade of the ancient huts at the top. Ever since then, he'd ardently watched for any signs of my physical struggle. I thought I'd hidden it pretty well, but apparently not.

"I want ye just as badly, mo chroí," Seamus said, tilting my chin upward to look at him. I rustled his red waves, sending a shower of grains of sand back onto the shore. "I just don't ye want to hurt yourself."

"Really," I said, not meeting his gaze. "It's not that bad."

"Catch yourself on, Jasmine," he said with a raised eyebrow as I stumbled once more. He scooped me up in one swift motion, his green eyes full of concern. I let him do it, despite how helplessly pathetic it made me feel that I could hardly stand.

He carried me to the water and descended into it with me, muttering something about my stubbornness. The moment my feet touched the water, I began to feel the soothing coolness of my transformation taking back over. At last I felt the sweet relief of my legs becoming one, and my body turning back into the form which the goddess of the seas intended for me.

The iridescent tail that I had been so terrified of the first time I saw it was admittedly beautiful. Greenish-silver in the sun, it sparkled like an opalescent version of an emerald as it appeared; each scale crafted with the intention of making me a magical creature of the Irish seas.

"Much better," I said as Seamus melted into the water next to me, his tail that looked just like mine materializing beneath the glass surface. The water was freezing cold, no doubt, given it was autumn in Ireland, but we were protected from it by our supernatural blood.

He touched my cheek affectionately, his muscular, freckled arms gleaming in the amber sunset.

"Atargatis calling ye back to the water," he mused, voicing my thoughts. We began to flit across the surface at a leisurely pace, turning toward the south.

"I hope Aisling wasn't too mad at me," I said, backstroking across the waves.

Seamus smiled. "Aye, well you're the Queen of the Seas now. Ordering your subjects around is something ye'll have to get used to, so it is."

"Very funny."

I didn't care that I was the Heir to an ancient mermaid crown. I didn't want anything to do with it. I wanted to find the stones before the other side could use them for evil, and that was it.

"It's for the best," he continued. "I know ye want to do this part alone."

Despite her strong objection to doing so, Aisling had eventually agreed to my request for her to return to Hy-Brasil and reunite with her own partner, Fintan, who was undoubtedly missing her very much by now. We would see her again soon, but I couldn't allow yet another person to take on my burdens. I was going to first set out to find my mother, reasoning that I had seen a concrete vision of her whereabouts, whereas the matter of the stones was more abstract. I thought–*hoped*, rather–that she might have information on where they were as well.

"Last chance," I said to Seamus as we swam further out into the open water. I pointed toward the general direction of the shores of Cobh.

Seamus didn't even turn to look at me, but his side profile revealed his jaw to be firm.

"I'm not going, Jasmine," he said. "Not without ye, ever."

"Well, you have some messes to clean up back home," I said. "Messes that are my fault."

I looked down at the water, the guilt of having torn him away from his normal life eating at me again.

"No, they're not," he said, his green eyes bright with sincerity. "And we have bigger things to worry about right now, aye?"

Of course Seamus' discovery of his selkie nature was much more of a problematic complication to his old life than mine. Considering both my father and my fiancé were dead, and everyone thought *I* was as well, I had nothing important to return to. He, on the other hand, had a successful career back in London, friends who were surely worried sick about his disappearance during their trip to Ireland, and his brother Aidan and Professor Liam Brennan who were entirely oblivious as to whether or not their mission to send him to the mystical land where the selkies of the Aran Islands dwelled had been successful. I wanted him to go back, at least temporarily, to let everyone know he was alright. To Galway first, and then London.

I thought my chances of returning to my own friends were much slimmer, given I had yet to hear of a Green Window that led to the Americas. Aisling told me point blank that she didn't think there were any until at least the Mediterranean, which meant a journey to Tampa could take a lot more time than I had to spare right now. I thought of Kiana often, of course, considering she had been the only friend of mine who had believed in my survival at any point. I held onto the unlikely hope that she could feel that I was alive in the way that Seamus had, even though she had abandoned the search for me when he hadn't.

But I could see Seamus wasn't budging, and I knew better than to try and force him. Despite the brevity of our time together, I sensed immediately that he was strong-willed. The man would never do a damn thing he didn't want to do...that was certain.

"Fine," I said, and we took a sweeping dive into the depths of the Atlantic.

I inhaled the salty water that breathed life into my lungs, instantly filtering out the filth of land-walker air, as I now called it. There was something so fulfilling about the nutritious ocean to me now, and the tiny slits on the side of my neck thanked me incessantly for satiating them once more.

"This way," Seamus said, reaching for my hand under the waves.

There wasn't much to see beyond endless slopes of sand as we made our way toward the ocean floor, flying at a speed that whipped my hair from my eyes. One thing I *was* looking forward to in Portugal was the variety of oceanic landscapes. I recalled it from my childhood when I lived there with my father, of course, but to see it from this new vantage point would be something different entirely. I couldn't wait to see the rainbow hues of fish and coral, which were now all part of my own environment rather than decorative accents to be observed as an outsider.

"How will we know where it is?" he asked, gesturing vaguely around the dark water.

"Oh, trust me, we won't be able to miss it," I said knowingly, gazing up at the surface to see that the sun had fully set and the sky was black.

The Green Window we sought was hidden within a coccolithophore bloom—a collection of microscopic marine algae. It was filled with calcium carbonate plates called coccoliths, which would make it look somewhat like an underwater cloud. The blooms' role in the removal of carbon dioxide from the atmosphere made them crucial to marine life, but I knew that they could be dangerous. Not to us, of course, but to the humans, maybe. I knew all about them given Raj's occupation as a professor of marine biology, and would be easily able to identify it once we were upon it.

I voiced this to Seamus, and he grinned as he shook his head in admiration.

"I dunno what a brilliant woman like ye is doing with me," he said, laughing. "Ye know something about everything."

"Please," I said, rolling my eyes as he swam in front of me. "Just the byproduct of being a professor's daughter."

My memories of Raj had always been fond, but now they held a deeper significance. Since embracing my nature as a creature of the sea, my recollections of conversations with him had evolved into vital clues essential for my survival. Raj's insights spanned a multitude of subjects—from marine life to geography, mythology, astronomy, and even history to some extent. *He* was the one who had known something about everything. As I embarked on the next phase of my destiny, I knew I would rely on Raj's wisdom more than ever. I only wished he could witness me putting it into practice.

"I think that's it," I said as we approached the swirling, underwater cloud. The seemingly celestial body churned in slow motion directly ahead, its mystical pink foam calling to us.

Seamus led the way and I grasped his arm tightly. I held my breath as the whirlpool enveloped us in its magical substance, the floating violet clouds beginning to noiselessly vibrate in preparation for transporting us to another place. Another sea, another country, another world.

CHAPTER 2

NOSTALGIA

"Feels like returning home to ye, doesn't it?" Seamus asked as we emerged to the surface off the coast of Porto.

"Sort of," I said quietly. I didn't know how I felt.

To some degree it did feel like coming home, because of all the memories I had here. Back when Raj was still teaching astronomy, he was posted at the University of Porto and we had spent three years exploring the entirety of the miraculous Iberian Peninsula. But Porto was also where I had fallen off the boat as a child and was marked by the mermaid curse that would alter the course of my life forever. I absently rubbed the silver scar on my palm that had been the catalyst for turning me into what I was. Seamus noticed me doing so, and he brought my palm to his lips and kissed it gently, reminding me that although it had happened for him in a different way, he was cursed, too.

The smell of the water was certainly one that stuck out vividly in my memory. It was a rich, earthy scent that I could nearly taste. I swallowed a mouthful of it, realizing there was no difference between drinking and breathing for me anymore. It slid down my throat with ease.

"Let's go," I said, pointing vaguely to the shore.

Our plan upon arrival was hardly sophisticated. There was nothing to do but to look around and hope that we were correct in assuming that the gem around Seamus' neck was a reliable guide in finding my mother. This was where I had seen her within it back on the Skelligs.

Unlike the luxuries that we had been afforded in Ireland, there was a lack of smaller islands just off the coast of the Iberian Peninsula, making it impossible to settle anywhere besides right next to civilization. In true merfolk fashion, we found a lagoon to lurk in that was just south of Porto, called the Aveiro. Calling it a lagoon was a generous term; it was really a shallow area of murky nothingness.

"Ready?" Seamus asked me as we slowed to a halt. We didn't dare go to the surface, but there was certainly not a ton of boat traffic near us. We were alone.

"Yes," I said, taking a deep breath.

I took the golden stone from his hands and looked into the near-translucence of it, willing myself to see a window. As soon as my fingers made contact with the hard edge, I began to feel the familiar warmth that indicated it was working.

I saw something, but I realized that this vision was different from the others I had already experienced. It was cloudy, as if there were a layer of mist pushing up against the walls of my mind, trying to prevent me from seeing what was happening. As I pushed back against it, I felt myself beginning to swoon in the water, and Seamus caught my arm.

"I've got ye," he said steadily.

And then I saw her.

Actually, I *was* her.

I saw my mother's red hair beneath me, and I was snaking through the water as quickly as I could. Her heart was pounding furiously–I felt like it was my own. She was taking shallow, labored breaths in the way one does when being pursued.

She whipped her head in all directions. Her changing line of sight made me dizzy since I was seeing through her eyes, and I wished she'd stop… until it occurred to me that she was doing it intentionally. She was showing me as much as she could of her surroundings. I didn't understand how it was possible, but my mother knew I was watching.

I felt as though I could vaguely hear her thoughts.

"They've found one," she seemed to be thinking.

They.

I knew who she meant. Cearbhall and Camila, of course. My heart sank with disappointment. They already had three of the stones, and now they had found a fourth. I didn't know how many there were in total, but the fact that they were ahead of us was enough to put me on edge.

"Where is it?" I replied, whispering into the stone.

She couldn't hear me. She kept swimming, and finally her eyesight landed on a coastline that I recognized. It was a tiny inlet bordered by towering rock formations that reached toward the sky; similar to Nohoval Cove. The wind was whipping violently and the sky was gray, but the water was the signature aquamarine of southern Portugal. Was this the Algarve region? There were only two people on the shore, one of them knee-deep with a camera and other strange equipment. The other was a young girl, clutching a book and a hat that both looked like they were one gust away from blowing into the ocean.

I finally understood. My mother wasn't there at all.

She couldn't directly speak to me, so she was showing me a memory instead.

"Now I know it's not what we had hoped," Raj said as we carried our beach chairs against the lashing wind. "But the sun's still out, and we came all the way here."

A large blast of cold air nearly knocked me off my feet, and I grabbed my hat before it became the property of the Atlantic. I was in a terribly sour mood, having been expecting a day of lazy relaxing in the sunshine while Raj took samples of sediment, rocks, and even small crustaceans if he was lucky. He had already begun his extracurricular activities of marine biology exploration in hopes that his interviews back at The University of Miami would go well. I had enjoyed our years in Portugal, but high school was waiting in America, and I already knew I'd have to repeat the ninth grade. I was ready to go home.

Instead of the picturesque day I had imagined, we had been given the worst weather possible and it rained the entire week. Even that morning when the thunderstorms finally ceased, we had debated driving down and saving the trip for another weekend instead. After all, we were going pretty far south of Lisbon and I hated the monotonous drive from the passenger seat as much as Raj hated to do it. There was simply no way to lug all of his oceanic exploration gear on the train, so it had been a massive undertaking for both of us. I think we both regretted it, even though he'd never admit it.

We reached the curved shoreline at last, and I was relieved to find that he had been right about the crowds, at least. There was nearly nobody else there, and I watched as the few tourists who had braved the wind inevitably gave up within the hour as their belongings went flying into the open water.

The cove was already quite secluded in comparison to others south of Lisbon, surrounded by massive cliffs that enclosed the shore in its own private circle of beauty. Even without the sunlight, the water reflected bright hues of rich turquoise, cerulean, and even hints of sapphire in the depths.

There was a cave nearby that looked irksome in the cloudy weather, but would probably have looked welcoming and cozy in the sun. I watched as Raj knelt in the shallows, picking up bits of this and that, and I eventually drifted off to sleep.

One of the stones was in that cave.

"Cearbhall and Camila are already on their way," she whispered to me.

"Praia do Calaveiro," I gasped as I came back to the present, turning to look at Seamus. "We need to get there now, before we look for my mother. It's urgent."

He didn't question how I had come to the conclusion; he was already nodding in agreement.

"Where is it?"

"We've got a bit more of a swim ahead of us," I acknowledged.

He followed my gaze south and flashed his brilliantly white grin. "Aye, well that shouldn't be a problem for us."

We took off like lightning once more, Seamus tossing me a piece of seaweed he had snagged from one of the lagoon's many twists and turns. It took all of me not to vomit immediately—it tasted shockingly different from the rich, nutrient-dense delicacy I had known back on Hy-Brasil and in Belfast. The seaweed in Ireland brought me back to life, but this…this tasted like what I imagined it to be when I was still human.

"That'll make ye miss the seaweed from Norn Iron," Seamus said with a look of disgust on his face that mirrored my own.

The swim took us longer than I thought it would. Perhaps I had been spoiled by the network of Green Windows throughout the seas surrounding Ireland—or perhaps I had overestimated how much water we could cover in a single day—but by the time we passed Lisbon, I was exhausted. Not even the teeming, colorful sea life around us could keep me alert. I flicked a bright red sea bream out of my way as I stifled a yawn.

"Let's go up," I said at last, pointing to the surface. "We have to be close by now."

We emerged and I saw the appearance of the familiar cliffs that lined the southwestern part of the peninsula. I scanned the shore as we came to a stop, looking for signs of the beach I'd only been to once in my life. I hoped I'd recognize it. The cliffs were climbing higher…surely it would be here soon…

"This is it," I said to Seamus excitedly, pointing at a large rock formation that jutted out into the sea just ahead of us.

I started forward, but he grabbed my arm.

"Wait," he said. "If Cearbhall and Camila are already there, we need a plan."

He was right. We couldn't just rush into the inlet and hope that the stone would be waiting for us, wrapped in a silk ribbon. But I was anxious.

"I just want a word alone with Camila," I said through gritted teeth. Her words spoken to me beneath Carrickfergus Castle still rang in my ears.

"Nothing is an accident…not even Raj's death."

"I understand it, believe me," Seamus said, acknowledging the validity of my hatred toward her. "But from what you've told me about these two, we've got to be strategic."

I had nearly forgotten that Seamus had never actually laid eyes upon either of the evil Amalgams of whom I spoke. He had only heard of Cearbhall and Camila through Aisling's retelling of what had happened to me when I had been kidnapped by them and taken to Belfast; both of them knowing I was the Heir of Atargatis before I did. It had been the stone of the North Sea's lack of reaction to my touch that had revealed that Oisin–Aisling's great-great-great grandfather and leader of the Belfast selkie clan–had tried to give them a fake. He had attempted to bargain the false stone in exchange for information on my mother's whereabouts. Unfortunately, Cearbhall and Camila had overpowered him and stolen the real stone, anyway. I momentarily mourned the fallen selkie leader.

Just as I was about to reply aloud, I heard something. Two whispering voices.

"Do you–" I began, but Seamus was already behind me, one hand over my mouth and the other around my waist, slowly backing us both away from the shore. His heart was pounding into my back.

It was *them*.

I looked over my shoulder as I realized there was a third heartbeat between us. It was the bright stone around Seamus' neck, pulsing in silent warning. I thought it might be Atargatis, telling us to proceed with caution.

As I strained my ears, I heard their voices clearly. They were coming from the inlet near the shore, echoing too far for a human ear to hear. I remembered Cearbhall telling me that our hearing develops later–something about it being superior to all other beings–and I prayed *he* hadn't heard *us*, already. One look at Seamus told me he was thinking the same thing.

"How the *fuck* did she escape?" Camila said exasperatedly, her voice sharp as knives as it bounced across the waves.

"Well, I told you not to let her go, but you insisted on me getting the stone," Cearbhall sniped.

Camila's scoff pierced the air. "Not *Jasmine,* you idiot. Her mother."

They were talking about our fateful exchange beneath Carrickfergus Castle, when the sea serpent known as the Ollphéist swept in to save the day, yielding to me, since it apparently answered to Atargatis. Supposedly all sea serpents did.

"She probably had more of the stones hidden somewhere," Cearbhall said with a sigh. "I wish we knew how *many* there were."

"You say that every single day," Camila replied coldly. "And yet you do nothing to seek out anyone who knows."

I breathed a sigh of relief upon hearing they didn't know the number of stones in existence, either. So we were even—at least in that way.

"If I knew who had *that* answer, I would have made hunting them a priority long ago," Cearbhall snapped back at her.

"Either way, Aine didn't have any others," Camila said dismissively. My heart froze at the sound of my mother's name. "I would have noticed when I questioned her the final time."

Cearbhall's high-pitched laugh traveled over the waves this time. "*Questioned* is a delicate term for what you did to her," he said.

My blood boiled. Seamus gripped my tensed shoulders tightly, anticipating my mad desire to fly to the inlet and rip Camila apart with my bare hands.

"I had to make sure she told me everything this time," Camila said quietly.

"Mmm or was it perhaps more that the fires of an old rivalry had been re-ignited once more?" Cearbhall replied coolly.

There was a long silence that followed. I didn't dare move.

Rivalry? What was he talking about?

"He should have been mine in the end," Camila replied severely. "Whether the magic that you *claimed* to have been there actually was or not."

He.

Did she mean...

"Well he wasn't. He was Aine's," Cearbhall said bluntly. "And now we have to deal with their bitch of a daughter."

I would have gasped, had I not been so terrified of being overheard.

So *that* was what Camila's goal had been. She had wanted to... be with *Raj.*

I felt the sticky seaweed threatening to come back up as I imagined such a thing. But how...how on earth had they even *known* one another? My mind worked furiously as I tried to piece it together. Across oceans, different timelines...it couldn't be possible. I *did* recall her saying she had spent some time in Florida. But even so, my dad was in his sixties when he died. And Camila had told me herself that she'd been several years younger than *me* when she'd changed. She could only be in her late thirties by now. That meant she was well over twenty years younger than my dad...*how—*

His student.

As soon as it crossed my mind, it became abundantly obvious. Camila had to have been one of his students at Miami. It was the only possibility that made sense, as disgusting as it was. But the romantic desire between them couldn't have been mutual...not Raj. No way. He'd never. Based on the bitterness in her voice, it didn't sound like it was.

"Now let's go find this godforsaken stone," Cearbhall mumbled upon Camila's non-answer. That was the last I heard of their conversation.

I was shaking.

"Easy," Seamus said quietly into my ear, but his voice was dark rather than reassuring. He, too, was connecting the dots in his head, but we both knew we didn't have time to dissect it now.

"My dad–" I began, but he shook his head.

"Jasmine, we've got to get the stone," he said urgently. "That's first."

He was right, and I knew it, but my head was spinning.

"How?" I said, almost hysterically, my mind unable to focus on anything other than the disturbing discovery I had just made. "They've already beaten us here."

Seamus looked toward the shore and back at me, biting his lip to conceal what I knew was a mild smirk.

"I've got an idea," he said. "But ye won't like it."

CHAPTER 3

BRUTE FORCE

s much as it pained me to admit, it was as solid of a plan as we had time to concoct.

The advantage Seamus and I had over Cearbhall and Camila was that—as far as I knew—they were unaware of his existence. Back when they had initially kidnapped me, I had no hope that I'd ever see Seamus again, because I had no idea he had become a selkie, too. Even if Cearbhall and Camila had been told that someone was looking for me by one of the other Amalgam spies on Hy-Brasil, they had never seen Seamus themselves.

We sped to the shore quickly and silently enough to see Cearbhall and Camila disappear behind an archway that seemed to lead to an underwater cave. I stayed and kept watch at a distance as Seamus slithered below the surface, lurking in the shadows of the now late afternoon created by the looming cliffs of the small inlet.

And the plan?

Again, it was rudimentary at best. I had described Cearbhall's physical stature to him, and ultimately we'd come to the conclusion that Seamus was simply going to take the stone by force.

"I don't think it'll be too difficult," he said with a shrug.

I was a realist, therefore I agreed. Seamus was tall, muscular, and generally formidable when angry, whereas Cearbhall was certainly much slighter. Additionally, Seamus had the advantage that should it come to a real fight, he could land-walk and Cearbhall could not.

"If I have to, I can drag him onto the shore," Seamus reasoned. "He can't do much harm with a fish tail on land."

"Right," I said. "But don't underestimate either of them. Cearbhall and Camila are cunning and dangerous. They're also likely armed, and we're not."

Seamus acknowledged my warning, but he was ready to go.

"Let's put this wee stone to the test," he said, tapping the yellow gem that had enabled our communication once before. "You distract Camila, and I'm going in."

As much as I didn't want him to go on his own, I knew it was the only way to ensure an even fight between him and Cearbhall. I also knew this plan meant *I* would get my moment alone with Camila, whether she liked it or not.

"Not the first test run I would have chosen," I muttered under my breath as I watched Seamus go, feeling we were putting far too much trust in the gem.

Once Seamus was outside the cave, he nodded my signal. I took the large rock I held in my hand and hurled it directly into the inlet where it cracked loudly against the rock wall. We waited a moment, and then Seamus flitted behind a large boulder just to the side of the entrance. He lurked below the water, eyes barely over the waves.

Sure enough, Cearbhall had done exactly what we had hoped and sent Camila out to investigate while he continued to look for the stone. I suspected there was a degree of distrust between the two of them, and I knew Cearbhall wouldn't let her be alone in the suspected hiding place of the treasure.

Camila exited the watery cave in a flash of her tail and looked atop the waves inquisitively. Seamus remained hidden behind her, and my heart nearly stopped as I thought she might have sensed his presence. Seeing the enemy standing so close to him terrified me, but I waited as patiently as I could.

Not yet, not yet.

Seamus nodded again, and I hurled another rock further down the shoreline where it bounced off of the cliff's wall. Camila's sharp gaze then snapped out to the open sea–unfortunately right to where I was positioned. I dropped below the water instantly.

Shit. Had she seen me?

When I emerged, I kept my eyes narrowed as slits and remained as close to the surface as I could.

I saw her squinting vaguely in my direction. The sun had risen by now, but the sky was painted with clouds that gave me a fair amount of shade to hide within. Seamus, as planned, slid into the cave behind Camila's back, so uncharacteristically silent and stealthy for a man of his height. I had learned the water had a way of disguising our true nature in that way.

I threw one more rock down the shore to draw her further away from the cave, but my stomach flipped as she now seemed to deem the disturbance unimportant. She flashed around, her tail flipping out of the water as she propelled herself back toward where Seamus had just gone.

No, no, you need to go investigate...

I must have made a sound or disturbed the surface in some way, because she then stopped in the water, turning slowly out toward the open ocean.

Oh no.

She locked eyes with me immediately, and the realization of how poorly executed our plan was hit me in the face. I shrunk backward, but it was too late. How could we have thought this would work?

I made my thoughts as loud as possible, begging Seamus to emerge from the cave.

Get back out here. Now.

Camila then disappeared below the surface of the water like a serpent as she made her way directly toward me. I flitted to get away from her, but it was useless. Even if I could get to the shore, my transformation on land would be too slow and she'd slip away. No, I would have to face her in the water.

And then the malevolent woman with the iridescent scar stamped across her face was upon me, her hands reaching for my hair. Her fingernails dug into me like claws and she laughed cruelly as she dragged me under the dark water.

"You *really* lack your father's intelligence, don't you?" she said from behind me, her arm across my throat in a tight hold. "I'm disappointed that this was the best plan you could come up with."

I was livid at the mention of Raj, the anger inside me reignited for my moment of reckoning with her.

"We wanted you to work with us," she said simply. "But since you've so adamantly refused, we'll have to kill you instead."

"Get the *fuck*—" I said, but thought of a better way to use my mouth other than cursing.

I bit down on her forearm as hard as I could and she shrieked in pain, letting me go as a stream of cloudy, silver blood emitted from her wrist. I took the moment of brief distraction as a blessing, flying behind her as quickly as I could.

It was surprisingly simple—I had no idea how I'd done it, but I had her in a headlock within seconds.

But once I had her there, I didn't know what to do. She was taken aback as well, apparently having assumed I had no real fighting skills. Which I didn't, as far as I had known. Her breaths were shallow.

"No, the reason you want to kill me is because you want revenge," I said as I regained myself. "First, you killed my father because he didn't want you, and now I'm next. Isn't that right?"

She howled with laughter, even as she struggled.

"Oh, you hold quite the undeserving opinion of your father.

Raj was just like every other man," she cackled. "You really think he didn't answer my advances?"

"*You* hold a high opinion of *yourself*," I said fiercely.

She was talking nonsense, trying to catch me off guard.

"So did he," she said with soft poison in her voice. "Your father wanted me so badly that he took me right on his desk in his office."

"You're lying," I said, but my own voice cracked with uncertainty.

"How would you know?" she replied. "It's not like you can ask him yourself."

Fury blinded me. I wondered where within me this brutal rage had come from. But I couldn't stop it, especially not when she started gasping. I tightened my hold, and something sick within me reveled in hearing her struggle. I couldn't explain it, but I felt my own mouth curving into a wicked grin at the prospect of my revenge being this easy.

But I couldn't do anything serious just yet. I had more questions for her.

"Where's my mother?" I demanded, my voice booming across the waves. I had forgotten all about Seamus coming to find me. In fact, I hoped that he wouldn't just yet. Not until I was done with her.

Camila didn't reply.

"You're in no position to withhold secrets," I shouted. The venom within my own voice was unfamiliar; it sounded like it was coming from someone else's mouth. "Not from *me*."

"You are no one," she said.

I realized my hands were crushing her windpipe, and I loosened them only for the sake of hearing her gasping answers.

"You're wrong," I said, the villain inside of me now entirely unrestrained. "I rule the Seas, remember?"

Why did I *say* that?

I felt the fragility of her bones within my hands. Her neck was like a twig, begging to be snapped in half. The anger for what I had lost was rising like a wave, preparing to crest at any moment as I brought the full force of my fury down upon her. In one way or another, I knew this was the person responsible for taking my father, my mother, *and* the love of my life away from me.

Matt...my heart stopped as I pictured my dead fiancé's innocent laughter that sounded like the musical notes on the piano he had so skillfully played. His blue eyes, so full of pure joy at all times. The handsome features of someone who didn't deserve anything that happened to him, because he had nothing to with any of this. He was nothing more than a careless casualty in Camila's pursuit to murder my father. As I thought of the kind-hearted man I never got to spend the rest of my life with, I was paralyzed by wrath.

"What you did to my family," I said softly, whispering directly into Camila's ear as I maintained my grip on her throat. "Will look like *kindness* compared to what I'm going to do to you."

My words cut the space between us with a knife.

I think I was as shocked to hear them coming from my own lips as she had been to hear them. Had I been standing, I was sure I would have staggered. She said nothing, and I could feel her losing air. Air or water—whichever she was trying to breathe.

I didn't know what to do next, but someone else made the decision for me. I felt myself being dragged away from Camila with such powerful force that it nearly knocked the wind out of me. She was left there, sputtering for a moment as she steadied herself on the rock where she had attempted to smash my head only moments ago. I knew she wouldn't pursue me, because she was physically incapable of doing so.

"What the—" I started, but I looked up to see it was Seamus who had me in his grasp. His strong hand was wrapped tightly around my comparatively tiny arm, dragging me away with the power and speed of a lightning bolt.

Around his neck was not one, but two glimmering stones.

One was the golden gem I had grown to know, and the other was a nautilus-like specimen with beautiful coils harboring the iconic swirling imprint of bright moonstone hues in every color. It was the signature rainbow design of an iridescent ammonite. It was beautiful.

"You got it," I whispered incredulously, now naming the iconic stone *the* Iridescent Ammonite of Iberia in my mind. I knew he'd succeed, but *still.* "How?"

"A lot less force than what ye were up to back there," he said curtly, and his tone took me by surprise. "Now houl your whisht until we get out of here."

He had never told me to shut up before except in my dream, and even then, it had been spoken on the cusp of sensuality. This time, the generally playful phrase seemed real and serious. He was *mad.*

"Where are we going?" I asked, having no idea what direction we were headed as we were now far out into the open ocean and deep beneath the waves. I didn't think he knew, either, to be honest.

"Back to Ireland," he replied through gritted teeth.

I tried to pull away, but his grip was iron.

"We can't!" I shouted. "My mother, she's—"

"That can wait," he said simply. "Ye heard the two of them. They've no idea where she is."

"I don't care!" I yelled, the anger from moments prior still pulsing through my veins. "We don't have time, we—"

"Ye need to go back to Ireland," he said steadily, eyes still directly ahead.

I noted the distinction in his words.

"Excuse me? *I* need to go back to Ireland?" I challenged. "What are you—"

"Aye, ye heard me," he said fiercely, but without raising the volume of his voice–which somehow made it worse. "What exactly were ye planning to do with that woman back there,

Jasmine? Kill her with your bare hands?"

Well, yes, actually, that *was* what I had been planning to do. I couldn't say that out loud, though.

"Exactly," he said, glancing at me sideways. "Ye lost your damn mind."

"No, I didn't," I shot back. "You have no idea what she's responsible for. She's the reason Raj and Matt are dead. And she —she tortured my mother!"

Seamus then finally came to a halt in the open water. The sand whipped below us as he turned to me.

"So ye want to be just like her, then?" he said, his green eyes filled with what looked more like concern rather than anger, now that I was looking directly into them. "You're supposed to be the *hero* in this situation, Jasmine. *You're* the one with honor!"

I said nothing. I wasn't ready to be ashamed yet. I was still full of rage. And I wasn't a hero. Not even close.

"I didn't even *know* that person ye were back there," he finished, his voice even lower.

"Well maybe you *don't* really know me!" I exclaimed angrily, staring at the sand below me.

I knew my words would sting, because it brought the facts to light. Our connection was undoubtedly fated and magnetic, but we had truthfully spent very little time together.

However, as soon as I said it, I regretted it. He had risked his life to find me, and no one does that for someone they don't believe they know in their heart.

Seamus clucked his tongue in disappointment and muttered an Irish curse that I assumed meant something along the lines of, "*Christ almighty.*"

I didn't say anything else. He grabbed hold of my arm again as he let out a frustrated sigh and took off at top speed once more. I did very little to assist, suddenly desiring to be weightless and carried away with the tide.

Camila's words describing her forbidden intimacy with Raj

rang in my ears as we flew across the sea, threatening to make me physically sick. Could my dad, my *hero*, really have done something so immoral as sleeping with a student? *Her?*

But even if her words were true, did I really have the capacity to kill her? To kill *anyone*? I could hardly believe the hands around her neck had been mine. As much as I wanted to blame it on Atargatis and the magic that connected myself to the ancient sea goddess who had at one time lost so much control of her own power that she had accidentally killed her own *lover*, I knew it had been all me. My flashes of anger from when I was a land-walker were still fresh in my mind. Like the day I screamed at my best friend on the Cliffs of Moher, thinking the same thing–that those words couldn't have been my own.

But they had been, and now I'd never get to take them back. What was wrong with me?

The Green Window containing the coccolithophores bloom was upon us once more, the telltale pink plumes sprouting up on all sides. We had gotten there much faster than I thought we would have considering how far we'd traveled. I felt the familiar lurch of my stomach as Seamus pulled me into the current with him. He wrapped his arm around my waist and we fell into the push and pull of the underwater tornado.

Just as I felt the ocean beginning to overpower us, I noticed that the plumes seemed to be changing color. They were spinning too fast, too wildly, and transforming from a rich, pink glow to a bright, electric blue. I didn't remember this from last time…

"Seamus—" I said, and I saw the matching look of confusion on his face.

"Something's wrong," he said in alarm, but it was too late. The plume had closed in on us.

CHAPTER 4

LIKE MAGIC

*A*idan McCarthy stood on the edge of the rock in the exact same place he had waited every morning for the past month. The water was uncharacteristically still for this time of year, but the October chill of coastal Ireland nipped at his ears in the incessant way to which he had grown accustomed, having lived on a boat for the past several years.

He tried to get there around the same time every day, but it wasn't always easy. He *did* have a real job to attend to, after all. But the promise he had made to himself–as well as the promise his younger brother had made to him–kept him consistent. Seamus was out there, and his mission to find the girl he was in love with had to have been successful…he needed to believe it for his own sanity.

They had only just begun to make amends for their years of estrangement when Aidan took Seamus out on the water to seek Hy-Brasil. As he had watched his brother jump into the sea, he felt a horrific wave of fear that he'd never see him again. That he'd never get to tell him everything was alright between them. He hoped Seamus knew that, but he needed to be a man and say it to his face.

Since his usual source of mythological mysteries, Mrs. Byrne, had drawn a blank when it came to places he could seek the selkies besides their disappearing island that he couldn't see, Aidan had traveled down other avenues for information. After some incessant prodding of locals of the Aran Islands, (there weren't many, mind you) he had gathered that there had been some peculiar sightings of vanishing fish tails around an equally elusive location known as The Wormhole–also called *Poll na bPéist* if you asked someone who had better Irish than him.

The rectangular rock formation certainly *looked* like a place where selkies could emerge from the bubbling depths, but it was so tourist-ridden that he couldn't imagine how it could be done without the creatures being seen. Well, at this time of year it wasn't particularly busy, he supposed. He looked around anxiously as the late morning sun crossed over his head and once more felt the cloud of desperation descend upon him.

Seamus wasn't coming. Not today.

But someone else was.

This particular someone had become so reliably punctual that Aidan nearly found himself hoping for his appearance just for the company he provided, but he shook the silly thought. The only reason this visitor came at all was because Aidan had made the critical mistake of bringing a sandwich the first time he came to pay his respects at what felt like his brother's watery grave.

"There ye are, ye wee skitter," he muttered to himself.

The great fluffy, golden dog came prancing across the rock with his wild, purple tongue that wagged jovially as he sniffed the promise of food Aidan had in his pocket. He held out the small bit of dried meat and the dog leapt down from a height that would have alarmed Aidan, had he not seen the beast do it several times before. He was surprisingly agile for such a large animal.

"I suppose yer getting greedy now, aye?" he said, reaching out and petting the dog's furry ears as they went horizontal in excitement. "I'm gonna have to start bringing more for ye."

The dog then looked at him hopefully with his wide, brown eyes that made Aidan sigh with regret. He wanted to take the thing home with him, of course, but he couldn't. A boat was no place for a dog. This particular one, big as he was, would need a place to roam free and run about. He couldn't take that away from him.

But then again...he *was* a stray. He had asked around the island and everyone seemed to pitch in their fair share of scraps for the animal, but he certainly had no permanent home or regular meals. And it *was* getting colder now. The locals called him "Halo" but for some reason, Aidan kept gravitating toward the nickname "Hero" instead. The dog seemed to answer to either; likely because he'd answer to anyone who held his next snack.

The fluffy canine then licked Aidan's hand affectionately before departing swiftly for the edge of the mysterious pool. Aidan followed him, peering over the ledge. It seemed so obviously full of magic and mystery, but he didn't understand it. To think his brother was so deeply connected to something this supernatural was hard to believe, but then again, Seamus had been confident he saw the isle of Hy-Brasil in the distance before he jumped. Why rule out the possibility that one of the fish tails the locals saw here belonged to his brother?

Hero let out a loud "*ruff*" that made Aidan jump.

"What's that?" he said, following the dog to the edge where he was sniffing intently.

The dog stuck his golden nose nearly into the water, and Aidan resisted the urge to yank him backwards, superstitious of whatever magic might lurk below. Perhaps he truly believed The

Wormhole *was* the serpent's lair as it was named, or perhaps he just had a much more direct line of sight into the impossible than most people.

He moved closer and saw what the dog was looking at–there was a distinctive glow within the depths of the swirling pool. Something silvery, sleek, and quick. Aidan dropped to his knees to look in after it. He wanted to reach his hand out and touch it...

Hero quickly circled the perimeter of the limestone hole before beginning to bark furiously from the other end. Aidan ran over to join him and–

"What the FECK is that?!" he exclaimed at the top of his lungs, tumbling backward onto the thin slice of rock that separated the edge of the rectangular pool from the open ocean.

"Hello there! What's the craic?"

Aidan blinked uncontrollably as he simply could not believe his eyes. In the pool below was a young lad, even younger than Seamus, staring up at him with eager blue eyes and sandy hair that he was shaking off in the same manner as Hero, who had also gotten soaked in the splash.

"Jaysus, Mary, and Joseph..." said Aidan, too frozen to stand.

"Ye look an awful lot like someone else I know," the boy said, shaking his finger. "I'd wager you're related to a man called Seamus?"

"That—that's right," Aidan said, barely able to breathe. "How do ye—"

"A *mucker* of mine, as he would say! I've picked up a bit of his Norn Iron speak from my own bride-to-be, Aisling. She's from an old Belfast family. In fact, they're much older than you'd even believe. But sometimes I can hardly understand her as well!" the boy exclaimed, swimming around the serpent's lair with ease as if it were no more than an oversized bathtub.

"Well, anyway, I know Seamus a bit. But I knew Jasmine first. And Aisling, who I mentioned, is actually Jasmine's cousin, if ye can believe that! Their mams are sisters. So I guess ye could say Seamus is a friend."

Aidan wanted very badly to speak, if only to quiet the boy in front of him, but he was still in shock.

"Well, I've actually been looking for *you*," the young man continued, now scratching Hero behind the ears as if they had known one another their entire lives. "Seamus has sent word."

The sentence brought Aidan back to his senses and he sat upright, jumping to his feet.

"What's he said?"

The young man laughed and waved him off.

"Not to worry! He's fine! He's on his way to Portugal," he said simply, as if the country were merely next door. "And he's been reunited with Jasmine and all that. So there's nothing to worry about. Everything's fine, *so it is!*"

He flashed a wide, expectant grin, and Aidan stared at him blankly.

"Seamus says it all the time," he said. "The man adds it at the end of sentences, even when it makes no sense to do it! I'm Irish, too, but my family's from all over. So I don't really—"

"Who—who are you?" Aidan interrupted him, his voice faltering in disbelief.

"Oh, my apologies, I'm Fintan," he said, extending a hand to Aidan. "Should've led with that, I suppose!"

Aidan took the lad's hand, somewhat reluctantly, fearing for a moment that he would be dragged into the water along with the creature. But no, of course he had no ill intentions. Aidan shook hands with him and started speaking again as quickly as he could so Fintan wouldn't begin again.

"So ye know Seamus," he said. "Was that all he said?"

"Oh, no!" Fintan said. "He wanted me to tell ye that there's no need to keep waiting for him, but he'll come to see ye as soon as he returns from Porto."

"Aye, and when's that?"

Fintan looked distraught by this question.

"Oh…well, I don't know," he said, as if he hadn't thought about it. "I suppose it could be weeks. Maybe even months. They're looking for the stones of Atargatis."

The stones of *who?*

Nevermind. Not important.

"And I suppose ye'll be coming back to let me know, then?" Aidan pressed, sensing it was tough to hold the lad's focus. "Or ye plan to bring him here when he's returned?"

"That's a grand idea," said Fintan.

"So I'll still need to keep waiting here, then, won't I?"

Fintan seemed puzzled by this, and Aidan rubbed the bridge of his nose as he attempted to maintain his patience.

"Ye know what, I appreciate it," he said finally. "I'm glad to know Seamus is alright. That's all that matters for now."

"Right," Fintan replied warmly. "Well, I suppose I'll be going, then."

With that, he flicked his tail in the air and dove back into the bubbling pool, disappearing within seconds as if he had never been there at all.

Aidan blinked wildly around as the dog came trotting back over to him, nuzzling into his leg.

"What's his name?" came a voice from behind Aidan that made him jump again.

"Huh?" Aidan said, horribly startled. He whirled around to see a man and his young son, clearly tourists, preparing to take photos of the mysterious pool in the optimal morning light.

"The dog," the man repeated in his American accent. "He looks just like our Chow Chow back home."

"Oh, his name's Hero," Aidan said as the young boy approached the dog tentatively. "Go on and pet him, he likes it behind the ears."

The small boy reached out and scratched Hero's furry head,

smiling widely as he did so. His father watched in amusement and then looked toward the bubbling pool.

"Amazing, isn't it?" he said to Aidan, pointing to the swirling water as the sunlight sent sparkles across the surface. "Almost like magic."

"Sure is," Aidan agreed.

PART II

EXPLORER

CHAPTER 5

KINGDOM UNDER THE SEA

"*W*here..."

I couldn't say the words, because I already knew.

One look at the massive, spiraling towers and columns that lined the glittering, underwater castle encased in seaweed confirmed it with my absolute confidence. The legends from my childhood, the bedtime stories…they were all real.

I was in Atlantis.

The city was expansive and miraculous, as I had always assumed it would be. But the castle at the center was entirely unlike the sunken, ancient pyramids I had always associated with the lost city in my mind's eye. The obvious signs of elegance and magic that sparkled within the windows of the towers made me eager to go inside—just to see who could possibly live within them. The rainbow network of coral and collection of seaweed that grew in front of the castle reminded me of a wild garden that, although vastly overgrown, was lush and perfectly methodical in its positioning. It reminded me of a much more colorful version of the underwater entrance ramp to Hy-Brasil.

Surrounding the castle were endless rows of other various buildings with purposes I could only imagine as it was nearly too overwhelming to take in. Directly above us was a thin veil of shimmering, dark blue matter that seemed to protect the city from the rest of the sea, similar to the misty haze that isolated the Irish selkie paradise from the human eye. Just above the veil was a massive collection of Great White sharks, swimming back and forth and presumably guarding the magical city. The entire place seemed to have a white glow to it, with flecks of aquamarine whirling throughout at lightning speed. It took me a minute to realize that the flashes of electric blue shapes were actually tails. Mermaid tails.

The look of shock on Seamus' face was enough to momentarily quell the tense atmosphere between us.

"Can you *believe* this?" I asked.

"No, no I can't," he said, shaking his head as he put an arm around my shoulder.

"Should we—" I began, not knowing what we should do at all. I glanced at his chest and wondered if we should hide the stones, but something about this place told me we would find allies for our cause here.

This was not a place of evil. I could feel it.

Seamus and I started off at a slow swim, flitting through the glittering clouds of water as I tried to make out the distinction in conversations happening all around us. It seemed to be a mixture of English, Portuguese, and perhaps Spanish, which would make sense given where I geographically believed us to be.

When I got my first, close glimpse of the inhabitants of this magical place, I froze in awe.

While our own tails were a bright, iridescent green that nearly looked silver in some lights, the tails of these merfolk were a shocking, electric blue flecked with scales that glowed pink and white as the light from above bounced off of them. Their eyes were lamplights like our own, but with hints of various shades of blue from bright cerulean to rich sapphire. Their skin seemed warmer than ours, not only in color, but in actual temperature. I could nearly feel their body heat radiating as we passed through the throngs of merpeople. Some of them turned to observe us with mild curiosity, but no one seemed to have any particular interest in us beyond a quick glance; as if they had seen our kind before.

The city was filled from top to bottom with rich, teeming ocean life that completely intertwined with the human-like residents. The array of creatures that whirled past me revealed countless varieties of fish from all families: from the Electric Blue Acara and black and orange Flowerhorn of the Cichlid family, to ordinary gray fish of the Mooneyes as well as guppies, neon rainbowfish, German blue rams…there seemed no rhyme or reason to *what* could exist here, as if all of the waters in the world contributed some of their own inhabitants to the colorful settlement.

We reached the center of the city where the castle was positioned, and I saw no guards in sight. Could it be possible that we could simply swim right through the front gates? And who lived here? A king and queen? My only experience with the world of mermaids was limited to the environment on Hy-Brasil, where tensions between Amalgams and selkies were the only spheres of political power. To my knowledge, there *was* no absolute ruler or official governing body of Hy-Brasil.

"Jasmine!" came an urgent voice from behind me and I knew who it was before I turned. "Oh, thank *Manannán!*"

The mass of red hair crashed into me with force that sent me flying into the castle's moonstone doors as my cousin thanked the Irish god of the seas that she found me. I gripped her back tightly for a moment before Aisling pulled away from me with her eyes shining. Her fiancé, Fintan, was right behind her as he engulfed Seamus in a brotherly hug.

"How did you–" I began, looking between the two of them,

not comprehending how she knew we'd be here of all places when we didn't even fully know where we were. Then it occurred to me that of course she would be aware of other mermaid settlements, considering she had known she was a selkie for most of her life.

"I followed the two of ye after I went back to get Fintan who had gone to send word to Seamus' brother," she said. Before I could scold her for doing so, she cut me off. "And when I didn't see ye, I thought ye might have gone the wrong way. I forgot to mention there's another Window that looks similar."

"Yeah, thanks for warning us that there were two," I said sarcastically. "They look exactly the same."

She scoffed playfully. "Oh ye didn't notice it's a completely different color?"

"We were a bit distracted," I said, glancing at Seamus. I looked for an indication of either anger or truce in his face, but saw neither. I actually couldn't read him at all, and I didn't like it.

"Come on," Fintan said, eagerly leading the way through the doors as they swung open with ease. "Ye can see where the rest of my family lives."

"Your family?" I asked curiously, flitting my tail to keep up with him.

"My father's side!" he said excitedly.

I nodded and glanced at Aisling who was moderately reprimanding Seamus for wearing the jewels so openly, but she also agreed that the people of Atlantis were the kind to be trusted.

I knew Fintan from his mother, Sorcha, and I had indeed harbored suspicions on whether or not the dark, somewhat brooding Lachlan that was Sorcha's current mate was actually his father. The sandy, golden hair and light eyes of both Fintan and his mother made me wonder.

We flitted through the grand entrance hall that exuded opulent elegance in every way—the sunken speculations from both history books and mystical rumor were nowhere to be found. The walls were the same glimmering white from outside, but flecked with streaks of pink and blue that brought the castle to life. Where there wasn't sand, there were slabs of white marble adorned with twisting patterns of waves and other symbols I didn't recognize.

Directly ahead of us was a grand, central room with a massive statue of–

"Holy shit," I said. "Is that…"

"Atargatis," Seamus said, looking between me and the statue.

I had only seen her likeness captured once–during the time when I was taken to the cult-like meeting of the Amalgams. That particular statue from the dark cave on Hy-Brasil was sinister in nature, with Atargatis' black eyes gleaming spitefully as she gripped a dagger in her long, clawed fingers.

This statue had the goddess of the seas depicted in an entirely different manner.

Here sat–or bobbed–a graceful, beautiful ruler that held in her arms the limp, dead body of whom I assumed was her mortal lover she had mistakenly slain, according to the legend. Her expression was grave as she acknowledged her error, and her tail rose up behind her while her weapons rested on the floor. A crown of ornate shells sat upon her head and had clearly been carved by a meticulous hand, with detailed lines that emphasized the beauty of the ocean's natural spoils.

Upon the seaweed-wrapped throne behind her sat her mortal daughter, Semiramis, the legendary queen of Assyria, from whom my father was descended. The white stone statue was heavily muscled and fierce, but undoubtedly benevolent.

Aisling smirked from beside me.

"You'll be *extremely* welcomed here," she whispered, and I felt a shiver run down my spine. "I planned to bring ye anyway, since Fintan's father would be a grand ally for us."

Seamus reached for my shoulder. I welcomed the gesture and tried to meet his gaze, but he didn't look at me. He stared at the statue in awe and I knew his thoughts mirrored my own. This statue was a symbol of how wildly and irreversibly our lives had changed since the truth had been revealed. This was what I had to live up to.

"Is that my son from the Emerald Isle, returned to the warmth of Iberia at last?" came a booming, powerful voice from beyond the statue. Fintan grinned widely and flew across the foyer where his father received him in a crushing hug.

He spotted Aisling and his smile stretched even wider.

"And *there's* the woman who's responsible for stealing my son away from me!"

Fintan's father didn't necessarily *look* like his son, but their mannerisms were identical. While he had darker features and brown hair that seemed to glimmer with flecks of gold in the light, his kind eyes were bright with the same eagerness that was ever-present in his son's attitude. He did not wear a crown, but he didn't need to. The way he carried himself told me immediately that he must be the leader of this grand kingdom.

The man had golden cuffs on both wrists that were adorned with bright blue stones—maybe sapphires—and a chain around his broad chest that held a glistening orb filled with some sort of swirling substance that reminded me of a storm cloud. His tail was the same sky blue as everyone else we had seen in the city, and he was heavily muscled. He looked like a warrior.

Aisling rushed to embrace him as well, rolling her eyes at his comment in a playful manner that told me they were all well-acquainted. Of course they would be, it was her future father-in-law.

"I'm sorry for your loss," the man said quietly, embracing her tightly. "Oisin was a great leader and warrior among us, and he will be sorely missed. I fought alongside him in many wars, and I owe him my life."

"Thank you," Aisling said, patting his hand that held hers as she acknowledged the death of her great-great-great grandfather–I still didn't know how many generations–likely for the first time, seeing as it had happened only days ago.

Fintan's father then noticed Seamus and I lingering in the background, and he looked to his son for an explanation.

"Father," Fintan said, floating backward to join us. "I've brought someone very special to see ye."

"Hello," I said nervously.

Fintan smiled encouragingly. "This is Jasmine. I'm sure you've heard of her by now…she is the Heir of Atargatis."

The man's dark eyes went wide with the same look of reverence that embarrassed me the first time I saw it in Oisin's countenance back in Belfast when he realized who I was. I instinctively began to shrink into myself, but Seamus' hand of encouragement on my back made me stand–*float*–a bit taller. I smiled at the impressive leader in front of me and he beamed back in response.

"Jasmine," he said, reaching for my hand before he decided against it, bowing deeply instead. "Atlântida serves the Queen of the Seas."

I noted the Portuguese version of the city's name and smiled. It sounded positively beautiful as it rolled off of his tongue, like a secret magical code spoken only to those who were fortunate enough to find it.

"Thank you," I said, and paused awkwardly, realizing I didn't know how to address him.

"Artur," he said simply, as if anything beyond a first name was unnecessary. He was humble. He looked to my right, and Fintan jumped to introduce Seamus.

"Seamus," Artur repeated, surveying the gems around his chest. He looked upon them not with hunger or covetous greed like Cearbhall looked at his own, but with respect and admiration. "These are stones of Atargatis?"

"They are," Seamus responded, meeting the man's eyes as they shook hands.

"Though I believe in leaving the stones alone, I am impressed," Artur replied, and I could tell he meant it. "This latest clan of Amalgams has been seeking them for quite some time, and already you have discovered two of them."

"We also want to leave them alone," I said hurriedly. "But the Amalgams–"

"They've left you no choice," Artur finished my sentence for me. "I know."

I nodded appreciatively, seeing he understood that our intentions were pure.

It dawned upon me, as I saw the second gem hanging around Seamus' neck, that I had no idea how the confrontation with Cearbhall had gone. There had been no time to discuss it yet, and now as I saw it glinting on his chest in its colorful magnificence, I was burning with curiosity as to how exactly he had gotten it.

Artur must have noticed a degree of exhaustion that shadowed my face, and he looked toward Aisling and Fintan.

"Let our guests get comfortable before we dive into business," he said to his son. "I assume you wish to discuss an alliance?"

Aisling and Fintan nodded. I looked at them to take the lead in replying, but they deferred to me. I hoped that my heritage was not going to set the precedent for my taking on a leadership role in our group, but I sensed it already had.

"Well–we actually kind of ended up here by accident," I said, embarrassed. "But–"

Artur waved off my concern. "It happens more often than you'd think," he assured me with a smile. "Go rest. We can discuss later."

We were told to meet back in the main hall after we had rested, and I noticed the light fading outside the archways that lined the walls of the marbled palace, signaling sunset in the underwater kingdom. I wondered if the same was going on above the surface, or if we were enveloped in our own, private universe. I'd believe either scenario to be possible.

From where I was, it seemed anything was possible.

55

CHAPTER 6

RECAP

Fintan showed us where we would be staying. It was a bright, ivory tower situated on the south end of the castle where we flitted easily through the glass-less stone window.

We entered a grand room that looked much more like a human dwelling than anything I had expected, and I was relieved to see something so familiar. It had dark blue walls and flowing curtains that danced lightly in the waves against the cutout in the stone where I could peer out at the city beyond. There was a large mirror, a dresser, and even a small side chamber that vaguely resembled a bathroom given there was a large tub in the middle filled with some sort of swirling, purple liquid. I wondered what it could be, but I was too tired to ask.

Lastly, there was actually a *bed*. Not that Seamus and I could do anything useful in it with our tails, but I was admittedly looking forward to resting on something other than a rock.

"Haven't seen one of these in a while," I remarked to Fintan as I admired the rich, crushed velvet sheets of soft blue.

He laughed. "Yeah, my mam's taken to selkie life much better than Artur's embraced his change," he said simply. "He still likes to hold onto some of the more *human* way of doing things."

I noted the distinction in his words, and I had to ask.

"Changed? Has he not been one of us for long?"

"Oh no, it's been a long time now," Fintan said, clearing his throat and now suddenly avoiding eye contact with me. "But my father–well, he's an Amalgam. Not like the others of course, but he is."

I was taken aback. Of course, I had no reason to assume one way or another, but I had grown so accustomed to villainizing the majority of Amalgams, aside from myself. I held out hope that there were others out there who believed in the just side of the cause when it came to the stones, but how would I ever know? The only group of them I had ever met were all under Cearbhall's thumb.

"I've got to dial down my accent now that I'm back here," Fintan said with a laugh, attempting to fill the awkward silence that had descended upon us. "Artur says he can barely understand me when Aisling and I visit! I'm sure ye get it, Seamus! Since your mother might've been one of the ancient selkies, just like my own mam…and whenever I'm around Aisling, her being from Norn–"

"Fintan," I interrupted, as I had learned it was the only way to get a word in with him. "How *is* Sorcha?"

I deeply regretted the way in which I had parted from Fintan's dear mother, the one who had sheltered me, taken me in, and showed me the general ways of being a selkie before either of us knew anything about who I truly was. She had shown me kindness, and I had disappeared without a word when I had been kidnapped by Cearbhall and Camila. From her perspective, it surely looked as if I had gone willingly. I hoped she knew the truth now.

Fintan saw the sadness in my eyes and reached for my shoulders.

"I promise, she's not mad," he said, and I believed him. "I explained everything to her, and she just wants ye to be careful."

I smiled back. "Please send her my best when you do see her again."

"I will. Oh, and she was also thrilled to find out about *this* lad," he said, slapping Seamus on the shoulder. "Last she heard, ye were a land-walker."

Seamus raised an amused eyebrow at Fintan before glancing at me.

"Yes, I told her about you," I said curtly.

The subtle smile on Seamus' face vanished nearly instantly and I felt the tension between us return with a vengeance.

Fintan, being the bubbly person that he was, had no sense of it. I cleared my throat to indicate that Seamus and I needed a moment alone, but he continued to look around the room with an absent-minded smile on his face. He was oblivious.

"Fintan, would you mind–" I began.

"Oh, of course!" he exclaimed, looking between the two of us as realization dawned upon him. He cleared his throat and looked around awkwardly. "I'll just be going, then!"

He disappeared from the room in a flash of green and silver. I watched him fly down one of the castle's passages before turning to Seamus, who had barely said a word to me since our arrival. He was leaning against the dark blue wall, arms crossed as those malachite eyes of his looked directly into my soul.

"What?" I asked, my voice sharper than I intended. I wouldn't necessarily have said his stare to be *stern* in nature, but his countenance was certainly not one of approval.

"Ye know what," he said. "What the hell was that back by the shore?"

"No," I said firmly. "You tell me how you got the stone first, then we discuss what I did."

I wasn't going to allow our conversation to be derailed by a lecture on my anger issues while the rainbow gem rested against his chest with no explanation.

He shrugged. "I took it."

"No shit," I snapped. "Tell me how."

Seamus smirked and I wanted to wipe it clean off of his face, but as he told the story, I couldn't help but grin, too.

"I swam as slowly and quietly as I could, but I knew he could tell that I was there," he began. "They have these senses that I don't think ye and I have fully developed yet."

"Like animals," I agreed.

He nodded. "The cave wasn't a normal one. I started to feel like I was falling asleep while I was swimming, and it took everything in me to stay awake. Finally, I saw the melter in the corner just before he disappeared below the dark waves. So I followed."

"Go on."

"We went through this cloud underwater that seemed to flip the entire cave sideways–kind of like how it feels going through a Green Window. Like ye can't tell which way is up. I thought he was leading me on, but I had to go where he went, aye?"

"Right," I said, tensing.

"We kept swimming and I thought, how *deep* is this feckin' cave? And just when I was about to turn around, I saw it. The stone was glowing, but not like this one," he said, tapping the yellow gem that looked almost pale in comparison to the rainbow of the Iridescent Ammonite beside it. "It was more like it was whispering, begging both of us to take it. So I waited until he closed in on it. I wanted him to touch it first, just in case. And then he turned around to face me."

"Followed me, have you?" Cearbhall said to Seamus, his lamplight eyes glowing in the darkness of the cave.

"I've come to take what's mine," Seamus said, pointing to the stone.

Cearbhall was amused by this, and scanned his opponent's body for something. A marking. He wanted to see if he was an Amalgam.

"I'm not one of ye," Seamus said, answering his unspoken question. He nodded at the gem again. "Now ye give me the stone, or I take it."

"What on earth would *you* need with this?" Cearbhall answered in patronizing tones, but Seamus saw through it. He had the strangest feeling that this man seemed to already know who he was. How that was possible, he didn't have time to contemplate, but he felt uneasy.

"That's my business," Seamus said. "Same reason ye want it for yourself, I assume."

"Surely you don't need such gems to impress a woman," Cearbhall said, surveying Seamus up and down. He swore the bastard nearly licked his lips. "You have other admirable...traits."

Seamus wrinkled his nose in disgust. He reached for the stone, but Cearbhall caught his hand with surprising swiftness and precision. His grip was fierce.

"I don't think so," Cearbhall said with soft venom. "Even if it's for the goddess you serve. That's why you want it, isn't it? A present for *her?*"

Seamus said nothing, debating his next move. He could snap his wrist in half, but not yet. The man was more agile than he looked.

"Oh, so I'm right," Cearbhall said as Seamus remained silent. "You *are* the pawn of Atargatis' Heir. She's sent you down here to avoid facing me herself."

Seamus still didn't move, his mounting anger pulsing through him as he looked for which part of Cearbhall's throat he'd grab first.

Cearbhall chuckled.

"Let me ask you," he said silkily. "Does she make you *bow* to her? Or do you do it voluntarily?"

That was enough.

Seamus twisted from Cearbhall's grip while his other hand had the man pinned against the wall of the cave within seconds. A brief look of shock flashed and faded from the evil Amalgam's face almost instantly as reached a claw forward to scratch Seamus' face. He narrowly dodged the blow, while Cearbhall's eyes shone madly with delight, as if he thought it to be amusing. Seamus swiftly ripped the stone from his grasp while his other hand crushed the water from Cearbhall's lungs.

"I leave without killing ye one time," Seamus said fiercely. "There won't be a second."

He took one last look at the villain before he cracked Cearbhall's head against the solid, rock wall at the bottom of the cavern in a sweeping motion that was *just* hard enough to knock him out. Seamus then shot straight toward the surface as best as he could find it in the dizzying waters. He fought through the swirling clouds and willed himself to find his way out, the new stone beating hotly against his palm.

As soon as he reached the surface, he removed the necklace he already had on in an attempt to string the second stone alongside the first, but before he even had time to imagine how to do it, the fossil sealed itself to the chain and clanked into place next to the yellow gem. It was as if each knew that it belonged with the other. They were reunited; like sisters.

"The wee stone got me out," Seamus said as he concluded his story, patting it against his chest. "I'm sure I wouldn't have been able to find the surface without it. It was like a magnet to the exit."

I looked at him, dumbfounded by the simplicity of him physically overpowering Cearbhall. I knew he would be capable of doing it, but to knock him out cold...I had expected Cearbhall would have been armed beyond his own claws. I shuddered at the thought of him sinking one of them into Seamus' handsome face. I started to reach for his cheek instinctively, but I had other questions.

And qualms.

"First of all," I said as evenly as I could. "How *dare* you get on me about what I did to Camila after what you did down there. How is cracking his head against a wall any different than me choking her out?"

I couldn't bear telling him that Camila had revealed to me that her romance with Raj was mutual. Angry as I was, I couldn't say the words out loud.

"Jasmine," Seamus said, rubbing his nose in exasperation. "I don't care what *I* have to do, but I don't want ye to have to do the same."

"Why?" I questioned. "It's *my* war we're fighting, don't you see? This is my responsibility!"

I was the reason we were here, under the sea. Not him. It was *my* lineage that obligated me to find the stones. He truthfully had no reason to be part of this at all.

Seamus didn't agree, which I already knew.

"Ye think ye need to be killing people left and right?" he shot back. "Because you're the Heir to some mermaid's throne from centuries ago?"

"Oh so *that's* what it is," I said, eyebrows raised as I challenged him. "What Cearbhall said about serving me—*bowing* to me. It bothers you, doesn't it? Because it threatens your *masculinity*."

I had once again struck a nerve–I could tell. Unlike the majority of men that I knew in the twenty-first century, Seamus had hints of traditional male dominance in his personality that I had only seen flickers of in our brief time together, but I knew they were there. I had, admittedly, always been the more authoritative personality in any romantic relationship I had ever been in, so the dynamic was certainly new to me. Taking the lead was my way, and I didn't know any other. Maybe it was because I had grown up with just a father. I didn't think Matt ever minded it, being the gentle, kind soul that he was.

But Seamus was not Matt, and the sooner I stopped comparing them, the better.

He was silent for a long moment before icily replying to my question.

"It's *my* job to kill or die for ye if and when the time comes," he said severely. "Not the other way around."

"I–that's just—" I began, but I couldn't think of the appropriate response. I was taken aback.

I softened, despite how frustrated I felt. No one had ever said something like that to me before. Given my generally undemanding existence as a human who hadn't regularly faced life-and-death battles with evil mermaids, there had never been a reason for a statement so profound. From anyone, let alone a romantic partner.

Die for you.

I suppose he had already proven that he would when he came to find me on Hy-Brasil.

"I know you believe that," I said quietly. "But we're supposed to be in this together."

He reached for my hand and gently pulled me closer to him. I let him, floating easily across the room as I met his gaze.

"We *are* in it together, but it doesn't mean I want ye to have to do things that will hurt ye for longer than they'd hurt me," he said, his hand on my chin while the other stroked my back. I melted into his touch because I knew how much he meant it. "I love ye too much to see ye suffer, a stór."

I realized then that I didn't often say the words out loud to him, but of course I felt them. I loved him so deeply that it took me by surprise, particularly considering the actual duration of time we had known one another, and what I had been through just over a year ago.

I closed my eyes briefly, recalling the life that had been stolen from me...the one that made me believe I'd never feel this way about anyone else ever again.

But if I were being honest with myself, I didn't feel the same way about Seamus that I had felt about Matt.

My love for Matt had been sweet, blissful, and dreamy like a fairytale. We had absolutely no trials and tribulations to deal with in our nearly perfect existence back then–in a world where I didn't know any other one existed.

The love I had for Seamus couldn't have been further from that feeling. It consumed me in a manner that told me it was a bond written in blood. We were connected in a way I couldn't explain, and his dedication to joining the hunt for the stones purely for the quelling of a threat we didn't fully understand yet...well, I knew it was the kind of love that both of us would die for.

"I love you, too," I said at last.

"And I have no shame in saying I *would* bow to ye," he said seriously. "I hope ye know that."

I remembered him dropping to the ground on Nohoval Cove, with no purpose other than to serve me.

"I know."

CHAPTER 7

ALLIANCES

Aisling came to get us as the sun was setting, and the view outside of the tower was breathtaking.

I found myself flitting as quickly as I could among the cloisters just so I could catch a glimpse of the glittering sunlight between the arches. Since I had primarily experienced the dark, moody greens of Irish selkie life within the grayest part of the Atlantic, the refreshing, colorful brightness of Atlântida was magical to me. It was as if someone had painted the city exclusively with liquid moonstone and then laid a rainbow on top of it.

Seamus took my hand as we shot down the side of the spiraling towers and back into the main hall where we were to discuss our plans with the others...and hopefully eat. The seaweed from the coast of Porto still gnawed at my stomach with its pungent taste, and I hoped a castle this grand would have better options.

"My utmost apologies," said Artur as we entered the room. There was a large, marble table laden with platters of every food I could possibly have wanted from my human existence in addition to a generous spread of various colored seaweed. "I should have offered refreshments long ago."

"You eat real food?" I blurted out before I could stop myself, recalling the strict diet of the Aran Island selkies and the only thing I had eaten since I changed. Seaweed *was* actually deli-cious–in addition to being vital to our health–but I eyed the skewers of shrimp and chicken in the center of the table with definitive longing.

Fintan grinned as his father answered.

"I'm sure my son has mentioned that I miss my human exis-tence more than most of our kind," Artur said. "It certainly won't taste the same, but I like to keep some traditions of the land-walkers alive."

I took an eagerly grateful bite of chicken, and discovered immediately that he was correct. It absolutely did not taste the same. I found nearly everything on the table aside from the signature plant snack of mermaids to be rubbery and foul-tast-ing, and I wondered how Artur could stomach it.

Grateful I had gotten a small plate, I returned to the buffet to pick off a few pieces of the purple seaweed–a color I had not yet seen in the delicacy. I chomped happily and felt my strength returning as I glanced at Seamus who had already devoured four strands of it.

"The blue's the best, I think," said Fintan, handing him another.

There were several others milling about the room, setting the table and clearing things away, but they all began to disperse as Artur cleared his throat to discuss business. He had a silvery-white goblet in his hand adorned with jewels, and one appeared in front of each of us immediately as he raised his glass.

"To the Heir of Atargatis," he said.

I blushed furiously and raised my glass out of politeness, wondering what could possibly lie within it since we were...underwater.

I glanced at Seamus who was wondering the same, but took a deep drag from the cup, nonetheless. I followed suit and tasted the most delicious liquid I had ever had in my life.

It was the color of rich, dark sapphire, and had an instant warming quality to it. I sipped it gratefully, feeling like I was drinking the most comforting tea in the world near a fireplace on a chilly winter evening. The way it reacted with the water was pure magic–swirling like a thick cloud of liquid that moved too slowly to become one with the rest of the water that made up the ocean around us. I finished my cup in two gulps.

"Before we begin our quest for the stones, there is also the matter of your mother," Artur said, and my heart leapt in surprise. I hadn't expected him to know anything about her. "Aisling tells me that Aine has escaped, and you have seen a vision of her? That's what led you to the Iridescent Ammonite?"

He spoke her name with familiarity that was not lost on either Seamus or myself.

"Ye know Jasmine's mother?" Seamus asked, my own excitement reverberating through his words.

Artur smiled. "I do," he said. "But I haven't seen her in many years. Tell me what your last vision was, if you don't mind recounting it."

I told him about how she led us to the cave near the beach in Portugal by sending me an old memory, and his expression was one of deep intrigue as he listened to my story.

"I don't know where she is now, though," I concluded. "I haven't tried looking into either stone since we got here."

"This is magic I have only ever guessed at," Artur said, sitting back in his marble chair and looking at us contemplatively. "Would you mind trying again now?"

I set my goblet down, realizing it had miraculously refilled itself. I wondered if it was alcohol, considering how it had melted away my shyness that I had felt upon entering the grand palace of Atlântida only hours ago. Or maybe I was just comfortable again, surrounded by people I trusted, with Seamus' reassuring hand on my tail.

I looked into the golden gem that Seamus held in front of me, once more willing myself to see beyond its barriers…to use it as a window to somewhere else. I closed my eyes and felt everyone in the room hold their breath.

"Ye got it," Seamus said under his breath.

We waited and waited, but nothing came. I tried the same methodical practice with the Iridescent Ammonite, but to no avail. They all tried to conceal their disappointment from me, but I saw their faces fall.

"Not all hope is lost!" Fintan said brightly through another mouthful of seaweed. "What about Niamh?"

"What?" I asked. "Who's Niamh?"

Aisling shot him a look and then tried to conceal it, but I had already seen.

"My mother," Aisling said with a sigh. "I told ye she land-walks often, if ye remember that from back at Carrickfergus."

"Of course," I said, recalling how Aisling had explained her mother's absence from under the castle on the fateful day of Oisin's death. I wondered, if she had been there, if he would still be alive.

"Well she's been trying to track your mam on land," she said. "Since your mam's escaped Atargatis' Pools, she might be land-walking where the Amalgams can't get to her. But I didn't want to get your hopes up before I heard anything."

While I appreciated the thought, I was irritated at being left in the dark.

"How much of all of this do you think she knows?" I asked, generally gesturing to myself.

I had only vaguely communicated with her through our strange visions, and of course I had no idea if *she* could see *me* through the connection the stones had opened between us. I thought it unlikely, given the manner in which she had shown me the memory of the beach.

"Well, if my mam finds her, she'll know everything soon enough," Aisling said with a shrug. "But so far there's been no luck in Ireland. We thought she'd go back there first, after she missed ye in Portugal…"

My heart sank again. I had tried to keep my expectations realistic. I knew it wouldn't be easy to track her down across the globe, but I had hoped she'd somehow *sense* where I was. Of course that felt like foolishly wishful thinking now.

Artur glanced between us before voicing an opinion I knew he wasn't sure I shared.

"If Jasmine wishes, she can continue her search for her mother," he said. "But I believe the stones are a more pressing matter."

I looked at Seamus who nodded to me. It was a curt, decisive nod, and I knew he was right. Looking for my mother would have to be our secondary priority. I had hoped we could do both simultaneously, but it didn't seem possible right now. I had to trust that Aisling's mother would do everything within her power to bring her sister home.

"Yes," I agreed with a sigh. "The stones first."

"Alright then," Artur began, addressing me with his dark blue stare. "It is no secret that the people of Atlântida remain highly isolated from the other seas. You should know that we do not involve ourselves in conflict unless there is a great threat."

"And you shouldn't have to," I said quickly. "This war with the Amalgams…it's my battle. I would never ask you to put your people at risk."

"Told ye," Aisling muttered under her breath. I shot her a look. Artur smiled kindly back at me.

"You misunderstand me. I disclose the nature of our people in order to emphasize how strongly we support you. The people of Atlântida have always believed Atargatis to be our Mother, our Goddess, and our Protector," he said. "We will not see her Heir's hidden treasure stolen by the Amalgams who wish to use it for evil."

I couldn't help but look at him inquisitively, knowing that he, too, was an Amalgam. Of course he had different opinions, but I wondered why. He seemed to understand my confusion and answered it swiftly.

"When I was marked and changed many years ago, I did not share the sentiments of my Amalgam brothers and sisters because I already knew other merfolk and their beliefs," he said. "The Amalgams tried, many times, to enlist me in their cause. But I remained on the side of those who believe that Atargatis' gems are to be revered, left alone, and perhaps not necessarily understood. I do not believe any single group or peoples should attempt to harness the power of the Seas."

I wondered how he had known mermaids back when he was a human, but I didn't think it was the right time to ask. Everything he said aligned with how I felt about the stones, and that was all that mattered.

"Cearbhall and Camila's gang from Hy-Brasil," I said, certain he was familiar with them as well as their true nature. His own son had once befriended them, but after what had happened beneath Carrickfergus and Oisin's death…surely everyone knew they were the enemy by now. "They've mentioned the stones hold the *power of the Seas,* but I still don't know what they mean by that."

"No one really knows," Artur said. "Only the true Heir would be able to harness them for their full power, but they can certainly cause destruction on their own should they gather more of them."

I had heard this before, and I was certain I'd hear it again.

"And there are others," Artur continued, biting his lip as he stared into the distance. "The chase for the stones has always been in the background of our history under the Seas. Cearbhall and Camila merely have them in their grasp at this moment. But there were others before them, and others will follow."

He spoke severely, telling me something I had already suspected when I happened upon the grand kingdom in which we now all sat. This conflict was much bigger than a small cult off the coast of Western Ireland.

"But our side has two of them now," he said, pointing to Seamus' chest.

I didn't know why Artur saying *our side* made me feel better already, but it did. Perhaps it was because anyone could take one look at him and know he was a fighter who didn't make a habit of losing.

"Do you know how many of them there are?" I asked. "The stones."

Artur shook his head regretfully and my face fell. I thought he wouldn't, given the eavesdropping I had done on Cearbhall and Camila back in Portugal. It seemed no one knew that, either.

"There was an old legend of seven stones, for the Seven Seas," he said. "But after them being revealed in so many in strange places, there's no way of telling if that's true or not anymore."

"There have been five discovered already," I said, counting those that I already knew about. "There's the green Tsavorite of Manza Bay that Cearbhall found, the bright blue Larimar of the Antilles brought to Hy-Brasil by Camila, the yellow gem from Professor Brennan's office that led Seamus to me, the Iridescent Ammonite, And the–"

I glanced up at Aisling who was staring into her lap with regret. I knew she was thinking of the failed heist against Cearbhall and Camila back underneath Carrickfergus Castle. When Oisin tried to give them a fake stone of the North Sea, and my heritage was revealed instead.

"Aye, and the one that was stolen from Oisin," she said. "The one I failed to protect."

"No, Aisling," I said sincerely, wishing I could reach all the way to the other end of the table to grab her hand. "That wasn't your fault. You were protecting me."

She smiled appreciatively at me, but I saw the pain that lingered behind her eyes. I knew how she felt. Fintan rubbed her gently on the shoulder. I would steal the stone back. I had to.

"I wish I could tell you we had a stone in our grasp to tip the scales," Artur said. "But as I said…I've never believed in seeking the stones unless it's absolutely necessary."

I nodded.

"Would you keep them here, once we find them all?" I asked. "For protection?"

I looked around and thought the castle seemed the safest place for them. At least that I knew of, given my limited knowledge of other underwater settlements.

Artur smiled back at me, perhaps flattered by my haste to trust him.

"We can discuss where the safest place to hide the ancient treasure of Atargatis will be when the time comes," he said.

"Fair enough," I replied. The protection of the stones would be a significant burden to whoever took it on, and I suddenly felt mildly embarrassed for asking such a favor.

"And for you," Artur said, turning to Seamus. "The stones act as your connection to her as well?"

Seamus nodded. "It's how I found her and Hy-Brasil when I was still a land-walker."

Artur's eyes grew wide at this proclamation.

"You don't mean to say you've just changed?" he asked, looking for the telltale signs of an Amalgam on Seamus' skin. Of course, he found no such thing. "You have the Irish selkie blood in you, do you not?"

"I do," Seamus said. "But it wasn't until I met Jasmine that I was–"

"Called to the Sea!" Fintan exclaimed, making me jump. I had nearly forgotten he was there. "I remember ye telling me that.

Like touching Jasmine's hand sent an electric shock down your arm."

I blushed, recalling the same memory from Galway. I opened my palm now, and Seamus traced his finger along my scar from beside me.

"Amazing," Artur said quietly. "Another mystery of the legend of Atargatis to unfold."

I saw a muscle in Seamus' cheek twitch with a hint of a smile, and I wondered what he was thinking. The peculiarly strong connection between us *had* been apparent when we first met back on land, of course. But as Fintan retold it to Artur, I thought it possible that I had somehow awakened the long-lost selkie blood within him. I suddenly pictured myself as a seductive sea monster, luring my prey to my fated journey beneath the black waves. I hoped he didn't see it that way.

"The precise number of stones is of utmost importance," Artur said, bringing my thoughts back to the present. "Otherwise, we're flying blind."

I waited anxiously as he took a deep breath.

"There is not a person *alive* who knows how many stones lie in the seas," he said. "But there is someone that's dead."

We all stared at him blankly.

"Someone that Cearbhall and Camila would never know about," he continued. "Because this man is a land-walker, and has never been anything else, despite his desperate wishes to be one of us."

"Who is it?" Seamus asked. "Where do we find him?"

Artur sighed. "He walks with a morbid company," he warned. "And because of my limitations—being confined to the sea—I'm not personally acquainted with The Santa Compaña of Santiago de Compostela. But I *do* know their story. Are you familiar with the legend?"

I gulped as everyone else shook their heads in confusion.

Unfortunately, I knew it well.

CHAPTER 8

DEALINGS WITH THE DEAD

I reached into the deep recesses of my mind, remembering Raj's retelling of the ancient procession of the dead from Iberian folklore. I wouldn't let Camila's poisonous words about my father cloud the memories that I had. The memories that I needed to solve the mysteries of my new life. I relayed the story to the others as best I could.

"The Santa Compaña," my father began, his glass of port swishing in front of him as we finished up dinner.

I was gnawing on his best attempt at recreating the pastel de nata from the place down the street, swallowing the miniature custard with significant effort. It was insufferably dry, but I didn't have the heart to tell him how bad it was.

"The Holy Company," I interjected with my mouth full before I could stop myself.

Raj smiled with amusement and approval. He had pushed me to learn both Portuguese and Spanish alike before our move, and I was trying my very best. I was horribly unskilled with languages, but luckily the simplistic translation was the same in both.

"Very good," he said. "The Santa Compaña is a legendary belief in the rural northwest Iberia, specifically Northern Portugal, Galicia…other parts of Spain. Do you want to hear the most famous story?"

"Do I have a choice?" I said with resignation.

It was a storytelling night, and this was long before Raj had made any friends on staff at the Universidade do Porto. I was the sole audience member present for his narration of traditions and lore.

Raj howled with laughter. "Oh one of these days you'll regret not listening to your old man's tales with intrigue and excitement, you know."

The eleven-year-old version of myself could never have guessed how true that statement would become.

He cleared his throat. The air outside was warm with the breeze of early summer, but not yet riddled with the sweltering heat that would soon descend upon the region with a suffocating force. We left the window open and I listened to the gentle lapping of the waves on the ocean, hardly comprehending how lucky I was to be experiencing the formative years of my childhood on the coast of the Iberian Peninsula.

"One of the most famous stories involving the Santa Compaña is that of a villager who unknowingly became part of the spectral procession," he said. "Let this be a cautionary reminder of the dangers of wandering alone at night and the consequences of encountering the supernatural."

He paused for dramatic effect.

"Okay!" I exclaimed, seeing he expected a response from me. "I won't wander alone at night."

"Good. Our story begins with a man named Juan, known for his curiosity and general fearlessness. One night, while returning home, Juan took a shortcut through the dark forest. As he navigated the twisting paths, he noticed an eerie mist begin to envelop the trees around him…"

"Let me guess," I said. "He walks right toward it."

"They always do," Raj said, somberly shaking his head. "Suddenly, Juan heard the faintest sound of footsteps coming from behind him. He whirled around and was petrified to see a procession of ghostly figures emerging from the shadows!"

I gasped, as a reliable audience member should.

"They were all carrying torches and were shrouded in spectral robes. At the head of the procession was a figure bearing a cross, his face obscured by a hood. Frozen in fear, Juan watched as the procession drew closer, realizing with horror that he himself was becoming one of them. He was now part of the Santa Compaña."

I gulped. I wasn't scared, of course. I was already eleven years old. But…the wind outside suddenly seemed to develop a slight chill. I shifted in my seat, imagining ghostly figures flying through the window of our house, trapping me in their march.

"Desperate to escape, Juan tried to flee, but found himself unable to break free from the grip of the evil forces that bound him…bound him to the *dead.*"

"Does he escape?" I asked, unable to handle the suspense. But I knew Raj would drag out the story.

"For hours, Juan was forced to march alongside the ghosts, his mind consumed with fear and desperation. As dawn approached, the procession began to fade away, leaving Juan shaken and questioning whether or not what he had experienced was real…and was he even alive?"

The chill was definitely there. I moved to close the window as my father continued.

"Haunted by his dealings with the dead, Juan returned to his village, determined to warn others of the dangers that lurked about at night. From that day forth, he became a fervent advocate for caution and vigilance, spreading the tale of his encounter with the Santa Compaña as a warning to all who would dare to venture into the night alone."

"Scary," I said, and I sort of meant it.

"What's the lesson here?" Raj asked in his best professor's voice.

"Um…don't walk alone at night," I said, shrugging. "Or wander into a strange mist."

"Well, yes," he said. "But the story of Juan and the Santa Compaña is a reminder of how thin the barrier between the world of the living and the realm of the dead truly is."

WHEN I FINISHED, I looked back at Artur whose face was grave.

"Your retelling is much more folkloric and glamorous than the reality of the procession," he said darkly. "The Santa Compaña often takes anyone who wanders into their midst and forces them to become part of their march forever. But a new leader is chosen every century, and this century's leader, fortunately for us, knows a great deal about the stones of Atargatis. He sought them himself for many years. He met his death long ago in Cyprus, in one of Atargatis' Pools."

"How…?" I began.

"Duarte, as he's called, was deeply infatuated with the idea of becoming one of us," Artur explained. "He sought to turn himself into a creature of the sea by entering one of Atargatis' Pools after supposedly having a vision of her at the temple in Hierapolis. He claimed he had her blessing to become like us in order to truly be with his soulmate in the afterlife, Nabia."

"The Iberian Peninsula's goddess of water?" I asked, speaking aloud for the sake of others who didn't know of the myth. I knew very little of it myself, other than it was extremely unclear. Sometimes she was depicted as a water deity, sometimes not. I always envisioned her with a mermaid tail, but perhaps given my heritage, my predisposition to that image was easily explained.

"Exactly," Artur said, impressed by my knowledge. "Duarte said he had dreams of him and Nabia together every night that were real, futuristic visions she had impressed upon him. And Atargatis, being a sympathizer of love for a mortal, supposedly blessed their union. Of course it was nonsense, but Duarte was so adamant it was true that he said he'd wait for Nabia until she came for him. He turned to the procession of the dead, deciding to walk the peninsula for eternity until she called him to the Sea. And he's still doing it, nearly a century later. Still waiting."

"A dedicated man, that is," said Fintan, pointing at Seamus and momentarily breaking the tense atmosphere.

"I was gonna say a daft eedjit, but sure," said Seamus, grinning in response.

"Tell us," I said to Artur. "What do we need to do?"

"You will need to alight for the mainland," he said, glancing down at my tail. "Unfortunately, given the curse that befalls me… I will not be able to join you."

"I understand," I said.

I was so quick to reply that I didn't notice the glances being exchanged behind my back as Artur continued, looking directly at Seamus.

"You'll need to walk with the Santa Compaña long enough to get Duarte to trust you, and then you'll ask him how many stones there are. If he inquires as to why you seek them, you will *carefully* tell him of our mission. I suspect he will be more inclined to take the side of those who want to protect the Seas rather than rule them, given his love for Nabia," he said. "But be very careful to ask only for the *number* of stones, not their locations. He will not tell you that."

"How do ye know?" Seamus asked curiously.

Artur's face grew dark.

"He won't want to feel used. He will want to feel helpful," he said. "Trust me."

I noticed that the conversation seemed to have somehow

developed to exist exclusively between Seamus and Artur, so I interjected.

"So how will we be able to see them if they're dead?" I asked. "And when do we go?"

No one answered me. I looked around in confusion.

"You know I can land-walk, right?" I blurted into the silence, wondering if somehow Aisling and Fintan had failed to mention that the Amalgam curse had evaded me to Artur. "Because I'm, well…you know."

I allowed my voice to fade, not wanting to sound like I was boasting. After all, I was hardly proud to be the Heir of Atargatis, considering the responsibilities it laid upon me.

"She can't be in the sun," Fintan said quietly, glancing at me. "She—"

"I'll be going, not her," Seamus said, nodding as he cut him off.

"No, you won't," I said quickly. I looked at him incredulously, but he didn't turn to meet my gaze.

Fintan looked between his father and myself while I sought support from Aisling, but I found none. She was nodding in agreement with Seamus. Based on Artur's expression, I got the sense that she and Fintan had already mentioned this information about me to him, and I felt betrayed.

Artur sighed and looked up at me.

"Jasmine, this could take *months* to accomplish," he said. "With the curse of being an Amalgam constantly at war with the spirit of Atargatis who also doesn't want you on land…we don't know what kind of lasting impact something like this could have on you. After all, you're the only one of your kind."

"Not to mention the excruciating pain it will cause," Aisling added. "And the likelihood of the Company trusting *two* of you–"

"I'm fine!" I said, much louder than I had planned. "Why are you–"

"No, you're not!" Aisling shouted, slamming her hands on the table more aggressively than I expected from her. Even Seamus started in surprise. "Ye forget, Jasmine, that *I* was on Skellig Michael, too. I saw ye stumble in pain. I saw your agony!"

"But–" I began, but Seamus squeezed my hand to silence me. Aisling wasn't done.

"And I thought...when I heard Seamus talking to ye in the monastery while I ran up there after ye–when I *told* ye not to do it," she said, shaking her head. "I thought I was going to walk into the room to see him standing over your fecking corpse."

She choked slightly, wiping what I assumed would have been a silver tear from the corner of her eye.

I said nothing. I hadn't realized how much it would have hurt her if something had happened to me...but I guess we were family.

I glanced sideways at Seamus and saw that he and Aisling understood one another. I would lose this fight.

"I can't let ye go," he said quietly to just me. "I'm sorry, a stór, but that's my final word."

I studied him, desperately wanting to argue, especially considering his *insufferably* authoritative language. *My final word.* Oh, he would pay for that comment.

But ultimately, I couldn't dispute the decision, because I knew he was right.

I had felt the searing sunlight on my legs, knowing it was Atargatis' curse punishing me for going against her wishes. Maybe it was the trace of the Amalgam curse as well. Artur was correct in saying there was no way of knowing what the source of my pain was. Not without asking Atargatis herself.

Either way, I knew I had only endured the pain on land for short periods of time while I was...distracted by other physical sensations. And lastly, the Iberian Peninsula was certain to be sunnier more often than Ireland. I simply couldn't be the one to do it.

"Alright," I said, resigning at last. "Fine."

I then rose silently from the table and floated from the hall, unable to focus on anything other than the sanctuary of the blue bedroom where I was going to sulk. I knew Seamus wanted to follow me, but they all had business to discuss. So I let them.

LATER THAT EVENING, Seamus came through the window of our room, his burgundy hair shining like firewood in the moonlight. I initially thought I'd pretend to be sleeping, but I couldn't stand the thought of being shut out of the plans entirely. I sat up on the velvet bed, bobbing ever so slightly as the gentle waves of the deep ocean fluttered my tail back and forth. There was a magically crackling fireplace in the corner that glowed in selenite serenity like the rest of the sparkling kingdom underwater, and it cast a light on his face that showed me how regretful he felt.

"I'm sorry, Jasmine," he said.

"I know," I said with a sigh. "I just don't want you to fight my battles for me."

"There's nothing I wouldn't do for ye," he said simply, shaking his head. "But ye misunderstand me. I mean I'm sorry for the pain I've caused ye. In the Skelligs, and in Nohoval Cove. The sun was out…it was selfish of me to put ye through that."

I recalled those memories and the blissful ecstasy I felt when we were physically together in the closest way possible.

"Don't be sorry," I said, my hand on top of his.

I wanted to tell him how incredible those moments were to me, that I didn't care what price I had to pay for them, but I couldn't find the words.

"When all of this is over, I swear I'll find a way to fix it for ye," he said seriously. "I'll not let ye suffer like this any longer."

Fix it, I thought. *Fix* me, *because I'm broken.*

Again, he seemed to read my mind and I didn't need to say anything else. He took my chin in his hand and kissed me deeply, sending the familiar spark flying across the connection that existed between us.

"I don't want you going to The Santa Compaña," I said as I pulled away. "There are other versions of the story–plenty of them–where Juan doesn't ever escape. Where he becomes part of the company forever."

"Ye were told some gruesome bedtime stories as a wee one," Seamus said, attempting to make me laugh. It worked for a moment, until I remembered who had told them to me. My dad.

I looked into my lap, wanting to tell Seamus what had been on my mind since the cave. I was terrible at expressing my emotions, but I needed him to know what Camila had said to me.

"She told me that they were *together*," I said in nearly a whisper. "When I had Camila by the throat in Porto, she told me it was mutual between her and Raj."

Seamus looked stunned for a moment, but he wiped it off his face immediately for my sake. He knew he had to be strong since I wasn't.

"I know ye don't want to be disappointed in your hero," he said evenly, voicing exactly how I felt. "But don't let her take the positive memories of your father away from ye. She has no right."

"I just can't believe it," I said, shaking my head in resignation.

I noted that Seamus didn't seem to doubt the truth of Camila's words the way that I had, and I wondered if I was horribly naive.

"Don't let her have the power to change your opinion of him," he continued. "Your father was a great man, no matter what mistakes he might have made. He was human."

I put my head in my hands. "Humans *are* weak, aren't they?"

"Aye, so it's a good thing we're *not* humans anymore," he replied, grinning.

I smiled and put my head on his shoulder. Seamus was strong in any capacity–human or selkie. His sturdiness was one of my favorite things about him. It was the only reason I was allowing him to go to Spain at all…because I knew he was resilient enough to do it.

"You could still walk away," I said into the silence, the irony of the phrase not lost on me. "This is the perfect opportunity for you to disappear on the Iberian Peninsula. I wouldn't be able to follow you for very long."

"No, I can't," he said, plainly not willing to humor me. "I'd never want a life that didn't have ye in it."

I looked up at him, his beautiful green eyes firm with promise.

"I told ye back on Skellig Michael that I'd die if I didn't have ye," he said. "I meant it."

CHAPTER 9

LOGISTICS

*Y*et another plan that put Seamus in incredible danger was devised, but this time I felt he'd at least be well-equipped to execute it.

How he was to walk among the dead undetected was a dangerous act of deceit that we would all need to take part in, but Artur would be the one to administer the potion that would make it possible.

"You're *sure* this will work?" I asked for the tenth time as Fintan's father flitted back and forth in the way I had learned that merpeople pace.

The cloudy orb that the great leader of Atlântida wore around his neck was filled with a thick liquid that was created from the dead souls of the hidden city, and it would cloak Seamus–for a short time–in a disguise that made him appear, well…dead. Artur had acquired the morbid relic through an ancient ceremony of underwater death that involved bleeding soldiers out should they die in battle. The fallen warriors in this particular brew were from some epic war nearly a century ago, but he assured me there was plenty more of it in storage.

"And why do ye keep this on hand?" Seamus asked, shaking

the orb that contained the potion known as the Nuvem Morte, voicing the question everyone else had been too afraid to ask. "Just in case ye fancy a wee dander into the afterlife?"

Artur nodded, and I began to see the humorous personality of his son poke through his own mask that he likely put on for those with whom he was unfamiliar. We were all–in a way–now family, and I could certainly tell he was getting more comfortable with us.

"Actually, you're not far off. Although, I often visit the less inviting of the two realms associated with the afterlife," he said. "The gods of the underworld find it rather impolite to be visited by a living being who doesn't at least pretend to be dead."

"Of course," Seamus said, suppressing a laugh as he shot a glance in my direction.

Artur continued. "I often visited Aed, lord of the Irish underworld, during my time in Hy-Brasil for counsel. I still call on a good amount of those unscrupulous beings, despite the fact that I don't generally agree with them," he said with a shrug. "They have magic that I don't, so when I ask for help, I try to be respectful. Hence the potion."

He spoke quickly, and noticeably avoided his son's gaze as he mentioned the Irish selkie paradise. I glanced at Fintan and wondered what had truly happened between his mother and the man that was before us. A question for Aisling later, perhaps. I also vaguely wondered what sorts of magic the gods of the underworld had that Artur didn't, and why he would need it... but it wasn't the time to raise the question of ethics. I had already decided I trusted him.

As far as the geographical strategy for reaching the morbid company was concerned, it was relatively simple. The five of us were to travel through a Green Window that would dump us off as close as we could get by water to Santiago de Compostela, the capital of Galicia in Northwestern Spain. If all went according to plan, Duarte would tell Seamus how many stones there were, and we'd move on with our search, at least knowing what we were up against. I didn't know if I hoped there were plenty more or just a few, knowing that either way, we were already behind the other side *and* we'd have to eventually steal the other gems from them as well. I couldn't even begin to surmise a plan on how we'd do that. Strong as he was, I didn't think Seamus knocking Cearbhall out cold every time was highly strategic.

Seamus had higher expectations for his encounter with Duarte than Artur, those of which he revealed to me once we were alone.

"Of course I'm asking the bastard where the rest are," he said bluntly, blatantly dismissing the leader of Atlântida's warning. "I'd be daft not to."

I put my head in my hands.

"You're killing me," I said. "First I have to sign off on you going without me while I wait offshore like some useless side-kick, and now you're going against Artur's *only* specific warning."

He shrugged dismissively. "I'll find the right way to do it."

I knew he would do it whether I consented to it or not, so I didn't press him further.

The week or so leading up to our departure involved a myriad of preparations including Seamus training one-on-one with Artur, both physically and mentally. Seamus had never had a need for rendering a weapon of any kind other than his own fists, but I suspected it wouldn't be difficult for someone like him to learn.

It was the psychological training that I thought might pose a challenge, because there were several factors at play other than Seamus' inherent strengths of sheer will and resiliency. He would need to maintain his sanity while under the influence of the toxic potion, and would need to outwit Duarte, who had centuries of practice in trickery. Artur warned us of the deceptive ploys that had been used on other mortals in the past to reveal their identity, thus removing the protective layer of the Nuvem Morte entirely.

The most terrifying of ruses was one that could be played upon Seamus by the potion itself. Although it was designed to shield a mortal being from the potential dangers of the dead, The Nuvem Morte could lead Seamus to hallucinate so severely that he could forget he wasn't actually one of the Company. He could simply forget he was alive. And if that happened…I could guess the consequences.

"Where does the procession end?" I asked. "I mean, what if Duarte doesn't trust him before they finish their march?"

Artur shook his head. "The legends say it's an endless loop all around the northern part of the Iberian Peninsula," he said with a shrug. "It goes on for eternity."

I shuddered as I imagined the ghostly figures traipsing across the continent with Seamus in their grasp while I waited help-lessly in the sea for *eternity.*

No, I couldn't allow myself to think like that.

"You'll need to get comfortable wearing one of those," Artur said to me, gesturing to the stones on Seamus' chest. "I want you to keep one for the sake of communication."

"Will it work?" I asked. "With him masked by the Nuvem Morte?"

"I don't know," Artur admitted. "But having the stone, whether in life or death, will also give Seamus credibility with Duarte. I want each of you to have one on you at all times from now on."

"I'll take the Iridescent Ammonite," I said as Seamus went to separate the stones. "I want you to keep the original one."

The one that had brought him back to me. I needed the miraculous yellow gem to do it again.

"And this goes without saying," Artur said, turning to Seamus, who was sharpening a silver blade. "*Do not* show it to him until you're sure he trusts you."

* * *

THE AFTERNOON BEFORE WE LEFT, Artur broke the news to me that Aisling and Fintan would be going with Seamus as well. I was furious, primarily because it meant I would now be completely alone except for Artur's company for the foreseeable future. The only glimmer of hope I had for the following days, weeks, or even months that Seamus was gone was Fintan's bubbly personality and the gift of Aisling's steady reassurance she carried with her at all times.

"Why the hell do *they* get to go?" I countered, not caring to watch my language in front of the great leader. I felt like I was arguing with Raj all over again, begging to be allowed to do something that *all* of my other friends were permitted to do. But not me. No, I had an early curfew and an endless list of rules that made no sense to anyone but him.

"Jasmine," Artur said patiently. "Aisling and Fintan will need to keep their eyes on Seamus periodically. I would have thought you'd be happy, knowing someone's looking out for him."

"Mmhm," I grumbled reluctantly.

Aisling and Fintan were to bring extra supplies of the Nuvem Morte just in case another dose was needed. Considering one dose could last up to three months, I sincerely hoped it wouldn't be necessary.

"Can ye tell me one more time what exactly happens when I take it?" Seamus asked in a pathetic attempt to change the subject. I was sure he and Artur had been over it a hundred times already. But as I looked at him, realizing we were splitting apart for an unclear amount of time *again,* I didn't want to waste a moment of it with pointless bickering.

Artur made a face of mild disgust.

"Well, like I've said, it tastes like shit," he replied. "But you will become a shadow of yourself, invisible to most mortals, but clear as day to The Santa Compaña. You have to keep reminding yourself, in every way that you can, that you *are* indeed alive underneath the film of death. Or else–"

"I die," Seamus said, voicing my guess.

Artur nodded and I hung my head.

Seamus glanced at me. I let out a cluck of disapproval, but it was riddled with resignation since there was no point in voicing my opinion about something that was already a done deal. I knew he had to do it.

We had only a few hours between Seamus' final preparations and dinner that would inevitably be followed by an early night given how exhausted we all were. Feeling mortifyingly inferior due to my physical limitations, I slinked away to our room while the others talked over the remaining details.

Not long after, Seamus appeared in the marble archway and beckoned to me.

"I want to show ye something," he said with a twinkle in his emerald eyes that made my heart flutter, despite my sour mood. I smiled back. After all, it wasn't *him* I was annoyed with. It was myself.

I followed him down what I would have called a hallway, considering it was architecturally designed to mimic one of a grand palace of Iberia, but was adorned instead with pillars and balconies that had no carpets, no steps, and no walkways. There was nothing other than a series of breezy airways lining the castle filled with the rich, nutrient-dense water of Portugal. The white marble flashed around us as we sped through the maze, and I suddenly thought Carrickfergus was extremely gloomy in comparison to this grand estate.

We flew through a doorway where an invisible wall brought me to a screeching halt. I could have likely pushed past it with force if I tried, but I was stopped by a silent warning. There was something, though I couldn't identify what it was, telling me to wait and prepare to appreciate what was beyond. As I floated there in anticipation, a thin film of sparkling blue and white emerged like a soft, translucent curtain.

"What is this?" I asked, and Seamus' answering grin was enough to tell me it was something that would make me very happy indeed.

"Artur wanted to create a safe haven for himself when he realized he could never land-walk in the real world," he said. "He tried using other, darker types of magic to see if it were possible in another place…in a small world he built on his own. But he tried to harness the dark magic for good."

"Magic from the gods of the underworld?" I inquired, reaching for the thin film, now on fire with interest for what lay on the other side.

Seamus nodded.

"I guess those yokes were the only ones who would help him with something like this," he said. "A massive undertaking, so it is."

The fact that the benevolent leader of Atlântida–the one with whom I entrusted Seamus' life–was regularly conversing with gods of the underworld surprisingly did not bother me. Perhaps because I knew instinctively that if anyone could turn dark magic into light, it was him.

Or perhaps because I knew what it was like to feel hopeless as an Amalgam, and that had I not escaped the curse because of who I was, I would have tried *anything* to land-walk again.

Seamus continued. "It didn't work, sadly for him. But it works for me. And Fintan," he said. "He's the one who showed me."

"Oh," I said softly, feeling a significant stab of sadness for Artur. Not even with all of the magic in the world could he create a place where he could be happy or escape his curse. I hoped he was still trying. I hoped he hadn't given up.

"So what exactly is beyond it?" I asked, reaching for the barrier again. "I mean, is it a room? A world…?"

Seamus held my shoulders tightly before letting me through.

"I don't know if it'll hurt ye or not, Jasmine," he said seriously. "It's not real, and there's no sun, as far as I've seen. But I still don't know."

I nodded and he shot me a warning look.

"Ye tell me immediately, and please be truthful with me," he said. "If it hurts, we leave, aye?"

"I promise," I said, and I meant it, even though I desperately hoped it wouldn't be the case.

It had only been a couple of days, but I missed being on land. To think I could do it freely, in a safe place, far away from the immediate threat of the Amalgams and the stones… I needed it, especially considering this was my last night with Seamus for-well, I didn't know how long. I couldn't think of it without choking up.

"And ye'll see things on the way there," he warned me. "Things ye might not want to remember. But it won't last long."

I didn't care. I nodded bravely.

"Let's do it."

He took my hand and pulled me through the sparkling fog. I resisted the instinctive urge to hold my breath. Air or water, I didn't need to.

I could never have prepared for the whirlwind of emotions that followed me through that thin barrier, lasting what felt like a lifetime and a millisecond all at once. I saw a million scenes flash before my eyes that confused me, made me so happy I wanted to cry, and brought me so much despair that I thought I'd never emerge. It was as if every memory from my birth until the present was rushing past me in a timeline that existed only in this miniature galaxy.

I saw Seamus, carrying me up the hill on Skellig Michael with the sun in his hair as he told me everything was going to be alright. Then I saw Matt, smiling broadly as he opened the car door for me on our first date and my heart leapt as I brushed his fingers. Kristen and Marissa sitting behind to me on the campus shuttle back at school, whispering about whether or not they should invite me to sit with them. Kiana embracing me as we tossed our high school graduation caps in the air, our heads thrown back in careless laughter. Raj as he snapped photos of me at my middle school spelling bee from the back row, mouthing the letters even though I begged him not to do it. Tears of happy remembrance welled in my eyes.

Next came the hard memories. Those that I never wanted to see again.

Me screaming at Kiana atop the Cliffs of Moher, my curse words sharply reverberating in the howling wind. Matt's mother, Rose, crying on my shoulder at her son's funeral. Christian's hands shaking on the podium as he recalled his favorite memories with his best friend who lay motionless in the casket in front of him. My first session with my therapist when I couldn't bear to look at her, because it meant the tragedy that had happened in my life was real. The days, weeks, and months, where I didn't eat or sleep, and I withered away to nothing.

Lastly, when I awoke under the sea beneath the Cliffs and realized that everyone thought I was dead, because Jasmine Atarga committing suicide was a very believable possibility.

I furiously blinked away the tears invoked by memories from my old life, the horrible moments of my past threatening to consume me with their vivid cruelty.

The water was black all around me, and long-fingered, white hands were pulling me to the ocean floor where I would be imprisoned for eternity. I was being dragged to the bottom of the melancholy sea of my own making. I was going to die here. I was going to drown.

But just as I started to feel like the bleak waves would take me under, I saw something else. There was a tiny light far above the surface, calling to me and telling me there was a reason to keep trying. To keep living, even when it seemed impossible. It reminded me faintly of the feeling I had as a child, reaching over the side of the boat in Portugal, and perhaps even when I saw a silver streak in the water below the Cliffs of Moher…but I knew it wasn't the same.

This was something that beckoned me to reach for it for my own good, not my demise.

The faint glimmer I saw wasn't sunlight, but rather a vibrant, opalescent moon. It was a benevolent silver sphere that welcomed me like a cozy night around a campfire rather than one that hung above monsters of the night. The hands that clawed at me loosened for a moment, but a moment was all I needed.

Hope swelled in my chest, and I shot straight to the light.

CHAPTER 10

UTOPIA

I gasped for air as I emerged on the surface, Seamus' hand clutching mine.

I wiped a tear from my face as I turned to look at him. I traced his strong jawline, as if to remind myself that he was real. That he, among many other things, was worth living for.

"What..." I began, unable to finish my sentence. He knew what I meant.

"I think it's only the first time where...where ye see it all," he said, studying me. "I didn't see as many of the memories this time. Are ye alright?"

"I am," I said breathlessly. I was rattled, and chilled to the bone with a feeling that was adjacent to fear...but I was alright.

I spun around in the dark waves to see where we were.

We were floating off the shore of a small island situated in an endless, twinkling sea. The moonlit, tiny oasis looked like Nohoval Cove, Hy-Brasil, and even a bit like Inishmore all in one. I knew before I asked, but I did anyway.

"Does it look different for everyone?"

Seamus nodded. "I see a version of Ireland, though," he said. "What about ye?"

"Me too," I said, beaming. "Something like that."

We made our way toward the shore under the bright, white stars and I looked up at the sky, watching the hues of blue and purple sprinkle the blackness of night.

Seamus held my elbow to support me as it still–even in paradise–took me longer than him to transform. He was immediately human again, and I remained on the sand like a pathetic, sitting duck for longer than was comfortable. I tried not to let it bother me as everything else seemed so perfect, and I waited patiently. At last, I felt the tingling in my lower body that signaled the beginning of my change. I brushed my hair from my eyes and squeezed the excess water out of it while I waited.

I wish my hair would dry, I thought absently, recalling the wet, sandy mess I had been on Skellig Michael and Nohoval Cove. It was so long these days, and being underneath Seamus on a beach certainly added to the incessant tangles. Then something strange began to happen in another part of my body besides my legs.

I felt a tingle in my scalp, like someone was cracking an egg on top of my hair. I gently shook my head, and ran my fingers through my waves, watching the moisture on each strand seem to disappear at my touch. With one final gust of light wind from the island breeze, my entire head of hair was completely dry.

"Woah," I said breathlessly. I had no other words. Seamus laughed as I looked up at him in amazement. Whether it would work outside of the oasis room or not, I didn't know. But I thought I had just learned to harness a tiny bit of magic.

Seamus watched me carefully as my tail began to melt away, and I held my breath, bracing for the pain, just in case. I *would* tell him if it hurt, but not until after we–

"How is it?" he asked, glancing at my tail in worry. "Ye promised—"

"I would tell you," I said earnestly as the tail began to shimmer away and was replaced by the beautiful flowing skirt I had known from before, only this time it was blue with flecks of purple glitter. I asked if he saw the same colors and he laughed, nodding. Whether it was the moonlight or the magic around me that protected me from Atargatis' scorn, I was completely comfortable.

Both of us now relieved, Seamus wrapped his arm around my waist as I moved to stand. I was much less clumsy than the last time I had changed, and I hoped this would be like riding a bike—that it would get easier each time.

"What do ye think?" he asked.

I looked around in wonder, thinking it was the most beautiful place in the world. I voiced this to him and he agreed.

We wandered the island's shores and I was sure we could have made our way around it in less than an hour, considering how tiny it was. The moon above was our only guide, and I had no idea what kind of laws of time constrained us here. I suspected there weren't many. Maybe none passed here at all.

"Not bad to be alone for a bit," he said absently as he placed an arm around me and looked up at the sky. I nodded in agreement.

Seamus' tall, tennis player-like build looked even more impressive on land as the height difference between us became abundantly obvious once more. Our time in Nohoval Cove had been only days ago, but we had been…on the ground most of the time. I remembered now how I constantly had to look up at him when he spoke to me in our human lives, and it reminded me of how shy I had been when he leaned over me at the bar back when I first met him. I couldn't believe there had ever been any feelings besides the easy comfort that existed between us now. He surveyed me in the same appreciative manner and kissed me on the forehead. There was no one here but us.

"How on earth did Artur *build* this?" I asked in amazement, watching the sapphire waves gently kiss the shore.

As I looked out at the ocean from the breathtaking shore, I wondered how it could possibly have been magicked by anything other than pure goodness. But then I remembered the barrier through which I had come. Given the whirlwind recount of my rawest memories, it seemed that with blissful joy came an equal amount of pain and sadness. There had been darkness before the light, no doubt. Perhaps the lords of the underworld had made a bargain with him, exchanging a bit of one for a bit of the other.

"Ye'll have to ask him," Seamus said, shrugging in disbelieving admiration.

"I will."

I *would* ask Artur, during the potential months that I sat and waited for news in the palace, like a pathetic princess whose prince had gone to battle for her. I tried not to think about it, not wanting to spoil the perfection of where we were.

"I don't want to leave ye again so soon," Seamus said softly, voicing what was on my mind as he tucked my hair behind my ear. "Not after I just got ye back."

"I know," I replied, my throat tight.

We hadn't explicitly addressed our upcoming departure at all during the time he was training with Artur, because I had wanted him to remain focused. I hadn't wanted to add to the stress he was inevitably feeling. I also knew he must be afraid to some degree, even though he was excellent at hiding it. Even though fear alone would never stop him from doing what needed to be done.

"But the sooner I go, the sooner I can return and we can start beating these bastards to the stones," he said. "And stealing the others back from them."

"That's true."

I had a horrible flashback–likely prompted by the memories that were just hurled at me as I passed through the mist–of the morning I said goodbye to Matt for what I didn't know would be the last time. I had lazily fluttered my eyes open and closed, neglecting to say anything meaningful to him. I had watched him go, taking everything I had for granted.

I looked at Seamus now, praying that there was no inevitable fate that was waiting to take him away from me, too. He was slightly possessive of me in his own way, but he didn't know I felt the same sensation for him. The love of my life had been taken from me once, and I didn't think I would survive if it happened again.

Of course, I didn't know how to voice any of this. I never knew how to say anything substantive when the occasion called for it.

"Seamus, I don't want you to go," I finally said in a small voice —a sharp contrast to the ferocity of my actual thoughts. "What if I asked you not to do it?"

"Ye know I can't do that," he said, rubbing the back of his neck. "It needs to be done."

"I know," I replied. "I just wish I could do *anything* that could help us."

"Ye can, Jasmine," he said seriously. "Ye spend your time here, learning as much as ye can from Artur. Look into the stone, try and feel the presence of the others. And when I get back, we'll go get them. And your mam."

I groaned as I thought of my mother, hiding in some godforsaken place in the middle of nowhere while she ran from the Amalgams who had put a price on her head simply for birthing me.

"She's your blood, Jasmine," Seamus said with a smile, reading my thoughts. "So we know she's a fighter."

I nodded and he bent down to kiss me. He swept an arm beneath me to pick me up, pressing me close to his chest as if I was light as air. As I felt his solid arms against my own, I realized I probably was.

"What do you see?" I asked as I traced my finger around the stone that rested against his chiseled chest. "When you cross the veil to get here?"

"Memories," he said. "The good and the bad."

I waited to see if he would elaborate without me prying,

glancing down at the script tattoo on his forearm. It was his late mother's name, Saoirse. It was a reminder of his selkie mom that had lived a horrific life riddled with abuse from her mortal husband—Seamus' alcoholic father—and eventually killed by what we now knew was the malevolent Green Window in Belfast. The mother that Seamus' older brother, Aidan, had called a demon of the seas when he found out what she was, only because he wanted to save her from the cruelty of the horrible man who had trapped her in a loveless marriage.

"I see the memories with Aidan, when we were wee ones," Seamus said, wandering aimlessly on the shore. "The days when mam used to take us to the sea, to museums, to school. He was older than me, but we still did a lot together. The three of us."

I pictured a young Seamus with his older brother whom I still had not yet met, but felt I knew already. I imagined the two of them, several years apart, but still looking like mirror images of one another. Aidan had lighter hair in my mind, since that's how Seamus had described him, and a significantly thicker beard, since he had mentioned his brother's superior facial hair on multiple occasions as well. Saoirse had to be beautiful, considering Seamus' own features. I saw her in my mind's eye with flowing hair and green eyes that smiled kindly upon the two most important people in her world.

"...and then I see the days when she didn't come downstairs because she couldn't walk. Because that bastard had made it so," he finished quietly.

I gulped, squeezing his arm affectionately.

"But when it's the good memories, I see ye," he continued, his smile returning in the moonlight. "The day I first saw ye back in Dublin, that long black hair falling down your back as ye walked out of the Jameson distillery...and I thought I'd do anything to know your name."

I let out a hollow laugh.

"You didn't even notice me until later that night," I said.

I had actually been mildly irritated by his lack of attention paid to me—or any of us, for that matter—after our whiskey tasting. I remembered how James had been the only one who approached us at all, and his redheaded Irish friend seemed entirely disinterested in the four American girls at the bar.

"Oh that's not true," he said seriously, shaking his head. "I couldn't stop looking at ye. Like I knew, even then, there was something pulling me to ye. I had to know ye, no matter what. And later that night, after I talked to ye, I knew I'd never care to know another woman again."

My heart thundered, but I knew he wasn't lying. There was no reason to do so.

"I assumed you only came to talk to me later because you saw no one else was," I said, blurting out my most vulnerable thoughts as I remembered staring at the chipped varnish on the bar, waiting for my cider and feeling highly self-conscious because I had no idea how to flirt anymore. That version of myself seemed so far away now. She was so unlike me—so weak and insecure.

For this, he had a quick response that surprised me.

"No one talked to ye because I had already staked my claim earlier in the afternoon," he said with a smirk. "Not a feckin' chance I was letting Harry step in...I know what the British accent does for American girls."

I laughed, and didn't care if I let slip something that went to his head.

"It was *your* accent I couldn't stop thinking about," I said truthfully. "*Sláinte.*" I repeated the Irish word for cheers just as he had said it to his friends that day. I remembered how nice it had sounded, rolling off his unique, Northern Irish tongue. He grinned so widely that I could have sworn he was blushing as he reluctantly tore his gaze from my own.

"I didn't know that," he said at last, looking back up at the moon.

It was so unbelievably surreal…to be in this setting, in this fantasy, made-up world that couldn't be real but somehow was, discussing normal things like the first time we met one another. Which hadn't been that long ago at all…and yet, it felt like I had known him a lifetime.

"And I wanted to know your name too, *Seamus*," I said quietly, reaching up to touch his cheek. I gently ran my finger down his jawline and across his lips, him closing his eyes as I did it.

"I love when ye say it."

I didn't need to say what I wanted. He knew, and he wanted it, too. Tonight was to be savored. It was for something other than the urgent, passionate need we'd had back in Ireland. He carried me further onto land, setting me down gently in the sand just where it met the rocks that rose to the hills beyond.

"Let's avoid the monastery if there is one this time, aye?" he said, smirking as he recalled the first time we had ever been intimate with one another. To have done what we did in an ancient place of holy worship such as that had been…well, it was something that would not have been looked upon favorably if I were a Christian.

I laughed and agreed, pulling him toward me on the ground. He kissed me gently and then slid his hand up the back of my neck, his fingers softly intertwining with my black hair. I kissed him back slowly, taking my time as he pressed down on me with a mild force that reminded me he could–but wouldn't–turn me over and do whatever he wanted to me at any moment. I inhaled his scent of autumn and campfires, doing my best to memorize it in case it was a while before I got to smell it again.

He was ready for me almost immediately, and I for him, so we met in the middle and I let out a gasp. He groaned in a manner that sent an electric current flying through my body, as if he was already an instant from losing himself, but wouldn't do it for the sake of waiting for me to capture my own pleasure. I let the waves wash over me repeatedly as he breathed softly into my ear, the sound of my name on his lips.

Even though I didn't want him to go to Spain, I had no doubt in my mind that his mission would be successful. My opinion of Seamus was that above all other things, he was entirely unwilling to fail if he made a promise. Especially when it was a promise made to me.

"That's my lovely girl," he said into my ear in his thick Belfast accent, allowing the faintest hint of dark seduction wash over the passionate love we were making.

I couldn't hold back the wave any longer, so I slipped beneath it.

I hoped there wouldn't be too much time in between this night and our next just like it.

CHAPTER 11

DEPARTURE

I wasn't going on land, of course, but my request to join the others in the departure was granted. We met in the main hall first thing in the morning, this time all of us much more sullen than the last time we had gathered at the large table.

Fintan had packed up a generous amount of seaweed for each of them to take, but I knew the amount he could hide in his pockets wouldn't last Seamus more than a few days. Supposedly our kind could go a long time without eating, but with the potion already dwindling his strength, I was afraid of what the lack of real sustenance would do to him.

As Seamus placed the orb of Nuvem Morte around his neck and I noted he would be going on land somewhere other than an island, I voiced a question regarding our transformations to Artur. It was one that I had been only moderately curious about until that moment, likely prompted by the sparkling skirt I had appeared in the night before.

"The clothes," I asked the leader of Atlântida, considering he seemed to know more about the magic of mermaids than anyone else I had met. "How does that *work?*"

Back on Hy-Brasil, the land of everlasting sunlight, I had

seen how the others emerged onto the shore in dark green skirts and kilts that were perfectly suited for the climate. I myself had never tried transforming back then, having been told I couldn't as an Amalgam. But once I did alight on Skellig Michael, I had been in the same attire. It had always puzzled me, but I was certainly grateful I hadn't appeared naked, of course. When I had turned into a *selkie* for the first time, on the other hand, I hadn't been so lucky. After my tumultuous fall from the Cliffs of Moher, I had relied on my hair covering my chest until I reached Sorcha's anemone home where she kindly tossed me a bra made of shells. It was the same one that I wore now.

"Oh, it's quite genius, actually," said Artur in the same excitable manner that Raj had always adopted when an academic question was asked of him. "The magic behind what one is wearing when they appear in their land-walker form has everything to do with camouflage. It's designed to give us a disguise that allows us to blend in with others around us, no matter how supernatural we might still appear to be."

I frowned, trying to piece it together.

"But I was in the same skirt on Skellig Michael in October," I said. "And back in Nohoval Cove...at that time of year, no one would be wearing those clothes."

"Neither were ye, for very long," Seamus said quietly next to me. He remembered that skirt very well—he'd taken it off more than once in that short period of time. I elbowed him and suppressed a laugh.

"Ah, well that means that the two of you were completely alone, then," Artur said, oblivious to his comment. "If someone *had* happened upon you, you would have noticed a very quick costume change. It's all about blending in."

Unbelievable. In our world of magic and mythology, there was an answer for *everything*.

I then told him about my miraculously dry hair from the

night before, but it was Aisling who answered me about that phenomenon.

"Oh, I could have showed ye that magic," she said. "I would have on Skellig Michael, but ye were a bit preoccupied, if I remember correctly."

"Easy," I laughed under my breath as I remembered her nearly walking in on Seamus and I…in the middle of something.

"It'll happen naturally when you're in a place where it makes sense," she continued. "But on the islands, ye need to give the magic a bit of a reminder that ye want to dry off."

She flitted away and Seamus glanced at me.

"I don't mind it when you're wet," he said, winking as he grinned. I elbowed him again.

As the Green Window Seamus and I had traveled through to get to Atlântida was no more than an elusive, moving cloud, I had no idea where we would go to enter back through it. Artur answered this question immediately as he led us down into what would have been considered the dungeons of the castle, had we not already fully been submerged underwater.

We entered a bright, beautifully lit room with vertical pools that lined the walls like windows in all different colors. Their liquids swirled within sparkling nebulas that looked similar to the veil of the magical room I had entered last night, but with an ever-present stream of bubbles that reminded me of the Wormhole back on Inishmore. There were purples, greens, blues, and whites…every color I could think of lined the walls. Each pool's contents remained separated from the water all around us, defying the laws of physics once more.

"All Green Windows to other parts of the world, yes," Artur said. "I was too tired of trying to find them in the wild through trial and error, so I installed some that take me to my favorite places. I can usually alter them a bit, if we need to get to a more specific location. For example, the one we're taking today is usually routed for Porto, but I made some adjustments."

"Wow," I said softly, taking in all of the possibilities. I had already digested the fact that the world was so much more accessible to me as a mermaid than a human, but seeing this solidified it. With the vast collection of Green Windows right in front of me, I could go *anywhere.* Maybe I would, while I waited for Seamus to return. Maybe I'd go after some of the stones—if I could come up with some guesses as to where they were—on my own.

"Hy-Brasil's window is over there," Artur continued, pointing to a green swirling pool at the very end of the hall with flecks of bright, electric orange and white within it. It was certainly Irish.

A pool much closer to us churned on the marbled wall with waters of bright red and white, like someone had melted a candy cane in a jacuzzi and turned it sideways. Sparks of black emitted from it in bursts of what was unmistakably thunder or lightning.

"I like having a preview of the weather," Artur said with a shrug. "That one's to Belfast. I added it once I realized Fin would be there more often than here or Hy-Brasil."

"Can't say I'm surprised it's raining in Norn Iron," Aisling said as she observed the magical, swirling flag of her home.

The Window we sought was red and yellow as it beckoned us with the signature colors of the Spanish flag. Clear skies, it seemed, as there was nothing emitting from the pool aside from a light, warm breeze and quiet, peaceful bubbles.

I absentmindedly hoped it wouldn't be too sunny before I was bitterly reminded that it didn't matter. I'd never see the land-locked city of Santiago de Compostela, because I wasn't going any further than the shoreline of Northern Spain. I shook the negativity from my thoughts.

"After you," Artur said, gesturing to Aisling and Fintan. They grasped hands and shot through the portal, vanishing with ease.

Seamus took my hand and we went next; I allowed myself to be pulled through the whirling current while Artur brought up the rear.

The journey was nowhere near as turbulent as the Green Windows I had experienced previously, and it would have been almost pleasant if we hadn't been headed to such a morbid mission. I watched as the serene blues flashed past us; the glimpses of coral, fish, and general sealife welcoming us to a much calmer part of the ocean than the one where I had initially become what I was. The dangerous Cliffs of Moher and the sea below them were positively terrifying in comparison to the tranquil paradise through which I was being propelled now. At one point, I could have sworn I saw the flash of a mermaid tail in the same silver-green shade as mine, but it was gone before I could observe any closer.

"Here we are," I heard Artur call from behind us.

I prepared to dive out of the tunnel of water as I always did, but there was no need. The current came to a gentle stop that allowed for all of us to catch our balance with ease. I knew why Artur preferred creating his own highways across the ocean rather than relying on those that nature had given us–he could ensure both a smooth entrance and exit ramp if he designed them himself.

Seamus rubbed my shoulders as we looked toward the shore. I never would have known it by sight alone, but Artur had told us that the Window would place us off the coast of Pontevedra; specifically near the Parque Nacional Marítimo-Terrestre de las Islas Atlánticas de Galicia. It was a national park with towering mountains that looked almost like the Skelligs. Almost, but not quite as impressive, in my opinion. As I looked upon the similar landscape, I felt the familiar aching nostalgia for Ireland.

"Closest I could get us," Artur said apologetically, knowing it was still quite a swim through the Ría de Arousa before it wound its way to land.

The waterway would eventually trickle off into a small river–Río Ulla–that would get Seamus, Aisling, and Fintan as close as possible to Santiago de Compostela by water. But even then, they'd have quite a journey on land between the tiny villages south of the capital. This would be as far as Artur and I would go with them. He was worried about the possibility of such a large group of us being seen.

The others flitted away in feigned casual conversation in order to give the two of us a final moment of privacy. I looked at Seamus, willing myself to be strong. He was coming back. He was going to accomplish the mission, and then we'd be one step ahead of the other side.

The orb of the Nuvem Morte glimmered around his neck, and I imagined what he'd look like when he gulped it down. What he'd feel like. It pained me that I couldn't do this with him, or in place of him. I touched his freckled cheek softly, wanting to remember every distinct feature of his handsome face with as much detail as possible. Again, I pushed away the memory of the last time I saw Matt, unwilling to acknowledge any parallels between the two occasions. This would *not* be the last time I saw Seamus.

"Come back," was all I could say.

"I will," he promised, green eyes blazing. "I love ye, a stór."

He kissed me urgently one time. When he let go, he swiftly whisked around before I could reply. I nodded, not hoping for another moment as I knew it was useless to delay the inevitable.

Aisling had told me she learned a bit of magic from her mother that kept things dry underwater, and I had asked her to write a small note on my behalf. I then slipped it inside the cuff that Artur had given to Seamus to wear around his wrist, hoping it stayed put and revealed itself to him when he needed it. It was something minor, but I thought it was important. I had placed it there to remind him that he was alive, in case he started to forget. In case the potion infected his mind.

Artur and I watched them go, all three disappearing as the murky waterway narrowed to a slit of a river. I hoped Atargatis' stones would keep Seamus and I connected like they had before. This time, I had one of my own in addition to the citrine around his neck, so I had to believe the likelihood was strong.

"He will return," Artur promised. He spoke with conviction that I know he honestly felt, and I tried to believe the same. I stared absently into the bay, now entirely devoid of any sign of merfolk aside from ourselves.

"How can you be sure?" I asked.

"I've lived through many wars, seen and trained many warriors," he replied. "Seamus is a fighter."

I imagined Seamus draining the deadly poison from the swirling orb in one sip. He would do it without hesitation, fully knowing it would turn him into a spectral nightmare.

PART III

SCHOLAR

CHAPTER 12

WORLDS APART

The first day was long.

If I leaned into my old melodramatic tendencies, I would have called it torture. But I wasn't allowing myself to spiral like I had the last time I experienced hardship relating to losing someone I loved. Because this was not the same as last time. I wasn't losing anyone.

I had clutched the rainbow Iridescent Ammonite with all my might when I went to sleep the first night without him, willing the connection to exist again. But my telepathy failed me, and my loud thoughts were met with radio silence.

I didn't leave the palace the entire next day, despite Artur encouraging me to see more of Atlântida since so much of my time had been spent within the confines of the castle. I didn't even leave my room.

At last, my appetite finally got the best of me. The following morning, I floated lazily downstairs to find Artur seated at the table, flipping through what appeared to be a collection of maps and charts of the Seas. His eyes were narrowed in focus, but they brightened as he saw me emerge.

"Glad you're up," he said, and another place at the table

instantly appeared, donning a bowl of fresh fruit that sat atop a bed of rainbow seaweed.

I carefully picked around the strawberries, knowing the only thing that would satiate me was the mermaid snack that I once abhorred but now couldn't live without. I took a grateful bite, using my fork as I saw Artur doing the same. Even though it was the only way I had ever consumed food since turning into a mermaid, I thought it would be considered rude to eat with my hands in front of him.

"How are you?" he asked kindly, surveying me in the same way that Raj used to when he could tell his daughter was troubled, but didn't want to pry. I appreciated his approach and smiled back warmly.

"I'm okay," I said honestly. "I just wish I knew what was happening out there."

He nodded in understanding and pointed to the stone around my neck. "Anything yet?"

"No," I said flatly.

"Not *yet*," he corrected. "Soon, I expect."

We ate in peaceful silence while I drank yet another strange substance that looked suspiciously like human coffee, but found it to be a deliciously sweet brew that tasted just like chocolate as I remembered it from my human life. It was the only familiar taste that translated to my mermaid existence, it seemed. I drank it deeply.

"I'd like for you to look over these maps I've marked," he said, sliding the miraculously dry parchment toward me. They floated through the water as if they were weighted and magnetic, ending up in my hands without needing to reach for them. "I've placed dots where I think some stones may lie, and I want to see if you can find a pattern. Or if you have any guesses of your own."

I knew a lot of this was fruitless until Seamus returned with answers from Duarte, but I appreciated Artur keeping me busy. I briefly flipped through the maps and shook my head, coming up blank. There were dots all over Asia, South America…some north of Russia. I had no idea where to begin.

"All guesses," Artur sighed. "Based on a number of conversations with others throughout the world who are long dead by now."

I saw no sort of rhyme or reason in his methodology, but my eyes lingered on the entirety of the Middle East, feeling certain that Atargatis would have hidden at least one near her own home. I tapped the vast area vaguely and Artur nodded in agreement.

"Syria," I said quietly. Where Raj's family was from.

My family. Atargatis.

"Yes," Artur said contemplatively. "I think so as well."

"A short coastline," I said, tracing my finger along the tiny patch of the Mediterranean Sea that lined the country's western border. "Not much for us to work with there…"

"Who says it's in the water?" Artur offered.

I shrugged, having always assumed they'd be in or near the water. But then again, the citrine had been sitting in Professor Brennan's office in Dublin. Sure, the stones had all originated from the sea, but there was no telling how many times they could have changed hands…it overwhelmed me.

"Shit, that's a good point," I said at last.

We poured over the maps for another hour or so, Artur explaining the anecdotal evidence he had for believing where some of them were, but both of us agreed it was like finding a needle in a haystack. We would simply have to go there, and I'd have to *feel* them.

Even though they wouldn't have the advantage of my sixth sense for finding the stones, I tried not to imagine Cearbhall and Camila having a similar strategy session to ours. I hoped they were as stupid as they were cruel.

I shifted my focus to another continent and saw a mark that made my stomach sink.

"*America?*" I asked, looking at the red dot that hovered just outside of my old home. Tampa Bay. Off the coast of Anna Maria, specifically. "You think there's a stone of Atargatis hidden somewhere near the United States?"

Artur's brow wrinkled in confusion as he studied my doubtful face.

"Why wouldn't there be?" he asked sincerely. "I suspect there's at least one on every continent."

I laughed. "Well–it's just–America is so...young," I finished lamely, wondering how he thought it possible that my silly little country with less than three hundred years of history could harbor a several centuries-old secret. Of course, the *land* had existed before that, and plenty of inhabitants as well. But still...I had never considered it. Probably because I had no desire to return to my homeland at all, let alone the Gulf Coast of Florida specifically. The more time I spent away from it, the better I healed from what I had lost there.

He shrugged and took another bite of what looked like bacon and eggs. I wondered how he could possibly enjoy it, but guessed he probably did it for habitual reasons more than anything.

"I think checking it out is worth a try," he said with his mouth full of food, reminding me once more that he was, indeed, Fintan's father. "Are you familiar with that area?"

"Oh, yes," I said with a slight laugh. "I used to live there."

His eyes lit up with excitement that made him look much younger than he was.

"Why not take a quick trip, then?" he suggested. "Just to see. If we don't find it, we go back another time."

He spoke of it so casually, as if flying across the world to look for a stone in Florida was part of an insignificant side quest rather than a critical mission.

"Don't tell me you have a Green Window to Tampa Bay," I laughed. The room in the dungeons was big, but not *that* big.

He acknowledged the absurdity of it and shook his head.

"No," he admitted. "But I *do* have one that leads to Havana. It's not terribly far, is it?"

"Probably not for us," I said with a shrug, seeing the distance between Cuba and The United States in a different light than I would have a few months ago. With creatures of our speed, it would probably be like sprinting the length of a football field.

We agreed to go the next day, and I was exceedingly grateful for the chance to leave the kingdom. As much as I wanted to further explore the gleaming city, I found its peaceful isolation to be quite lonely since Artur and I were the only inhabitants of the castle. Others often came and went, but I didn't know how to introduce myself. The thought of venturing out and meeting *real* merfolk–the kind that had likely only ever known this type of existence–severely intimated me. I wondered if that was how Artur felt all the time; like an outsider amongst his own people. Aisling and Fintan seemed to rarely visit, though I still didn't know why.

I spent the rest of the morning reading, deciding it was time that I take advantage of the vast collection of ancient books Artur had in his study. He had found a way–perhaps via counsel of the lords of the underworld again–to preserve an entire library with the same drying magic I had already seen employed on smaller documents.

"It's all yours," Artur said sincerely when I asked for directions to the grand room. "I'm thrilled that someone other than myself gets to enjoy it."

The study was down the same passage as the Room of Windows, and it was one of the most beautiful libraries I had ever seen. In place of wooden shelves that would have been typical in a land-walker's study, Artur's books were nestled between rows of neat, white stone cases and surrounded by a circle of marbled columns. There were globes littered throughout the cove of academia, and I was reminded of Raj. If my father could have *seen* this place...

I flitted around the vast collection aimlessly for several moments as I took it all in. There were endless volumes penned by unfamiliar authors, which wasn't surprising–I couldn't know them all. But several books were written in languages whose origins I couldn't even begin to guess. If there were dialects lost to those of us on land, there had to be an equal number of them lost under the sea, I supposed.

I lazily perused the rows until I remembered I had come for a specific reason. At last, I thought I found what I was looking for.

The real story of Atargatis.

Not a legend retold to me through someone's words out loud, but written down on paper, in a concrete place where I could read them for their truth. It was inside a massive book that could very well have been from ancient Mesopotamia had it not been for the relatively modern-day English in which it was written. Well, that was if you considered the late 19th century to be modern-day, according to the publication date on the back.

I flipped to the very end of *Legends of the Middle East* where I tracked the index to Atargatis' page.

Atargatis, sometimes called Derceto or Derketo (Greek):

The most famous version of the Atargatis myth originates from the city of Ascalon in ancient Syria. According to this legend, Atargatis was a mortal princess who fell deeply in love with a shepherd named Hadad. Despite the vast differences in their social status, their love for each other was pure and unyielding.

She bore him a child, Semiramis, who would later grow up to become the Queen of Syria. They were happy. But one day, in the midst of their intimacy, Atargatis accidentally killed Hadad. She was so distraught by her grave mistake that she threw herself into the water in an attempt to drown herself. She was almost successful, but the gods would not allow it.

The gods took pity on Atargatis and transformed her into a beautiful mermaid, allowing her to survive in the waters she loved so dearly. As a mermaid, she retained her divine powers and continued to watch over the waters, blessing fishermen and sailors who honored her with offerings and prayers.

Throughout the ancient world, Atargatis was worshiped as a goddess of fertility, protection, and the life-giving waters. Her cult spread across the Near East, leaving traces in the religious practices of various cultures, including those of Mesopotamia, Syria, and Phoenicia. Even today, remnants of her worship can be found in archaeological sites and historical texts, a testament to the enduring legacy of this enigmatic goddess.

I flipped to the next page expectantly, but that was it.

I sank back in disappointment. Nothing about Amalgams. Nothing about the stones. It was simply a book from the human world that knew nothing of what truly lay beneath the surface of this ancient legend.

I shelved it once more, irritated by the text that was written by someone who could never have guessed what we were all truly after.

I scanned the other shelves with diligence as I desperately sought a volume that might speak to the legend through a more mystical lens. Perhaps somewhere in ancient history, there was another person like me…someone who had fallen into this world of mythology and tried to understand it. Surely *someone* would have documented the wars that were happening under the sea.

My search was fruitless. There was nothing (at least in a language that I could read) within Artur's magical collection that could tell me more than I had already heard from his own mouth. We were all navigating this journey alone.

I sighed as I looked around for clues, knowing I wouldn't find them here.

CHAPTER 13

BACK TO THE BAY

The following afternoon, I met Artur down in the chamber where the Green Windows were bubbling, casting shadows of vibrant color upon us like moving artwork on the walls. I watched as he seemed to be adjusting something on the frame of the magical pool that was illuminated with red, white and blue, knowing it signified Cuba rather than America.

"Almost got it…" he said, running his hand down the left side and staring into its depths.

The window responded to his touch, beginning to gurgle furiously with excitement.

"There we are," he said, backing away from his work with satisfaction. "This should get us a bit closer to Florida now."

He motioned for me to go ahead of him, and I remembered the hesitation I used to experience before vanishing through the magical portals that took me all over the world. Not anymore. I plunged headfirst into the wall that catapulted me to another continent.

"Here we go," Artur's voice came from behind me as he, too, threw himself into the current.

We whipped through the water, the buzzing of sea creatures

all around us as the various blues and greens of the ocean flew past me in a whirlwind of beauty. I hardly had time to take it in before we started to slow down. I supposed, in the grand scheme of the oceans, the distance between Portugal and Cuba was rather minimal.

The swirling waters came to a halt and I broke through the surface, the whirlpool shooting me toward the light above. I gasped for air and found that the sun was delightful while I was still a mermaid–the beams of heat I hadn't felt in so long hit my face with a force that warmed me to my core. My selkie blood had kept me comfortable in Ireland, but *this* was real warmth.

I saw the shores of Havana in the distance and remembered suddenly that Camila, who I now decided was my mortal enemy, was from Cuba. She had told me so back on Hy-Brasil. Now knowing she must have been a student of my father's at the U in Miami, I shuddered as I imagined her lurking in this same sea.

Before I could dwell on the nightmare, Artur turned to face us north.

"I'd love to take a detour," he said, motioning behind him. "But sending you on land to fetch cigars and rum for me seems like an unfair exchange."

We took off with lightning speed toward the United States, the bathtub water of the Gulf of Mexico enveloping us in its eternal sunshine. I felt a tiny surge of nostalgia as we veered west past the Everglades. Just on the other side of the state would have been my old home in South Florida, the place where I had lived with my father for most of my life. I almost wanted to take a turn and see it again, but we had somewhere else to be. I had to go back to the place I feared the most.

Tampa.

It had been home to me for a few years, but it wasn't anymore. Even when this was all over and we had the time and freedom to land-walk as we pleased, Seamus and I would never live there. We'd go back to Ireland–land or sea, depending on my pain tolerance. The thought of it brought me courage, and I clung to the shred of hope that it would be sooner rather than later. I patted the stone on my chest and gave it a kiss for good luck.

Artur wore a cuff on his right wrist similar to the one he had given to Seamus, and I wondered why he wore it other than for the storage of small, insignificant items. He seemed to glance down at it every now and then, as if the stones encrusted within it brought him peace the way the one around my own neck did.

"Is this area familiar to you?" he called to me.

"Sure is," I said quietly, my stomach turning.

We slowed down near Sarasota as we agreed it was time to look–or, rather, *feel*–around for the stone. Artur was mainly reliant on me, of course, but I had been more than honest when I told him I didn't know how the magic worked. I had no idea if I'd be able to sense it again.

Artur smiled and looked around. "Anything?"

"Not yet," I said, and we trailed on.

We were growing ever-closer to the point where the bay broke from the ocean and back to the shore. I looked up at the familiar, frighteningly high Sky Bridge above our heads that connected South Bradenton to St. Pete. I had always hated that bridge.

The water below it, just east of Fort De Soto Park, had been the scene of Matt and Raj's accident. I hadn't realized how close we were. When I saw it, I froze.

"I—I can't go in there," I stammered, panic beginning to close in on me as the bay seemed to do the same.

I didn't know we'd be passing it…but of course we would. Why hadn't I thought of this? Why had I agreed to do this?

I couldn't be here. Not in these waters.

Artur turned to me, his expression filled with confusion and alarm.

"Jasmine, what's wrong?"

"I–" I breathed, my heart pounding as the cars zoomed back and forth on the bridge above. "Do you not–"

Of course he didn't know. How would he?

How would Artur have a clue as to who I was before I discovered I was destined for a throne of ancient mermaids? Back when I was just Jasmine, Professor Atarga's daughter who was *surely* a disappointment because she didn't even go to grad school. Or when I was Matt Taylor's significantly younger girlfriend who was probably only with him for his money because he was a doctor. I had certainly never told the leader of Atlântida who I really was, and even those under the sea who whispered about me after my existence became known...they would never have known *this* part of my past. The part I had run away from in the first place.

"Jasmine?" Artur asked hesitantly, but his voice was far away.

I didn't reply, and before I knew it, he was guiding me out of the bay by the shoulders. I was unable to feel anything beyond the distant humming of the cars and boats beyond...I would certainly never be able to hear the stone like this.

We were back in the open ocean before he spoke, the shore of St. Pete Beach glimmering faintly in the distance.

"What happened to you here?" he asked kindly, his dark blue eyes searching me.

I opened my mouth, and everything came rushing out at once, like the floodgates to my emotions had been forcibly thrown open. Once I started, I couldn't stop.

I told Artur about Matt and Raj; how my friends had broken the horrible news of their deaths to me on the morning of my engagement. How I ran away to Ireland hoping to escape it all, and ended up meeting Seamus who I fell so deeply in love with that it poisoned me with guilt. I told him how I fell off the Cliffs and ended up on Hy-Brasil under the care of Sorcha–Artur's own estranged partner–who told me what I had become. Once I was scooped up by Cearbhall and Camila, he knew the rest of the story. I was breathing heavily, the sobs above the waves so much more prominent than those I could have wailed in the silver smoke of mermaid tears under the sea.

I spoke for a long time without pausing, but Artur never wore an expression other than meditative patience and understanding. When I finally finished, I looked up at him with pleading eyes. I hoped he wouldn't think me a coward after everything I had revealed.

"I didn't know anything of your true past," he said quietly. "I should have asked you earlier."

"I just feel so weak," I said, all pretenses now dropped. "Like I can't get out from under what's happened to me, no matter what I do. It's pathetic."

He shook his head and took me by the shoulders.

"It's the opposite, Jasmine," he said. "You have been incredibly brave."

"It doesn't feel like it," I said, thinking of how I wept when Seamus left. How I clutched the stone like some helpless damsel in distress, pleading for him to come home.

"You have emerged victorious from the trials in your past," Artur said. "And I know you'll do it again. What's happened to you has made you a fighter."

"I'm not," I said honestly, shaking my head. "I couldn't even finish what needed to be done when I had Camila in my grasp back in Portugal. I just froze, and then we let her go."

"Do not mistake mercy for weakness," Artur said warningly. "It takes far more strength to spare someone's life than to send them to their death."

I nodded, having nothing else to say. I could tell he meant what he said, and who was I to question the wisdom of the great leader of Atlântida? We bobbed above the waves in silence for a moment before he spoke again.

"Your friends," he said quietly, looking back toward the bay. "Those from your trip to Ireland. They think you're dead?"

"Everyone does," I said. "Seamus and I planned to go back eventually, to clear some things up…but there's been no time."

"There's time now."

I stared blankly at Fintan's father, who so closely resembled my own the way he looked at me now. Like he was going to push me to do something difficult, because he knew it was the right thing to do.

"I can't," I whispered. "I can't face them."

"You can," he said firmly. "And you should. They will want to know that you're well. Don't let this curse that has befallen you win."

"I'm surprised you're encouraging me to go on land when that's what we just sent Seamus to do," I said quietly. "Because I couldn't."

"This won't take nearly as long as that," Artur replied, pointing to the bay. "What do you need? Sunset and a couple of hours at most?"

He was serious. He really wanted me to do it. I bit my lip apprehensively.

"Do you want your friends to continue believing you've taken your own life when the truth is that you're the happiest you've ever been?" he asked.

"Am I the happiest I've ever been?" I said rhetorically, gesturing to the tears that hadn't yet dried on my face above the waves. I wiped away the thick, silvery wetness with my forearm.

"With Seamus, it seems you are," he said simply. "You can be happy while also taking responsibility for your destiny, you know. Both of you have shown that already."

"Both of us shouldn't need to," I said. "It's *my* burden, not his."

Artur chuckled. "Oh, there isn't a burden of yours that he wouldn't gladly shoulder for you. *That* much is obvious."

I looked back toward the bay. I didn't want to. I *really* didn't want to.

But Artur was right…it was wrong to let my friends think I

was dead. I owed them the closure, if nothing else. I had already left them in the dark once, and they had pulled me out of the depths of despair, only to have me abandon them again. I had to make things right.

The sun was already beginning to set. I *could* do it.

"Alright," I said finally. "Let's go…before I change my mind."

CHAPTER 14

ARTUR'S TAIL

e shot across the bay as quickly as we could, staying close to the ocean floor out of fear of being spotted. The autumn in Tampa was actually quite a nice—and popular—time to be out on the water. There were a number of cruise ships docked at Sparkman's Wharf, and I tried my best to read the large clock and calendar near them that marked the date.

"Six," I murmured to Artur. "I can't read the date, though."

He looked at me curiously. "Would that make a difference?"

"I suppose not," I sighed. "But it would be nice to know if it's a weekend or not."

He pointed to a sign above the beer garden in the distance. It was the same one I had been to countless times because it was walking distance from both of our places, even before Matt and I lived together. I had laughed here with him, enjoyed happy hour drinks and talking about nothingness…in another life.

Thirsty Thursday, the sign read.

Perfect. If there was one thing Kristen would be doing on a Thursday, it would be having a drink.

And I thought I knew exactly where. I hoped she hadn't changed much in the few months since I'd seen her.

"And now we wait," Artur said, falling back to float atop the waves. I did the same.

We lingered as the sun continued to sink, and I broached the subject of the oasis room. I wanted Artur to know how impressive I thought it was.

"It's lovely," I said as he beamed with pride at his invention. "But I'm sorry to hear that it didn't work for you. I'm sorry that you can't land-walk, even there."

He waved in dismissal. "I'm just glad someone gets to enjoy Utopia. Although, the passage there can be quite jarring the first time you do it."

I recalled the rush of harsh emotions I had experienced on my journey into the sparkling sea; the memories that nearly broke me flying directly alongside those that brought me back to life.

"Why?" I asked. "Why does the passage show you such... severe memories?"

"It's payment," he said seriously. "Payment for entry requires one to acknowledge the hardships of reality. Only then can you enjoy the spoils of Utopia...when you know it can never be real."

"That's profound," I said, and I really meant it.

Artur nodded and laughed. "Well, I hoped to design it to show each person something different. Their own version of perfection. What a true *Utopia* would look like to them."

I smiled. "Seamus and I both see versions of Ireland. The green parts, not the cities. The inlets, cliffs, and little islands...all jumbled into one."

"That means you both really love it there...you see it as home," he said.

"What do you see?" I asked.

"I see Ireland as well, actually," he said. "Dublin, though. I pop up in the River Liffey."

"Interesting," I said, amused by his answer. "It's quite filthy, isn't it?"

"Now it is, but it wasn't back then," he said wistfully. "That's where I saw Sorcha for the first time."

"Oh?" I asked politely. I hoped he'd tell me more, because I was more than moderately curious about his love affair with Fintan's mother.

"I was a human when I met Sorcha," he continued.

This took me by surprise, considering Sorcha had been the one to tell me that mermaids couldn't physically *desire* humans once they were changed…it wasn't biologically possible. There were a few things Sorcha had told me that I didn't necessarily believe were wholly true, and considering how I still thought of Matt longingly now and again, I wondered if this was one of them.

He must have known exactly what I was curious about, and he spared me from asking.

"Oh I wanted Sorcha. She didn't want me," he said. "Not really. She treated me like a friend. At least in the beginning."

Considering they ended up having a child together, I didn't see how that was the case, but I waited patiently for him to tell his story.

"I lived in Lisbon for a large part of my life, but I was in Dublin for months at a time frequently in those days. It took a lot longer to get there by ship, of course," he said, winking at me. "I'd always make time to see the Irish girl I met by the river that I couldn't get out of my head. I fell in love with her, and when I found out what she was, I begged her to change me. But she wouldn't."

"I thought only Amalgams could change people?" I asked.

"Well, she had been in battle against Amalgams already and had at least one scar to prove it," he said. "It doesn't change anything about a real mermaid if they're marked by one, other than giving them the power to do it themselves. To make other Amalgams."

I was shocked to hear this. I had never even thought of the possibility that any others besides those who were damned to the seas forever could have the power to do it–the power to change humans. I wondered how many Amalgams on Hy-Brasil had marked other selkies with the burden. I didn't respond, thinking of the scar on my own hand. Did that mean...

I didn't want to know. I'd *never* do it.

"As I mentioned, the Amalgams have been searching for the stones for a long time," Artur said. "This latest wave of Cearbhall and Camila is just another crew rising to power."

I was trying to piece together a possible timeline in my head, but I had no concept of mermaid history or which conflicts had preceded the one we were facing now. Artur knew what I was doing once again.

"Yes, I'm certainly old, Jasmine," he said. "But Sorcha's older. She's seen a lot more war than I have."

I nodded, urging him to continue.

"So one day, we were on holiday in Western Ireland, visiting her family. Of course she didn't tell them that I knew what she was," he said. "None of them would've cared anyway, I expect. They weren't the best people. But I was insistent on going to The Wormhole on Inishmore–"

I let out an amused chuckle recalling the Green Window of the Aran Islands, and he grinned in response.

"Of course I didn't know what it was back then," he laughed. "I wondered all morning why Sorcha was so adamantly against us going to see it. It was a major tourist destination, after all."

He paused before letting out a sigh.

"And then, because I'm an idiot, I *fell in*."

I looked up in alarm, wondering how the mermaid portal didn't tear him to shreds or suffocate him. "What happens if a human falls in?"

"They don't work for humans, so typically nothing," he said. "But Sorcha's arm was locked around my own, and she came tumbling in with me. Once we were inside, the current started to pull, and I would've died if she hadn't marked me right then and there. I changed halfway through, just when I had nearly run out of air."

I was horrified by the dark turn his story had taken. I knew it was impolite to ask, but he had told me this much so far. I asked him my most pressing question.

"Does Fintan know?"

"Yes, he does," sighed Artur. "We told him when he was old enough. And then it took him a long time to forgive me. To believe that I hadn't done it on purpose, in order to force his mother to change me."

I said nothing. I had secretly been wondering the same. The coincidence seemed too unlikely.

"The truth is, Jasmine," he sighed. "I wanted to be with her so badly that I understood why everyone thought I had done it on purpose. Some days I think I would have eventually tricked her into it, if only to be with her in every way possible. Of course, I didn't realize what being an Amalgam really meant…physically."

"I understand," I said, feeling a distinct pang of sadness for his misjudgment. I remembered the days when I thought Seamus was lost to me forever because of what I was. "So what happened then?"

"She didn't believe me that it was an accident, and therefore couldn't forgive me. But she was already pregnant with Fintan," he said, his eyes glazing over with regretful remembrance. "I knew she loved me, even though she never said it."

So maybe *that* was why Sorcha told me the things she had. She didn't want me to believe it was possible to love a human. Maybe because she wished it wasn't.

I should have known, considering Seamus' own parentage consisting of a selkie mother and human father.

I tried to imagine how Saoirse could ever, at any time, have loved Seamus' horrible father. But then I had a sick thought.

Maybe she hadn't. Maybe he had forced her.

I recalled the original selkie legend told to Seamus by Mrs. Byrne, the witch from Cashel that had given him the clues that led him to find me. It was one he already knew from childhood—the tale of Thady Rua O'Dowd, the Irish clan chieftain who trapped his selkie bride on land by hiding her pelt. Even though I knew doing so wasn't *really* possible given the true nature of our transformations, the sentiment was the same. Forcing a selkie woman to stay on land against her will. It seemed horrifically obvious now, and my stomach churned.

"Once you find out, the mother is supposed to stay in her land-walker form until giving birth," Artur said, continuing his tale. "And then we toss the baby in the ocean after it's born and see what happens."

His statement caught me off guard as I had been so lost in my dark thoughts.

"What?" I barked out a laugh despite myself. "You do *what?*"

"I mean, we're gentle about it, and some superstitious parents avoid it, I've heard…but that *is* what most of those with the selkie blood do," he said with a shrug. "Not that it's always revealed right away, of course. Some transformations happen much later in life. No one knows why."

All of the discussion surrounding the technicalities of pregnancy as a mermaid made me instinctively clutch my stomach, even as I laughed.

But no. There was no way…I couldn't be.

I gulped. That was the *last* thing Seamus and I needed right now given the hardship we were facing—and would continue to face—on a daily basis. Artur must have known what I was thinking and gave me a curt, warning raise of his eyebrow.

"I hope you two are being careful, Jasmine," he said, and my face practically lit on fire with embarrassment. This was *just like* talking to my dad. Only he wasn't my dad, and that made it even worse. "Maybe ask Aisling to um…provide you with some guidance."

I thought I would die as I nodded, only now realizing how careless Seamus and I had been.

Would the symptoms be the same as a mermaid? I tried to remember the few times I had land-walked since our first…*union* on Skellig Michael. I had done so back in Nohoval Cove, and again in Utopia…but none of those times had been particularly lengthy in duration.

Had I felt anything strange back then? Nausea? Headaches? I honestly couldn't remember any physical sensation other than the kind that had me sighing his name. I hadn't gotten my period, but I assumed that was just because I wasn't human anymore. I tried to count the amount of times we had been together within the past month, and I was suddenly terrified. What was I *thinking?*

But there was admittedly a tiny part of me, a nearly nonexistent part, that wondered what it would be like.

Even though it felt almost forbidden to picture it after such a short amount of time, I already knew that Seamus would be an incredible father. Being the fierce protector over me that he was, I was certain he'd be the same with a child. And like a large majority of other humans on the precipice of marriage, I *had* wanted children back in my old life. Matt had wanted them so badly, too. Of course he had; he was a pediatrician. He would have been a phenomenal father, too.

I remembered the day when I had had a terrifying, very real pregnancy scare. It happened at a time well before I was intrigued by the idea—or even open to it, for that matter—of motherhood.

Becoming a parent was the fodder of nightmares to me, but apparently not to him.

·   ·   ·

"I CAN'T…" I said, shaking as I held the test in my hands.

I was already over a week late, and I was never late.

Matt looked at me with soft eyes and smiled from across the granite countertop of the island. The space between us felt enormous, despite his kind, comforting demeanor that assured me we were in this together. He couldn't understand.

"Jazz," he said gently. "What are you afraid of?"

"Everything," I admitted, imagining what my dad would say if I told him I was pregnant out of wedlock by a man who was nearly a decade older than myself. The boyfriend he had yet to meet. The boyfriend I had been dating for less than six months.

I was so fucked.

Matt looked me up and down and sighed, kissing me on the forehead before he made his way to the window of his apartment. His much-nicer-than-mine, *adult* apartment. Because that's what he was. An adult. Someone who would be capable of being a father and providing for a family. Meanwhile, I was barely out of college. He crossed his arms and turned to me.

"I'll take care of you, you know," he said in a small voice. "If… if you don't want to be with me."

I knew what he meant. He was a doctor. He was opening his own practice within the next couple of years. He had money, and I had nothing.

"What?" I exclaimed, nearly dropping the box on the floor. "How could you say that?"

He tossed his hands in the air in frustrated confusion. "What else could it be, Jazz?"

I was breathless as I sputtered out my next words. "The fact that I'm…that I'm twenty-two years old and nowhere near ready to be a mother!"

"We'd figure it out together," he said. "You wouldn't be alone."

"Do you…do you want to be with *me?*" I asked, fearing the crippling feeling of rejection. "Or are you saying you'd rather pay me off?"

"No, no, no, *Jasmine*, please," he said with his sincere smile and kind eyes that were utterly incapable of lying. He rushed back to my side and grasped my hands. "I'd ask you to marry me right now, if that's what you wanted."

"It's not about that," I grumbled.

Marriage scared me, too. How did he not see he was making this *worse?*

"For what it's worth, I'd love for you to be the mother of my children," he said as he tried to meet my gaze, but I couldn't look at him. "But I won't push you. I won't be upset no matter what happens. And we can decide–"

"*We? We* decide?" I shouted, fear-induced rage rising in my chest. "How *dare* you even suggest that *you* would get to have a say in what *I* do with *my*–"

He held up his hands in solemn surrender that quieted me instantly.

"Jasmine, that's not what I meant," he said calmly, and I felt my heart rate slowing as I saw his earnestness. "I would never suggest it's anyone's choice but yours. I am a *doctor*, remember?"

I sighed, my hands still trembling as I turned the box over again.

"I know," I said. A doctor for *children* specifically, at that.

"Take the test," he said. "Please."

So I did, and I could have sworn I saw a flicker of disappointment in his face when I told him it was negative.

I REALIZED that I had no idea how Seamus felt about children. Or marriage, for that matter. Although I felt our souls were connected, there were a lot of practical, real-life things I didn't know about him. I didn't often think about it, considering how little time we had for such topics over the past few weeks, but a memory like the one I had just recalled reminded me just how important those types of conversations were.

But realistically…what would it change now if we disagreed? I hoped we wouldn't, but I wanted to be with him more than I wanted anything else.

"Looks like it's time," Artur said, bringing me back to the present. I swiftly removed my hand from my stomach where it had lingered during my daydream, and watched the final rays of sun fall beneath the surface.

"I think so," I said. "And you'll–"

"I'll be right here waiting for you," he promised. "Take your time."

"Okay," I said slowly, turning toward the shore. Toward the people who were living normal lives, entirely oblivious to the two half-humans lurking in the bay.

He smiled encouragingly. "Go."

I paused just as I was about to get out of the water, remembering something from Artur's story of his own life.

"I've never seen her scar," I said. "Sorcha's mark you said she had from the Amalgam. I spent several days with her before I left Hy-Brasil, and I never saw any markings on her."

"Yes, well," Artur blushed. "It's in a rather–intimate place."

"Oh," I said, my cheeks burning. I wished I hadn't asked.

CHAPTER 15

PARTIAL TRUTHS

I snaked through the busiest part of the wharf, avoiding the tourists' eyes as best I could. It was arguably the most populated area of downtown Tampa, but I had no other choice. I found a small patch of sand behind the small dog park that was now abandoned given the time of day. It would have to suffice.

I willed my transformation to go faster as I felt the chatter increasing on the street behind me. Just as I began to panic, I looked down to see the familiar green, silk skirt fluttering in the wind. Because I was in Florida, I didn't look out of place at all in the island getup. Much like it had in the oasis room when I thought of it, my hair dried instantly with a gust of wind. Camouflage, indeed, I smirked. A searing pain shot through my leg and I froze, but it vanished almost as quickly as it had come on. Either way, the sun was gone now, and I wouldn't be here long.

Brushing off the skirt as best I could, it occurred to me that for the first time ever as a land-walker, I also had *shoes.* Every time I had been on land so far, Seamus and I had been on a beach. I had never even thought about the need for footwear, and I laughed as the beige sandals on my feet seemed to perfectly fit the disguise of a human on a vacation in Florida.

Here goes nothing, I thought, making my way across the small dog park and onto the sidewalk where normalcy began.

The Water Street district was just around the corner. It was a place that I had resolutely avoided the entire year I grieved given what I had learned at a restaurant there, despite living in a condo directly above it. I glanced upward at the silver building I knew, all of the windows lit up with the lives of others who existed so similarly to how I had back then. I tried to count the windows to find my own place, but I stopped as soon as I reached what I thought was my old floor. I didn't want to see it.

I caught my reflection in one of the windows below and was met with a shocking sight. There were mirrors all over Artur's castle, but I hadn't spent much time looking in them. I hadn't really *studied* my appearance in a long time, and it was surreal to do so now.

My eyes were still brown, but with a distinctive hint of bright, electric green lining the irises that was impossible to miss. My long black hair was rich, thick, and cascading in voluminous curls down my back. My arms were toned with muscle I certainly had not had during the months I failed to eat a single square meal, and I looked so much better–no, *healthier*–than I had the last time I had been here.

I rounded the corner and saw two of Kristen's old favorite places. Marissa may or may not be with her given it was a week-night. Kiana was definitely not here since she lived in D.C., which was highly disappointing, considering she was the one I really wanted to see. She was the one who had continued to look for me the longest when I went missing. She continued to believe in me, even after I had been a horrible friend to her.

My heart pounded as I looked through another window.

Sleek, golden hair in a high ponytail on top of her head, and shoulder-length auburn waves right next to her. I'd know the two of them anywhere.

I stood in the street, frozen with indecision as I alternated between telling my friends the truth, half of it, or an outright lie. Surely they would have heard from James—Seamus' best friend that they had met in Dublin—that Seamus was also gone. He'd vanished without a trace, too, after all. Maybe Aidan had an alibi for him, but I couldn't imagine what it would be.

Should I tell them we ran away together? We *did*, in a way. I didn't need to specify just how far we had gone, did I?

I felt myself shrinking away from the entrance, and I knew I had to go in now or I'd never do it.

I swung the door open to the restaurant and I barely heard the hostess as she asked me if I wanted a table. I thought her gaze lingered upon me curiously for a moment longer than was polite, and I realized with a jolt that she could very well have recognized me from the news. I was sure I'd been all over it, both here and in Ireland. Even with my supernatural features, my face was still probably familiar.

"No, thanks," I replied, avoiding eye contact. "I'm meeting someone here."

The two of them must have recognized my voice, because they both turned around at the same time. Kristen's face went blank with shock, while Marissa's glass fell straight to the floor and shattered, sending blood red wine sweeping across the white tile.

"Hi," I said.

"What...the *fuck*?" Kristen said breathlessly, and I understood. She was looking at a ghost. "We thought–"

"I know," I said quietly, the guilt of what I had put them through descending upon me with unrelenting force. They had likely accepted my death months ago...I didn't even know how long it had been, actually. I couldn't remember when exactly I had fallen from the Cliffs. Maybe August? Or was it September?

Marissa said nothing, but took it upon herself to move all of us to a booth for privacy. The hostess didn't object, noting that the restaurant was relatively empty and there was something very odd happening between the three of us. We sat for a moment before Kristen reached across the table and embraced me tightly, a single tear falling down her cheek. Marissa followed suit, the expression on her face unreadable.

Their hugs weren't the familiar embraces of friends relieved to see one another. They were confused and afraid. They were cold.

"I'm sorry," I said. "That's what I want to say first."

There was a long pause that nearly suffocated me. Just as I was about to speak again, Marissa cleared her throat.

"I can't say we forgive you until we hear an explanation," she said shakily, taking me by surprise. Usually the meeker of the two, I had expected a softer reception from Marissa. But she was hurt, and that was fair. It was the second time I had gone rogue on them in a year.

"I know," I said. "I–"

But she cut me off. "Just when we thought we had you back, you disappeared again," she said quickly, blinking away what I thought was a tear behind her thick glasses. "Where did you go? Why didn't you call?"

Her voice trembled as the words rushed out, like she had rehearsed what she was going to say in the mirror but never thought she'd actually get the chance.

Kristen, on the other hand, shook her head incredulously, eyes unblinking. She spoke before I could reply.

"Jasmine, do you…do you know that everyone thinks you're dead?"

Her voice cracked. I had never seen my most confident friend waver in this way.

"Yes," I said quickly. "But–I'm not."

"Answers," Marissa demanded, wiping the now streaming tears from her eyes. "Now."

I sighed. How much could I tell them?

"I've been with Seamus," I said slowly, and this was met with a collective sigh that contained a hint of annoyance I couldn't miss.

"Well I'm sure James will be relieved to hear that," Kristen said, her usual sarcastic demeanor emerging as her shock thawed beneath the tension. "You know they've been trying to get Seamus on a missing persons list for weeks, but Aidan won't do it?"

"Aidan?" I asked quickly, wondering if Kiana had told them what she had researched with Seamus. I didn't think so, but I couldn't be sure. "How do you know Aidan?"

Kristen waved dismissively. "I don't. But when Seamus didn't show up to work for the third week in a row, in addition to failing to answer anyone's calls, James finally got a hold of Aidan. Apparently he has all these cryptic answers about Seamus going sailing with him and somehow he's never near the phone."

I wondered what else Aidan could possibly have said to quell their concerns, and found that I had no better ideas. It seemed like he was simply buying time until Seamus returned. Fintan had told us he'd sent word…but how practical would it have been for Aidan to tell James that a selkie had appeared on Inishmore, assuring him that Seamus was alright?

"Jesus, Jasmine," Marissa said, shaking her head. "You have no idea what kind of a mess the two of you have caused."

Don't get angry, don't get angry, I thought to myself. They're just humans. They can't understand.

"Look at me," Marissa said. My gaze was locked on the table, trying to think of what else to say.

My eyes met hers and I knew she was studying the strange color of my irises. They probably looked even more supernatural to her than they did to me. *Had* Kiana told them her suspicions about the selkie legends? I doubted it, considering Seamus had told me that Kiana stopped believing in them herself. But just as I thought Marissa was preparing to draw attention to the changes in my features, Kristen interjected.

"Where did you guys go?" she asked. "It's been almost *two months*."

So *that* was how much time had passed. Did that mean it was late October? Maybe November? My concept of time was warped, but I couldn't dwell on it—they were staring at me expectantly.

"Portugal," I said. *Not a lie, not a lie.* "And then Spain."

"Why?" Kristen pressed. "I mean, why not tell us you wanted to…run away with him? I obviously would have told you not to, but we *were* all rooting for you two."

"I don't know," I said lamely.

I couldn't look at her, because "running away" with a guy wasn't something I'd ever do, and she knew it. Despite how distant I had become from them, they both knew damn well I wasn't the impulsive type. If I met her eyes, she'd see right through me.

Marissa looked at me intently before softening ever so slightly.

"Jasmine, does he treat you well?" she asked seriously, the shadow of her former self coming to the surface. "I mean…are you okay?"

"If you're implying he kidnapped me–no, he didn't," I snapped before I could stop myself.

She hardened again, sitting back in her chair. Kristen rolled her eyes, and I knew they had grown tired of my sudden outbursts of anger. I didn't blame them. I sighed, trying to find a way to tell a version of the truth.

"I'm sorry, I just wanted to explore this thing with him before I said anything to you both," I said, knowing it was a weak explanation, but I had nothing else.

Neither of them were put at ease by this.

I knew I couldn't answer their questions unless I told them everything, which wasn't an option. I had certainly considered it—as it would technically be the easiest thing to do—but I feared their reactions.

They had already thought of me as mentally unstable before all of this happened, and telling them I had become a mermaid would send them over the edge. They would think I'd snapped. As much as their opinions of me were already destroyed, I wanted to at least preserve the notion that I was *sane*. And I could definitely never show them what I was. They would be terrified.

"So do you like…love him?" Kristen asked bluntly. "You must. In order to do something this stupid."

"I do," I said simply.

She looked back at me with mingled worry and frustration.

"Where is he?" Marissa asked sharply. "Is he here with you?"

"No, he's still in Spain," I replied. *Offer nothing extra*, I told myself. *Nothing but the truth you can tell.* "And I'm going back."

"So you just flew all the way here to tell us you're alive instead of calling from Spain," Kristen said skeptically. "We're honored."

"Kristen," I sighed, begging her to meet me halfway so I didn't have to lie anymore. "Please. I'm trying."

"I just don't get it," she said under her breath as she leaned back in her chair.

Marissa studied me behind her thick frames. "Are you going to call Kiana?"

"I can't," I said, and both of them clucked with disapproval. "I was hoping one of you could tell her."

Kristen scoffed loudly, having reached the end of her patience.

"You owe Kiana a massive apology, and you think we're going to tell her that you showed up in Tampa to tell us you ran away with some guy you met in Ireland…all while allowing everyone to think you were dead?" she said. "You think she deserves to hear that news from *us*?"

"I think she'd understand," I replied coldly.

I truly believed she would, when she heard my friends' description of my appearance. She would know Seamus had been right all along. She was smart, and she would figure it out. I had to believe that she would.

There was a long, painful pause as the food they had ordered came to the table and they begrudgingly offered me a spring roll. Luckily I had no appetite for their type of food now, so when I declined, it was sincere.

Marissa's engagement ring caught my eye, and I realized that she had surely chosen her wedding date by now. I once thought I'd stand up next to her on her big day, but I'd never be asked to be a bridesmaid now. I wondered how Kristen was faring since her split with Christian–she had broken up with him over the summer before our trip, but of course in my selfishness, I had never asked how she was doing. I never thought of anyone besides myself back then.

As I looked at the two people across the table from me, I realized I hardly knew anything about them anymore.

Since I had nothing more I could say, and they had done nothing to indicate openness to reconciliation, I decided the conversation was over. I stood to leave and they stared at me, lost for words.

"I know it won't be today, but I hope you can eventually forgive me," I said, the silvery tears starting to well in my eyes. I didn't care if they noticed the strange phenomenon. "I didn't want to hurt either of you. I really didn't. And I appreciated everything you did for me."

No response, just stoic faces. From their perspective, I'd abandoned my nearly ten years of friendship with them for a guy I met two months ago. *That* made my stomach turn.

I only had one sentence left in me, so I said it.

"I guess I just wanted you to see me one more time... so you can let me go."

I didn't look back as I swept out the door and into the street, knowing I would never see them again. The silver tears were now flowing uncontrollably, and I ran for the water as fast as I could, wishing I had felt the physical pain of my Atargatis' curse instead of this.

145

CHAPTER 16

NOVA VIDA

Artur was kind enough not to press me for information when I returned to the water with tears streaming down my face while simultaneously insisting I was fine. As soon as I hit the waves and my legs were replaced by my tail, I felt the familiar physical relief of being back where I needed to be.

I felt moderate emotional relief as well, having at least revealed to my friends that I was alive. Even if they hated me for it, they knew the most important part of the truth.

"The stone isn't here," I said definitively, wiping my eyes before descending under the waves. "I would have felt it if we were in the bay."

"Are you sure?" Artur asked gently.

I nodded, bringing my attention back to the task at hand. Throughout my life, I had often distracted myself from acknowledging my feelings by throwing myself into objective tasks, and I saw no reason why I couldn't do the same this time. The stone. That's why we were really here.

"I am, actually," I repeated, clearing my head and voicing a suspicion that now came to my mind. I repeated Camila's words regarding Raj's death that she had spoken to me beneath Carrickfergus Castle. How his death wasn't an accident, leading me to believe she had at least been present for it, if not orchestrated it herself. Artur nodded contemplatively as I spoke.

"So you think Camila may have already found the stone that was here," he said. "If there was one?"

"Maybe," I said with a shrug. "She claimed the stone was from the Antilles, but that's not terribly far from the Gulf of Mexico. And I just…don't feel anything here."

Nothing but self-pity, anyway, I thought.

He didn't look entirely convinced, but given the accessible network of Green Windows in his own basement, I thought we could try again another day. Today's task had been accomplished, even though it left me feeling worse than I had before I had done it. I didn't regret it, necessarily, because I had known all along how Kristen and Marissa would receive me. I had been a terrible friend to them well before all of this happened. I didn't deserve their forgiveness.

As soon as we got back to Atlântida, I flitted up to my tower for solitude. It was now the middle of the night, and I just wanted to sleep so I could dream the horrible day away.

I pictured what Seamus would say if he were next to me now, lying in our soft, velvet bed under the sea.

"That's alright, mo chroí, they'll forgive ye eventually. We'll try again."

But Seamus wasn't here.

It then hit me how ridiculously selfish I was being—whining about my friends hating me while Seamus was fighting a perilous battle on land with the dead. I shifted my focus to him, begging the universe to keep him safe. I drifted off to sleep, talking to him through my thoughts.

It didn't work. I was greeted with a nightmare.

· · ·

I WAS BACK in my beautiful condo in Tampa that I shared with Matt, soaking in my bathtub. He was standing above me at the sink, staring down at me. I looked up into his cobalt eyes that were clouded with puzzlement and…what else was that? Fear?

Yes. It was most likely fear, because just below the surface of the water was the distinct outline of my iridescent tail. I was a mermaid.

"What happened, Jazz?" he asked, shaking his head in dismay. "Marissa and Kristen told me you were dead."

As was customary for him, he looked exceptionally handsome, even with his brows wrinkled in worry. He was wearing a crisp, beige linen suit without a tie, personifying effortless sophistication while his dark brown hair tinged with subtle curls caught the final rays of sunlight that streamed in through the window. When his hair was cut short, he looked like a celebrity on the red carpet, and when he let the curls grow a bit longer, he looked like a professional hockey player traveling for a game. Either way he presented himself, his refined features were so elegantly structured to perfection; like he was too lovely to be real.

"I'm not," I said lamely, gesturing to my general appearance. "I'm just…this now."

I reached for him, trying to grasp his hand. He backed away, nearly stumbling across the slick tile as he went.

"Matt," I said, my voice strained. "Come on…it's me."

He looked around in all directions before finally resigning and sitting on the floor next to the tub. I propped myself up on the edge with my elbows so I could meet his gaze.

"Your eyes are different," he said. "*You're* different."

"Well, yeah," I laughed. "I have a tail."

He didn't laugh. He looked like he wanted to cry, which made me want to do the same.

"What's wrong?" I asked, reaching for his hand again. This time he took it, but reluctantly.

He ran his hands over my own and I noticed that I was wearing my engagement ring—the one that had somehow been salvaged in the accident that took his life. In real life, I had only put it on my finger one time before tearing it off and placing it on a chain that I wore around my neck for months after his death. It was something everyone thought was odd, but I couldn't bear to part with it entirely back then. Matt had never even gotten to give it to me himself, and it was so unfair.

"Everyone has been worried sick about you," he whispered. "Why didn't you call?"

I looked at him, desperately wanting to explain, but how could he not understand? Didn't he see that I had no choice but to become what I was? Why did *no one* seem to understand that I didn't voluntarily leave everything behind? If I had had a choice—

Would I have chosen otherwise?

"Are you going to come back home and marry me?" he asked, his hand still hovering on my ring finger.

"I—" but my voice caught in my throat. Of course I would. But how? How could we be together now? He wasn't even *alive...*

"I have the strangest feeling you don't love me anymore," he continued, and then he looked into my eyes, piercing me with his deep blue stare that was filled with nothing but goodness. Kindness and goodness that I didn't deserve. "Is that true?"

I stared at him blankly.

"Of course it's not!" I said desperately. "How could you think that?"

He didn't respond to me, but looked out the floor-to-ceiling window wistfully.

"I miss loving you," he said, and I saw a tear forming in the corner of his eye. Oh no, I couldn't see Matt cry. To see *him*—the happiest person I knew—shed a tear...it would kill me. He was too bright. "I miss being with you."

"Me too," I whispered, knowing what he meant.

I thought of our intimacy, remembering the romance beneath our soft sheets when he'd laid his entire heart out before me. Just around the corner from this bathroom was the master bedroom we'd shared; I could picture the white curtains and miraculous view of the bay sparkling below. It was the room in which he had made love to me gently and purposefully, like I was a piece of breakable, rare art. Like I was to be revered and handled delicately because of how valuable he believed me to be. I missed it so much it hurt.

"Do you?" Matt asked. "Even when you're with *him*?"

I froze. How did he know about Seamus?

No rules of logic in dreams. That's how.

"What–what are you talking about?" I stammered.

He looked into his lap before his gaze returned to the window where the sun had set. The gray of the evening descended upon us, and nothing but my tail illuminated the room.

"When he makes love to you," Matt replied quietly. "I don't think you remember me at all."

I felt like I had been punched in the stomach, hearing him acknowledge that I was with someone else. I looked down at my hand and saw the ring had vanished.

When I looked back up, Matt was gone, too.

Even my subconscious knew it was being unusually cruel. I was violently jolted awake in the dark blue chamber, and my eyes remained fixated on the marbled ceiling of my room until the sun rose again.

I chose to get lost in my thoughts while staying awake, because the alternative of trying to sleep them off had proven much worse.

Matt had certainly been a much different lover than Seamus, but oh…it broke my heart to hear that he thought I could ever forget him and the way he looked at me on those nights. I kept those memories closer to my heart than he knew.

And his words asking me to come home rang in my ears. I wondered what I would have done if everything had been different. What if there had been no accident, and I had ended up in Ireland anyway? What if I'd been called to the sea, destined for my new life with Seamus, but Matt was waiting for me back home?

I stopped myself.

Hypotheticals had no place in my mind during the darkest hours of night.

* * *

ARTUR SEEMED to notice my generally sullen behavior, because he sent someone up to my room once the day had begun. Someone to hang out with. Someone my age.

"Hello," came a voice from the doorway. Within it floated the outline of a brown-haired woman with glowing, dark skin and a bright blue tail. Next to her bobbed a companion who matched her stunning countenance in nearly every way. They were both strikingly beautiful, and undoubtedly brother and sister.

"Hi," I answered awkwardly.

"Artur says you haven't seen Atlântida at all yet," she said. "We'd like to show you around, if you want to come with us?"

I glanced out the window at the brightly glimmering city and shrugged. It *was* a crime that I had not yet explored any of it. I had barely been here, actually, with all of the Green Window travel. I was curious about the mystical, lost city, and I felt a sudden urge to leave my room and *do* something. Anything.

"Sure," I answered with a smile, sincerely grateful for the offer.

The woman returned it warmly.

"I'm Diana, and this is Benedito," she said. "My brother."

"Nice to meet you," I said. "I'm Jasmine."

"We know," said Benedito. "I mean, Artur told us about you being *The Heir.*"

"Please," I said, rolling my eyes. "Don't."

Diana patted me on the shoulder playfully. "It's for your own safety that he told us," she said. "So we don't take you to the *dangerous* parts of Atlântida."

I raised a skeptical eyebrow as I glanced outside of my tower and at the prosperity that lay beyond and below. "Are there any?"

Benedito laughed, his bright blue eyes twinkling in a very Fintan-like manner that made me smile. "Not really."

We took off down the marbled halls of the castle, presumably so my two tour guides could show Artur that they were indeed doing what they had been asked–or told–to do. He was at the table and I nodded at him gratefully. Anything to distract me from Seamus' absence was welcome, and he knew it. I grabbed a piece of seaweed on the way out.

I found myself wholly enamored with the sparkling buildings from which merfolk whizzed in and out, bubble trails following in their wake. A few people *did* notice me this time, as if they had heard rumors of guests of some kind being in the castle. After a quick glance or whispers, they generally looked away and left me be. I appreciated it.

The most magical part of the city, which I had noticed upon my arrival, was the constant circling of sharks above the veil that sealed us off from the rest of the ocean. I pointed up to them, and Diana smiled.

"Yes, they protect the barrier. But a lot of families keep them as pets," she said. "They're actually quite docile."

"Really?" I said, laughing faintly and not fully believing her as the menacing tails whipped back and forth above my head.

Diana and her brother guided me through a labyrinth of white stone pillars that towered almost to the height of the sharks as they formed a majestic barrier that encircled the city.

This part of Atlântida resembled the depictions of the lost city I had seen, the ancient architecture inspiring a sense of historical mystery.

A massive archway of white marble flecked with gold emerged in the distance, marking the culmination of our journey through the cityscape. Just beyond it, the barrier of blue mist loomed; a dreamlike cloud shielding us from the vast expanse of the open ocean. Below the archway, a pool shimmered with a bright, electric blue substance swirling within it.

"This is the healing pool," my new friend said as she led me to the pool's edge. "We call it the Nova Vida. It will cure most ailments…and generally just makes you feel better."

Water within water. It was a strange phenomenon to behold as I watched the swirls of smoke emit from the pool before transforming back into droplets of dreamy liquid, flickering across the surface like tiny lightning bolts. The faint fog that hung over the surface of it exuded a welcoming energy, and I wanted to dive in immediately.

I gathered that it was a relatively popular social headquarters as well, because there were several others lounging in and around the pool, laughing and talking about…whatever it was that merpeople laughed and talked about, I supposed.

I was now extremely curious as to everyone else in the city's origins and lives…had they always been creatures of the sea? Was it rude to ask?

"Want to go in?" Diana asked, looking me up and down. "It might do you some good."

It was her polite way of saying I looked like hell, no doubt. I thought it was a fair observation.

I followed her and Benedito into the pool and took a sweeping, graceful dive that was like falling in slow motion. I melted into the strange substance, allowing it to fill my lungs as I took a deep gulp of the liquid lightning that sent a shock of undeniable nourishment pulsing through my body. I immediately knew that even one breath of these waters would bring me back to life if I were an inch from death.

I stayed at the bottom of the pool for a long, peaceful moment, feeling as though the waters were waking me up from a long, deep sleep. I emerged on the surface where the misty fog danced around my eyes lazily and saw the siblings were grinning expectantly at me.

"Incredible, isn't it?" asked Benedito excitedly.

"Yes," I acknowledged with amazement, churning the liquid in my hands as it floated and fell in defiance of all laws of matter.

Diana floated toward me and leaned against the marble edge of the pool with her hands behind her head.

"This is the endless source of healing waters bestowed upon the city of Atlântida by Duberdicus, the god of the oceans–if you're familiar with Lusitanian mythology," she said. I nodded and beamed at her words—the two of us would certainly get along. "And all healing waters throughout the world are sourced from this pool."

"Where else are they?" I asked, flicking the sparks from the water's surface with my tail as I closed my eyes and floated on my back. "The other healing waters."

"Oh, all over the place," Benedito said as he took a large gulp of the shocking blue substance; a gesture that would have been disgusting in a regular public pool. But not this one. "All over the world there are lakes and rivers where Duberdicus has magically gifted a small bit of this water, because he thinks it's unfair that so many places are landlocked away from the sea."

I had heard of healing pools and other bodies of water with medicinal properties being sprinkled throughout the world, but never believed in any of it. There was so much I believed in now that I hadn't before.

"I've been to one in Florida, actually," said Diana, looking at me. "Isn't that where you lived before you were one of us? Artur mentioned that."

I shifted uncomfortably, hoping Artur hadn't disclosed *everything* about my past in Florida. I assumed he wouldn't.

"Yes," I said. "Where in Florida?"

"Ponce de Leon's Fountain of Youth," she said simply, running a hand through her brown curls. "In the northern part. St. Augustine."

I laughed out loud. "No way," I chuckled, thinking of the corny tourist attraction near Jacksonville. "Are you serious?"

She nodded, plainly not understanding why I thought it was so funny.

"It's always crowded, so we had to sneak in at night," she said.

"And these humans came as some sort of late-night dare to jump in the fountain," Benedito joined in as he recalled the memory. "So we had to hide our tails and wait til they left."

Probably students at whatever university was there. Flagler, I think it was called?

Something then occurred to me that I hadn't thought of since leaving Ireland. These were Portuguese merpeople–at least, that's where they lived now–and they spoke about a place that they would have had to land-walk to get to. Was that possible? I couldn't believe I had never questioned it before. I had always thought of it as a trait unique to selkies of Ireland and Scotland, considering the legends about us hiding our pelts on land until we wished to return to the sea.

"Diana," I said. "Can you–can all merpeople land-walk?"

She looked at me blankly. "Well, sure, besides the Amalgams."

Benedito let out a huff of disapproval at the mention of them, but Diana checked him.

"Artur is an Amalgam," she scolded him just like a sister does. "They're not all evil."

I sat back, contemplating. To learn that mermaids and mermen walked on land *all over the world* was hard to comprehend. I wondered how many times I had been near one and not known…on a plane, in a restaurant…

"Are there a lot of them?" I asked. "Of *us*?"

Diana shook her head and laughed loudly. "Oh, no, Jasmine," she said. "We're definitely a rarity."

"Interesting," I said quietly.

"There's the dynamic duo," came a voice from behind me. "Causing trouble like always, I assume?"

Diana and Benedito were smiling and waving to someone, so I turned and leaned against the edge of the pool to see who it was.

A newcomer was swimming toward us, and his tail was unlike any I had ever seen. It was a deep, rich onyx with flecks of light pink and orange littered throughout the scales. There was a massive scar running down the side of the tail that was the same color as the one on my palm—as if an Amalgam had raked their claws down it while he was already a merman. After hearing what had happened to Sorcha, I guessed that was exactly what had happened. His skin was nearly white as marble aside from the faint shadows cast by his muscular frame, with features so blonde and light that I assumed he couldn't be from here.

"Hello," he said, noticing me. His crystal blue eyes flickered to the stone on my chest and I wondered if he knew who I was.

Ew, I stopped myself. Even thinking of myself in that way—as if I were someone *important*—was revolting.

"This is Jasmine," said Benedito.

I extended my hand to shake the blonde merman's. He kissed it instead, but not in the endearing way Fintan had done back when I first met him on Hy-Brasil. It lasted a bit longer than was decent, and I fought the urge not to shudder. I pulled it away swiftly the second he let it go.

"Elias," he said, his aquamarine eyes not leaving my own. They were piercing and bright, surveying me with an intense curiosity that made me uneasy.

"Hi," I replied, caving and breaking our eye contact first.

"Jasmine just got here," Benedito continued. "So we're showing her around."

Elias raised an interested eyebrow at me.

"Ireland? Or maybe Scotland?" he asked, looking at my tail that was visible just below the misty surface of the water, not knowing he had answered my silent question regarding different tails indicating different parts of the world.

I nodded. His gaze flickered to my hand, and I instinctively closed my palm. But he had already seen my scar.

"Hy-Brasil, Ireland," I said, even though I felt entirely false for acting like I had ever actually lived there. I truthfully didn't know where else I would consider home. Carrickfergus didn't quite feel right, either, even though that's where Aisling lived. I had no permanent place under the sea yet.

"Oh, I might need to leave then," he said, flashing a grin of bright white teeth at me. "I didn't fare so well last time I was around an Amalgam from Hy-Brasil."

He gestured to the gash on his tail, answering another question of mine. I tried to mask my shock.

"She's not like them," Diana answered a bit more sharply than I thought necessary. "Don't you know who she *is?*"

Elias looked at me again and his eyes dropped to the rainbow Iridescent Ammonite around my neck once more.

"Oh so that's *you,*" he said with amusement. "I apologize for not bowing to my *queen.*"

"Funny," I shot back lamely. I knew he was seeking banter with me, but I had no energy for quips. I couldn't tell if I liked him or not, but Benedito and Diana seemed to be friendly enough with him, so I didn't think too deeply into it as he slid into the pool with us. He closed his eyes and basked in the medicinal waters.

"What brings you here to Atlântida?" he asked me lazily after a few moments, eyes still closed.

Artur had warned me about the city of Atlântida wanting to

stay out of conflict, and I didn't know how each individual would react to the information that the Heir of Atargatis had come to enlist their leader in a treasure hunt for the stones they all likely thought were best left alone. So I refrained from telling him anything meaningful.

"I'm friends with Fintan," I said at last. "And Aisling."

This was clearly not the answer he was expecting, and suspicion flashed behind his eyes as he opened them. He ran his tongue contemplatively across his very pink lips as he kept eye contact with me, as if debating what to say.

"Fintan and Aisling haven't been here in a while," he said carefully. "I'm sure Artur is grateful you brought them back."

"I guess so," I said, and I let silence fall between us.

Even after Artur told me why he did, I couldn't believe that the light-hearted Fintan could hold a grudge with anyone, especially his own father. It sounded like those who lived in the city were well aware that their leader's son chose to spend very little time here.

"Where are you from?" I asked suddenly, now gesturing toward his tail. "Black and orange…?"

"Scandinavia," he said. I could have guessed as much given his…blondeness. I noticed that he looked me up and down with no discretion whatsoever while he spoke, and I didn't know what to make of it. "Norway, specifically. But my mother's side of the family is from here, so I'm back for a while."

I thought briefly of the origins of the Little Mermaid in Denmark, and wondered with wild curiosity what life was like for Scandinavian merfolk. Did they have a Hy-Brasil? I didn't want to ask him, thinking the Heir of Atargatis already ought to *know* what mermaid life was like all over the globe. I would ask someone I trusted. Artur, maybe. I thought of the books in his library, knowing I would be better off trying to find otherworldly volumes once more down there rather than pointlessly chatting with strangers in a jacuzzi.

"Have you been?" he asked. "To Norway, or any of the Scandinavian nations?"

"No, but I'd like to go," I said, sighing as I thought of Raj's teaching job at the University of Stockholm he had just started before...before *it* happened.

"Artur has Green Windows all over that part of the world," Elias said with a shrug.

"I should ask him to take me," I said, nodding.

"I'll take you," Elias offered, taking me by surprise. "If you're up for it."

His voice was steady, smooth, and certain of himself. As if he didn't care at all what I thought of his boldness. I didn't know what to say. Of course I wasn't *up for it.* I would never go across the world with some random guy I didn't even know—

Nevermind. I guess I *would* do that, considering that was exactly what I'd done with Seamus. But that was different. I'd never do that with *him.*

Diana and Benedito's sibling bickering that had been buzzing in the background of our conversation then became too loud to ignore, and I was grateful for the interruption that spared me from responding. They were arguing about where the next batch of healing water would be sent, and who would be taking it. Benedito said he'd offered to do it, but his sister had shut it down immediately.

"You act like I'm a decade younger than you or something," he said, laughing. "We are *twins.*"

"Well *you* behave like you're a decade younger," Diana shot back. "If you went up there, I bet you wouldn't even be able to find your way back without a Green Window that leads right to our doorstep."

"Would you blame me? There are like a hundred entrances to Atlântida," the twin grumbled in response.

I tried not to notice Elias' gaze continually flickering to my chest as I decided the conversation between us would not resume. I told myself he was looking at the stone, even though I sincerely doubted it. I shifted ever so slightly, adjusting the straps of my sea-shelled top that I now realized was far from modest.

When he finally rose to leave us after what felt like hours later, he bent down to kiss Diana's hand and then mine, his lips lingering far too long on my skin once more.

"Lovely to meet you," he said silkily. "I hope I'll see you around."

He reached for my left hand this time. I knew instinctively that he was looking for a ring as his thumb gently grazed my fourth finger. He—nearly undetectably—smirked when he didn't see one, and it annoyed me beyond belief.

Seamus' soul was mine and mine was his. I didn't need a stupid piece of jewelry to prove it.

CHAPTER 17

THE WORLD SERPENT

"How was your day with the twins?" asked Artur as I returned to the castle's main hall. "The Nova Vida was to your liking?"

He was sitting at the table with several scrolls laid out in front of him that looked like navigational charts of some kind. I wondered what sort of business–aside from treasure hunting–he attended to as ruler of the grand city.

I glanced at my reflection in the mirrored tray that was resting on the stone table, noticing some color had come back into my cheeks. The bags under my eyes had vanished, and I was certainly in a better mood than I had been that morning, despite my mildly off-putting interaction with Elias.

"Yes," I said truthfully. "It was lovely."

He invited me to join him for dinner and I was pleased to find that my appetite had returned as well. I scarfed down the seaweed platter that appeared in front of me before another one immediately repopulated in its place. The sapphire liquid I had found so delicious a few nights ago also appeared in my goblet, and I drank it gratefully. I slurped two full glasses before I slowed down.

"That's the good stuff," said Artur, pointing to it.

I nodded. "I can tell."

We ate in silence for a few more moments before I got up the courage to ask him what had been on my mind.

"Artur, I was wondering about other mermaid life... throughout the world," I said slowly. "I feel embarrassed that I don't know anything about any of our kind besides Irish selkies. And a tiny bit about the Portuguese merpeople that live here."

"Oh, it's nothing to be embarrassed about," he said, waving his hand in the air. "How would you know? You just became one of us a few months ago."

I beamed appreciatively. I hadn't suspected he'd judge me for my lack of knowledge, but it was nice to hear him say it.

We agreed to meet the following morning with Artur promising I could ask as many questions as I liked. I was excited to once again exercise my brain in a way that reminded me so much of Raj and our study sessions. When Seamus would comment on the fact that I seemed to know something about everything, I knew I owed it all to my father. I wondered *what* he would think of my life now if he could see it. His scholarly self would be fascinated. He'd want to know everything there was to learn, just like I did.

I floated up to my tower and rested in the window while I watched the sun go down. When it did, I tucked myself into the sapphire sheets and kissed the Iridescent Ammonite around my neck, telling Seamus goodnight.

I didn't have any nightmares this time, presumably thanks to my soaking in the Nova Vida's healing waters.

I didn't even dream.

* * *

IN THE MORNING, I flew down to the main hall where Artur was waiting for me. He tossed me a bite of seaweed before beckoning for me to follow him. We were wasting no time today, it seemed.

"If you liked the library, just wait until you see this," he said excitedly.

We passed the oasis room but I didn't dare peek through the doorway–it was a place I'd never go without Seamus. It would make me miss him too much.

We continued on past the study where I had–unsuccessfully–sought more books on Atargatis, and instead shot through another white marble archway that led to a room that instantly darkened as we entered, revealing a beautiful replica of the night sky.

I looked around for signs of a thin veil that would take me to another universe like the oasis room had, but there was no definitive barrier here. There was just a loose, swirling cloud that surrounded us in magical hues of dark blue and purple. Constellations from both our universe and others I didn't recognize sparkled above us, seemingly inviting us to explore them all. I remembered going to planetariums within science museums as a child...none of which could hold a candle to this place.

"I don't remember if I mentioned this, but my dad was an astronomer," I said suddenly as Artur watched me marvel at the room. "Well, a marine biologist more recently. But when we lived in Porto, he taught astronomy."

"Ah so you must recognize plenty of these, then?" Artur said, gesturing to the arrangement of stars sprinkled across the night sky.

"Sure do," I said, spotting the outline of Libra instantly–Matt's sign. I wondered what Seamus' sign was. I registered with a sinking feeling that I actually didn't *know* his birthday. He didn't know mine, either. I didn't even know how old he was. Not that it would change anything now, but it was unbelievably surreal to realize. We had to be close in age, of course. But still...

Questions for when he returned, I supposed.

When. Not *if.*

Artur then waved his hand in the air and the sky began to shift, the stars whirring around one another and rearranging themselves in a new pattern. The light brightened and I shielded my eyes as the room vividly transformed, revealing a massive, three-dimensional globe in the center.

"Wow," I said softly.

Artur reached up and tapped the globe. It spun madly.

"Where to first?" he asked.

I looked up at him in dismay and he laughed.

"No, not literally," he said. "*That* would be amazing. But we'll be able to see."

The wonder of the magic that he had created in the palace overwhelmed me and I didn't know where to start. I supposed I'd begin with where I was most curious, given my conversation at the Nova Vida yesterday.

"Scandinavia," I said. "Norway, specifically."

"I *do* think there's a stone of Atargatis there," he mused with approval. "An old friend of mine once thought so, too."

He snapped his fingers to bring the spinning globe to a halt.

The invisible magnifying glass that controlled our vantage point then narrowed in upon the beautiful country. It showed me the sweeping fjords that lined the entire western coast, the collection of islands that existed in the sea beyond, and the white snow that blanketed it all. I watched as merpeople–all with black tails flecked with orange and bits of pink–flitted in and out of the water, leaping through the waves with the whales. I knew they would have been undetectable to the human eye given their speed, even if they hadn't been in such a remote place where so few people could venture.

"There are endless inlets lining the coast, as you can see," Artur said, pointing to an area just south of Bergen. "So the merfolk there don't really have *one* place they reside, like here and Hy-Brasil. They don't have much of a sense of community, from what I recall. A lot of Scandinavian merpeople are just free roamers throughout the seas."

"That must get lonely," I said.

I remembered Sorcha mentioning the nomadic lifestyle that some of our kind adopted. Back then, I had assumed she only meant selkies from Ireland. It seemed so obvious now that there were so many other populations. I wondered if Elias was a free roamer, considering how he alluded to his time in Atlântida being temporary.

Artur shrugged. "I'm sure it does."

I studied the fjords that continued to flash across the globe in front of us, and the sweeping landscapes were so alive I felt I could nearly taste the water. Puffins colored the terrain with their bright beaks, and seals barked loudly in the distance like the water dogs that they were. I wanted to reach out and touch the snow.

"Have you been here?" I asked Artur as I continued to watch the endless movie of Norwegian wildlife.

He nodded.

"I have. I took Sorcha to see the Northern Lights in Tromsø, many many years ago," he said. "And we stayed, wandering through the fjords for a long time. It was beautiful there."

I wondered what 'many years' and 'a long time' were to him, considering he had already alluded to his old age, but then I thought of something else.

"Will the Scandinavian merpeople help us?" I asked. "Against the Amalgams. If we need them?"

"I don't know," he said, his face darkening. "There's quite a large population of merpeople out there that empathize with the wrong side of our cause for whatever reason. I worry that Scandinavia could be the first to fall should there be a war."

War.

The word stung, but I supposed that's exactly what it could become.

Even if we found all of the stones, the Amalgams would try to steal them back. And we'd still have to take theirs. Considering so much of our effort had been focused on finding the stones rather than deciding what to do with them afterward, I didn't know how we'd ever truly end this conflict. There would be no diplomacy or treaties—of that much, I was certain.

"But if it comes to war, there is another, extremely powerful ally in the Scandinavian waters we can tap," Artur said, breaking into a grin. "Given your ability to command the serpents of the seas."

I raised an eyebrow, thinking he greatly overestimated my abilities. To say I could *command* them was generous. I knew it was supposedly one of my *powers* as the Heir, but I was far from harnessing it. The serpent beneath Carrickfergus spared me, but I don't think he necessarily *listened* to me.

"Which one?" I asked.

Artur grinned. "Jörmungandr, otherwise known as The World Serpent," he said. "And I'm warning you, it's much more fearsome than how Norse mythology has captured it."

And of course, because of my father, I knew about this one as well.

"Think about the kinds of samples you'll be studying in that part of the world," I said. "Off the coast of Sweden, Denmark, and Norway...it'll be incredible."

We were in Raj's study as he prepared for his trip to Stockholm, a voyage whose purpose was to determine whether or not he could see himself posted there to teach. He had been offered the position in the marine biology department, and had changed his mind at least three times. As he always did when he was indecisive, he had gone on one of his tangents about history that began in one part of the world and ended in another, and somehow turned into a theoretical discussion of each nation's oldest legends along the way.

I had at least successfully led us back to Scandinavia with the questions I asked. Matt sat in the corner, smirking at me as he knew what I was doing.

"Maybe Professor Brennan will come visit you and he'll take you diving," Matt added, shrugging.

Raj scoffed. "*I* taught the *laddie* how to dive, don't get it twisted, my boy," he said, dragging his poor attempt at an Irish accent out as he mimicked his friend. Matt grinned. "But you're right, it would be fascinating to explore those waters. I never have."

I stood and spun the globe that sat on his desk. I landed on Norway.

"I can picture you on a boat amongst the whales," I said. "Frolicking between the endless fjords, discovering hidden caves and wildlife you didn't even know existed."

Raj looked wistfully at the vast dark blue area of the Norwegian Sea on the globe.

"There's so much out there to be discovered," I said encouragingly. "You have to go!"

He sighed. "You're right," he said. "I've actually always hoped for a diving encounter with Jörmungandr."

"Oh, here we go," I said under my breath.

Matt leapt to his feet. "No, let's hear it," he said, smiling with sincere interest. "I love a good Raj Atarga lesson of lore."

"See," Raj said, pointing to Matt and looking at me. "This is the kind of enthusiastic audience I expect when I teach my classes. But these kids at Miami, they couldn't give less of a shit."

I rolled my eyes. He was so dramatic. Just because *one* student had fallen asleep during his lecture on the nocturnal feeding behavior of the Dendrophylliidae family of coral…

"Anyway," he said, happy to oblige with Matt's request. "In the depths of the Norwegian Sea, where the water meets the sky, there lies the fearsome creature known by the name Jörmungandr. The World Serpent."

"I have chills already," I said. Raj shot me a look before continuing.

"Produced by the union of trickster god Loki and the giantess Angrboða, the serpent grew at an alarming rate, coiling itself around the ocean floor. As it grew, the serpent's presence became known to the world, and rumors flew that it could encircle the whole globe," he said. "Some whispered that Jörmungandr's scales shimmered like jewels, reflecting the color of the ocean's depths."

Matt nodded his head, intrigued.

"But it also possessed a fierce and unpredictable nature. Its movements could stir storms, churn the seas—"

"Generally cause disasters," I said, trying to get us to the point.

"Exactly," Raj replied. "Now, the gods themselves were afraid of the World Serpent's power. They knew that Jörmungandr's presence could bring about cataclysmic events, threatening the very stability of the world. Thus, they sought to contain the serpent, to bind it beneath the waves and prevent its wrath from unleashing chaos upon the world."

"Only after a tireless effort and great sacrifice did the gods manage to chain Jörmungandr at the bottom of the ocean, using unbreakable bonds forged by dwarves. There, beneath the swirling currents, the World Serpent lay imprisoned, its immense form coiled and dormant, but still potent with ancient magic."

"Despite its captivity, the legend of Jörmungandr endured as a reminder of the primordial forces that shaped the world. Some whispered that one day, when the bonds that held it weakened, the World Serpent would rise again, heralding the end of days in a final, cataclysmic battle known as Ragnarök."

"Ragnarök, like Thor?" asked Matt.

"Very good, my student of Norse mythology," Raj said, grinning.

"No, I've just seen Marvel movies," Matt replied with a shrug. "Don't give me that much credit."

MY EYES WENT WIDE with horror as the magical room's rendition of Jörmungandr now flashed before me. Whatever I had expected from my father's story, it wasn't this.

The beast had almost human-like qualities in its face, but it was certainly not one of us. It looked like a serpent descendent of Cthulhu–the blue and black monster had two distinctive tails in addition to four tentacles that emerged from its back as well as bright, gleaming yellow eyes.

"This is not how I pictured it," I said softly at last.

"He's a shape-shifter, which makes him incredibly dangerous and hard to find," said Artur. "They say he can even sometimes appear as a woman or man, depending upon with whom he negotiates."

I tried to imagine the creature of horror turning into a normal person. I couldn't.

"I'll note that to my knowledge, Ragnarök did not happen and Thor never slayed the thing," Artur said, seeing that my level of intrigue had not wavered.

I chuckled hollowly at his joke as the monster stared down at me.

Could this thing–this creature of nightmares–really answer to *me?*

CHAPTER 18

BOLD STATEMENTS

On the tenth day following his departure, I finally heard from Seamus.

Well, I *felt* him.

The stone lit up atop my chest and gently tapped against me in the middle of the night. I felt it, and then it was gone. It seemed to say, "I'm alright, I love you."

I hoped I was right.

Nighttime had long since cloaked Atlântida in darkness, but now I was wide awake. I stared out the archway that led to the open ocean and made my way to the window, watching the few stragglers of the night zoom by below. The city was filled with quiet whispers of lovers making their way home in the early hours of the morning, and I yearned for my own. I kissed the stone gently in reply, telling him I loved him too.

I wondered, then, if Seamus could feel me dreaming of him when I finally fell back asleep.

I was lying on a beach with his dark red hair in my face, brushing against me and tickling my nose. I couldn't hear what he was saying–it was as if I were replaying an old memory on mute.

But I didn't need to hear. I felt Seamus press against me with his muscular frame, and I gently kissed the freckles on his forearm that was propped up next to me. He smiled back at me and closed his beautiful green eyes as he rested his head on my neck. I ran my fingers absently through his hair, looking around to see where we were.

The beach was one I recognized, but I couldn't remember in which part of my life I had seen it. It was flat–devoid of the cliffs that lined the shores we had been on in Ireland and Portugal together, so it couldn't have been one that I had ever been to with him before. The sand was white as snow, and I suddenly became obsessed with recalling its name.

Was it in America?

Yes, the wind seemed to answer as the hum of voices around me became clearer in my head. They were speaking English. It was somewhere in St. Pete, Florida, I thought. Yes…there was the famous pink hotel just behind me.

Seamus kissed me softly on my neck again before rising from my chest. He was being uncharacteristically gentle as he swept a strand of my hair aside. I closed my eyes.

"I love you," I said quietly, wishing I had said it more before he left.

"I love you, too," he said, bending down to kiss me. I noticed that all hints of his signature accent were suddenly gone, and he spoke in burdened tones.

I opened my eyes and saw it was now Matt who was leaning over me in the sand, not Seamus. His blue eyes were wide with sadness like they had been in my last dream.

I gasped, but no sound came out.

"You'll choose me, won't you?" he asked innocently, grains of sand sprinkled throughout his glossy hair.

He reached for the chain around my neck and found the

Iridescent Ammonite rather than the gem I knew he had been looking for. He had been hoping to find the diamond ring. It had been on my finger in the last dream–where was it now? In real life, it sat on my dresser back in Tampa, collecting dust. I'd never see it again.

"You stopped wearing the ring," he said quietly. "But I understand."

He wasn't angry, just incredibly sad. Matt was never angry. I didn't think he knew how to be.

I sputtered like an idiot. "I–"

"But Jasmine, tell me you will," he said, his voice now alert and urgent as he clasped my hand. I sensed he couldn't hear me, because he talked over me as I tried to respond. "Promise me you'll choose me."

He saw the flicker of doubt in my eyes before I could attempt to mask it. His face fell.

"How can you know after such a short time that he's right for you?" he said, his voice cracking ever so slightly. He was so kind, and it was excruciating to see him distraught. "You don't even know him."

"I *do* know him," I said, but again, he didn't hear me. I was speaking into a soundproof abyss.

"I loved you for so many years," my dead fiancé breathed as his dark eyelashes blinked away a tear. "I can't let you go."

I couldn't take it anymore. I needed to wake up. I begged my subconscious to release me.

"If he makes you happy for now, that's all I can ask for," he continued. "But after that…I hope you'll choose me. In the end."

In the end.

Why did he have to say that? What did he *mean* by that?

"I can't promise anything," I said before I could stop myself, and apparently those were the only words he heard, because he fell back on his heels and released my hand in defeat.

As if triggered by my harsh words, the sky suddenly turned black.

A violent crack of thunder was followed by an intense shower of rain that would have suffocated me had I not been able to breathe underwater. I choked on it anyway, wiping the rain from my eyes so I could see.

Lightning struck the shore in a white, blinding light that revealed Matt was now lying motionless on the beach in front of me, covered in blood. The sea roared behind him as a massive serpent rose from the water. I screamed.

I stood to run, but I couldn't. I was a mermaid, and my tail wouldn't transform.

It was too far for me to drag myself into the water; I had nowhere to go. I looked at Matt desperately again, but I knew he was already dead. His corpse was staining the shoreline a sickening ruby red, and the blood was endless. It was flowing all the way from the tip of my tail and straight into the sea that started to burn with flames of the same color.

I couldn't help him, and I was going to die here, too. The fire from the sea would engulf me. It was coming for me.

But then Seamus appeared, bending down to scoop me up in one swift motion.

"I've got ye, Jasmine," he said steadily, rising to his feet. His eyes were steel as he looked down at the dead man on the shore. "I can't help him, but I've got ye."

I SHRIEKED IN TERROR.

I know I did, because I woke up and heard the tail end of the petrifying sound. I quickly clapped my hand over my mouth, hoping I hadn't disturbed Artur below. I blinked furiously, attempting to remove the scene of Matt's dead body from behind my eyelids as fast as possible. I had dreamt of both Seamus and Matt plenty of times, but never together. I didn't like it at all.

But what was the *meaning* behind these past scenes?

In my first dream, I had been so flustered by the discovery that Matt knew I was with someone else. And now, in this subsequent scene, he was asking me to choose him...*in the end.* His choice of words haunted me–did that mean the afterlife? Was it really possible that he had been talking to me from beyond the grave? I didn't want to think so, but nothing felt impossible to me anymore.

Even when I inevitably compared the two men in my mind–something that wrought extreme guilt upon me–I had never thought about *choosing* between the two of them. Not seriously, anyway.

But if I had to...

Seamus would want me to choose honestly. He would have to know that I picked him because I wanted him more. Because I couldn't live without him. He could be dark and even mildly dominating, but he had honor. It wouldn't be enough for him to have me against my will. He would need to *win* me.

But Matt...Matt would have no such reserve. He would beg for me on his knees. He would plead for me to pick him, no matter what it cost.

And if it ever came to that, I didn't know if I could say no to him.

* * *

ANOTHER WEEK or so passed in which I spent a great deal of time educating myself on ancient mermaid lore from across the world with Artur as well as formulating guesses as to where the other stones might be. He was still entirely convinced that Duarte would only give Seamus the information regarding the number of them, but I held out hope that he would get more than that out of the ghost.

I also spent several of my mornings in the Nova Vida by

myself, finding that it brought me peace just as much as it improved my physical health. It was a positive way to start my day, even if the effects didn't last very long once I emerged. Magical as it was, it couldn't erase the constant feeling of fear that gnawed at the hole in my chest. I had hardly felt Seamus' presence at all since the faint heartbeat, aside from his reappearance in a series of nightmares that always seemed to end with him carrying me out of a fiery sea while I watched Matt bleed.

I had asked Artur if we could go looking for my mother while we waited, but this was met with an adamant *no*.

He told me it would put her at more risk, considering the target that was on both of our backs–especially mine. I was protected by the barriers of Atlântida, as well as the people here that were disinterested in my presence–if they even knew about it. Artur had been very literal when he said the residents of his city rarely took notice in matters of the outside seas. I scowled at the thought of wasting time that could be spent seeking Aine, but I *did* understand. I hoped that she was safe, and that Aisling's mother had some sort of lead as to where she was. I would owe her everything if my unknown aunt brought my mother home safely.

When I wasn't busy studying mermaid mythology or treasure-hunting in both the study and constellation rooms, I was with the twins. Diana and Benedito were easy to be around. They asked very few questions beyond the surface-level kind, and they showed me all of the interesting sights that Atlântida had to offer. As I should have expected given Artur's preferences, the city was set up very similarly to a human metropolis, with shopping centers, restaurants, and even public parks aside from the Nova Vida. I was mildly interested, knowing that the inside of the castle was still my favorite place to be. I wondered how the humble Artur had ascended to the throne–not that there actually *was one*–in Atlântida, but Benedito and Diana didn't really know.

They mentioned it may have something to do with an alliance with Duberdicus.

"He's old," Benedito said with a shrug. "I've never known anyone else to rule here."

I had just begun to wonder where the twins' slippery friend, Elias, had gone when he made a sudden appearance one morning while the three of us were lounging in one of the gardens at the palace. Artur had given me the "day off" from real lessons and as much as I had feared that having too much free time would cause me to spiral, I found I was actually enjoying it.

Benedito and Diana were playing a rather rudimentary game of checkers in the sand with shells of different colors while I sat tucked away, studying a map as I scanned for Atargatis' Pools.

I had been told there was a cave of them in Cyprus, where my mother had been imprisoned, but Artur and I thought there might be another in Syria, Iraq, or even Kuwait. We also assumed that a stone would be hidden within one of the Pools, so I was examining every possible body of water I could find throughout the entirety of the Middle East. But who knew if her Pools were natural bodies of water? What if they were crafted by humans? I knew the goddess' old temple in ancient Hierapolis was entirely landlocked in modern day Pamukkale, Turkey. But no, there would be no use land-walking to the abandoned temple...she wouldn't leave something as valuable as a stone of the seas there...or would she?

"Hello," said a voice next to me, causing me to jump. Elias floated gracefully onto the bench beside me. "What are you looking at?"

I made no move to hide the maps and instead handed them to him, my eyes aching. Although I still didn't want to say anything about the stones, I supposed there was no harm in telling him I was doing research for my own curiosity's sake. "Looking for the Pools of Atargatis."

His eyes flashed with dangerous excitement.

"Going to pay a visit to your Mother, are you?" he asked.

White-hot anger surged through me for a moment before I realized what he meant by it. Of course he had no idea about my *real* mother being imprisoned there. He was making a joke referring to Atargatis herself. The Mother of the Sea. I let out my breath.

He must have noticed my tense demeanor, because he raised his hands in surrender, leaving the maps suspended in the water.

"Yikes," he said, breaking into a grin as he laughed nervously. "Are you alright?"

I snatched the maps back. "I'm fine," I said. "But no, I'm not planning on going there right away."

Whether he was disinterested or simply wanted to ease the tension that I had caused, he changed the subject.

"I heard about your trip with Artur back to America," he said.

I looked up at him and thought I saw something like empathy or pity in his eyes for a moment, but then it was gone.

"Yes," I sighed.

How *much* did he know about that trip? What had Artur told him exactly? I wasn't even aware Artur and Elias were further acquainted beyond the relationship of ruler and subject, but I suppose I had never asked.

He studied me. "Did you enjoy it? Feel nostalgic?"

"No," I said honestly. "Too many terrible memories there."

He waited for a moment before speaking again.

"Your friends," he said. "They'll forgive you."

So he *did* know a bit more about it.

I was mildly irritated with Artur for divulging the details to him, but then I remembered he had sent Diana and Benedito to my room when I sulked after Seamus' departure. He was trying to make me feel comfortable in the city. He was trying to help, in the poorly executed way that was customary for a dad. Especially a dad that had no daughters of his own…he didn't have a clue. I softened.

"I don't think they will," I said sadly. "And my *best* friend wasn't even there. She lives in Washington, D.C., not Tampa. She's the one to whom I owe the strongest apology."

"Well, if she's your *best* friend, then she's the one who's most likely to forgive you," he reasoned.

I smiled. He was actually being sincere and empathetic, which were sentiments I didn't expect from him after the only exchange the two of us had ever had.

"I hope so," I said.

He was quiet, but his turquoise eyes were still locked on my own.

"If you want to tell me more," he said. "I'll listen."

Even though it was wildly out of character for me, I accepted his invitation. I supposed it was easier for me to confide in a stranger, because I knew he didn't have a vested interest. He didn't really care, so it didn't really matter.

"Right before I fell from the Cliffs, I got into a fight with Kiana. And I never got to apologize," I said. "I regret it so deeply, because she actually helped Seamus look for me for a little bit."

"Fell off the Cliffs?" he inquired curiously.

"Oh…well, I fell off The Cliffs of Moher in Ireland," I said. "And then I turned into this." I gestured toward my tail.

He looked shocked, but I didn't elaborate further. The longer I existed as I was, the less important my origin story became. At least that's what I wanted to believe.

"Anyway, I can't help feeling like she gave up because she was still mad at me," I said. I was reaching the point of oversharing, so I stopped at that.

"Nah, that's not it," he replied, shaking his head. "It's impossible for people who aren't like us to ever imagine this world could be real."

"Seamus did," I said simply. I wondered if Artur had told Elias about him, too. I clarified anyway. "My boyfriend."

The word sounded so painfully immature when I said it out

loud, and I blushed furiously. *Boyfriend.* Seamus was so much more than that.

"Well, it's different when they're trying to fuck you," Elias quipped, and it caught me entirely off guard. I actually laughed.

"In all seriousness," he continued, grinning. "I'm sure one day you'll get to apologize to Kiana, too. And she'll just be happy to know you're alive."

I sighed. "Maybe one day."

We sat in silence for a while and I glanced down at his tail. The bright mark of an Amalgam was branded across the sparkling obsidian from his hip all the way down to where his knees would be if he were in his land-walker form.

"Can I ask?"

"You can," he said, but he didn't elaborate. So he would make me.

I humored him. "How'd you get that scar?"

He sighed, running a hand through his nearly white-blonde hair. "As you know, the Amalgams of Hy-Brasil don't believe in the same things we do here," he said. "About Atargatis."

"Right," I said. I knew better than he could imagine.

"Cearbhall, I'm sure you know him," he continued, and I froze. He noticed my stiffness and replied, "Yeah, that's my opinion of him as well."

"I was in Manza Bay when he found the Tsavorite," he continued. "I had helped him track it down, because he claimed someone else was after it. Someone nefarious."

I nodded, wondering how the slick Elias could have been outwitted by Cearbhall.

"Of course I was too stupid back then to realize he was seeking it for himself. For his clan to use for evil," he said. "I tried to fight him for it, but I was weak back then."

It took everything not to raise a doubtful eyebrow at that statement, acknowledging the broad shoulders and thick chest muscles he had that nearly rivaled Seamus'.

Nearly. Not quite.

"So he dragged this down my tail and now I'm hideous," he concluded.

"Sounds like something he'd do," I remarked.

Elias nodded. "I thought I'd pay him back in the end, but it didn't work out," he said. I waited for him to continue. "I gave Oisin a cheap piece of sea glass that looked enough like one of the stones to try and trick Cearbhall into trading with him, but I guess you know that part of the story."

I gaped at him, recalling how the stone's lack of reaction had proven my heritage. How it had unraveled everything. "That was from *you?*"

He nodded and then shot me a mischievous grin.

"You really messed that plan up," he said. "Thanks for that."

I scoffed, but playfully.

"Apologies," I said. "Next time you need to give me a heads up."

His blue eyes pierced mine once more. "I will."

"But you can still land-walk," I said, recalling what Artur had told me about being marked by an Amalgam as a true mermaid.

"Oh, yeah," he said. "It doesn't affect me beyond the fact that I can now do it to others if I choose."

If I choose. I didn't like the way he said it...as if he thought it was some great gift he now had permission to use. I absently looked at the scar on my own hand.

"Yes," he said. "You probably can, too."

"I'd never," I said immediately, and I meant it.

I'd never bring the curse upon someone, no matter what. Elias didn't challenge me, and I wondered if he had already done it himself. It wouldn't necessarily surprise me, given his arrogant nature I had sensed the first time I met him. But after seeing a glimmer of sincerity within him now, I hoped not.

"It's interesting to me how Atargatis can be interpreted so differently by all of these various cultures," I said, wanting to break the silence that had fallen. "She's a humble hero in Atlân-tida, a ruthless ruler to the Amalgams, and a respected–but somewhat insignificant–deity to the regular selkies of Hy-Brasil."

Elias nodded contemplatively.

"And what is she to you?" he asked. "Besides your ancient ancestor."

I hadn't fully formed an opinion yet. I certainly feared her, considering how I felt her cruel wrath every time I transformed in the sunlight. I recalled the daggers that ran down my legs on Skellig Michael and how Seamus had carried me up to the top for the smallest bit of shade that brought instant relief. I knew that she did it to me because she wanted to drag me back into the water. But I *did* wonder how much of it was because she was trying to make me into the hero she wanted to be. After all, she *was* helping me find the stones. I could feel her pushing me along.

Elias watched my side profile as I mulled it over.

"I'm scared of her," I admitted. "But I want to believe she's good."

I had to. I had to trust that the Mother of the Sea was rooting for me.

"What about you?" I asked him. "What do you think?"

His pink lips curved into a wicked smile as his electric eyes glinted with mischief.

"I think she's an alluring and tantalizing warrior," he said, looking me up and down the way he had in the Nova Vida. "And if *I* were the man lucky enough to share her bed, I'd never leave her unattended. Only a fool would."

I stared at him blankly, horribly taken aback by his forwardness.

My heart thundered in my chest and I didn't know what to say or do. I was flustered, and he knew it. Watching me squirm seemed to satisfy him, and he did nothing but smirk as he rose from the bench and flitted away. He approached Diana and

Benedito, who were completely oblivious to what had just occurred.

After an appropriate amount of time that would not arouse suspicion, I fled to my room. Once there, I dropped the sheer curtain of sparkling waves that I had learned (following my night of horrific shrieking and an embarrassing breakfast encounter with Artur) soundproofed the room completely. I screamed as loudly as I could.

"What the *hell* was that," I shouted into the mirror, criticizing myself with pointed rage.

Guilt consumed me, even though I had done nothing wrong. I had, of course, not returned his advances in any way. The thought of doing so repulsed me. But the way it made me *feel* when he said that...

It made me angry because I hated that I felt he was right.

I *knew* Seamus was out there, fighting for me because he had to. Because he was a warrior who would do anything for me. But it didn't change the fact that I *hated* him being gone. The fact that I missed him so much it hurt. What happened with Elias, on top of the dreams I had been having, was enough to set my progress right back to the day Seamus had left.

I didn't leave my room for another two days.

CHAPTER 19

OTIMA

*A*rtur finally came to get me himself, after Diana and Benedito's attempts were unsuccessful. I had brushed them off telling them I was physically ill, something that both of them knew wasn't true considering my frequent visits to the Nova Vida.

"Jasmine," Artur said from the doorless door frame, sounding just like Raj. "Out."

I rose from the bed and he looked me up and down with concern.

"Let's go," he said.

"Where?"

He sighed and motioned for me to follow him. "You need to eat."

"I'm not hungry."

My stomach growled loudly, giving me away. I meandered down to the passage in defeat, taking my sweet time. There was more seaweed, of course. But there was also a steaming mug of chocolate. I *did* love the chocolate drink.

"What's going on?" he asked. "You're a shell of a person."

"Technically, I'm not a person."

He actually laughed at my comment before turning serious once more.

"You've been acting sullen for days, and I thought we had gotten past that," he said. "How can I help you?"

I sighed, knowing I would be far too mortified to tell him what had triggered my sudden reclusion, but as I opened my mouth, tears began to form instead. I let out a dry sob into the water where the silver strands of liquid were immediately lost, and he rushed to my side.

"What if he doesn't come back?" I choked out, burying my head in his shoulder. He put his arms around me and gently patted me on the back like a child.

"He will, Jasmine," he said with certainty. "You need to have some faith."

"I've barely heard from the stone," I sobbed. I had tried to stay distracted, but the uncontrollable wave of fear that I felt for Seamus' safety took me under at last.

"I know, I know," Artur comforted. "But I told you, the connection with the stones might not work under the influence of the Nuvem Morte."

"What if he thinks he's dead?" I whispered as a chill ran down my spine. The magic of the poisonous potion was strong...it was very possible he could have already forgotten it all. Our mission. His life. Me.

Artur patted my head gently once more. "He could never forget he's alive when he has *you* to live for. Believe that."

* * *

MY OUTBURST of tears seemed to have alarmed Artur to some degree, because we were immediately back to our fast-paced schedule of learning the following morning. I would have been embarrassed by the amount of times he had seen me lose control of my emotions, but I didn't have time to be. We were right back to business.

"I want to start working on harnessing your powers," he said simply at breakfast.

"What powers?" I asked. "Controlling my visions?"

Please, I thought. *Teach me how to keep the nightmares away.*

"Aside from the visions," he admitted. "I can't help you there, unfortunately."

My face fell. Of course not. I wondered if anyone could.

"I want to start by testing the limits," he said simply. "Of your control over the sea serpents."

"The Ollphéist didn't really *listen* to me, necessarily," I said, recounting the incident at Carrickfergus once more. "He just chose to go after Camila and Cearbhall instead."

"Did you try to command it?" Artur asked.

"No, I thought Oisin had it under control," I said uncomfortably, recalling how all I had done was swim as fast as I could away from the beast. Aisling had then sent me through The Green Window to Skellig Michael, and I never looked back. And because I failed to help him, Oisin had died.

Artur tapped his chin thoughtfully before shrugging.

"Let's go to the library," he said.

I followed him back to the shelves, and asked him about the magic that kept the pages dry.

"As I said, I like to keep things a bit more *human* here," he said, laughing. "I couldn't live without my books, so I had to learn how to make it work."

"Can you teach me?" I asked. I told him about the note Aisling had written for me, and I suddenly wanted to know. Was magic inherently gifted to us as merpeople? Or did we have to learn it?

"It'll take some practice," he said. "But certainly."

He sped away behind a row of stone shelves and returned quickly with a roll of soggy, blank parchment. It looked exactly as one would expect a loose scroll to appear under the sea–flailing about in the waves because it didn't belong there. Artur pressed his hand to it and blew a thin stream of bubbles directly onto the paper. It looked like he was whistling.

The parchment dried instantly, and we were able to hold it in the exact same manner as we would have had we been above the waves and in a regular library. The sensation was unbelievable; like a tiny, invisible shield had descended upon the paper that even my own hands could not penetrate.

"Now you try," he encouraged, tearing off a small corner of the remaining parchment and handing it to me. "Focus on why you want to dry it–like you *need* to read a message someone's left for you. Or in this case, since the paper's blank, you *must* write something down before you forget."

"I can't think of anything," I murmured to myself, tapping my chin.

"It can be anything you want to write down," he said with a shrug. "Anything you want to say."

I thought of my conversation with Elias about Kiana.

I'm sorry, I thought, as loudly as I could. *I'm sorry and I wish I could tell you myself.*

I closed my eyes and Artur handed me a pen. I grasped it tightly and touched it to the page where I was sure it would immediately push through nothing more than a mess of melted paper.

But it didn't.

I felt the pen touch the parchment as solidly as it would have on a regular slab of marble had it been on land. I furiously scrolled the words out of fear that the spell would break before I was finished, and then I blew a thin, steady stream of bubbles over the top of my work.

When I was done, I gingerly opened my eyes, hoping I had been successful. I glanced down at the words and smiled. The paper was dry–only directly above the letters rather than the entire sheet as Artur's had been–but the words were certainly there, written in my own, terribly illegible hand. It wasn't bad for a first try, I thought. I then looked at the pen that I was still gripping tightly. I half expected a feather quill and ink pot, but it was a simplistic ballpoint. It said *Universidade do Porto* on the side and I roared with laughter.

"The barrier protects the city, but we still get garbage down here," Artur said with a shrug. Then he beamed at me and slapped me on the shoulder. "Well done, Jasmine."

Now feeling moderately accomplished, I was ready to get to our actual task. Artur pulled down a volume that looked newer than the rest and flipped to a page that showed a map of Portugal. Off the western coast, there was a sketch of yet another frightening sea serpent that I supposed could have been a cousin of the Ollphéist–except it had wings and therefore more closely resembled a dragon. It certainly didn't look like the World Serpent.

"Portuguese waters, 1848," he read. "A vessel named the Iara–"

I let out an amused huff. "That's ironic," I said, noting the ship's name being an ode to the Brazilian mermaid legend.

"Indeed," Artur mused. He had grown accustomed to my mythological knowledge by now, so he simply continued reading. "'The crew of this particular vessel claimed to sight a massive sea serpent between St. Helena and the Cape of Good Hope. They could see–hmmm it's listed in metrics here, but your *American* purposes–about four feet of its head, and another sixty feet of it slithering below the surface.'"

I studied the drawing of the frightening beast but said nothing.

"She's really more like fifty feet," he said. "They liked to exaggerate for dramatic effect in the 19th century."

I looked up at him, noting the present tense of his speech. "You don't mean–"

"I told you we don't get involved in conflict very often here," Artur said. "So she's actually quite benevolent. Would you like to meet her?"

Well. Not really.

We left the library and descended even further into the depths of the castle, down hallways I had not yet explored.

We reached a wide garden that was similar to the one in which I had been reading a few days prior, but there were no tucked away cloisters reminiscent of academia down here. Instead, there was nothing but a few benches of marble and sprawling rainbow seaweed plants. In the center was a stone statue of a sea serpent sitting beneath what looked like another mighty ruler–this time a king rather than Atargatis–who stood victorious over the slain bodies of what looked like hundreds of water demons with forked tongues. I wondered who it was.

Then I saw it.

The massive dragon-serpent, dark sapphire scales running from nose to tail, was sleeping in the sand, its nose emitting puffs of peaceful bubbles. I gasped.

She sensed our presence and awoke, revealing two massive, bright pink eyes that zeroed in on us immediately. I saw no chains of any kind holding the beast to where she was. I quickly backed away, terrified, and slammed directly into Artur who laughed at my apprehension.

"Invisible to humans, strikingly beautiful to us," he said. "Her name is Otima."

"Great," I said, translating the Portuguese word. And she was, indeed, just that. I hoped she wasn't *violenta* as well.

The creature lazily made her way over to us; half-floating, half walking as her claws stamped the sand. She revealed a pair of great wings and strong legs that helped her glide effortlessly across the ocean floor in a manner I thought was far too graceful for her size. Her claws were sharp as knives, and she had a swishing tail topped with jagged spikes that could have crushed me instantly. I looked at Artur incredulously, wondering how on earth he could have ever tamed this fearsome beast.

"Only if Atlântida is threatened would she ever strike," he said, petting her nose as if he did it all the time. The creature seemed to like it, bending further to make it easier for him to reach. "We have had peace for many years, so she has no need."

I looked up at the grand beast and she noticed me as well, turning her pink eyes to me. I thought she was trying to talk to me.

Hello, Mother of the Sea, she seemed to say, speaking directly into my mind. My eyes went wide and she seemed to chuckle as more bubbles emitted from her nose.

She then did something I could never have predicted. The beast dipped her massive blue snout directly to the ocean floor in some sort of invitation. I almost backed away again as she extended a claw, but I knew she was asking me to take it.

I tried to imagine it was the paw of an extremely friendly dog. I reached both my hands for it and put one on top of the shiny, blue scales, and one on the bottom as if I were going to shake it.

A light began to emit at my touch. Nothing too bright, but a faint, lazy glow of pink that seemed to offer friendship. Alliance.

Your servant, I heard her voice in my head.

I released her claw and floated away slowly, my eyes wide in wonder.

"Well, I think that settles that," Artur said.

I was mesmerized by my connection to the magnificent crea-ture, and I wondered if the Ollphéist of Strangford Lough would have reacted in the same way had I reached for his claws. Actu-ally, I couldn't even remember if he even *had* claws. Most snakes did not, but I could tell that the magical sea serpents that I supposedly commanded were not *most snakes*. Either way, I thought he would probably have smashed me into the wall like an egg.

* * *

THE NEXT DAY, Artur brought such positive news that my worries about Seamus were nearly forgotten for a singular moment.

"Aine's been found," he said, grinning widely. "She's completely safe and will be awaiting your return to Ireland. She's in Belfast with Niamh."

I sank back in relief. My mother was home. She was with her sister, and I'd see her soon.

"But Cearbhall and Camila know about Carrickfergus Castle," I said, biting my lip. "How do we know she'll be safe?"

"They're land-walking for now," he said with a shrug. "Remember the Amalgams can't do that."

Thank Manannán they couldn't.

"And besides, Niamh has some of Oisin's magic. She's laid another protective spell on the castle," he said. "A new one."

I went to the Nova Vida after that, my heart feeling lighter than any other time I had been there. I was relieved that my mother was safe, and that she knew *I* was as well. I had never met her, of course, but hearing of her brought me back to life. I couldn't wait for our reunion. I was so busy imagining what she'd be like in real life that I was hardly even bothered when Elias came to torment me later that afternoon.

I hadn't seen the Norwegian merman since his inappropriate comment, partially by my own design. Any time Diana and Benedito mentioned Elias coming to join us, I had made up some excuse or another to return to the castle and shut myself in my room.

Unfortunately, the castle wasn't safe, either. Artur had revealed to me that he actually thought the Scandinavian pest could be helpful in our mission, and therefore he had told him about our search for the stones. I couldn't imagine how he could be useful, considering I had grown to think he was nothing more than an arrogant prick.

"Your valiant hero has still not returned?" Elias questioned as he lurked behind one of the cloisters in the garden where I had come to seek some quiet time. I shut my book, seeing that serenity was no longer a possibility.

"Don't you have your own house to stalk around?" I asked sharply, wondering *why* everyone in Atlântida felt so comfortable simply entering the castle where their leader dwelled. I had noticed so many comings and goings of different people that I gave up on learning their names. I also gave up on the idea of any privacy. They were all a bit too familiar, if you asked me.

"I do, but I'd so much rather be in yours," he said as he floated next to me.

I noted that all pretenses between us had been dropped, and it seemed he'd now resort to openly provoking me.

"It's not mine," I said flatly, dodging him. "Not for long, anyway."

Something flashed in his eyes. "You're not staying?"

"No," I said. "When *Seamus* returns, we're going back to Ireland." I purposefully emphasized his name, letting it slowly roll off my tongue.

"Happily ever after," Elias said, his blue eyes locked on mine. I didn't look away.

"Exactly," I said coolly.

"Has he built you your dream home in the luxurious streets of the shining city of Dublin?" he pressed mockingly. "Or perhaps you'll live in a *wee* cottage in the country, tending to your cows?"

I scowled, thinking of our perfect Irish paradise from Artur's hidden room. I wanted to see it again, but not without him. I was afraid it might not even look the same if I went in alone.

"I don't know exactly where yet," I replied.

I didn't even know why I felt the need to answer him. To acknowledge his taunts at all was letting him win.

"No ring, no house," he clucked his tongue disapprovingly. "I wonder *what* you see in a man that doesn't provide for you."

His audacity was infuriating, especially considering I had almost believed him to be sincere only days ago. I opened my mouth to say something vulgar when he cornered me at one of the cloisters.

"You deserve a palace," he breathed in my ear, his hand grasping the frame above my head as he leaned in toward me. It was the closest he had ever dared get to me, and I wondered *where* he got the nerve. "After all, you are a queen. A *goddess*."

It wasn't a compliment, but a fact. I was Atargatis' Heir. I *should* live in a palace and rule the Seas once I had all the stones. But I didn't want to. Not at all.

"I'll choose my own destiny, just like Atargatis chose hers," I said, slipping away from him. He let me go, watching me too hungrily as I disappeared around the corner.

CHAPTER 20

THE WARRIOR RETURNS

*B*efore the following dawn, I felt the Iridescent Ammonite's call.

My heart leapt out of my chest with excitement, and I scrambled to hold it close to me. I listened.

It continued to reverberate loudly. It was pounding.

It's done, it seemed to say. It was Seamus' voice.

I swam down the hallway as fast as I could, darting across the grand hall and directly into Artur's chamber–I didn't care how rude it was to wake him in the early hours of the morning. I flung the moonstone doors open without knocking and showed him the glowing stone.

"Does this mean what I think it does?" I asked, terrified of being disappointed.

"Yes," Artur said confidently, shooting out of bed like a bolt of lightning. "Let's go, now."

We both tore out of the chamber, across the bright, moonlit marble of the main hall, and straight down into the Room of Windows. My heart was racing a million miles a minute.

"You remember it's a bit of a swim once we get there," Artur said, handing me a piece of bright pink seaweed before tucking a strand into one of his cuffs on his wrist for Seamus. "And he'll need the extra kick after what he's been through."

I nodded and gulped it down quickly before we vanished through the bubbling water that sent us swirling and whirling to another sea. I felt an electric shock of energy pulse through my veins as my eyesight noticeably sharpened.

"Let's go," I whispered to myself.

We emerged into the early hours of the morning and wasted no time. I followed Artur up to the light of the gray sky as he chose to flit across the surface where we were the quickest. Whether it was the miraculous seaweed or the anticipation thrumming in my chest, I felt like a car engine that had been supercharged, rocketing through the water so quickly that I couldn't even see the shore. Everything flew past me in a blur of color and I looked down at my arms—they were illuminated like glow sticks against the black water.

We flew past the shores of the Iberian Peninsula into Northern Spain when I saw the familiar inlet where I had watched Seamus leave well over a month ago. I truly didn't know how much time had passed. My heart was pounding in anticipation of our reunion—as excited as I was, I was also terrified to see what state he'd be in. I had no idea what to expect.

"I'm going to get him," I said.

I thought Artur might protest, but he didn't. Whether it was because the sun had not risen yet, or because he knew I would do it either way, he nodded encouragingly.

"Go."

I zoomed to where the body of water began to narrow into the river, melting into the stream while leaving nothing but my eyes above the surface. He would be somewhere around here...

I checked the stone against my chest, and its bright glow hadn't faded in the slightest. The thumping heartbeat was strong. He couldn't be far.

I hoisted myself up on land as the river was reaching its

narrowest point. I knew there would be no one here and it was safe to wait for my transformation. It was the spot where we had agreed to meet when it was over, and I looked around like a hawk for any sign of him. As my tail started to melt away, my immediate instinct was to set out on foot in search of him, but the stone held me back. It told me to stay right where I was. The sun was up, but I couldn't even think of the pain. If it was there, I didn't feel it.

And then I saw him.

Covered in what looked horribly like blood had it not been jet black, he was walking slowly–staggering actually–but walking at least, to the edge of the river where I was standing. I knew he hadn't traveled on foot the full distance, considering it would have taken well over seven hours to do so, but I couldn't surmise a guess as to how else he had done it.

It didn't matter. All that mattered was that he was there.

He held a sharp blade in his hand that was dripping with the same substance that was splattered across his face. His hair was long and unkempt, the usually auburn locks stained dark as night as they stuck to his face that was slick with sweat. His skin was paler than the moon that had faded above us to make way for sunrise.

Bloodied and bruised as he was, I knew before I even asked that he had accomplished his task.

He had won, because he was a warrior.

"Seamus," I gasped, sprinting toward him. He saw me too, and he welcomed me as I crashed into his arms.

"Jasmine, *Jasmine*," he repeated again and again, gripping me tightly as if his life depended on it. "It's you."

He breathed deeply into my hair and I knew what he was doing–he was trying to make sure I was real. He was trying to ensure that this wasn't a trick of the toxic potion that had nearly killed him.

I pulled away quickly to see if there was any damage. He was drenched in sweat, marked with several cuts, and covered in a foul smell that I realized must have been the scent of the dead... but overall, he seemed unbroken. I could tell now that the black liquid was certainly blood, although it couldn't have been a human's. I shivered.

I touched his face and brushed a lock of his hair from his eyes as I kept my tears at bay. I let out a deep breath for the first time in over a month.

"Are you hurt?" I asked quietly.

"No, a stór," he said, his voice heavy as he took my chin in his hand. I looked up at him and saw that his eyes had black circles beneath them—he looked like a ghost. Which, in a way, he was. He noticed my surveying eyes and put me at ease.

"The Nuvem Morte," he said thickly. "It's not fully worn off yet."

That's right. It would last up to three months unless...

Unless the dead found you out for your truth should you try and deceive them. That was what Artur had said.

Unlike Artur's dealings with the gods of the underworld who were well aware he was alive, Seamus *had* attempted to deceive The Santa Compaña. I looked him up and down and thought his frame was much too solid to have only taken the potion a month ago. My stomach churned as I wondered how he had gotten out alive. I knew he'd tell me everything, but not here. Not now.

"Where's Aisling and Fintan?" I asked worriedly.

"Safe," he promised. "They fled on land, but they're on their way back. They weren't pursued. They'll be fine."

We traipsed back into the water, him nearly falling in as we approached the shore. We transformed quickly into our selkie selves, Seamus wincing slightly as I watched him cautiously. The dried blood that covered his body started to wash away, but his ghostly pallor remained. I reached for his arm, but he patted my hand in reassuring dismissal.

"I'm alright," he said, but the gash that ran from his shoulder and well past his elbow said otherwise. I took one look at it and knew immediately that it was no ordinary cut. Where there should have been a raw, ruby red mark of a fresh scar, there was a deep line of sinister obsidian instead. A black mark to remind him of his time with the dead.

The Nova Vida, I thought to myself. That's where I'd take him when we got back.

Artur was waiting for us in the open water, and he slapped Seamus on the back as he beamed with pride. He acknowledged the scar but didn't seem too concerned, which put me at ease. He handed Seamus some seaweed and I saw the tiniest hint of color return to his freckled cheeks as he swallowed it.

"You get what you needed?" Artur asked, but it was rhetorical. He knew as well as I did that he had.

"Aye," Seamus replied, wiping the dried blood from his face. "The bastards made me work for it, but it's done."

PART IV

RISK-TAKER

CHAPTER 21

BATTLE SCARS

*A*rtur agreed with my plan to take Seamus straight to the Nova Vida, so we went to the healing pool as soon as we returned. He knew we wanted some privacy, so he left Seamus and I to go alone. It was still early in the morning, and I was relieved to see that it was completely deserted.

I poured the magical substance over Seamus with my hands, watching the strange sensation of waters with different densities interact and swirl about, their miraculous properties bringing relief to his wounds that were already beginning to heal themselves.

He closed his eyes and I gratefully watched the pool bring him back to life. The waters were also forcing the Nuvem Morte to fade—his freckles colored the lines on his face once more as they reappeared, and the ghostly pallor disappeared from his countenance. He was cleansed of the remaining black blood as it vanished in the depths of the pool, erasing all physical traces of what he had been through. Physical, not psychological, I was sure.

"Better?" I asked. He had not experienced the sensation of the healing waters prior to his departure, since neither of us had discovered it yet back then. I thought of all my peaceful mornings here and knew this was exactly what he needed.

"Now I am."

He opened his emerald green eyes and reached for my face. I could feel relief radiating from him in the hungry manner in which he kissed me; as if he were still trying to prove to himself that I wasn't a ghost. I wrapped my arms around his neck, his familiar scent of campfires and autumn leaves rushing into my nose and warming me to my core. He lifted me onto his lap and cradled me in the pool, tracing a finger up and down my arm.

"I am so feckin' relieved to see ye," he breathed, pressing my head into his chest. His voice was dark.

"Me too," I said, letting out a dry sob. "Don't ever leave again."

I knew I sounded pathetic, but I didn't care. I was exhausted from weeks of worry and putting up walls of feigned strength in front of everyone but Artur, acting like I was doing nothing aside from patiently awaiting his return. The morose attitude I had adopted in Seamus' absence was chillingly similar to the emptiness I had felt and displayed following Matt and Raj's deaths, and I didn't ever want to experience it again.

"No, Jasmine," he promised, hands sinking in my hair. "I won't."

I suddenly felt the strangest sensation that we were being watched, and I was right. I looked up and saw the last person I wanted to see, lurking around the pool.

It was Elias, and I wondered how much he had eavesdropped.

"Apologies," he said silkily. "I didn't mean to interrupt. No one's usually here this early. Well, I guess sometimes *you* are, Jasmine."

Seamus turned around to see who it was, and I saw a shadow of annoyance flash across his face at the familiarity in which Elias spoke my name. I could have died, because Elias had never actually spoken to me when I came here early in the mornings. I hadn't seen him at all, which meant he had been watching me.

The two men had also never been acquainted–since I had met Elias after Seamus had already left–which made it even worse.

"This is Seamus," I said, my hands still on his shoulders as his grip on my back tightened ever so slightly. "Seamus, this is Elias. One of my–friends."

I hated the word, and Elias knew it. We were *not* friends.

"Hey," Seamus replied. He spoke evenly enough, but with a clear tone of dismissal.

"She's been dying for you to return," Elias said, staring at me in amusement while I fumed behind Seamus. "I've hardly seen her smile in weeks."

"Well it's a good thing I'm back then, aye?" Seamus said, shifting to rise out of the pool while I moved aside, his own smirk emerging as he sized up the intruder.

They both now had massive scars that scraped down their bodies, and I glanced between the two of them, wondering which was worse. Because it hadn't healed in the pool, I knew that it meant Seamus' new wound was permanent. I couldn't imagine what kind of creature could have inflicted it upon him; the black mark ran nearly the full length of his arm and glinted like liquid onyx in the faint sunlight that streamed down from above.

"I guess so," Elias said, not even pretending to address Seamus as he looked directly at me with his blazing, blue eyes. "See you around."

"Who was that feckin' melter?" Seamus said to me as Elias flitted around the corner and vanished from sight.

I shrugged.

"He's friends with these twins Artur introduced me to. Diana and Benedito," I said. And then I added, "He's actually the one that gave Oisin the fake stone. To trick Cearbhall and Camila."

Seamus looked as if he might say something smart, but thought better of it.

"Well he can't be all bad then, I suppose," he said with a dismissive sigh. "Want to head back?"

"Sure," I said, feeling the tiniest bit awkward for a reason I couldn't explain. I shook it off immediately, feeling stupid. Elias seemed to thrive in his pursuit of pestering me, but that didn't mean I'd ever taken his bait. There was nothing I had ever said to him that I wouldn't say right in front of Seamus.

When we arrived back at our tower, we sped immediately past our room and I knew where we were headed. We were going to the oasis room. *Utopia,* as I had come to know it. Seamus was going to tell me what had happened in Spain, and he wanted to do it when we were completely alone.

"If you're not ready to talk about it yet..." I started as we floated through the doorway.

I was never one to push others to relive their trauma so soon after it had happened. It took me months to go to therapy after Raj and Matt's deaths. Even then, it had been several sessions before I said anything meaningful. Seamus didn't seem like the type who feared saying what was on his mind, but I didn't really know for sure.

"No, I want to," he said earnestly. "I need ye to know the things I did."

I didn't like the distinct note of graveness in his voice, but he took my hand and we crossed through the door to the magical room where the sparkling blue barrier invited us to escape. We entered the only place where we could be alone—the magical world where nothing could hurt us.

As we crossed through the veil of memories that enabled our entry to Utopia, I braced myself for the rush of emotions that were to come, but they didn't. Or if they did, they seemed so much more insignificant this time. My mind was elsewhere–I hardly saw them at all.

We landed in the water with a gentle *splash* and paddled toward the shore, Seamus' strong hands guiding me from behind. The sand was perfectly cool and the moonlight above was bright enough to light the dark shadows on his face. The Nuvem Morte had faded in the healing pool, but traces of it remained. My tail melted away slowly, but as I made to stand, Seamus placed a hand on my shoulder and joined me back on the ground.

"Ye may want to sit for this."

And then he launched into the most terrifying nightmare that I could imagine, and my hand stayed clapped over my mouth for the majority of the warrior's tale.

CHAPTER 22

THE SANTA COMPAÑA

Seamus, having no idea where exactly The Santa Compaña would be, had waited in the shadows near the Cathedral of Santiago de Compostela until nightfall. It seemed like the type of place where something like this would occur. The potion had begun to work almost instantly, and he could tell he was fading from notice of others in the street the longer he stayed tucked away.

The sun finally set and he looked down at his own arms, finding he was nearly translucent in the moonlight. He caught a glimpse of himself in one of the glass windows of the old church and confirmed that all signs of life had been drained from his face. His skin had faded to a sickly pallor, and he felt he wasn't far away from disappearing entirely.

"I'm alive," he told himself, even as his heart slowed and eventually stopped beating.

The heartbeat, from what he remembered, had been what connected him to Jasmine through the stone last time. He hadn't known whether it was hers or Atargatis' pulse that he felt, but knowing his own wouldn't be consistent made him certain their connection would be much more challenging this time.

The street fell eerily silent as the clock passed the hour of three, the usual nightlife of Spain much quieter in this docile region. He listened intently for any sign of life—or death, he supposed, was more accurate.

Then he heard them.

The dulcet tones of those whose hearts no longer thrummed with blood came from the east, and he turned to follow the whispers. The Santa Compaña were approaching the square where he stood, and he could only hear them because he was one of them.

"Who is there?" came a slick voice; the personification of midnight.

Seamus hesitated for a moment before emerging from the shadows, facing the ghostly army clad in white robes that marched with hoods over their heads and torches in their hands.

"Have we another Juan in our midst?" said the leader, the only one wearing black. It had to be Duarte.

His joke of the last mortal who had fallen prey to their trap was met with a ripple of laughter and Seamus' heart would have pounded had it not been incapable of doing so.

But no. Duarte saw him, and he knew instantly that the leader of the morbid company believed he was dead.

Seamus turned to face the others and choked back a scream. They were worse than skeletons–horrific beasts of twisted shapes and deformed features that seemed to have been carved by the devil himself. He could not imagine these beings in front of him to have ever been alive at all, and he wondered how long they had been aimlessly wandering the entirety of the Iberian Peninsula as corpses. He wiped his face blank as best he could, and he said nothing.

"Duarte, he's too young," hissed someone to the leader's right.

Duarte removed his hood to reveal a cruel, crooked grin that was weather-worn beneath sunken cheeks that were filled with decaying matter.

"Who are you and from where do you hail?" he asked. "Do you wish to join in the procession?"

"I'm Seamus of Ireland," he responded. There was no reason to hide his identity. They wouldn't give a shit, either way. "I wish to pledge my allegiance to The Santa Compaña."

The leader looked amused by this statement.

"Ireland? You're a long way from home, *laddie*," he said mockingly.

Without missing a beat, Seamus said, "I met my death in the waters of Iberia."

Duarte surveyed him briefly, deciding his origins were of little importance. "And how far will you go for your allegiance?" he asked. "How deep is your desire to be one of us?"

Seamus looked him over contemplatively. He decided he better go all in with his charade, and replied simply, "I'll do anything."

The crowd of the dead chuckled at this, apparently having witnessed a trick of this nature before. Duarte stepped forward and surveyed Seamus.

"You *are* young," he said, reaching a clawed finger up to touch his cheek. Seamus forced himself not to flinch. "Why would you choose this form of death when someone could await you on the other side?"

The other side, meaning Heaven or Hell, he assumed. Anywhere other than this purgatory of mindless wandering.

"She doesn't," he said bluntly.

Remembering the man's story, he risked it all with his next sentence. He knew he needed to plant the seeds in Duarte's mind that the two of them could be one in the same; that they could share the same loss that led them to eternal misery. Artur had told him this much.

"My woman is lost to the sea, a maiden of the waters that can never be mine. Not even in the afterlife," he said.

Duarte tried to hide it, but a trace of understanding—and

perhaps even alarm that Seamus might know something about him—flashed in his eyes.

"Then you will complete a task for me," the leader of the dead said. "To prove your loyalty."

Seamus nodded gravely, knowing he had no choice but to do it, whatever it was. It was the first step in infiltrating the nefarious company, and he'd need Duarte's respect as well as his trust to get him to answer the critical question. The question to which no one–not even Cearbhall and Camila–knew the answer.

"What is it?" he asked, not taking his eyes off the disgusting creature, no matter how badly he wanted to do so. "The task."

"You will drink the blood of a human," Duarte said. "It is our way."

Seamus didn't react at all.

"Show me which one."

He willed himself numb as the beginnings of a sick ritual formed. The titters of excitement in the crowd were loud, but Duarte silenced them as the procession floated through the walls of the church. Seamus hadn't been in a church in a long time, and he never imagined *this* would be his first time back.

His body morphed through the wall easily and he was immediately placed on the other side, where massive golden arches extended straight to the sky. Reaching for Heaven, he supposed.

Heaven. A place he'd been told his whole life was reserved for him if he lived honorably and righteously. It was a place he'd never see after he did this.

The Santa Compaña followed Seamus down the aisle and to the altar, the pillars rising on either side of him, trapping him in. He reached the altar where a young woman lay, whimpering. Her chest was rising and falling in sharp, jagged breaths as she clutched at the binds that held her to the marble. He was reminded brutally of Aslan the lion on the stone table, or Jesus Christ on the cross, if he were being more literal. He had hoped the human in question would already be dead, but he felt foolish for that now as he looked upon the victim that was placed before him. Of course they would make him kill her first.

She was tragically beautiful, her brown eyes full of sadness in a way that made Seamus' heart hurt. He willed himself not to see Jasmine in her expression, but their features were so similar. The same curve of their mouths, the same soft, olive skin. The same jet black hair that fell like a curtain of silk past her shoulders.

"Please," the woman begged. "Help me!"

Seamus looked down at her, expressionless. He knew Duarte was watching him.

The evil leader then descended upon Seamus and whispered into his ear.

"You'll use this, and then you'll drink her," he said, handing Seamus a brutally sharp knife with glinting garnets on the handle.

The Virgin Mary stared down at Seamus from the stained glass above, telling him this was his last chance to turn back as he took the blade from Duarte's hands. He thought of all the times as a child he'd been in a place just like this, praying to her for forgiveness for trivial matters like fighting with Aidan, getting smart with his teachers...things that didn't really offend God at all.

But he did not tremble. He couldn't let The Santa Compaña see that this was breaking him. He closed his eyes as he blocked out the woman's sobs, asking himself if he was really capable of this. Of murdering someone who was entirely innocent.

He took a deep breath and turned the knife over in his hands. He willed himself to bring forth the darkness within him, and shut out the light. Who was he, after all, to determine right from wrong? It was wrong to murder someone, of course. But wasn't it also wrong to let down the woman to whom he had pledged his very soul? The woman he promised he'd die for? Wasn't *this* a form of dying for Jasmine? Killing his soul? He looked up at Mary, begging her to understand.

But he wasn't a Christian. Maybe he had been once, but not anymore. And he was certainly already a sinner in God's eyes. He misused the name of the Lord on a regular basis, had taken Jasmine–and plenty of other women before her–to his bed without the sacrament of matrimony, and he had absolutely never honored his father. With three of the ten commandments already broken, what was one more?

No, he was far from holy. Religion looked him in the face and mocked him.

"The clock is ticking," Duarte said from behind him, sending a shiver down his spine.

Then something occurred to him.

"Why her?" he asked Duarte bluntly, staring into the terrified face of the woman on the altar.

Duarte met Seamus' gaze, daring him to say he was afraid. His eyes, lifeless as they were, seemed to beg him to say he couldn't do it. The leader did not reply to his question. He wouldn't.

Then Seamus heard the faintest whisper from a voice he did not know.

Heard it or *felt* it, he wasn't sure. It was a voice that spoke with utmost authority and clarity, ringing through his ears to tell him something important.

"It's a ruse," it said.

He didn't know what made him believe it, but he thought it might be Atargatis. Or God. Maybe not the one he had known as a child when he sat in church pews and confessionals, but perhaps another. Seamus didn't know how many there were anymore.

He froze, the dagger in his hand now slick with sweat.

"Not able to do it?" Duarte asked, a cruel grin creeping onto his face as he and the company began to close in on him. "A shame…"

The voice did not speak again, but Seamus knew he hadn't imagined it. *It's a ruse.*

"Seamus, you wouldn't really do this to me, would you?" cried the woman from the altar.

No, that voice was too similar to Jasmine's to be real.

He thought now that whatever he looked upon was no woman. It was a trick–this victim was one of the hallucinations that Artur had warned him about. This creature on the altar was an evil being…maybe even Satan himself. There was no way to be sure, but he had to believe it. He had to tell himself that was the case, or else he'd never convince himself to do it.

Seamus moved swiftly. He lifted the woman's head off the stone, resting it on his own chest for a single moment before dragging the blade across her throat.

Black smoke emitted from her neck like Dracula himself had returned, and she transformed into a cackling, evil demon that rose from the ashes to join Duarte's side.

Seamus stood right where he was, not daring to back away in a sign of weakness or fear.

He had been right.

"Have I proven my worth to your satisfaction?" he said coldly, looking directly at Duarte.

Both the demon and Duarte's eyes were shining with approval.

"Indeed you have," the demon said, shapeshifting back into a woman. But this time she had white blonde hair, pale skin and black eyes–all traces of her innocence had vanished. "But you still need to drink my blood."

She presented her wrist to him and Seamus went numb. He willed himself again to rid his mind of any thoughts other than completing the task at hand. He'd do it.

"On your knees," she said with ferocity, her dagger-like teeth bared in a way that reminded Seamus so deeply of the terrifying dream he had once had of Jasmine. The one he had had back in Ireland, before he knew what she really had become. When she had dragged him across the sand and shape-shifted between his lover and a monster.

He met the demon's stare.

"I kneel for no one," he said.

Then he took her wrist in his hand and slit it with deadly precision. Liquid black pearl began to seep from the wound, and the demon shuddered with something that sounded disturbingly like pleasure.

Seamus brought it to his lips and drank.

His vision went red and he felt nothing. He didn't think or taste. He didn't process what he was doing, or even conceptualize the texture of the hot liquid in his mouth. The dead spirit within him seemed to take over the remaining goodness that glimmered in his soul, and he prayed he'd be able to remember he was alive again when it was over. But he couldn't think of that now.

The demon tossed her head back in ecstasy as Seamus inhaled the drops that flowed freely from her until she told him to stop.

She ran her clawed hands through his hair and then lifted his face to meet hers, grinning with joy at the sight of her own black blood dripping down his neck. Seamus feared momentarily what curse this would unleash upon him, but Artur had told him the Nuvem Morte would protect him from anything regarding the dead. The potion was an invisible, impenetrable shield that made him invincible to the poisons of the underworld. He would not be physically harmed, no matter what the demon's blood was laden with.

But what the Nuvem Morte wouldn't do, unfortunately, is make him forget what he had done.

"I sense that you're an excellent lover," the demon whispered to him through a thick mist that Seamus sensed secluded her words from anyone but him.

He pulled away in disgust, wiping her filthy blood from his mouth. It took all of him not to spit it at her feet.

But Duarte. He needed Duarte to trust him.

Seamus said nothing as the creature disappeared in a cloud of black smoke. The church was silent, the procession behind him seemingly in awe of what he had done.

"Excellent," Duarte said to him. "You will come with me, now."

Seamus sighed nearly undetectably, the blood still warm in his throat.

At least his plan was working.

CHAPTER 23

FROM THE DEPTHS OF HELL

For the next several days, Seamus did very little aside from wait. It was too soon to ask questions of Duarte. The demon he had enlisted in his tricks had left once satisfied that Seamus had completed her task, but she would return. Seamus heard whisperings from the other members of the morbid company that she would come back with a vengeance, eager to trick him again as she had so many others.

"She doesn't like to be outwitted," one of them said.

It didn't frighten him, because Seamus knew something that none of them did. He was not truly one of them. He was alive, and he could not be harmed.

Weeks went by, and he felt his confidence wavering as his efforts with Duarte were proving to be a difficult, slow burn. He kept track of the days by marking a brick on the side of the Cathedral, and each time he did so, he was more distressed to see how many had passed.

He tried to forget the scene at the altar, but it came to him at all hours. The Nuvem Morte, of course, deprived him of sleep, so he was forced to live the nightmare in the daylight through hallucinations.

The thought of returning to Jasmine and telling her what he had done constantly plagued his mind. He imagined the expression of horror on her face and it filled him with despair each time. Would she ever look at him the same, knowing that he had committed murder after being convinced by nothing more than a faint whisper from no one? Would she ever be able to kiss him again, knowing the blood of a Satanic creature had been on his lips?

The only thing that kept him alive was the small note he had found from her. The one that he kept tucked away in the magical cuff from Artur that he wore on his wrist.

"I love you. Don't forget you are alive."

He had to believe that she wouldn't see him as a monster—that she would understand why he had done it. Because if it meant getting what he needed for her, he'd do it again. He'd do anything for her, because that was his duty.

As the leader of The Company, Duarte led the way in all matters of importance. The aimless wandering that never ceased involved the haunting of sacred places throughout Santiago de Compostela and the hills beyond, as well as seeking humans to drink. Seamus learned quickly that the drinking of the demon's blood was the initiation ritual all had to endure, and it would change their tastes to desire nothing else besides human blood for the rest of eternity.

Since Seamus was not actually dead, he was repulsed by this notion and had to subject himself to eating human food when and if he could acquire it without being noticed. It weakened him greatly, but there was no option for the sustenance of seaweed in the landlocked city.

Whenever the others cornered humans wandering on their

own late in the night, Seamus bowed his head in shame. He didn't help them. He watched them all suffer and die.

There had been no one new added to The Company in well over a hundred years, so they were all fascinated—well, as fascinated as the dead can be—by Seamus's appearance. They wanted to ask questions of his desire to become one of them. He repeated his answer regarding his maiden damned to the seas as many times as he could, in hopes that Duarte would notice. He tried incessantly, and unsuccessfully, to get Duarte to disclose more about himself.

It was one evening in the Praza da Quintana de Vivos where Seamus believed his efforts were finally coming to fruition.

They had been seeking more tourists when Duarte beckoned for Seamus to step aside with him.

"Demonio requests your presence tonight," he said. "Underground."

Seamus nodded and followed him across the square. Duarte slipped through the wall and led him into the dungeons of the church where he had committed his act of murder well over three weeks ago. Or had it been even longer than that? He panicked for a moment, realizing that he was already starting to forget the exact duration of time that had passed. He needed to get this feckin' job done.

The Cathedral had been eerie to him when he first arrived, but now he was used to it. He caught a glimpse of himself in his reflection on the gold pipes that lined the stairwell, and found his eyes had sunken even deeper and his skin was now completely white.

Just when he thought the winding staircase would never end, Seamus was dumped out into a vile smelling dungeon where a black altar sat at the front of the poorly lit room.

"Here he is," Duarte said, stepping off into the shadows and leaning against the wall.

As Seamus entered *Demonio's* lair (as he had learned she was called), he came to a halt. She was sitting perched on a throne of solid gold, her white hair this time slicked back into a bun and was clad in black armor. She was prepared to fight him, it seemed. He nearly laughed, knowing how easily he could break her. But again he was reminded of Artur's warning of hallucinations. He saw a relatively slight woman, but it could easily be a trick of the mind. He didn't know what she could shape-shift into. He wiped the smirk off his face before she saw it.

She rose and came toward him, her eyes scanning him hungrily. Seamus stood completely still as she approached, and she seemed to grow taller as she did in order to match his gaze. She reached out her hand and he recoiled instinctively, which made her roar with laughter.

"You act like you don't know me now, young Seamus?" she cackled.

Studying him intently and finding nothing that resembled discomfort in his expression, she continued.

"I've had many men and women *drink me,* you know." She brushed her wrist against his mouth and he wanted to rip her throat out, but he forced himself to remain stoic. "But none who brought me so much pleasure as *you.*"

He looked down at her with disgust.

"I'm sure you're curious as to why I've summoned you here tonight?" she asked.

He did not reply.

"I *did* want to find out if what I suspected about you was true," she said, circling behind him. She spoke into his ear and ran a finger along his jaw. "If you're as passionate a lover as I hope."

The very pit of Seamus' stomach lurched in revulsion.

Oh, *fuck* no. Not that. Anything but that.

She saw his expression of horror that he could not conceal this time and laughed.

"You know most men would be honored to be asked to the

Demonio's bed," she said, and her eyes flicked to Duarte. "I have never granted *him* such an honor. So I'll ask you again."

"No," Seamus said firmly. Demonio reached her hands around him from behind and he shrugged her off with force.

Anger flashed within her eyes and she disappeared into her black cloud of smoke, reappearing at her throne.

"How honorable of you," she said, her eyes wide in feigned innocence. "To remain loyal to the one you love, even when being offered a night with me…"

When he didn't reply, she continued to taunt him.

"But she's a maiden of the sea, is she not? They aren't offered the same afterlife as humans like you."

Seamus glanced at Duarte, but the leader of the Compaña made no indication that he had his own personal ties to this truth. He attempted to quiet the hot anger rising in his chest for the sake of not arousing suspicion. He spoke evenly.

"Aye, she is of the Seas," he said.

Demonio smiled cruelly at him. "So you'd rather be celibate for *eternity* than betray her?"

"Correct."

"How intriguing," she said. "I've never known a man that would choose such an alternative."

He said nothing, feeling horrifically suspicious that she was toying with him. Like she knew he was a fraud.

"Unless," she said with a soft venom that reeked of cruelty. "You still have hope of returning to her, because you have lied. Because you yourself are not dead, and you have falsified your presence here."

The demon tossed a tiny, crumpled up piece of paper at Seamus' feet and he bent down to pick it up, already knowing what it was.

I love you. Don't forget you are alive.

Seamus' blood ran cold. How the demon had found it, he didn't know.

"I'll need an explanation for this," she said softly, and Duarte muttered some sort of curse from behind his back. "Why did you come to our Company if you are not truly one of the hopeless dead?"

Seamus looked between her and Duarte, thinking fast. He knew it was risky, but he had to reveal it now. He turned directly to the ghostly man, desperately hoping that there was an unknown rift between the two of them that would allow Duarte to hear him.

He said the only thing that he thought would jar Duarte the most, and he'd figure the details out later.

"I am the Heir of Atargatis," Seamus said firmly. "And I've come to reunite ye with Nabia."

Duarte's eyes, full of death only moments before, went wide with renewed life that reflected his shock.

"You lie," he whispered, but he was hopeful. Seamus saw it in his eyes.

Demonio looked between them sharply, plainly not understanding of whom they spoke. Good, Seamus thought. It was just as he expected. She was not of the Sea. She was from Hell, and knew those pits alone. It was an advantage for him.

Seamus then revealed the gem that he had had kept tightly pressed to his chest for days. Even in its smoky appearance, shrouded by the mist of the Nuvem Morte, it was clear that the stone was magic.

"It would glow at your touch," Duarte said, his face falling before turning to one of stony anger. "If you were the true Heir."

As if in answer to his doubt, the stone began to emit a faint light.

It slowly grew, illuminating the floor before the walls, the ceiling next...Atargatis, or Jasmine–he didn't know which–was helping him.

"Impossible," Duarte breathed. "Where is Nabia?"

"You fool!" hissed Demonio. "You would forgive this traitor? What message would that send to the rest?"

Seamus nearly pitied the man for promising he could reunite him with his centuries-lost lover, but remembered the horrific act Duarte had forced him to commit. The one he made all members of the Company commit. He hardened once more. There would be no mercy…not when the fate of his and Jasmine's world was at stake. There were forces, just as dark as the demon in front of him, at work under the sea right now, and every moment he wasted here was another one where Cearbhall and Camila could be tracking down the stones. Or worse–finding and recapturing Jasmine's mother.

Seamus looked firmly at Duarte. "I need ye to tell me how many of these there are." He motioned to the stone around his neck. "Then I'll reunite you with Nabia."

Duarte looked like he might oblige, but the demon cut in.

"Enough!" she said, having lost patience with their exchange. "You will pay for your deceit."

She then brought a blade that seemed to materialize out of nowhere down through the air, but Seamus was quicker. He leapt to the side and grabbed Duarte by the back of his neck, something that he had questioned was even possible considering they were both ghosts, but it worked.

He fled up the stairs, crashing through walls as he heard the hurried steps of the demon behind them. It was an even fight–she could flash to other sides of walls with her cloud of smoke just as quickly as Seamus and Duarte could disappear through them.

Demonio screeched with rage as she burst through the floor of the church and into the pews, shattering the stained glass windows with her black cloud of terror. Seamus paused only momentarily before pressing through the nearest wall and up another flight stairs. He was climbing and climbing with Duarte's neck still in his grasp. Had the man fainted in fear?

Something occurred to him as his feet made contact with the solid ground. He couldn't actually fly. And they were headed straight for the top towers. There would be nowhere else to go.

"Shit," he said under his breath, realizing he had trapped himself as they emerged on the roof. He looked around wildly for an escape when Duarte slipped from his grasp.

"Oh no ye don't," he said, lunging for him. Without fully meaning to, he pinned Duarte to the ground where his head hung over the ledge of the massive cathedral.

Duarte laughed.

"I can't die twice, you fool," he said.

Seamus looked at him, desperation descending upon him. "Please," he said at last. "Tell me how many there are. And I swear I'll find Nabia and bring ye two together. Ye have my word."

Duarte studied him.

"You are not the Heir of Atargatis," he said. It wasn't a question.

"No," Seamus answered honestly.

"But you do know the Heir," Duarte said, pointing to the stone as it continued to glow. "I can see that she's the woman of whom you spoke. Would you die for her?"

Seamus looked at him gravely. "I already have."

Demonio then materialized before them, forcing them both back from the ledge with her black wind.

Seamus leapt to his feet, but felt himself being lifted into the air by the cloud. The Nuvem Morte within his body flickered as Artur had said it would–should his ruse be discovered. He could feel his bones cracking as the demon tightened her grip on him through the cloud. She raised him high into the air before slamming him directly onto the stone roof. He braced himself for severe impact, but it was moderate. He was still protected, but not for long.

"The cloud of death is my favorite ruse," the demon laughed cruelly as she saw the holographic figure of Seamus becoming more solid. She slammed him into another pillar–this time he felt the full force. "Oh and you're even more alluring when you're *alive*."

Seamus looked at Duarte from the other side of the roof, praying the man would find an alliance with him. He tried to stand, but his head was spinning.

"But first, *you* will be punished for this," the demon said, rounding on Duarte. "For being so careless and not seeing that this was the Nuvem Morte at work."

And just when Seamus began to lose hope, the ghostly man silently slid a dagger across the roof from behind his back, the garnet-handled blade landing right in Seamus' grasp.

No way, Seamus thought, snatching up the dagger. It gave him renewed strength, and he silently leapt to his feet, the demon's back still to him as she descended upon Duarte.

He crept behind the massive shadow where the demon was bent over Duarte, torturing him with her suffocating black cloud. Trusting nothing other than his instinct and Atargatis' thrumming beat that was now hot against his chest, he reached into the cloud and plunged the knife where he thought the demon's heart might be if she had one. His own arm was torn by something sharp in the process, but the dagger landed on its target. His own ruby blood splattered across the roof, churning with the black blood from Demonio.

The smoke flashed a bright red before it rose higher in the sky, and liquid midnight began to pour from it like a storm cloud. The demon's limp body hung in the center of it.

The thick, black blood continued to rain from the cloud, flooding the roof with a vengeance and drenching Duarte and Seamus in the process. He wiped it from his eyes, seeing it entirely differently this time as it dripped down his face, neck, and chest. It was a sign of triumph rather than a humiliating act of service.

He had done it. Demonio was dead, and Duarte would respect him for it.

Duarte looked up at him from the center of the pool on his hands and knees. The sun was beginning to rise in the distance.

"I owe you a debt for this," he said to Seamus. "I cannot die again, but what she could have done is much, much worse."

Seamus looked at him, stony-faced. "You know what I want."

"There are ten," Duarte replied immediately. "Ten stones."

"And where are they?" Seamus asked, desperate to get in another question before the ghost disappeared at the break of day. He was no longer one of them–he'd never see Duarte again. Damn Artur's warning about not asking too many questions.

"Which have already been found?" Duarted inquired.

Seamus listed them furiously, willing the sunrise to hold off.

"As far as I know, there's the Larimar of the Antilles, the Tsavorite of Maza Bay, the...yellow one from the North Sea," he began, listing the stones that were in the enemy's hands. Neither him or Jasmine had ever seen the stone that Cearbhall and Camila had taken from Oisin, but Aisling swore the fake looked just like the real one, and it had definitely been a yellowish green.

Duarte nodded, now seemingly intrigued by how many had truly been tracked down. "The Chrysoberyl. That's the one from the North Sea"

The sun was nearly up, so Seamus pressed on. "The Iridescent Ammonite of Iberia...and this one," he finished.

He held up the miraculous, golden gem that had started it all. The flecks of light within it seemed more prominent now in contrast to the gray of Duarte's faded existence.

"The Citrine of Cyprus," he said.

Seamus nodded, recalling Professor Brennan's original discovery of the gem. Duarte looked contemplatively at him.

"If they haven't been found already…there is one in each of the following places."

Seamus listened intently, knowing his life depended on remembering the man's next words.

"One lies in Nóregr, one in Yamato, and… the rest are in the homeland of Atargatis herself."

Seamus stared.

Where the *fuck* were those places?

It wasn't in any way directional, but it was more of a lead than he already had. And it was all Seamus was getting out of the dead man. The sun was just behind the buildings ahead, and the ghost in front of him vanished.

He prayed Jasmine would be able to figure the man's words out. She knew damn near everything—she had to know this.

CHAPTER 24

UNSPOKEN THOUGHTS

"**D**o ye know?" Seamus asked me urgently as he finished his story at last.

I was so shaken that I could hardly sputter the words out, but of course I had to.

"Nóregr means *North Way*–the old Norse word for Norway," I said, my mind working furiously. "Yamato…I think before *Nippon*, that's what Japan was called. Yes. In very early texts. And of course Atargatis is from the Middle East. I know that's not much to work with, but Artur and I have some guesses…" My voice trailed off as I pictured the old maps from the study. Yes. We could figure this out.

Seamus grinned at me with relief and admiration.

"Christ, I knew ye'd get it immediately," he said before kissing me deeply. "The smartest woman that ever lived."

I could hardly breathe, let alone be flattered by his compliment. I sank into his shoulder as he placed his arm around me, pulling me into his chest.

"Seamus…I'm–" I began, now shaking in the sand of our oasis. The air was perfectly temperate, of course, but I felt a violent chill as I remembered something from his story.

The note. The stupid note I had left as a lover's reminder. My silly diary that I tucked away into his cuff in hopes that he'd read it at night when he was alone. It almost got him killed.

"I'm so sorry for the note," I whispered, my voice cracking. I was mortified by my carelessness.

He tilted my chin upward to look at him. His green eyes were piercing me with their concern and sincerity.

"No, no, Jasmine," he said seriously. "Don't ye see? The note is what kept me alive. There were days where I nearly forgot who I was. The potion is just as dangerous and more than what Artur warned me it would be. It changes ye…changes your mind. My time there felt so much longer than it was."

"Still…" I said, imagining him sucking the demon's blood. And her *liking it.* I had gone limp when he told me of Demonio propositioning him, not knowing how I could ever move on if he had granted her request to take her to bed. I could hardly imagine a *human* woman sighing Seamus' name without boiling with rage, let alone an entity of the undead. It made me physically ill, which was a sensation I hadn't felt since I had become the strong creature that I was.

But he hadn't done it. He had killed her instead, damaging his own soul in the process. I didn't know which act was worse.

He seemed to know what I was thinking, and he bowed his head in shame.

"I had to do it," he said. "I'm sorry, Jasmine."

"Sorry for what? You did what you needed to do to accomplish the mission," I said firmly. "Now we know how many there are. *And* we know the general location of each. I bet with the power of Atargatis, I'll be able to sense them once we're there. That's what I did last time."

As I talked quickly, I knew his mind was far away. I looked into his murky green eyes that were clouded with the haunting of the deathly existence in which he had lived for over a month. I was endlessly grateful it wasn't any longer. What would I have done if he had been gone for six months? A year? I shuddered as I imagined it.

"I couldn't think of the possibility of coming back to ye without answers," he said, shaking his head. "When she made me drink the blood, I didn't even taste it."

I thought of the time I had Camila in a chokehold back in Portugal. The utter blindness of my rage had been the only sense that controlled me. I knew with certainty that I wouldn't have struggled to snap her neck in half. I wouldn't have felt anything. I would have done it if it had been necessary, and I knew that Seamus must have felt something similar.

"I almost failed ye," he said.

"But you didn't," I replied decisively. "You came back with more answers than we could have hoped for. More than Artur thought you'd get."

Seamus looked up at the sky, the perfectly shaped moon reflecting upon the lapping waves that were all ours. I wanted to stay here, just like I had wanted to stay back on Skellig Michael. I wanted to remain lost in our own world of ease; where nothing mattered but us.

But that wasn't real. We still had a job to do.

He placed his hand on the back of my head and kissed me tenderly before standing up to pace—something I had never really seen him do. It was out of place for such a sure-statured person. He walked back and forth in contemplative silence, as if debating whether or not to speak again. I hoped he knew he could. I hoped—despite my inability to do the same—that he knew he could tell me anything. I watched him silently, the black scar along his arm glinting in the moonlight. I hoped no part of the demon had entered him through the mark. I knew Artur was confident in the potion, but since I had no experience with it, I feared it.

Seamus looked up at the sky before turning to me.

"The worst part is, I would've done it anyway," he said. "Even if Atargatis, or God, whoever it was, hadn't told me it was a ruse."

I opened my mouth to say something, but he wasn't finished.

"I would've killed her either way," he continued. "There's nothing I wouldn't do for ye, Jasmine."

His eyes looked straight into the galaxy. I nodded as if I understood, knowing I never fully could. He'd said it before, but now he'd proven it.

"I know," I whispered.

"Ye know when she told me to kneel and I refused," he said. "I thought of ye."

"Why?" I asked cautiously, even though I recalled our conversation regarding Cearbhall's taunts before he left. I didn't want him associating me with the demon. I couldn't bear the thought of Seamus viewing me as some malevolent queen to whom he was required to submit. That was what Cearbhall had made me out to be–that wasn't who I was.

"Because I won't kneel for anyone besides ye," he said.

I smirked, but quickly wiped it off my face as I saw how serious he was.

Seamus was dominant–I knew that. He truly found something significant in being demanded to bow to someone, and he simply wouldn't do it. I tried to imagine him pleading for mercy from anybody, and I couldn't picture it. It was not his way.

As I watched him standing in the pale light of the moon, the faintest traces of the potion of the dead still in his face, I thought it genuinely possible that he would kill someone with his bare hands rather than bow to anyone for anything. Anyone but me.

"I know," I said.

"Would ye kneel for me?" he asked, his hand stroking a lock of my hair from above. He looked down upon me with love and admiration, but there was a faint shadow of illicit temptation coloring his face. "If I asked ye to."

I looked up at him from the ground, realizing that I nearly was.

"Yes," I breathed.

I knew what he wanted me to do, so I did it. I felt no shame in admitting that there was nothing I wouldn't do for him, either.

I rose, but only to my knees.

* * *

"Are you pleased, *a stór*?" I asked, quoting what he had said back in Nohoval Cove. I sat back on my heels with the taste of him in my mouth, knowing he had to be.

"Aye," he said, falling gently into the sand next to me as he put his hand behind my neck and kissed my forehead. "I love ye, I'm sorry."

"Sorry for what?" I asked.

"Treating ye like that," he said softly. "I don't think ye like it."

"That's not true," I said, suddenly sitting up on my forearm. "I just don't like it in real life. When you try to tell me what to do."

He raised an eyebrow at me with a smirk.

"So I can order ye around as long as it's only in the bedroom?"

"Or on the shore," I said. "We haven't actually ever done this in a bedroom, you know."

"That's right," he laughed, but his face fell slightly. "I'd like to."

Sadness flickered across my face that I hoped he wouldn't notice, but of course he did. I felt an inexplicable, irrational surge of jealousy for any woman that had shared that experience with him in the past. The normalcy of just…going to bed with him and then *waking up* next to him. Without a tail.

"What are ye thinking?" he asked.

I sighed deeply, knowing that there was no use in saying something like it out loud, but I might as well reveal it all while we were talking about it. I couldn't tell him about my stupid jealousy over nothing, of course, but I could reveal my other thoughts to him.

"I picture you and I...what our lives would be like if we had a normal existence," I said quietly. "If we just bought a house somewhere. Got a dog. Lived."

He looked up at the stars and his mouth turned into a hard line. His expression was contemplative.

"Like what ye would have had with your fiancé," he said.

I regretted saying anything almost instantly, particularly in light of the dreams that I'd had while he had been away. I hoped they'd cease now that he was back.

"Seamus–" I began, but he cut me off.

"No, I understand," he said sincerely. "Ye were so close to a happy, normal life. And then all of this happened. It's natural to wish it hadn't."

"But I don't wish that," I said, carefully dancing around the truth of my thoughts that burned in my mind. "I don't wish I hadn't met you."

"Ye wouldn't have been in Ireland if–" he stopped himself from saying the harsh words as well.

I spoke evenly. "No," I agreed. "But don't you wonder...given how all of this happened. Don't you wonder if we would have still somehow found our way to one another?"

I thought of the questions I'd asked myself after my dreams while he was away. About the hold the universe seemed to have on the two of us, and how–even after such a short amount of time–I couldn't imagine my life without him. Even in another timeline, another life where I wasn't struck by tragedy at all... would I somehow have ended up with him? Given my fate, was Seamus the one I had been meant to find all along?

"I feckin' hope so," he said with a smile that I could hear curving on his lips without even turning to look. "But Jasmine, I'd give ye back your normal life with him any day to save ye from the burdens ye have now. If I had the power to do it."

"I'm the one who stole a normal life from you," I said, reminding him of the truth. "Not the other way around."

He shrugged.

"I'd take any kind of life with ye over one where I didn't know ye," he said. "But...I'd still want ye to have the house, the dog, all of those things."

"I want those things with *you*," I said, tears brimming in my eyes despite myself.

"So do I."

We could have them one day, couldn't we?

Then I remembered the searing pain in my legs that I felt in the sun. Maybe not. We were quiet for a while, until Seamus finally spoke again.

"But I know that if ye ever had to choose, you'd pick him, not me," he said. "And as much as I'd hate it, I wouldn't blame ye for it."

His words were far too close to what had happened in my dream. I was startled by them. I sat up and found he was already doing the same, leaning forward with his elbows resting on his knees.

"Why would you–"

"I'm sorry," he interrupted. "I shouldn't have said that. I only say it because I just want ye to know that I'd want the happiest, best life for ye. And that would have been with him, not me."

The fact that I couldn't agree with his assumptions nearly pulled me to the ocean floor with guilt. Yes, I *should* have wanted to choose my fiancé. I *should* have chosen my partner of several years who was ripped away from me rather than the man I met immediately afterward.

But I knew that should the hypothetical question ever come to fruition, I don't think I would want to pick Matt. No. After seeing Seamus return to me today, covered in blood, and knowing that he'd gone to a place worse than death for me...

knowing he had given up his very soul in the pursuit of what I had sent him to do. I thought I'd choose him.

I thought.

I couldn't say for certain, because seeing Matt's kind eyes filled with sadness as he came to realize that I loved another man more than him…it had broken me, even while I slept.

Of course I didn't say any of this out loud. I was a coward who sat in silence.

Seamus leaned over to kiss me but I could feel it was a soft, resigned gesture filled with the burden of knowing he was my second choice. It was as if he thought I was going immediately back to bed to dream of Matt in order to escape the life I had in reality.

"I love you," was all I said. I hoped it was enough.

CHAPTER 25

NEXT STEPS

I awoke the next morning much earlier than Seamus, and I decided to let him rest longer. He had slept most of the night and I only heard a few groans that indicated nightmares. I had expected worse, considering the horrors he had shared with me about Spain. I gently kissed his dark red hair before floating from the room and out into the hallway where the grand castle was silent.

Now that he was back, we'd rest a day or two while we mapped our best guesses of the remaining stones. Based on the information Seamus had gathered, a few of my joint assumptions with Artur were relatively accurate, including my suspicion that America did not harbor one of the magical gems, which was a relief. I didn't ever want to see Tampa Bay again.

One thing I did dread, however, was the confirmation of a stone's existence in Scandinavia. I had expected it after our discussion about Jörmungandr, but the thought of further enlisting Elias in our cause irritated me to no end. He was like a cockroach that couldn't be stamped out, no matter how much I avoided him.

But I trusted that Artur had a better read on the slimy asshole than I did. For whatever reason, the great leader of Atlântida seemed confident that the pestering nuisance of Norway was an asset for us.

"Oh if *this* is what your bedhead looks like, I must be missing out," came Elias' familiar voice from the shadows. "Not that I didn't already think I was."

I rounded on him, smoothing the back of my hair. It *was* messy.

"You better watch that mouth of yours," I said, and I was serious. Seamus would wipe the floor with him if he heard him talk to me like that, which was a fact that I thought Elias knew after meeting him in the Nova Vida.

"Why?" he asked. "Will your pet cut out my tongue for speaking to you?"

My pet, I smirked to myself, remembering how *I* had gone to my knees for Seamus only last night. And how I would do it again, whenever he asked. No, Elias had not a singular clue who played what role in our relationship. He couldn't imagine the world in which Seamus and I lived—one where we were equals.

When I didn't reply, he made a move toward me. "So you have come to seek my counsel at last," he said with grandeur. "I had a feeling this day would come."

"Enough with the theatrics," I said sharply. "Tell me where you think the stone is. Why Artur thinks you deserve to be part of this."

He threw his hands up in mock surrender and led the way down the hallway, zig-zagging lazily through the water as if we had all the time in the world. I glanced around for Artur, hoping he'd join us soon. I didn't love the idea of locking myself in the constellation room alone with Elias while Seamus slept.

We entered the room, and the sky immediately rearranged itself to display the grand globe again as I waved my arm. Artur had taught me how to command the room, and I was getting quite good at it.

"Impressive," Elias remarked.

I spun the globe with the flick of my finger and zoomed in on Scandinavia. The North Sea, The Baltic Sea, The Norwegian Sea…all of these bodies of water looked much bigger than I remembered, and I bit my lip nervously. How would we ever narrow it down? Couldn't Duarte have been more specific?

"*Where* in Norway?" I asked, overwhelmed.

Elias looked contemplatively at the map.

"Zoom in here," he said, pointing to a tiny collection of islands off the northwestern coast. Trondheim was the closest city name that I recognized.

"Keep going," he said, tapping his chin. "Right there."

"Henningsvær?" I inquired, frowning and narrowing in as far in as I could on the tiny island off the coast. "How do you know?"

"It's just a guess, but since I grew up there, I think it's a good one," he said with a shrug. "I've heard legends of the stone being hidden on one of these islands for years, but no one's ever seriously looked…there's a rumor that it might be on an island that's not always there."

"Like Hy-Brasil," I concluded, remembering the phantom island of Ireland as I traced my finger along the map where the Lofoten Islands were scattered. "But it could be *any* of these…"

"Presumably, you'll be able to feel it if you're near, won't you?" he said encouragingly. "I think it's a good place to start."

I sighed, feeling less confident in my abilities.

"Well, if it has to be in any Scandinavian archipelago," I said. "I'm grateful it's this one with a few *hundred* islands rather than the nearly thirty thousand in Stockholm."

Elias laughed, raising an amused–and maybe impressed–eyebrow at me.

"Is that the largest one in the world?" he asked. "Collection of islands, I mean."

I shook my head, still fixated on the Lofoten Islands as I tried to imagine us circling all of them, flitting aimlessly amongst the inlets for days or even weeks. "No, the largest is the Malay Archipelago. Between the Pacific and Indian Oceans."

"And what's the exact latitude and longitude of it?" he asked.

I looked at him curiously for a moment before realizing he was joking.

He roared with laughter upon seeing the look on my face, which would have annoyed me if he hadn't followed it with an immediate compliment. A compliment regarding an attribute of mine besides my looks, which was quite a change of pace for him.

"You're quite brilliant," he said. "There's a vast library of knowledge stored in that brain of yours."

"My father was a professor," I said simply. "I know a lot of random, seemingly useless shit."

He swam closer to me, and I knew he wanted me to look at him. I didn't.

"But it's quite useful now, isn't it?" he said.

I had to acknowledge how many times in the past few months since I transformed that my father's influence in my life had indeed saved me—or at least revealed something useful to me. It was like he was feeding me clues from beyond the grave. He was showing me the way.

"It'll be bright pink," Elias said, his eyes still on me. "The stone. It'll be Thulite, the national stone of Norway. I'm sure of it. Everyone says so."

"Hmm," I debated aloud. It seemed too obvious, but then again, the rosy gem was *just* unique enough to fit Atargatis' taste. She liked the less common jewels. There were no sapphires or rubies in her collection. I realized how much of my trust was being placed in Elias' guesses, and I knew I'd need to run it all by Artur first, anyway.

"Want to go now?" Elias asked.

I stared at him blankly.

"No," I blurted out without thinking. "I'm not going with you."

His grin faded and was replaced by a moderate scowl. "Why not?"

"Because–" I began, but I didn't know what to say. Because Seamus would be furious? Because I didn't particularly want to be alone with the slimy creature in front of me?

He looked me up and down with his turquoise gaze, apparently satisfied by my inability to voice a sound excuse. He approached me and reached for the stone that hung around my neck, and I didn't move as his hand brushed far too close to my skin. He touched the gem, marveling at the iridescent rainbow as well as the chest upon which it rested. I realized I was holding my breath, though I didn't know why. I was wildly uncomfortable, and he knew it.

"When you have them all," he said, still marveling at the stone as he ran his thumb across it. "I hope you'll make them into a crown."

"I won't," I said. "I don't even want to keep the stones. I just want them safe."

He looked disappointed by this statement, but I couldn't imagine what he had expected me to say. How many times had I already alluded to the fact that I didn't want *any* of this? That all I wanted was to secure the stones and move on with my life?

"But I want to see you covered in the gems that answer only to you," he said, his voice dropping to a whisper. "I can picture how marvelous you'd look. Like the real queen of the Seas."

He then reached out and touched me, running a finger up my arm that made me shudder despite doing everything in my power to avoid it. I tried to slowly back away, but he still held the Iridescent Ammonite in his hand. He laughed softly and it infuriated me. I wanted to slap him across the face for daring to touch me, but I couldn't move.

"I don't want to rule," I said severely.

"That's a shame," he replied, his gaze reluctantly leaving my chest and returning to my face. "I hope you change your mind."

The door behind us swung open. I instinctively flew backward from him as I peered into the doorframe.

Thank Manannán it was Artur and not Seamus. I didn't know what Seamus would have done if he had seen Elias' hand so close to my chest. To my throat. Probably throttled Elias' own, I guessed.

"My apologies," Artur said, entirely oblivious to the tense atmosphere he had just stumbled upon. "I was doing some research regarding a rare bit of pirate's treasure and lost track of time."

I raised an eyebrow, unable to tell if he was joking or not. "Another treasure hunt? Aren't the stones of Atargatis enough for you?"

He clucked his tongue and in a very Raj-like manner said, "Ah, Jasmine, there are always multiple endeavors of the Seas in which I am involved," he said. "But I agree, this one is the most important."

We then filled him in on everything we had discussed, and he agreed there was no time to waste.

"Ah yes, your father told me the rumors of a shadowed, alternate version of Henningsvær," Artur said with a wistful smile as Elias described the possibility of a disappearing island amongst the Lofotens.

He clarified as he noticed my confusion.

"Elias' father, Erik, and I fought alongside the Amalgams last time. It was a much more disorganized camp than this one of Cearbhall and Camila, though. They didn't even find a single stone before we brought them down."

"Is he the one that told you about Jörmungandr?" I asked, remembering the terrifying legend of the World Serpent.

Artur nodded. "Yes. Of course, back then we had no idea if there was a stone in Scandinavia or not. It was all hearsay. Erik is sending me a loud *'I told you so,'* from beyond the grave right now, I'm sure."

I nodded, understanding the dynamic between Artur and Elias at last. The Norwegian's father had been one of the great leader's best friends. I studied Elias, who had no semblance of pride or even recognition on his face. I couldn't read him at all.

"We leave tomorrow," Artur said firmly.

CHAPTER 26

PLANS & PROVOCATION

I left the room swiftly in order to avoid another potential one-on-one encounter with Elias, returning to my tower where Seamus was just waking up in the soft, velvet sheets. He had bathed in the Nova Vida, but it hadn't erased all of the physical side effects of his lengthy mission. His dark red waves were long and askew, and his facial hair was wildly overgrown. I smiled as I looked upon the unkempt version of the man I loved. I didn't care what he looked like. I was just so relieved he was back.

"I've missed it?" he said, sitting up in alarm as I floated through the door frame. "Why didn't ye wake me?"

"It's fine, I wanted you to rest," I said.

I dropped the shimmering curtain in front of the doorway before settling down on the bed next to him, allowing my iridescent tail to flutter lazily in the gentle underwater breeze.

"Aye, I needed it," he admitted.

I kissed him deeply, taking him by surprise, but I felt his lips curve into a smile as he immediately reciprocated. I ran my fingers along his muscular shoulder blades and leaned in closer, my lips on the side of his neck as he wrapped his own hands around my lower back. I then pressed him back down onto the bed, knowing we couldn't do anything *valuable* right now, but wanting to push it to the limit anyway.

Seamus seemed to feel the same way, because he instinctively reached for the hook that held my sea-shelled bra in place and undid it with one hand (I had always thought he was a little *too* good at that) before reaching up to admire the top half of my naked body. The human half.

"Christ, don't tempt me when I can't take ye," he said through a deep sigh.

He slowly ran his hands across my breasts before bringing me down to his mouth, his teeth gently scraping the most sensitive part of my body that he could reach while I was still a mermaid.

Gripping my waist tightly, he traced his thumb along the lowest part of my midsection where my skin met my tail, sending the familiar surge of longing pulsing through my bloodstream. I let my hair fall in front of me and he reached for a section of it before pressing it to his nose to inhale my scent the way I always did to him. Humans or selkies, we were constantly burning for each other.

I kissed him one more time before rolling to the side and leaning back against the bed frame, nothing covering me but my lengthy black hair.

"Sorry," I said with a smirk.

He looked at me sideways and grinned, shaking his head. "This feckin' tail is going to be the end of me, so it is."

"To be continued," I said.

I then launched into the recap of the morning, telling him of our plan to leave for Norway the following day. I saw a mild shadow of annoyance cross his face when he realized the "*we*" included Elias as well, but Seamus was wise enough to know that having a guide in our midst would be useful. Elias *was* from the specific part of Norway where we thought the Thulite was hidden, and his father had been Artur's closest ally…all of that was worth something.

"Seamus," I began tentatively. "Once we find the stone in Norway, can we—"

"Of course," he said without missing a beat. "Say it and it's yours."

I reached for his hand. "I just want to go back to Carrickfergus for a bit," I said. "I want to meet my mother before we seek the rest of the stones."

I didn't want to let too much time pass in between our discovery of one stone and the next, but I needed to go to Ireland. I had to know Aine. *Annie.*

"Aye, I assumed that was the plan," he said, and then he caught a glimpse of himself in the mirror above the dresser. "But I'll need a shave before I'm ready to meet your mam."

I laughed and traced a finger along his furry jawline. "I don't mind it."

"Can I ask ye one favor then, too?" he said tentatively, his gaze returning to my own.

"Anything."

He took a deep breath.

"Since we'll be in Belfast, do ye mind if we go…if the sun's not out of course–" he paused, but I already knew what he wanted to ask. He wanted us to go visit his mother's grave.

"Oh Seamus," I said, touching his freckled cheek. "Yes, of course we can."

He let out a light sigh of relief.

I wondered how often he had gone back to see it over the years. I was reminded of how much about his life I didn't know, and how desperately I wanted to. I wanted to see more of the place where he grew up…actual Belfast, not just Carrickfergus Castle's underwater dungeons. I wanted to know the history of who he was. And of course I wanted to meet Aidan.

Aidan. His older brother who knew only a fraction more of

what had happened to us than my friends. The one who had steered the boat that led Seamus to Hy-Brasil. The one who had teamed up with Seamus, Professor Brennan, and Kiana to find me.

The realization that I hadn't yet told Seamus of my field trip with Artur to Tampa during his time away hit me like a ton of bricks. In the rush of getting him to the healing waters followed by our discussion of The Santa Compaña, there had been no time for me to divulge the details of my own (much less arduous) experiences from the past month or so. I braced myself for his reprimand as I told him I land-walked, but it never came.

He nodded contemplatively instead as I concluded my story.

"I'm proud of ye for doing that," he said. "I know how hard that must have been, especially when they didn't react the way ye hoped."

I shrugged in what I hoped looked like a dismissive manner, but I was sure he saw through it. "I knew they wouldn't forgive me."

"It won't be the last time ye see them," he said as he tilted my chin upward. "We'll try again, a stór."

I smiled. It was exactly what I had thought he'd say.

As much as I didn't want to make him feel the guilt that I did, I felt that I needed to relay what Kristen had said about Aidan's poor attempt at covering up Seamus' disappearance.

"You know they told me that your brother's been making up all of these ridiculous excuses for where you are…and James has been worried sick," I said in a small voice. "Maybe we should pay a visit to your friends as well. To let them know you're alright."

His face fell. "My friends are mostly in London, if ye remember."

Of course. With all of our focus on Ireland, I had nearly forgotten that in Seamus' old life–his human life–he had actually lived in London for several years, and technically still did. *That* was where most of his adult life had taken place. James, Oliver,

Harry, Jack, and Benjamin–all of his friends I'd met on that trip–none of them were from Ireland. It had been the nature of his selkie roots that dragged him back home.

"The money I'm spending on that place while I'm not there," he said, breaking out in a grin as he shook his head. "It pains me to think about it."

I couldn't help but laugh, too, knowing how expensive London was.

"I want to see it," I said suddenly. "Where you live."

"Well there's no sun this time of year, I'll tell ye that," he said, and I could tell the idea of going back, even for a little bit, was appealing to him. I was sure he missed it to some degree. Unlike me, he hadn't been running away from anything when he left for his trip to Ireland. "Would ye really want to go?"

"I would," I said sincerely. "I love London, and–"

And I want to know everything about you, because I love you and I want to see every aspect of who you are. That's what I wanted to say.

But I failed to express my sentiments aloud, as was often the case with my limited way with words.

"I'd like that," he said. He was looking at me, but his mind was far away. "Being with ye in my place, waking up in my bed. It'd be nice to just see ye there, like I picture it in my mind."

I beamed as I started seriously thinking it through. The River Thames...we could easily get to London by water...yes, it was definitely possible.

But when?

The stones could take months, even *years* to track down. By then, what would have become of his life? The mess he'd left behind was already enormous, and it would only get worse the longer we waited.

I voiced this to him, and he agreed.

"When we go, I've got to think of a damn good excuse," he said, stretching his arms behind his head as he rose from the bed and made his way toward the window with a swish of his tail. "For where the feck we've been."

"I told Marissa and Kristen that we went to Spain and Portugal," I shrugged. "Which isn't technically a lie."

He paused at the window for a moment, the black scar on his arm flexing as he absently turned his hands over. He looked back at me intently, something behind his emerald eyes that I couldn't read.

"Or we could tell them–" he began.

I didn't know what he would have said, because at that moment, Artur appeared in the doorway with an eager smile plastered across his face. Luckily I had extremely thick, long hair, or he would have caught me entirely indecent.

"Aisling and Fin are back," he said brightly. "Come down."

As soon as he left, I threw my top back on and reached for Seamus' hand. The clouded look on his face lasted one more moment before he smiled. We'd figure out our excuse later.

When we reached the table, I saw the sun had already started to sink, signaling late afternoon. I hadn't realized how long I had been in the study that morning, and Seamus clearly hadn't realized how long he'd slept. Fintan and Aisling rushed to greet us and launched into the retelling of where they had been and what had happened from their perspective in Spain.

I tried to ignore the sixth, less welcome guest at the table, Elias, as he drank deeply from the goblet that was in front of him. Seamus gave him a curt nod of acknowledgment and nothing more.

"We had eyes on Seamus most of the time, even though we could never see the others. But then he disappeared for me. Maybe round the tenth day," said Fintan through loud chomps on his seaweed. "I thought, where'd the man go? But I know how the Nuvem Morte works...I know it's a tricky thing."

"I saw him a bit longer," Aisling said quietly. "Right up until the end."

"You've seen a relative die," Elias stated bluntly across the table, causing Aisling to sit up taller in surprise.

"Excuse me?" she asked pointedly.

Elias shrugged. "If you've seen a family member die in front of you, you can see the Santa Compaña more clearly," he said. "I thought everyone knew that."

"Well we're not from here," Aisling said, defending herself as Fintan—being the way that he was—didn't realize how much his candid speech irritated her. "I don't know the lore of Iberia the way I know my *Irish* tales."

"Well you should familiarize yourself with it," Elias continued, wholly unbothered by her attitude. "It's quite useful to be worldly and well-read. For example, *Jasmine* knows about mythology from all over the globe. It seems to be her specialty."

He then looked at Seamus and drained his glass.

"Did you know that, Seamus?"

Why? Why was he doing this?

"Aye, I knew that," Seamus said, meeting his eyes with a steely gaze of warning. "I think I know a bit more about her than ye do."

His words lingered in the air with definitive tension that even Artur couldn't ignore. The leader clucked his tongue and muttered, *"Play nice,"* under his breath.

Elias seemed to thrive in the discomfort he had created, running his tongue across his lips in the way I had learned he always did when he wanted to push buttons.

"Anyway," Aisling pressed on before he could say anything else. "Once Seamus went down into the dungeons, I lost track of him. But then we saw him again on the roof when–" she looked at me carefully, knowing I likely didn't want to hear the account of Seamus' brutal injury, but I nodded, insisting she go on. This retelling was for Artur. I ran my finger down the demonic wound on his arm, the origins of which I already knew.

"When the demon slammed him into the stone, the potion started to flicker him back to life, since they had discovered his ruse. Seamus somehow stabbed her, and the demon burst into flames..." her voice trailed off.

"Excellent work, it was," said Fintan in awe. "Ye should've seen him, Jasmine."

I flushed with pride. I wished I could have seen it, but only in a world where I already knew what the outcome would be. To see my victorious man, emerging from the black pool of blood from a Spanish demon he had slain...I reached for his hand under the table. He slid his grip behind my waist and tail, pulling me directly onto his lap instead. The gesture took me by surprise, but I welcomed it.

"*Anything to get back to ye,*" he said so quietly that I almost wondered if it was a thought inside his head rather than spoken words. I leaned backward into his warm, hard chest.

Elias' eyes were on me like daggers as Seamus traced my stomach with one hand and reached for his goblet with the other. The Norwegian was seething, and I genuinely couldn't understand why. I had truly shared nothing with Elias beyond two or three exchanges of pointless banter that almost always left me repulsed or offended by him. If he thought more of those conversations, I pitied him, because it was a clear sign that he was extremely out of practice when it came to winning hearts.

"...And we had our plan to split up anyway, so Fintan and I took the long way back," Aisling finished.

Her betrothed shot a knowing look at her across the table and I blushed as I looked down into my lap, not wanting to pry. They took the *long* way home—the one that involved some *alone time* it seemed. Good for them.

"I'm so glad you're back," I said to both of them sincerely. "Thank you for everything."

They beamed back at me.

"And we'd do it again," said Fintan, raising his glass.

Seamus absently stroked my arm and kissed various–innocent–parts of my body while the rest of the conversation went on, and I knew what he was doing. I didn't blame him, honestly. Elias was infuriating.

With the plan being to meet in the Room of Windows at dawn, everyone dispersed for the evening. Seamus and I opted for a swim in the moonlight before bed, given how late he had slept.

"I hope it's as easy to find as Hy-Brasil," I said, my mind returning to the mysterious Lofoten Islands where the stone would hopefully be hidden. "If it's not a real island."

Seamus let out a hollow laugh, undoubtedly recalling how he had stumbled upon the mystical phantom island off the coast of Western Ireland—by falling into the open ocean during the middle of a thunderstorm.

"Sorry," I laughed, remembering how I had been lucky enough to have a guide back then and he had not.

I yawned widely and he leaned in to give me a kiss on the head.

"Get some rest, a stór," he said. "I'll be up after ye soon. Something I want to talk with Artur about, first."

I floated lazily away from him, thinking of bright pink stones and islands where the sun was always shining. Seamus was back, and we weren't going to be apart for a long time now. Even though we were setting out for more danger, I felt perfectly at ease. Everything would be fine as long as we were together.

But before I could sleep, I had to take a quick detour to find Aisling. I needed to ask her about something that had been bothering me since my trip back to Tampa, as embarrassed as I was to do it.

I found her—thankfully alone—in the garden out front of the castle. She was cutting bits of seaweed for the morning, humming pleasantly to herself as she flitted to and fro.

"Can I help?" I asked.

She turned around and smiled at me. "I'd love the company,

cousin," she said, flashing a grin at me and tossing me an extra knife.

I sometimes forgot that while we had developed such a strong friendship already, we *were* actually family. I supposed that made Fintan my future in-law, too. The thought of having a family again was comforting.

"Are ye nervous?" she asked, surveying me closely.

She knew I didn't often discuss my feelings, but I *had* always felt comfortable doing so with her—even from the very first time I met her. I remembered thinking she was so meek and shy back then–two words I'd never use to describe my strong-willed cousin now. But she was kind and trustworthy. I knew I could confide in her.

I shrugged. "A little bit, but we'll have Artur with us."

She nodded in agreement. "He's definitely a good warrior to have on your side," she said. "Fintan doesn't love to visit him so much, but I hope one day he'll change his mind."

"Yes, I hope one day he'll truly forgive him," I said, and she saw that I knew about the history between her fiancé and his father. Her brown eyes looked at me with understanding.

"Sorcha is a severe woman," she replied. "She is kind, but damn, she can be unforgiving. I think that's why Fintan never let it go with his da. Because his mother's influence is so strong, so it is."

I recalled the white-blonde selkie that had first discovered me when I fell off the Cliffs and changed into what I was. She *had* always been quite obtuse, but I knew her heart was in the right place. Her bluntness originated from concern for those she cared about, and she did her best to protect everyone in her circle. I owed her a lot, personally, and I hoped one day I'd get to see her again to tell her how grateful I was for her guidance.

"What do you think of Lachlan?" I asked, my curiosity getting the better of me. He had been Sorcha's mate, but that was about all I knew of him. He had never been overly warm to me, but wasn't cruel, either. He had always seemed relatively superstitious when it came to legends about the shallows hurting our kind—something I learned quickly wasn't the case at all. I hadn't formed much of an opinion of him other than I thought he was slightly odd and not at all a proper match for Sorcha.

Aisling nodded and smiled.

"He's kind," she said. "He doesn't always come across that way, but he is. He cares for Fintan, too. Practically raised him."

I hadn't known that, and she could tell.

"When Fintan was young, Lachlan and Artur got into it over which was the better place to raise a child…here in Atlântida, or Hy-Brasil," she explained. "With the Amalgams being so prominent in Hy-Brasil, and Artur having his reservations about them, he was furious when Lachlan and Sorcha suggested it. But, ultimately he decided he wanted Fintan to be with his mother. He knew that if there were war again, Atlântida would be one of the first to be called to fight. He wanted to protect Fintan from that as best he could."

I tried not to shudder, knowing the war she spoke of could be right around the corner now.

"*And* Sorcha wanted him to marry an Irish girl," she said, flashing me a wicked grin. "So there was that factor as well."

I grinned. "Well he found a good one," I said. Hoping I wasn't being too nosy, I asked another question. "How did you two meet?"

Although they were both in Ireland, Hy-Brasil and Carrickfergus weren't exactly next door.

"Oisin," she said simply. "He knew Artur, as ye know. I wouldn't say it was arranged by any means, but damn they pushed for it."

I looked at her in surprise. I hadn't even considered their union to be anything other than voluntary. She saw what I was thinking and clarified.

"Oh no, it's not like that. I fell in love with him right away," she said, slightly blushing. "How could I not? He's so…full of light. Do ye know what I mean?"

My breath caught in my chest. I hadn't thought of the similarities between Fintan and Matt, but now I saw them. It was probably why I enjoyed his presence so much, even when he couldn't stop talking. There weren't a lot of people in the world like that–people who were always bright, no matter what kind of darkness surrounded them.

"I do," I replied with a smile.

We mindlessly, silently cut the seaweed for a while longer as I took small bites here and there of the different varieties. I avoided the pink, knowing it would provide a caffeine jolt that I didn't need right before bed. Aisling told me the pale green kind had a calming quality to it, so I eagerly reached for a few strands of it, thinking I could use a nice natural sleep aid before our big day.

"I need to ask you something," I said finally, my courage mounting given the intimacy of the conversation we'd already had. "About–"

She didn't reply, but took my hand and beckoned me to follow her across the garden. The moon was now high above the sphere where the sharks circled, and she reached down into a small collection of oysters that were ornately laid amongst the shells that lined the castle's walls. She sifted through them for a moment before finding one that was to her liking, slapping it into my hand and raising a knowing eyebrow. The dark gray shell popped open and there was a singular, gleaming pearl in the center.

"Take that for now," she said. "For emergencies only, mind ye. That there is not a permanent solution."

My mouth gaped open. "How did you—"

She rolled her eyes and laughed. "Jasmine, the man can't keep his hands off of ye," she said. "I thought of saying something to ye both back on the Skelligs, but I hated to ruin the moment."

"I appreciate it," I said, blushing furiously but laughing anyway.

She smirked. "Mmhm. I'll get ye some stoneseed root back in Belfast, too," she said. "That's a regular tea we'll brew for ye."

"Stoneseed root?" I asked curiously.

"Ye'd be surprised how often nature rivals modern medicine," she said. "There's also jack-in-the-pulpit root, thistles…that's just to name a few preventative measures."

"How do you know all of this?" I asked, impressed.

"Is it surprising, someone else knowing something ye don't for once?"

I blinked, but saw she was joking.

"Selkies and other mermaids in general have learned to live with what Mother Nature can provide us, ye see," she explained. "Out of necessity."

It made sense. I supposed Aisling couldn't very well make it to a pharmacy once a month.

"And the human methods wouldn't work for us anyway," she laughed as if reading my thoughts, which were fixed on my toiletries kit back in Galway that had my own prescription. "We're too strong."

That, we were. I popped the tiny pearl in my mouth and was grateful for my cousin's discretion. Despite the hollowness that I felt for the loss of my old, land-walker friends, it was nice to have one under the sea.

CHAPTER 27

WINTER WONDERLAND

"*T*ime to get up," came an infuriating voice from the archway that separated our room from the rest of the castle, indicating my privacy curtain of sparkling waves had been dissolved by an intruder. The sun wasn't even up yet, and I groaned at the sound of the world's most annoying alarm clock.

Who had told him where our room was?

I rose and saw that Seamus was already gone, while Elias lurked in the doorway with his signature egotistical smirk plastered across his face. I had just been enjoying the peaceful realization that my disturbing dreams had subsided in the wake of Seamus' return, but now my annoyance returned with a vengeance. My sanctuary of sapphire velvet now disturbed, I reluctantly rolled out of bed.

"*He's* already with Artur. Has been for hours," he said when he noticed me glance at Seamus' empty pillow. "Last minute preparations. I came to escort you."

I begrudgingly excused myself to the powder room where I freshened up in the way I had learned mermaids did, and took the extra step of braiding my long hair. We were going on land, presumably, and I needed it out of my face while I looked–and potentially *dug*–for the stone. I grabbed one small, blue sea shell and tucked it into one of the tresses near my ear. Just for good luck, because it reminded me of Atlântida.

I emerged a few moments later, and Elias unabashedly scanned my entire body. Once again, I thought that I was being very generous for not slapping him in the face.

"You're a vision," he said without a hint of sarcasm in his voice.

I rolled my eyes and swept past him with a huff of disapproval, the Iridescent Ammonite that I now never took off swinging back and forth as if to remind me of the time he had so boldly reached for it. We made our way down into the great room where Seamus was talking with Artur, Aisling, and Fintan. There were a variety of weapons–daggers, mostly–laid out in front of them on the grand marble table.

"You think we need those?" I asked in alarm.

"Aye," Seamus said. I noticed he'd shaved, and his hair was back to its normal length. I wondered *how* our kind got haircuts underwater, but assumed it was Artur's magic at work again. "We don't know what they're like up there."

He shot Elias a dirty look, and I saw a flash of anger surge through him as he connected the dots that the man had actually gone up to get me from our bedroom. Before he could say anything, Aisling began fastening a gold cuff to my wrist that mirrored both Artur's and the one Seamus had not taken off since Spain. I slid one small dagger with emeralds at the hilt into the magical bracelet for no reason other than the green reminded me of Ireland. Seamus did the same with his choice.

"There," Aisling said, patting my wrist and stepping back. "Ye look like a beautiful warrior, Jasmine."

"She does," said Seamus and Elias at the same time.

I wanted to die.

"We'll meet ye back in Belfast when you're ready, yeah?" Aisling said to me as she gave me a big hug. I had told her last night that we were thinking about spending a few days in London before or after Ireland, and she had told me a few days as a land-walker would be good for me. I agreed, but everything depended on what happened today.

I smiled at her and nodded.

Artur swept in front of me and led the three of us to the Room of Windows where the swirling pools greeted us once more. I looked around the marbled hall wistfully, hoping this wouldn't be the last time I saw it. Atlântida had been extremely lonely for most of the time I had spent here, but I couldn't help feeling a bit sad to leave the comfort of the grand castle. I hoped I could return at a time when exploration through the Green Windows was purely for leisure rather than necessity.

"Bergen was the best I could do," Artur said, referencing the Window's exit ramp. "And mind you, it's miserably cold up there right now."

"I thought our body temperatures adjusted?" I asked. "To the climate."

"Sure, but you can still feel it if it's cold enough," he said, shivering as he anticipated the chill of the Norwegian winter that was waiting for us on the other side of the portal.

"You'll like it, I think," Elias said quietly as he floated up next to me. He tried to meet my gaze, but I avoided it. "Norway."

I thought I would, too. I had always wanted to go. Matt and I had talked about doing a grand tour of Scandinavia when we went to visit Raj at the University of Stockholm, but of course that trip never happened. Back then, everyone told us we were crazy to want to spend the holidays in such a freezing destination and that tacking on Norway at the end would be absurd. But I thought seeing the Northern Lights would be worth it, and from the research I recalled, November through February was the best timeframe for maximum visibility.

. . .

"JAZZ, are you *absolutely sure* you don't want me to come there, instead? Florida in December is much more preferable than Sweden."

I scoffed as the voice of my father echoed through the room on speakerphone, and Matt sat in the corner rolling his eyes because we knew he'd react this way. Even if I thought he actually wanted to come back to Florida so soon after starting his new job, I wouldn't have imposed the pressure on him like that. He was slammed with both his new courses and the general learning curve of exploration of the Baltic and North Seas when all he'd ever really experienced in his career was the temperate part of the Atlantic off the coast of Florida or Portugal.

Matt came to stand over the phone.

"Raj, we're coming," he said. "Jasmine's been talking about the Christmas market thing forever—she's always wanted to go at that time of year."

"And God forbid we tear you away from Marine Ecosystems Dynamics," I added. "How would your class ever move on if they didn't have their papers on the Baltic Sea's brackish water expanse graded by Christmas?"

"It *would* disappoint a few of them," he said with a sarcastic sigh. "I frequently have students stay after class to discuss the link between historical significance, scientific discovery, and the economic core of the Hanseatic League."

"Well, good thing we have planes and indoor heating," I said. "So our journey of passage will be much easier than a 14th century trade route."

Matt looked at me, laughing incredulously. *"What the hell are you guys talking about?"* he mouthed.

I shrugged. Whenever I wanted to get something out of Raj, I just had to nerd out with him for a few minutes. It worked every time.

"Alright, fine," Raj said with a sigh. "We'll do Christmas here, then. And I guess by then you'll be–"

Matt started furiously coughing, prompting Raj to do the same.

"Gotta go, kids, a student's knocking on my door," he said, clearing his throat. "Let me know what dates you're thinking about when you get a chance!" He hung up the phone.

By then you'll be engaged, is what he was going to say.

I GAZED into the Window of all white, whirling water. This one, I could see immediately, was not like the others. This one was warning us of the weather so intently that there was no trace of the nation's flag colors at all. Just ice and snow.

"Ready to go?" Elias asked me, and then he had the audacity to reach out his hand as if I would take it. I didn't wait to see if Seamus had noticed the gesture, vanishing through the bubbling wall with Artur instead.

We flashed through a sea of bright blues that gradually became lighter, airier, and brighter, and I gathered it was going to be a sunny winter day rather than a gloomy one. My favorite kind, unless I had to go on land. I felt the ocean growing colder around me, like I had stepped into an ice rink wearing too thin of a sweater. The current was so incredibly strong that I actually feared I would somehow get lost in the whirlwind, and I reached to grab hold of Artur's tail.

The snow-capped peaks rose like towering castles all around us, and the water was so incredibly clear that I could see for miles. I smiled broadly as I saw a school of mackerel zooming beside me, and I wondered if they were trying to race us. I gave my tail an extra flick and all thousand or so of them responded with their own.

But we were faster. We left them behind us and a few minutes later, I finally felt the current beginning to slow. Our exit from the underwater highway was rockier this time, and I wondered if

Artur needed to do regular maintenance on these passages across the oceans.

As I emerged on the surface, I took a deep gulp of the invigoratingly cool water and closed my eyes in delight at its taste. Whether I was breathing water or air in my new existence, all I tasted was nutritious oxygen, and *this* was one of the most delicious varieties I'd had so far. I looked up to see the bright, fairytale buildings of Bergen lining the ocean and coloring the steep rolling hills in bright, primary hues. It looked like a Christmas village, topped in the snow of what I realized had to be November by now.

Seamus came up right behind me as he emerged from the current, shaking the water from his hair and leaning his chin on my shoulder. He had been to Norway before, and told me he couldn't wait to see the fjords from this perspective.

"It's beautiful," I said, looking up at the magnificence of a place that seemed magical all on its own, even without the presence of four supernatural creatures nearby.

We flitted along the coastline at a moderate pace, Elias pointing out places that he knew as we went, our keen eyesight serving us miraculously. I spotted the puffins I had seen from the constellation room's rendition of the country, and I kept my eyes peeled for any sign of whales. I glanced to my left and saw a faint shadow of sadness clouding Artur's face as he undoubtedly recalled memories of being in this place with Sorcha. Back when she loved him.

"Almost there," called Artur encouragingly.

We arrived at the Lofotens in less than an hour. The snaking archipelago offered countless waterways that wound around the mountainous beauty of Norway, and I wished I was here for any reason other than another dangerous mission. To explore the endless inlets sounded much more pleasurable than a treasure hunt at the moment. I hardly noticed the freezing temperatures as I drank in all the mountains, wishing I could land-walk them all, bright sun or not.

Elias had told us that somewhere near–or perhaps *within*–Henningsvær was where his father had suspected one of the stones was hidden, and we trusted that the wisdom of the late Erik was the best lead we had. We trailed toward it and I glanced in amusement at the soccer pitch that was situated right on the island, like a floating arena from a video game.

"Football," Elias corrected me.

We slithered around the shores, dropping below to the surface as we took caution not to be seen. I privately thought no person in their right mind would sprint outside to investigate a mysterious fish tail on a frigid day such as this, but I followed Artur's guidance.

The sun was now high in the sky, and I knew we wouldn't get more than seven or eight hours of daylight at this time of year. I hoped we would be able to retrieve the stone before nightfall, even considering the pain it would cause me if we went on land. As beautiful as it was by day, I thought the dark, winter waters might be frightening under the moon. I knew about Jörmungandr, after all.

I voiced this to Artur and he laughed.

"I don't think the World Serpent is lurking below the surface to snap at our tails," he said. "And he wouldn't hurt you, remember?"

I shrugged. Even if I was supposedly his master, I didn't particularly want to test out the theory today.

We continued to circle the perimeter of Henningsvær with Seamus and I both clutching our stones, hoping for any sign or signal. Elias was guiding us given his general familiarity with the area and where his father had suspected the stone might be, but it was quiet for a while.

Finally, as we rounded a bend that passed under a thin highway that connected the island to another, I felt something. I paused as I felt the ammonite grow hot against my chest. Seamus looked at me, and then down at his own, watching the Citrine glowing faintly beneath the waves.

"Hang on," I called to Artur and Elias who had gone ahead of us. They both turned and sped back toward us.

"Do you feel something?" Artur asked intently. He noticed the stones and I saw him hold his breath as I nodded.

I knew Elias had led us to the right place. It was close. I just didn't know where...

An eerie silence descended upon us, until I heard a song.

It was one of the most beautiful and tragically mournful sounds I had ever heard. It made me want to burst into hopeless tears and roar with radiant laughter at the same time.

It was a whale's song.

The volume was rising as it started to swallow me, the sound seeming to originate from within my own head. I couldn't turn it down. I faced the others.

"Hey," I said, drawing their attention to it. "Do you hear that?"

The three men stared at me blankly, and I realized they couldn't.

I felt myself falling behind the same membrane of silence that I always experienced in my dreams, only this time it was the voices of everyone else that I couldn't hear, not the other way around. I was deaf to the replies of Artur, Elias, and Seamus alike. The only sound that penetrated the barrier of my mind was the whale song. It was calling to me, beckoning me somewhere...to Henningsvær, it seemed.

But it didn't look like Henningsvær. Not really. Even though it had just been in front of me, the Norwegian island settlement now looked entirely different through the pink mist that had begun to descend over my eyes. I felt like I was disappearing into thin air, being taken somewhere else that was just beyond the world I knew.

Seamus looked at me in alarm. I reached my hand out for his, watching my fingers break through the thin, pink barrier. I grasped it tightly as soon as I caught it and pulled him toward me.

Rather than the sudden appearance on Hy-Brasil, this new passage felt as though I'd simply fall asleep and wake up somewhere new. Seamus broke through the mist to join me, and then both of us were enveloped in the pink film, isolated from the other two companions of ours who I now thought couldn't see us at all.

"Jasmine–" he started.

"Should we pull them through?" I asked, pointing to the other two who remained on the outside. "I feel like it's now or never."

He looked at Elias resentfully, but ultimately nodded his head.

"Aye, he might be useful," he said. He stuck his hand out of the mist and reached for Elias, dragging him inside. He fell into place beside me.

"Holy shit," he whispered as he entered and saw what we did.

Artur was next. I reached my hand for his, but the veil wouldn't budge. It wouldn't let him through.

"Land-walkers only, maybe," Elias guessed.

I wanted to tell him so he wouldn't worry about us, but Artur was brilliant. He would figure it out.

The mystical bubble told me it would be alright, and I nodded as if to tell it we were ready to go. It seemed to understand, because the pink light that surrounded us became so blindingly bright that I closed my eyes. Seamus and Elias did the same on either side of me as we faded from one universe and appeared in another.

CHAPTER 28

INTO THE FJORD

*M*oments later, I opened my eyes narrowly as slits, and saw a beautiful island that was nearly identical to Henningsvær as we had just seen it, but it was also markedly different.

For one thing, it was spring rather than winter, allowing for a clear line of sight to pure greenery ahead. There was a massive fjord calling to us, like mountainous gates promising that what we sought was indeed here. There was nothing outwardly supernatural about the place, but I could sense that there was magic surrounding us. The whale song was now far from tragic—it was joyful, alive, and awake. I shook away my dream-like state, returning to normal with one splash of the cool water on my face.

The stones against our chests were humming.

The Thulite of Nóregr was here.

"Alright?" Seamus asked me as he suppressed a yawn. It seemed the mist had a sleepy effect on all of us. Elias was rubbing his eyes, blinking furiously in the bright sun.

"I'm good," I responded. "Let's go."

We swam into the fjord, the towering rocks on either side

inviting us deeper into the mysterious island of–what I assumed was–eternal spring. I followed nature's skyscrapers with my gaze, wondering where within the obsidian cliffs the tiny gem could be hidden.

We approached a small rocky shoreline and I saw the outline of a few mermaids lounging and watching us with caution behind their eyes. I wondered if they would swim away as we reached the shoreline, but they didn't. I ignored them momentarily, as Elias and Seamus were both already stepping across the first row of pebbles and onto land. The island's magic placed them in nothing but black shorts flecked with orange, which was undoubtedly an ode to the signature colors of Norwegian fish tails that I had already seen.

I smirked slightly as Seamus towered at least three inches over Elias, a fact that I knew would likely piss him off for no reason other than height was one more thing Seamus had that he didn't.

Humility returned to me with a crushing force, however, when I followed them and Seamus did what he always did–helped me out of the water as I slowly transformed. I felt so weak. I hated it.

Elias looked down upon me in alarm as he saw my strained face.

"Does it hurt you?" he asked. Of course he had never seen me do it, and it probably came as a surprise to him that the *Queen of the Seas* couldn't do the simplest of tasks without wincing in excruciating pain. "To transform?"

"Sometimes," I grumbled, not meeting his eyes. "Usually just in the sun."

The three of us looked up. The sun streaming through the clouds was exceedingly bright. Magical as the island might have appeared, it was certainly the same sun that I believed Atargatis continually used to punish me.

"Ye don't have to come with us, a stór," said Seamus, crouching next to me.

Of course he already knew what my answer would be. Elias rolled his eyes, nearly undetectably, at the sound of my Irish pet name. I shot him a nasty look before replying.

"Yes, I do," I said simply. He looked as though he wanted to argue, but I nodded seriously. "I mean it."

At last I transformed and I ignored the sharp blades of pain that scraped the length of my thighs to my ankles, because we had a job to do. A soft, black skirt fluttered down my legs with a generous slit that I thought was a touch too seductive for the occasion, but I didn't mind it. My top half was covered with the same bra I had been wearing, but I watched in awe as the color of the shells darkened to onyx flecked with orange that sparkled as they caught the light from the sun. My cheeks burned as I looked up and saw both Elias and Seamus were openly marveling at my costume change.

I cleared my throat, knowing Seamus would drown Elias on the spot if he caught him staring at my chest.

The island was much less populated than Hy-Brasil, and the inhabitants were not at all friendly like the residents of the western Ireland paradise. The mermaids that dwelled here *looked* like Elias—black tails with flecks of orange and pink, and their typical Scandinavian light eyes and hair—but they had a strange, robotic quality to them that was almost…evil. They all looked the same as they stared after us with nothing more than mild curiosity—sitting stock still in the shallow water or on the shore like perfect, white Barbies. They irked me.

"What the–?" I began, and Elias shook his head in dismay.

"I dunno," he said sincerely, a visible shudder running through his body. "Not somewhere I'd ever live, that's for sure."

We trudged up the rocky shoreline and tried to ignore the stares at our backs. I knew what Seamus was doing as he glanced around at the strange creatures—he was counting, just in case we had to fight them. I hoped it wouldn't come to that, but I thought concealing why we were here, should they ask, was a good idea. I doubted they would, considering they didn't look like they could *think* let alone speak. We made our way into the fjord, and I didn't dare turn around again.

"Now what?" asked Elias as we ventured into the lush conifers beyond.

"Oh, you're asking us?" I said sharply, my irritation at my physical limitations not fully worn off yet. "I thought, being our guide, *you* would know."

He scowled at me and I sped up, making my way toward the mountain ahead as I had no idea where else to start. The humming had been a dull, consistent vibration within the stones since we entered the fjord, and I assumed we'd simply keep going until the pattern changed.

"Well I've never had a reason to go seeking a magical island," Elias called at my back. "I wasn't even sure something like this was here. That was just my dad's guess."

We'd much rather have your dad's help than yours, I'm sure, I thought to myself, knowing inherently that Artur's late friend would have been a much better companion than his pain-in-the-ass of a son.

"No one forced ye to come along, lad," Seamus replied in patronizing tones. "Would've been just fine if ye'd chosen to stay behind."

Elias, unfortunately, took the bait. Any questions I had regarding how bold he would be in front of Seamus were answered immediately.

"Ah, but I couldn't miss out on a chance to see those *legs* of hers," he said without a single hint of hesitation.

I froze. He would pay for that comment.

I heard a loud thump and I knew Seamus had Elias against some sort of hard surface. I turned around and I was right. He had the blonde pest pinned against the side of the mountain with one hand, the other relaxed down at his side as if it were truly no effort at all to keep the fully grown man suspended in this way. As I noticed how slimy Elias truly looked as a land-walker and Seamus' biceps in comparison, I suspected it wasn't much of one. I did nothing to intervene.

"Ye wind your feckin' neck in, or I'll do it for ye," Seamus said to him.

Elias merely cackled lightly as he was released. Seamus then stormed ahead, grabbing me by the arm somewhat forcefully as he went. I glanced back at Elias who mouthed to me:

"He's got a temper."

I shrugged.

As I expected, feeling the stone would be impossible under the tense circumstances. After walking for what seemed like ages and all of us collectively acknowledging that we had no idea where we were going, we heard faint sounds of whispers in the distance. It was the only deviation from the monotony, so we followed it blindly. Seamus pulled me closer to him as we pushed through a throng of particularly thick trees, shoving branches out of our way as we squinted to see what was ahead.

We came upon an opening that revealed we had climbed much further up the mountain than I thought, and directly ahead of us, tucked away like a hidden lagoon, was a lake of shocking, crystal blue. It was the culmination of the river that ran from the sea, and it was the only feature of the island thus far, aside from its inhabitants, that was undoubtedly supernatural. The only water I had ever seen come close to the same shade of electrified azure was the Lago di Braise in the Italian Dolomites, and that was being generous to the mountainous body of water. In the very center, presumably the deepest part of the lake, I could see a perfectly round circle of bright white.

This was where the magic was.

"How much you wanna bet it's in there?" Elias said.

Neither of us answered, but the stones did.

Both mine and Seamus' gems began to buzz with excitement at the prospect of being reunited with another of their sisters.

I nodded. "It's there, alright."

We made our way down the mountain, Seamus lifting me over various boulders and other obstacles since none of us had shoes. I reached the shore of the blue and white loch and felt a sharp pain in my leg that seemed to sweep the floor out from under me, knocking me flat to the ground.

"Shit," I said, reaching for Seamus' arm. But of course it was Elias' I grabbed by accident.

I swiftly tore my hand away and shook my head in dismay, embarrassed and wondering how many times I'd slow us down.

"Are you okay?" Elias asked, his blue eyes scanning my legs for injury. "What was that?"

"I'm fine," I said truthfully as Seamus helped me to my feet from the other side. "I–I just think she's trying to talk to me."

"Atargatis?" Seamus asked. "What's she saying?"

"She's telling me to go in," I said. I didn't actually hear her say it in my head, but I knew that's what she wanted. That's what she always wanted–*me*, in the water. Did she know what we were up to? Did she approve? I had to think so, as my legs were now positively throbbing at the shore of the lake where her treasure was hidden.

Seamus walked into the water with me, and Elias followed.

"No," I said to both of them. "I'm going alone."

Elias let out a cluck of disapproval at the same time Seamus said, "Catch yourself on, Jasmine."

I knew they would follow, but I still didn't wait for them. I could see that there was no gradual descent into the depths of this lake–the dark sapphire rim beneath me promised a sharp drop off into the abyss.

I jumped, taking a sweeping dive, and my tail re-appeared before I even hit the water.

The cerulean surface crashed over me with the invigorating

water of Norway once more. This time I was engulfed by an even richer texture–the waves felt like liquid gold that I could either drink or breathe.

I opened my eyes and saw nothing but blue, cotton candy clouds swirling in front of my face, inviting me to reach out and touch them. But the necklace continued to pulse, and I remembered why I was there. The rainbow Iridescent Ammonite of Iberia lit up to guide my way, illuminating a path to the circle of white water.

I followed the light down, knowing it wouldn't take long. My tail whisked me through the water, and I felt Seamus and Elias' presence–I didn't turn to look for them, but I knew they weren't far behind me.

I reached the floor of the lake where I saw the slowly churning, magical tube of bright white water that extended from the bottom all the way up to the surface. It looked like an underwater skylight from the heavens, and I saw there was a faint shadow of something within it. This had to be where it was.

I reached my hand toward the white film and pressed through it, my eyes fixed on the outline of whatever was in the middle… what was that? I reached further, now submerged in the white water up to my elbow. Almost there…

My fingers made contact with what was unmistakably a tiny box vibrating with energy. I knew, without a shadow of doubt, that it held the Thulite.

Could it really be that easy?

Of course not, because I discovered that the white column appeared to be a one-way barrier as I tried to pull the box back out. No matter how hard I tugged, it wouldn't budge. I felt the current pulling at me, trying to take me inside of it. I resisted, wishing I had legs so I could dig my heels into the sand.

"Come *on*," I said exasperatedly as the white water crept up my arm. I was getting sucked inside. As I struggled, I didn't even notice that the traces of Elias and Seamus had vanished from my peripherals.

I heard something coming from inside the swirling column that made me pause.

It was the faintest sound of beautifully elegant music. It was similar to the whale song, but this was unquestionably being played by a human's hands.

What was the instrument, though? I listened more intently...I heard strings.

It was a violin, and it was so charming that I simply had to listen. Yes, I'd stop for just one song...the box could wait. It would still be here when the music ended.

Listening to just one song couldn't hurt.

The wonderful sound began to wash over me, the notes begging me to close my eyes and fully enjoy them. As I did, I thought I began to recognize the melody.

Yes, it was definitely a song that I knew, although I couldn't name it. It was one that reminded me of Matt—one that I thought we had danced to long ago. I knew the waltz from a gala we had attended at his alma mater, The University of Georgia.

It filled me with sadness to do it, knowing that it couldn't last, but I allowed myself to slip into the nostalgic bliss of the memory from that night. The violin told me to, and I couldn't resist.

"YOU LOOK ABSOLUTELY BEAUTIFUL TONIGHT," he said to me, blue eyes twinkling as we swayed on the dance floor with the very few others that were still left. He placed his hand around my lower back and pressed me closer as he whispered his next sentence. "You shouldn't wear red. It's not fair to everyone else in the room."

I blushed furiously. "I had to dress to match the theme," I said. "Red for Georgia, you know?"

He laughed his musical laugh, his nose wrinkling as I ran my finger down the slight bump that it had. It was just one of the distinctive features on his handsome face that I loved so dearly. It was hard to choose a favorite, considering how everything about him seemed to have been sculpted with the intentional purpose of making him beautiful.

"I can't wait to make you my wife," he said into my ear. It was a sleepy voice in which he spoke, like he was sharing his dreams with me as they happened while he was still awake.

"Not yet," I teased, even though I knew he was the one. I had known for a while. "You *just* got out of school."

He laughed and rolled his eyes at my exaggeration.

"I seem to remember that *you* are the one who just graduated from college," he said, pulling away to meet my gaze. He looked at me with nothing but good humor and joy in his eyes, like he was just…happy to be there. Happy to be anywhere with me. That was how he always looked. "I, on the other hand, am an ancient relic of this place."

"I meant medical school," I corrected myself.

I ignored his comment about my own college experience, having been painfully insecure about our age difference since the very beginning of our relationship. It was something I never shared with him, because I knew he didn't understand. He didn't think seven years and some change was significant when you planned to be with one another for a lifetime.

But that's because he didn't hear the whispers of *'gold digger'* that I did when people found out what his profession was versus mine.

"Oh, yeah, I forgot about med school," he said, grinning. "That *did* take a while."

"*Doctor* Taylor," I said slowly. "It sounds a little too impressive to forget."

"Mrs. Jasmine Taylor sounds better," he said, swirling the name around in his mouth like a rich taste of bourbon.

I hadn't decided if I'd change my name or not. Jasmine Atarga was so…me. Additionally, I felt mildly guilty that Raj had no one else to carry on his own. But I *did* love how distinguished Jasmine Taylor sounded. It was elegant, and rang like a title more than a name. At least that's how it sounded in my head.

I didn't really care, as long as he was mine.

He kissed me and gently rubbed the fourth finger on my left hand.

"As soon as you say the word," he said seriously. "I'm doing it."

A SILVER TEAR was brimming in the corner of my eye. I should've let him do it sooner. I shouldn't have made him wait until I was in my late twenties. We would have had more time…more time in which we could have been husband and wife to one another.

Instead, he died as nothing more than my boyfriend. It stung to realize that I had been so worried about what other people would think that I altered my own life's path to avoid their judgment. I had cared about all the wrong things back then.

But now…now I was here, at the bottom of a lake in a magically altered version of Norway. And I'd never be Jasmine Taylor.

I realized with a start that I was now in the center of the white, swirling column rather than floating outside of it. The box that I knew held another stone of Atargatis was in my hands, and now I was even further away from getting out with it thanks to my daydreaming. I shook myself awake and pressed into the barrier. It was rock solid. I was stuck.

"Ah, we shouldn't take what isn't ours," said a deep, raspy voice. I looked up to see a strange creature floating above me. It was a dark-haired man with bright, red eyes and what I could have sworn was a forked tongue that ran across his sharp teeth. He was playing the violin while staring at the box in my hand.

Of course, I had allowed myself to be lured into a trap.

CHAPTER 29

SCANDINAVIAN SCHEMES

I gulped.

If only I had thought for one second about all of the mythology that I knew, I would have seen it coming.

I had fallen right into the clutches of the spiteful Nøkken–the Nordic water nymph that lured women and children into the depths of lakes and rivers by playing them songs on his violin. This creature was such a widely known menace that it had two other names, *Näcken* or *Strömkarlen*, depending on where you were in the world.

I tried my best to recall any stories of captives making it out alive and what they did to escape, but I couldn't think of a single one. Had I not been furiously thinking on my feet—or tail—I would have sighed at my stupidity.

"Give me a riddle," I said, guessing. "If I solve it, I get out of here with the stone."

"A riddle?" the creature cackled, tossing his pointed nose back as his garnet eyes glinted maliciously in the white light. "I am no riddler."

Shit, that wasn't it.

Payment of my own jewels, maybe?

273

"Then name your price," I said.

He looked me up and down condescendingly.

"You have nothing I seek," he said simply.

I noted this as strange, considering the Iberian Iridescent Ammonite was prominent on my chest. He surely knew what it was.

"So you don't want the stones of Atargatis? Why do you protect this one, then?" I tapped the box.

He shrugged. "To lure my prey."

Despite the desperation of my situation, I somehow didn't fear him. There was a way out of this, I just needed to think...I tried to buy some time.

"You won't kill me," I said. "That's not your goal."

"No," he replied. "But I will enslave you."

I wasn't familiar with this part of the legendary trickster's games. I looked around the thin, white tube, and saw the tiny outlines of other water nymphs beginning to appear, gazing at me with their hungry, red eyes. It seemed I would become one of them if I didn't think faster.

"Name your price," I said again. "Something else."

He knew I had nothing. He knew I was trapped. Even if Seamus and Elias had been closely following behind me, they couldn't get to me in here. Not while Nøkken had me in his trap. I was sure of it. I wondered if they could even see me.

I heard a faint screech in the distance that sounded awfully like another monster, and the nymph in front of me grinned wickedly.

"Oh, I didn't expect *this*," Nøkken said with relish, putting his violin back up to his chin as he prepared to play another song. My death march, I supposed. "Perhaps you're going to be eaten, after all."

I whirled around as the other water nymphs began to disappear through the white film once more, bubble trails flying in their wake. Their eyes were wide with fear and panic in the same way I imagined my own to be.

"What–" I began, but the trickster cut me off.

"I yield to Selma," Nøkken said, backing away as he began to play. The song was far from elegant this time. It was harsh, too loud, and too fast. "And it appears she has staked her claim upon you."

He vanished through the white water, leaving me alone in the column. I froze, knowing something far worse was coming for me. What the hell was a *Selma*? It didn't really matter, actually, considering I was locked in a chamber with no way of escaping whatever was on its way. The white film grew increasingly opaque, the bright light from above beginning to blind me.

Another ear-splitting screech rang through the water, and the barrier around me shattered like glass. It was gone in seconds, and the sapphire of the lake surrounded me once more.

Seamus and Elias were at my side immediately, both of them with their blades at the ready.

"Jasmine what happened?" Seamus yelled over the screeching. "We couldn't see–"

"Something's coming!" I yelled as I held up the small chest. "I've got it–it's in here!"

Seamus quickly took his dagger and dug it into the box, popping the lid to reveal the pink stone we sought. It glowed at my touch in confirmation that it belonged to the goddess of the Sea. Before I could attempt to string it around my neck with the other, a wave sent me flying. The sound of a violent beast roared once more.

From the depths of the water emerged a massive, aquatic dinosaur with eyes of red fire and small, tight knit fins that were sharp as knives along its black scales. I gasped as the prehistoric creature brought its tail down between myself and Elias, sending me backward yet again in another forceful wave. Seamus caught me from behind as I crashed into him before rushing toward the beast himself. The stone slipped from my grasp.

"*Shit*," I swore, and I scrambled to retrieve the pink gem. Elias snatched it above my head, and I looked up at him with relief for one moment before the truth dawned upon me. Before disappointment punched me in the gut.

He took off for the surface without a backwards glance.

I should have known.

Traitor.

I didn't have time to mourn his betrayal as Seamus was actively fighting the dinosaur, dodging the beast's sweeping motions with its tail. He then lunged for the creature and wrenched open its jaw, preparing to either rip it apart or drive his dagger in its mouth.

I forced myself to remain calm, recalling that Artur and I had tested our theory regarding the hierarchy of water beasts. This one *looked* like a dinosaur, but it was swimming…so it had to be considered a sea serpent…right?

I thought of my exchange of respect with Otima, as well as the Ollphéist. I didn't have a choice but to try.

"WAIT!" I shouted. Seamus' dagger was pulled back and his opposite elbow held the creature's mouth open–he was prepared to strike.

"Jasmine–" he said in alarm as he saw me approaching the beast. The beast whose mouth was one wrong move away from snapping his arm off.

I could do it, but I only had *seconds*.

I shot up to the dinosaur's face and showed it the Iridescent Ammonite of Iberia on my neck. I let it see my eyes.

It stopped and cocked its head ever so slightly. The ruby eyes searched me. Not maliciously, but not kindly, either. It was curious, and nothing more.

I reached tentatively for its scales, despite Seamus' look of concern. I touched the creature gently, and a small glow began to emit from its neck.

So Selma *was* considered a serpent. Or maybe I simply had ultimate control over all fearsome creatures of the seas–snakes or otherwise.

Well, except for nymphs and tricksters. They didn't give a shit about what the Heir of Atargatis had to say, apparently.

The serpent then seemed to question me, as if it didn't understand why I would be *here*.

The stone, I thought, hoping it could hear me. *I have come to retrieve what's mine.*

This explanation seemed to suffice, because Selma slithered back to the lake's floor in a benevolent manner, dipping its head as Seamus and I rose above it.

It was bowing to me.

"Come on," Seamus said, reaching his hand toward mine, reminding me of the urgency to catch Elias. I could marvel at my powers later.

We rocketed to the shore in seconds, but there was no sign of the traitor. I wondered wildly how deep his scheming truly went. Did he know of another way off the island–one that wouldn't require him to pass by Artur? Or would he lie to the leader of Atlântida and tell him we'd met our deaths in the lake?

And lastly…was he working with Cearbhall and Camila for the stones or someone else? My mind was racing as I felt irate anger pulsing through me. All of those times I thought I could have slapped him, I really should have. His unwelcome advances on me were *nothing* compared to what he'd done now.

"Go!" I yelled as Seamus' tail vanished and his legs returned. I knew my transformation would slow us down, and if Elias got away, we'd never see the Thulite again. "I'm right behind you!"

He looked at me regretfully, but knew I was right in urging him ahead. Seamus sprinted up the valley and into the mountain, clawing his way up the rock of the beautiful Nordic landscape until he disappeared from sight. The pain in my legs seared white-hot, and I had a horrible feeling I would be stuck here forever.

"No," I begged Atargatis. "I have to finish the mission. I'm doing this for *good.*"

I waited and waited.

At last, my tail finally melted to nothingness and my legs were granted to me once more. I sighed with relief.

I rose to my feet, watching the tail of Selma seem to wave goodbye to me as it emerged one time above the waves before disappearing into the depths of the blue lake. Stillness returned to the surface, revealing an innocent picture of serenity. There was no indication whatsoever of the trickery, destruction, and chaos that existed below.

I flew up the mountainside, my legs on fire as the sun was still blazing in the sky. I had no choice but to ignore the pain. I was desperate to get to Seamus and Elias before the stone was gone forever or before Seamus…no, he wouldn't do that.

Or would he?

I thought of what he'd done in Santiago de Compostela. But… that was different.

I tumbled down the other side of the mountain, ripped through the trees, and eventually made it back to the shore where I came to a screeching halt, my breath knocked out of me by what I saw. They were both on their knees, Seamus behind Elias with his blade pressed to the traitor's throat.

"No!" I shouted as I ran to them.

I looked at Seamus incredulously, but I could see that he believed he had good reason to do it. I stood above them both and looked down at Elias, all traces of his smugness now vanished from his terrified face. He trembled as he looked up at me.

"Explain yourself," I demanded of him, my voice cracking against my will. I was shaken, disturbed, and disappointed in myself for not seeing through his facade. Seamus did not loosen his grip.

"Jasmine," Elias breathed. "You have to believe me, I was coming back for you–"

"Enough," I said coldly, not allowing his eyes to truly look into my own. I turned my gaze to stone. "You would have left us there to die."

"Maybe him," he said boldly, tilting his head back. Seamus tightened his grip on the blonde hair and I thought he'd snap his neck if I didn't get to the point quickly. "But not you. I'd never."

His eyes flickered with hints of what could have been the truth, but I didn't trust him. I never would again. I said nothing.

"Cearbhall, he–he threatened me," he sputtered. "He made me–"

I cut him off. *Cearbhall* was all I needed to hear.

"You're a coward for deceiving us in order to protect your-self," I said at last, my voice dropping to a whisper. "Us, and Artur...everyone who trusted you."

I tried to keep the tears at bay, because I didn't want to give him the satisfaction of thinking he had any sort of emotional power over me. No, the truth was that if I were to cry, it was because I was furious with myself for being so foolish.

"Wouldn't you?" he asked me. The simple question, and the way he so genuinely thought of myself as the same as him, sent me into a rage.

"No!" I shouted. And then I steadied myself, speaking with the same volatile poison that I had used with Camila. "I'd rather die than dishonor myself like you have."

I picked up the beautiful pink stone that lay next to him in the sand, magically sealing it onto my chain beside the other where it vibrated in satisfaction at being reunited with its sister.

Seamus waited in anticipation with the knife. He would let me make the call.

"Jasmine, please," Elias cried, his blue eyes begging me to have mercy. I wanted to look away. "You *know* me."

Seamus regarded me with a touch of bewilderment, and perhaps even a flicker of alarm crossed his face. I could nearly hear the questions buzzing in his mind. Did the man before him, whose fate rested in his own hands, deserve mercy? Or was there an unspoken connection between the traitor and his own woman of which Seamus was unaware? And would I choose to spare him because we had forged some sort of bond during the long weeks he had been gone in Spain?

Gone because he was fighting my war. Gone because Seamus was quite literally descending into Hell for me.

No, Elias was nothing to me.

"I *do* know you," I said dismissively. "I've known exactly the kind of person you were all along."

I thought–if his expression showed the truth now–that my words stung. But it didn't matter. Not when he was working with the enemy.

I shook my head curtly at Seamus, signaling we would spare him, but we'd leave him here. Elias' betrayal wasn't worth damaging his soul.

Seamus lowered the knife and both of them stood. Elias rubbed his neck and opened his mouth to speak. He didn't get the chance, however, because Seamus swiftly hit him in the face and knocked him out cold. Elias hit the beach with a thud and I jumped, even though I had fully expected him to do it. I was glad he did.

He then took my hand and we descended into the water, neither of us saying a word. The small group of very blonde half-fish onlookers watched us in their same, robotic gaze as we passed, having observed the entire exchange in silence. I wondered what they'd do when Elias woke up, but I stopped myself from pitying him. All I wanted to do was get as far away from the eerie island as possible.

The sun was sinking, signaling late afternoon. I sighed with exhaustion as the pink mist met us instantly, allowing the whale song to fade us back into the real world.

Now that I had seen Seamus with his knife at Elias' throat, I realized that the time may very well come when he did need to kill for me. But today wasn't that day.

* * *

WE EMERGED from the pink mist where Artur was waiting for us. He saw who had not returned, and confusion shadowed his face.

"What–" he began.

"We got the stone," I said, holding up the Thulite around my neck. "But–"

"We left the Norwegian bastard on the island," Seamus said matter-of-factly. "Double crossed us. He's working with Cearbhall."

Artur looked at us in dismay before disappointment descended. I think he felt the same way I did. Elias was an arrogant asshole, but we thought that was the extent of his aggravating attributes. To think that his intentions had been more sinister than simply stirring the pot for the sake of pissing people off was disturbing to both of us, because how could we have missed it? Clouded by the additional fact that he had been Artur's late best friend's son…I knew that the leader of Atlântida felt like as much of a fool as I did.

"Erik would be ashamed," he said at last, shaking his head before looking at Seamus and I apologetically. "I'm so sorry I placed my trust in him."

"We all did," I said, avoiding Seamus' raised eyebrow. Of course *he* never trusted the snake. I wondered for a brief moment if there would be an '*I told you so*' conversation between the two of us later, but something told me Seamus wasn't that type of man. In fact, I didn't think he would waste his breath discussing

Elias ever again. To gloat simply wasn't his way, and I was grateful for it.

"Well, another of the ten stones has been secured, nonetheless," Artur said, slapping Seamus and I both on the shoulders with a sigh. "We're making progress."

I was still jarred by the betrayal, which led to my next negative and unhelpful comment.

"It doesn't feel like it."

Seamus and Artur looked at one another before the great leader spoke to me directly in measured tones.

"Might I suggest that you view today as a victory," Artur said. "And you *rest* before you go on to find the next one."

As much as I had hoped the same before we left that morning, it seemed impossible now. Elias' deception made me feel like I was losing my edge, and I didn't quite feel like taking a vacation. I felt uneasy, like we were falling behind. Like Cearbhall and Camila were a step ahead of us.

"We can't," I said, shaking my head. "The Amalgams, Cearbhall–"

Artur put up a hand to silence me.

"We have several advantages that they do not, thanks to Seamus' success with The Santa Compaña," he said. "We know how many stones there are, *where* they are, *and* you have a better chance of sensing them than they do."

I didn't bother voicing the doubt in my mind at the final part of his statement. How had they found the Larimar then? The Tsavorite? Clearly Cearbhall and Camila had some kind of ability to track the gems that rivaled my own…

"Take a minute to breathe, both of you," Artur said encouragingly. "Take a week."

Seamus looked at me and must have seen something in my expression that convinced him I needed it, because he was already nodding his head in agreement.

The matter of Elias aside, I knew that the repercussions of the emotions I had experienced within the white column hadn't quite faded yet, either. The memory of Matt's gentle voice in my ear was fresh; having been a far more realistic depiction of my time with him than any of my dreams at night.

I caught a glimpse of my own reflection in the glass waves and thought I looked like hell.

"Aye, I think that's a good idea," Seamus said, his eyes not leaving me.

"Back to Ireland, then?" Artur suggested as he motioned vaguely to the west.

I let out a sigh and deferred to Seamus. I was exhausted. I wanted relief and comfort, and I didn't know where I'd find that. I wanted to turn my mind off, and have someone else make the next call.

One of the things I loved about Seamus was that he instinctively knew when to take the lead.

"London, first, I think," he said decisively. "If that's fine by ye, Jasmine?"

"Yes," I said, surprised by the eagerness of my own answer. "Let's go."

I let out a sigh of relief. Time alone with Seamus in London was truthfully exactly what I wanted. To leave this search behind for a few days sounded like a dream, and I could see that he and Artur both sincerely didn't think of it as selfish to do.

I wanted to meet my mother, of course, but I hated the idea of doing so when I was in such a fragile state of mind. I wanted to meet her when I was at my absolute best. I wanted her to think her daughter was strong.

"That's easy," Artur replied kindly. "Straight shot that way."

He pointed slightly southwest and handed us each a piece of the magical pink seaweed that I knew would rocket us across The North Sea almost as quickly as a Green Window could. I took a bite gratefully and felt my physical battery recharging as my mental battery prepared to do the same.

"Thank you for everything," I said sincerely to Artur.

He had been so kind to me from the moment I met him, and his presence was a small reminder of the father I had once lost. During the long days when I felt so lonely and afraid for Seamus' wellbeing, Artur was the only person whose words I believed when he said everything would be fine. Dads have that power in a way no one else does.

"Of course," he replied. "There will always be a home for you in Atlântida, if you want it."

I thought of my cozy sapphire bedroom with the magical fireplace and smiled. We would certainly take him up on that offer.

"I will wait for your call for aid in finding the remainder of the stones…and war if it's necessary," he continued. "Atlântida will always answer the call of Atargatis."

I hugged him tightly, and I felt him tense slightly in surprise before warming to my embrace and gently patting me on the head.

"And you," he said to Seamus, hands on his shoulders. "You have a warrior's spirit. I'd say your father would be proud of his son, but I know what he thinks doesn't carry much weight. So I'll tell you that *I* am proud of you. And hopefully that counts for something."

I was taken aback to discover that they were more familiar with one another than I realized, yet upon reflection, it made sense. The two of them had spent countless hours training together before Seamus departed for Spain. I was aware that part of their training involved Artur's cautionary tales about the mental tricks that The Santa Compaña might play on him, and how they'd stop at nothing to break him. The hardships of Seamus' past would undoubtedly have surfaced during those discussions, as there was plenty of loss in his life that the morbid company could weaponize.

"It does," Seamus replied to him, smiling as he shook his hand.

We turned to depart for the open waters where we would go

our separate ways. Artur waved briefly before diving gracefully beneath the waves, and he was gone with a flash of his tail. I felt a subtle twinge of sadness as I realized he was going back to an entirely empty palace, his son and future daughter-in-law already having returned to the Emerald Isle. To be ancient and alone must be sad.

I wondered if that was why he kept the doors of the castle open at all times.

PART V

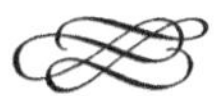

LOVER

CHAPTER 30

SEAMUS OF LONDON

*S*eamus and I whirled through the North Sea in the darkness that had now descended, the waves rising ahead of us in an endless sea of ink and white as the black water caught the light of the moon.

The tumultuous nature of the current would have been terrifying to a human, but it was a thrill for us. We rocketed across the top of the waves, the howling wind of winter seeming to urge us onward while the pink seaweed propelled us like lightning. As the moonstone fish flashed past us, I gripped his hand tightly and began to feel a combination of relief and excitement rapidly replacing my disappointment. Now that we were alone, Elias' betrayal already felt like a distant memory.

I reached up for his wrist with my other hand as a particularly powerful wave hit us both from the side. We swerved for a moment, my stomach lurching wildly, before immediately correcting our course. We looked at one another and burst out laughing, amazed by our own strength to fight back against the power of nature.

"Bout ye?" he sarcastically called over his shoulder to me, and

I grinned in response. He likely couldn't see my face through the dark ocean spray, so I shouted back to him.

"Never been better," I said.

Just two sea monsters, swimming across one of the most deadly and fearsome bodies of water in the world. What could be more peaceful?

As much as I longed to return to Ireland, I loved England as well. I was intrigued to see more of Seamus' real life–well, his *old* life–that I knew almost nothing about. I knew he had lived and worked in London for the past several years, but that was the full extent of my insight into his world.

Before I knew it, I saw land again. We slowed as we approached Southend-on-Sea where the River Thames began, and I spotted the faint glimmer of lights on the horizon that signified the fast-paced city. Big Ben called to us, reminding us of the time we now had to enjoy this unique version of human life. It wasn't endless, and it would be precious, but it was something.

Because of my keen, supernatural eyesight, I could see that the massive clock read the hour of four, and I yawned in response. Of course it was morning, not afternoon.

"Aye, I'm exhausted," Seamus said, doing the same. "We'll rest when we get home, a stór."

Home. It sounded nice coming from him.

"*Does* it still feel like home?" I questioned, asking the same thing he had asked me back in Porto.

"I dunno," he said, scanning the skyline contemplatively. I knew what he was thinking, even though he didn't harbor any resentment for his old life like I did. Nothing here would ever be the same for him again.

We ducked below the waves, watching the ocean floor carefully as the sand rose higher and higher. The water was filthy, but it didn't bother us considering our lamplight eyes. I didn't know where we planned to emerge, but we were still covered by the darkness of night, so I didn't worry too much about being seen.

Seamus seemed to have a spot in mind, so I followed him without question.

I remembered being here with both Raj and Matt, at very different stages in life.

RAJ HAD BROUGHT me as a child, during our years in Portugal, and I had wailed with frustration at the lengthy behind-the-scenes tour of the Victoria & Albert he had booked for us. It was something that I would have been thrilled to do now, but back then I couldn't understand why we would willingly commit to a tour of a museum that we could've breezed through on our own.

Matt and I had come to London during one of his medical conferences, so I had been mostly alone while he sat in seminars all day. I had wandered up and down the River Thames on both sides on a freezing December day, and I still recalled the mulled wine warming my belly as I looked up at the Tower Bridge in awe. It was my favorite landmark.

"You really do have morbid tastes when it comes to history," Matt remarked as we walked across the bridge, his own holiday drink staining his lips currant as he held my arm. I had been telling him about the mace I wanted to steal from the Tower of London so I could hang it on our wall at home, and he told me that a medieval weapon of blunt force wasn't exactly his first choice in decorative accents.

"I just think it's interesting," I remarked, placing my other mittened hand on his forearm. "And they weren't exclusively used as weapons, you know. By the Renaissance, they were mainly used for ceremonial purposes. To represent power and authority."

His musical laugh rang through the bitter winter air.

"Oh that's more tasteful," he said. "Fine, but you're the one taking it off the wall. I'm not getting arrested by the Crown."

I grinned. "Deal."

"What else did you do today?" he asked.

"Shopped with your credit card."

He let out a low whistle. "Oh, I hope you didn't find Bond Street."

I laughed softly. "There's a book exchange near the South Bank," I said. "So I spent a while wandering down there."

He smiled with the familiar look of admiration he always had in his eyes for me.

"Of course you did," he said. "What did you get?"

I had been carrying the tiny book with me all day, so I removed the gold-plated volume from my overcoat pocket.

"The Complete Adventures of Sherlock Holmes!" Matt exclaimed. "That's very…you."

He meant it as a compliment, of course.

"I've got to keep my wits sharp," I said. "Just in case there's ever a mystery afoot."

"I don't think anyone who's met you would ever describe your wits as anything other than sharp as a knife," he remarked. "You're way smarter than me, anyway."

I rolled my eyes. "You're a *doctor*," I said. "I didn't even go to grad school!"

"Why would you?" he replied with a shrug. "You'd run circles around those professors."

I blushed, because I had always been insecure about my lack of pursuing my education beyond undergrad. Whenever someone complimented my intellect, I couldn't help but notice that they always seemed *surprised* by it. Like they expected me to be Matt's decorative arm candy and nothing more. Perhaps it was a stupid chip on my shoulder, but it existed.

Matt never saw me as anything other than brilliant, despite him being the smartest person I knew. Well, aside from Raj.

.   .   .

"WHERE ARE WE GOING?" I asked Seamus at last as we rose back above the surface, passing all of the familiar sites: we were flying beneath The Millenium Bridge, past The Savoy hotel…the river was curving, and we were approaching Westminster.

"Almost there," Seamus said, flashing me a wide grin. I now had an intense level of curiosity for where he lived. I hadn't had the courage to go to my own place when I was back in Tampa, but I hoped that one day–before it went into foreclosure–I would get to go back to my condo. I didn't want anything from there, but there was a part of me that wanted to say goodbye.

We slowed at Chelsea Embankment Gardens, and it was quiet. I didn't know what day of the week it was, but we were still here far earlier than the regular hour of morning commuters. It seemed like a safe enough place for two sea creatures to turn back into humans. I thought the sun would remain hidden even after dawn, considering the typical gloom of London winters. I sincerely hoped it would, not wanting my physical challenges to spoil my time here.

"Up we go," Seamus said, throwing himself onto the tiniest stretch of grass beneath the Albert Bridge.

He transformed instantly and was clothed in attire that was far more appropriate for winter in England than our Hy-Brasil uniforms would have been. After Artur's explanation of how the clothing magic worked, I had been expecting it, but my heart still fluttered as the London version of Seamus emerged.

He was wearing something extremely similar to what he had been on the first night I met him–a dark green henley shirt that hugged his forearms tightly and light khaki pants. The only variation this time was that in place of sneakers, he had winter-proof boots and a long black jacket that was slung over his shoulder. I grinned in admiration. It was truly incredible magic.

"Handsome," I remarked, and his cheeks turned as red as his hair as he humbly shook his head.

He reached back into the water and pulled me up to join him.

The grass was slick with fresh, cold rain, and even with my internal thermostat, I still felt the chill that caused so many to withdraw indoors during this time of year.

"Sorry," I said, embarrassed as I always was for slowing us down. I also worried, after what had happened in Norway, that one day my transformation might not work at all. I shuddered at the thought.

"Don't be," he said sincerely. "There's no rush."

It was nice to hear him say it, but I didn't release the breath I'd been holding my chest until I saw the shadow of my legs begin to appear. The shimmery scales slowly melted away and were replaced by my knees, my shins, my feet…thank Manannán.

I finally stood, wobbling only slightly. I was in a chartreuse sweater, jeans, sneakers, and a winter coat that I certainly didn't recognize. The green both of us wore may have been an ode to Ireland, for all I knew. I shrugged. It would have to do for now.

"Don't worry," Seamus said as he noticed I was rubbing my arms in the chilly air, even with the new outerwear I now had. Selkie blood or not, it was definitely cold. "It's not far."

It wasn't. His townhouse was less than a ten minute walk from where we were by the river. The Chelsea neighborhood was quiet and peaceful in the early hours of the morning, and I saw the sky starting to turn gray on the horizon. We took a few turns down sleepy streets of colorful, mostly pastel brick buildings before reaching his own that was painted a warm ivory. I stepped across the threshold of the black door and my body instantly warmed like a toaster.

"I see they haven't turned the electricity off," I remarked. He had left a light on in the kitchen, and I wondered if I had done the same back in Tampa.

"I don't even want to think about it," he said, laughing.

I looked out the window while he went to get me a blanket, and I peered down the street toward the tiny intersection where one row of cozy homes crossed with another. I supposed the general afflu-ence of the area was why he felt confident enough in the simplistic method of hiding a spare key under the mat outside the front door, answering my question as to how we were to get in. He was clearly not worried about anyone trying to enter that shouldn't.

"What exactly do you do for a living?" I asked. I couldn't imagine anyone less than extremely well off could afford to live on a street such as his in London.

He let out an amused scoff. "Nothing, anymore," he said.

"No really," I said, genuinely curious. "I never asked you back in Ireland, even when we spent the entire evening talking about our lives. I want to know."

Of course, our topics of discussion had been much more intriguing than our respective professions. I don't think I ever told him what I did for a living, either. As the days passed, I myself hardly remembered. It seemed so unimportant now, but I was still moderately curious. I don't know what I had expected of his life in London, but him living in such a luxurious neighbor-hood wasn't necessarily on the list.

"Insurance," he said simply. "Nothing at all interesting."

I secretly agreed, so I didn't ask anything further.

I trudged across the checkered tile, observing how barren the place looked. It was tasteful and extremely nice, but it was certainly plain. It reminded me of my own, and how I had never done much to it after Matt's death. But I guessed for a man, the lack of warmth wasn't surprising. He scratched the back of his neck in what I realized was self-consciousness, and I nearly laughed. I wouldn't have cared where he lived or what it looked like.

"I don't really know how to decorate," he said nervously. "But I hope ye like it."

"You do?" I asked. A loaded question.

"Well, I thought I might keep it for us," he said. "Considering ye can land-walk when it's not sunny. The sun rarely shines here, in the winter at least."

I beamed.

"Alright," I said, thinking of my place. Matt had put it in both of our names. "Then I'll have to list my condo for sale. If I can figure out how to do that as a dead person."

"I want to see Tampa, too," he said quickly, ignoring my joke. "But I know ye–"

He stopped himself, but I knew what he was going to say. Something along the lines of, *I know ye don't want to go back there for a number of reasons.*

And it was true. The sunshine state was not the place for me. I was a broken selkie that couldn't bear the rays, and there were far too many of them there.

"I have no desire to return to Tampa," I concluded aloud for both of us.

"Fair enough," he said, brushing one finger down my cheek. He understood.

I was surprised to find that I did still feel the sensation of thirst, so Seamus brought me a glass of water from the fridge while I studied the small courtyard out back. Thinking it looked like a nice place to read, I could certainly see us returning. I could see us having a life here.

Seamus coughed up his own glass before I took a sip of mine, and I looked at him questioningly.

"That's disgusting," he sputtered. "Maybe because it's not saltwater."

I tasted mine and felt the same, but I swallowed it anyway, assuming we needed the same amount of water as humans did, if not more. Since we were in Europe, it was at least mineral water. I wondered how vile the nothingness of American filtered water would taste.

"Do ye want to rest?" he asked, and I nodded gratefully. The sky was lighter now, and the clock read that it was past five in the morning, but I needed a few hours of sleep.

He showed me to his bedroom and I hardly noticed anything about it other than how soft and comfortable his sheets were. I climbed into them and he joined me.

I passed out within minutes.

CHAPTER 31

LEARNING CURVES

When I woke up, I could tell it was late morning, despite the lack of sunlight visible behind the clouds out the window. Seamus' arm was slung around me from behind, and I was extremely comfortable as the little spoon.

After a few minutes, I turned around and buried my face in his chest while he began to awake, sleepily stroking my hair. I had thought about how nice it would be to wake up next to him like a real human in an actual bed, and my expectations were exceeded. It was lovely.

"Did ye get enough sleep?" he asked.

"I think so," I yawned. "For now."

He brushed his fingers along my back under my sweater as we laid there in peaceful silence.

"This is nice," he mused, eyes still closed as he read my thoughts.

He kissed my forehead and then my mouth, pulling me close to him with one hand as the other reached for the waist of my jeans that I hadn't even bothered to take off in my exhaustion. I traced my finger along his muscular forearm, avoiding the deep black scar. I didn't think it would be sensitive to the touch, but I didn't want to remind him of it. Not now, when we were so content with our ordinary existence. I wanted to forget we were anything but normal for a few days.

He gently brushed his tongue against my own, our lips not leaving one another's as he pressed me onto my back and got on top of me, his muscular shoulders hovering above me. I reached for his belt and he helped me with it, sparking the invisible flame between once more.

"I've wanted to take ye for so long," he said into my ear.

"Like you haven't already?" I asked as he slid my jeans off and ran his hands up my thighs. I rolled my head back, shivering at his touch.

"Not here, in my own bed," he replied.

I knew what he meant, because I felt the same way. He'd had every inch of me on the shores of Ireland and the magical beach in the oasis room, but this was somehow very different. This was how I pictured it happening originally when I first met him–the normal way.

He started to descend between my legs and I ran my hand through his burgundy waves, closing my eyes as I prepared for one of my favorite sensations, at last without the complication of sand.

Then I froze as the realization that I hadn't been a *real* human on *real* land in a long time came rushing back to me with an overwhelming force. As a mermaid, I had never felt insecure in any way because I was a biologically different species on beaches and in bodies of water where I was *naturally* supposed to be.

But being a land-walker in a city was different. I suddenly desperately wanted a chance to refresh more than anything else in the world.

I voiced this to Seamus, and he laughed heartily.

"I understand," he said, coming back up to meet my face. "But just so ye know, there'll never be a time I don't want the taste of ye in my mouth."

I knew he meant it considering the way his lower body felt pressed against mine, but I still wanted a shower. He busied himself in the kitchen to give me some privacy; a notion I thought highly chivalrous considering how many times he had already seen me naked. I was relieved to find an unopened toothbrush under the sink I could use, but that was about all I found in the way of amenities.

I opened the glass door and rolled my eyes at the singular bar of soap and bottle of shampoo that sat on the shelf, making a note to retrieve my own hygienic needs at some point in the day. While this refined version of Seamus existed, the lack of bathroom essentials reminded me that he was still limited by the constraints of being a male.

I stepped tentatively in the shower, remembering my dream when I had been talking to Matt from inside the bathtub and I'd had my mermaid tail. If the shower water touched my bare legs, would I immediately transform back into a selkie? Or did I need to be fully submerged? Was it limited to ocean or river water only? There was only one way to find out, I supposed. I turned on the tap and braced myself, waiting for several moments with my eyes closed, holding onto the door just in case my legs melted away.

But nothing happened. I laughed at myself, making a note to tell Seamus of my discovery in case he had been wondering the same thing.

It was around one in the afternoon when we both were cleaned up, and I felt revitalized as I stretched my legs, now confident that the dark skies of London would keep the pain away. I hadn't felt a thing since we got back to his place, and I was grateful Atargatis was giving me a break.

Despite knowing it would taste like dirt to me and probably have no impact on my energy levels, I felt like I needed caffeine. I sipped coffee in the kitchen and turned on the news that was on a continuous loop. I learned that it was a Thursday, and Chelsea had lost to Newcastle last night, one to three. Seamus checked on various things around his house, apparently pleasantly surprised with how well it had held up during his nearly three month absence.

"It's a nice place, but it's old, so it is," he shrugged.

He gave me a full tour of the townhouse, and I found it was much bigger than I had originally assumed. There was another spare bedroom and bathroom up the stairs, and a small rooftop terrace with an electric fire pit that looked like it would be cozy at night. In the office on the main floor, there was an extremely ornate, seemingly custom wooden poker table that sat next to his desk. I raised an eyebrow in surprise when I saw it.

"A gambler, are you?"

He smiled, arms crossed as he leaned against the doorway. "I don't have intellectual hobbies like ye," he said. He pointed behind the desk. "We should add some bookshelves back there for ye. Give the place some taste."

I looked around the office, thinking it could use a touch of academia. Maybe I'd add a globe...in memory of Raj.

"Sounds good."

"So, what do ye want to do tonight?" he asked, sliding behind me and placing his hands on my shoulders. I leaned back into him, looking out the front window as I felt the rush of being human again pound through my chest. To have the choice of what we were doing next was a novelty I hadn't experienced at all since I'd known Seamus. Even back when we met in Ireland, we'd always been on a schedule; always had obligations.

"I *would* like to go out," I said, remembering the rich dining and entertainment scene that existed in the magical city of London.

I turned around to see he was grinning widely. "I was hoping ye'd say that."

There was the minor issue that while we were at his house that was filled with all of his clothes besides the suitcase of lost belongings sitting somewhere in Ireland, *I* had nothing else to wear. As comfortable as the jeans and sweater were, I didn't quite feel like wearing them out to a fancy dinner in London. In general, I owned not a single human possession aside from the small ring with the triskelion symbol I had purchased in Galway. I was unsure of how to bring this up to Seamus since it seemed like a thing a man wouldn't understand.

"Um–" I began, but he spared me from voicing my problem as he had apparently already realized I no longer had a thing to my name. He quickly rummaged through a drawer in the kitchen and tossed me a black credit card with silver numbers on it.

"I should take care of a few things at my bank," he said, glancing at the clock next to the pantry. "Go get yourself whatever ye need."

"Oh, you don't have to–" I began, my cheeks turning bright red.

"I mean it," he said sincerely, ending the possibility of an argument. "Don't even think about it, aye? What's mine is yours, I hope ye know that by now."

I blinked, slightly taken aback by the profoundness of the statement, but I appreciated it.

We swept out the door to Sloane Square station and agreed to meet back at his place by five, which gave me a relatively narrow window of time to not only remember where the best shopping in London was, but find something suitable for dinner tonight as well as regular clothing for the next few days. Seeing as neither of us had phones anymore, we agreed to be exactly punctual if not early. Seamus said he'd pick up two iPhones while he was out, but I shut the idea down immediately.

"What are we going to do with those at the bottom of the Atlantic?" I said. I didn't need yet another expensive thing collecting dust back home while I ran away from the world again.

We hopped on the District line toward Upminster together

and prepared to part ways at Victoria station, the incessant traffic of the tube bustling all around us.

"Bond Street, Soho," he said, gesturing vaguely to the map over the door. "I truthfully dunno much about clothes…but that's the main area, so it is."

"Seamus, I really can't–" I began, my face on fire as I ran my finger along the card in my pocket. I was sweating. I had *never* let a man dote on me like this. Matt had tried to, and I had vehemently refused, having always been mortifyingly insecure about how much more money he had than I did–especially in the beginning when I was fresh out of college. I had tried my best not to offend him when he presented me with a Chopard bracelet on our first anniversary and I gaped like a fish, having never owned a piece of jewelry so expensive.

"Ye can," Seamus said firmly, green eyes locked on my own. "Enjoy it, and get anything ye want. I want ye to be comfortable here. This week, and when we come back."

I looked up at him shyly. "Fine."

"D'ye know London quite well?" he asked, as if it had just occurred to him that I might not as we exited the train. I smiled to myself, noting that he always seemed to assume I knew everything. "Or do ye want me–"

"No, I'm good," I said earnestly, knowing the clock was ticking and I wasn't going to be a physical burden in addition to a monetary one. "Go take care of what you need to do."

I still wasn't comfortable with the financial arrangement, but I saw that the man genuinely did not care. I half expected that if I showed back up at his house with nothing but designer bags, he wouldn't even question it. I had no idea what he actually did for a living beyond the vague term *insurance*–and now I was more than moderately curious. Whatever it was, it was apparently lucrative enough for him to send an American girl he barely knew running wild with his credit card in one of the most expensive cities in the world.

It turned out I actually did know London very well–I had always been good with public transportation and directions in general. Plus, I didn't have to go far. Without even looking at the map again, I hopped on the Victoria line for two stops and got off at Oxford Circus, thinking it was a good starting point.

I leisurely strolled up and down Carnaby Street that was already beautifully decorated for the holidays, and I was reminded again of my time here with Matt as I passed the world famous Christmas lights. I knew it was a touristy area, but there were a few hidden gems of boutiques tucked away on the side streets that I remembered from my last visit to the city. Additionally, I didn't want to venture too far from the tube, because I didn't have endless amounts of time.

I stepped into a shop that looked like it promised a good amount of variety, and left with a couple bags filled with reasonably priced items that would get me through the week including a pair of boots, some sweaters, and another jacket that was more suitable for evening wear than the one Atargatis had placed on me at the river's edge. Winter attire was my favorite kind to shop for, considering I never got to wear it in Florida. Not that I needed anything particularly heavy with the extra layer of heat insulation that my selkie blood provided me, but I did think it was a good idea to blend in.

"Oh!" I heard someone gasp from behind me in line, and I whirled around. I saw a woman fumble with a coffee cup, and I caught it midair with my left hand. She stared at me.

"Nice catch," she mused, laughing. "Almost dropped that right on your foot. Sorry about that."

"No problem," I replied. I smiled at her and handed it back, not a drop having spilled. She looked at me curiously and I made a note to check the appearance of my irises in the mirror. Did they look as supernatural and strange as they had in Tampa?

I thought of Kristen, and how I had made a similar catch with her Guinness back in Dublin. Back before I knew what I was and why I had suddenly developed incredible reflexes. I wondered what else I could do as a land-walker…

I tried not to think about the mounting receipts as I continuously tapped Seamus' card to the screens, feeling like the most spoiled woman in Soho. I browsed around Liberty for some makeup and hair tools, and then into Boots for shampoo and conditioner, given my observations from earlier in the afternoon.

The final item on my list was my outfit for tonight…and I wanted something impressive.

Seamus and I had only ever been around one another as humans in very casual settings–the Jameson distillery, of course, and various pubs in Galway and Dublin. I knew that whatever I chose to wear, he'd love, but I wanted something special, if for no other reason than to see his reaction.

In the window of one of the boutiques off Bond Street, I saw something that immediately caught my eye and thought of Kristen, who had told me long ago that red was my color. Matt had thought so, too.

I tried on the matching dark cherry set of pants and a low cut top, checking all angles in the mirror.

"My goodness, that looks amazing on you," said the shopkeeper in awe. "And with your *necklace.*"

I looked down at the stones that held the power of the Seas. She was right.

* * *

"Grand timing."

I turned and saw Seamus was rounding the corner outside of Sloane Square station right behind me. Darkness had already descended, as was customary for a winter afternoon in London, and I was glad to have an escort back to the house. Not that I thought I needed one for safety reasons in a neighborhood like his, but a soft snow was beginning to fall, covering the patches of ice that lined the sidewalks. I paused and waited for him to catch up.

He grinned and pointed to the bags I had in hand.

"Successful trip?"

"Yes," I said, blushing furiously as he placed a hand behind my back and bent down to kiss me on the head. "Thank you."

"Anything for ye, a stór," he replied.

We strolled at a leisurely pace, passing the coffee shops and other adorable houses that lined the streets of Seamus' neighborhood. Even after seeing them all, the ivory one with the black door was still my favorite.

"How much time do ye need to get ready?" he asked as he unlocked the front door.

I shrugged. "Maybe an hour?"

I took my time, noting that he seemed in no rush at all. I had learned over the years that it was a rarity amongst men to understand that it took time to get ready. Matt had always understood, much to the dismay of Kristen and Marissa. Their own boyfriends had been notoriously impatient with hair wash days and makeup routines.

This time when I re-entered Seamus' bedroom, I took more notice of what it actually looked like. The bed frame was made of dark cherry wood, matching the sleek dresser, and the walls were almost bare except for a Chelsea poster and a framed photo of him with a man who I guessed was Aidan, given their likeness. His older brother looked to be in his twenties in the photo, and Seamus in his teenage years. They had their arms around one another, and I wondered if it had been Saoirse who took it. I couldn't remember how old Seamus had been when she died.

The sheets beneath his white comforter were a dark moss, and I smiled, realizing that it seemed to be his signature color. Whether it was Ireland or his eyes that prompted me to do so, everything that was green reminded me of him.

I resisted the urge to further poke around, but noted that

there was no hint of a female presence ever having existed within the room. I didn't think there would be, considering how he treated me back in Dublin and of course how he treated me now, but I had been mildly wary of disappointment, nonetheless. I knew nothing of his romantic life prior to meeting me, whereas he knew everything about mine. I didn't know if I would ever ask at this point, because I knew that it just…didn't matter. There would be no one else ever again, for either of us. I was sure of it.

I stood in front of his full-length mirror some time later, pleased with the final product. My hair was falling well to the middle of my back, in loose soft curls of rich black that sparkled in a way my human hair had never been capable of doing. I had nearly forgotten how to use a curling iron in the months where I'd allowed the ocean to do it for me, but I was glad I had put in the extra effort tonight.

My makeup was relatively subtle–for no reason other than I had never been any good at it, having never had a mother or sister to teach me–but I ran a streak of black eyeliner on top that made my supernatural greenish-brown eyes pop. I suddenly felt inexplicably nervous, likely because I hadn't actively tried to impress a man with my looks in over a year. I knew I didn't need to with Seamus, but the sensation of *wanting* to was enough to make my stomach flip.

I stepped out into the living room where he was waiting for me, and he let out a whistle.

"*Christ,*" he said under his breath, doing nothing to hide his admiration as he looked me up and down.

"Forgot what I looked like on land, hmm?" I replied.

"Oh, no, that's branded in my memory for life," he mused, crossing the room and pulling me in for a kiss. "I just haven't seen ye like this in…"

He almost said "a long time," but stopped himself. Was three-ish months really a long time? That was how long it had been since we'd met.

"I can't believe that's all it's been," he said, touching my cheek as he spoke my thoughts.

"It feels much, much longer than that," I agreed.

He looked extremely handsome as well, wearing dark khakis and a navy button-down shirt that hugged his muscular chest and shoulders…no green tonight except his eyes. And of course the sleeves were rolled up to reveal his forearms, as was his signature. The demonic scar was certainly visible, but to a regular person I suppose it might have easily been explained as a plain tattoo with a strange shimmer to it.

I ran my finger along his actual tattoo of his mother's name on the opposite arm, noticing the solid black watch on his wrist. It had an almost entirely blank face aside from the number ticks and the brand name.

Hublot. I knew that one, having been on Bond Street only a few hours ago. The beautifully minimalist timepiece was exactly on brand for this version of Seamus that I was discovering–expensive as all hell, but subtle and sleek. It wasn't loud, flashy, or made of gold. It was just…sexy.

He peeled his gaze from mine after another moment and turned back toward the kitchen. "Drink?" he asked, gesturing to the wine fridge on the counter.

I swung the door open and peered inside curiously. It was a relatively impressive collection and I raised an eyebrow noting some of the years. I was certainly no sommelier, but I knew a decent amount about wine considering Raj's love of port. There had been far too many birthdays and Christmases where I defaulted to a bottle of something good rather than trying to reinvent the wheel.

"Do we still like this?" I asked, pointing to the shelves. "Alcohol?"

I assumed not, considering how terrible Artur's human food as well as regular mineral water had tasted to us. And coffee.

"Shit, I hope so," he said with a laugh. "Only one way to find out, aye?"

We uncorked a Sauvignon Blanc and he led me up the spiral staircase to the rooftop terrace, flipping on the outside light. He lit the fire pit I had noticed earlier, but there was no need. Had I been a human, I would have been freezing. But as a selkie with a blanket draped around my shoulders, it was perfect. The cold, November air was crisp with the scents of humanity and earth that made me feel alive.

"Come here," he said, reaching for my arm.

He pulled me onto his lap on the squishy chair and I watched the fire as we drank, discovering with relief that I *did* still enjoy the taste of wine. The first sip brought a wave of relaxation that melted the weight of the past few days from my shoulders.

I found it nearly impossible to believe that just hours ago, I had been trapped under a magical lake on a Norwegian island, attempting to bargain with a water nymph named Nøkken. Seamus rubbed my arm gently and mindlessly, signaling that his thoughts were far away as well.

"How long can we stay?" I asked, not wanting to know the answer, but feeling I needed it. "I'm worried about the stones."

He looked at me, his green eyes turning to amber as they caught the light of the fireplace.

"I think we should go to Carrickfergus a week from now," he said. "I want to give ye the life ye deserve, if only for a few days."

"Thank you," I said quietly. What I didn't say—out of shyness, I supposed—was that any life with him was more than I deserved. I had already been granted happiness with one partner in my life, and I couldn't believe I had gotten lucky enough for it to happen again.

"Shall we go?" he asked, finishing his glass.

We both still wore our gems, but his Citrine was hidden beneath his shirt. The Ammonite was glinting seductively on my exposed chest, the rainbow hues adding dimension to my overall colorful appearance.

I had placed the Thulite rather carelessly in my pocket, and Seamus recommended I embed it directly into the golden cuff around my wrist before we left.

"Aye, Artur showed me how to tuck the wee stones in there," he said. "Ye want it exposed or hidden?"

"Exposed," I said.

He wet his hand under the sink and then pressed his thumb to the gem, holding it for a few seconds like he was waiting for glue to dry. The pink stone seemed to melt the gold momentarily, sealing itself directly into the wall of the bracelet with a magical magnetic force. It glinted beautifully under the kitchen light, and looked as if I had picked it out at a jewelry store just as it was.

"That's amazing," I said, turning my wrist over.

"And solves the problem for where the rest will go as we find them," he said. "Beautiful as ye'd look, I don't think ten stones of Atargatis around your throat would be all that comfortable."

We put on our coats and stepped into the street. I thought of Aisling and Fintan, wondering if they ever did things like this. I knew they spent a few days in Spain, but did they have another dwelling on land that they used on a more regular basis? I found it hard to believe other selkies and mermaids didn't miss this type of living while perpetually under the sea. I had grown to appreciate who I was when I was a sea creature, but I needed this, too.

The heaviness I'd felt back in Norway seemed to vanish entirely as Seamus lifted me by the waist over a patch of ice and placed me gently on the other side. I felt light as air.

CHAPTER 32

FIRST DATE

We got off the tube in Mayfair, and Seamus led me inside a restaurant that smelled of deliciously smoked cocktails and general fine dining. It was beautifully decorated, with candles of soft gold plastered to the gray flecked walls where massive, copper statues of animal heads were lined up next to one another.

"Seamus," the hostess said, greeting him with bright familiarity. "Where have you been?"

He smiled back politely. "Away on business."

She nodded, as if this were a common occurrence. I had *never* seen the refined side of Seamus before until today, and it was highly intriguing to me. A house in Chelsea, and now a regular at an upscale restaurant in London's most expensive dining district? It almost amused me, because I knew it wasn't him. Not really.

I'd seen him swear like a sailor, knock a man out cold, and wrench open a dinosaur's jaw with his bare hands. He was rugged, no matter what he looked like right now. But I didn't mind it, since both versions were equally attractive to me.

"This is my girlfriend, Jasmine," he said.

I started at the sound of my name, wondering the same sentiment that had occurred to me back in Tampa. Would I be recognized as a missing person? My name wasn't extremely common, after all, and it hadn't happened too long ago...

But evidently Sky News had more interesting stories than an American tourist committing suicide in Ireland, because the young girl simply beamed at me from behind the stand without a hint of recognition in her face–just admiration that made me blush.

"Oh wow," the girl said, doing nothing to hide her awe as she took in my necklace, and perhaps my general appearance. I *was* supernatural, now, after all. "Such a pleasure to meet you, Jasmine. We'll take good care of you both tonight." She disappeared to grab our menus.

"Girlfriend," I remarked to him under my breath. "A little early to put a label on it, don't you think?"

I laughed at my own joke—the term sounded so immature given what we actually were to one another.

Seamus shook his head and grinned broadly. He then turned to look at me and opened his mouth to respond, but the hostess returned.

"This way," she said with another bright smile.

She led us to a table up the winding copper staircase, near the balcony overlooking the dining room below. A grand piano was staged in the center, where I was sure someone would inevitably sit down to play soon. My chest tightened for a moment, remembering the last time I had seen an empty piano at a restaurant—the time when Matt never showed up to play it because he had been in the accident that took his life.

No, I wasn't going to think about that tonight.

The server came to take our drink orders and Seamus deferred to me.

I ordered a gin cocktail, and him a Blanton's on a big rock. An order Matt would have placed.

"American bourbon?" I asked. "Are you trying to impress me?"

He laughed heartily as he took a sip of the dark liquid. "Bourbon's my favorite. To tell ye the truth, I don't like Irish whiskey at all."

"Ironic," I said. "Considering we met at the Jameson distillery."

He shook his head as he swirled the glass.

"That's just a Dublin tourist thing I had to do, aye?"

Before I could respond, our server returned with two small pours. No, *tiny* pours of something dark.

"Jack sent these up for you when he heard you were back from Ireland," she said, placing the delicate glasses on the table. "A *wee* taste of Emerald Isle whiskey." She exaggerated the accent the way I always did, and I laughed.

Seamus looked up at her in surprise.

"He didn't," he said.

"He did," she replied, smirking as she walked away.

I didn't know what it was, but I sensed it was *very* expensive.

Seamus shook his head incredulously before he handed me the small glass. I smiled back at him as we tapped them together.

"This will be the first and last taste ye get of that," he said, laughing. "Because no feckin' chance I can afford a bottle of it."

I raised an eyebrow and drank deeply, surprisingly thrilled with the taste.

"Oh shit," I acknowledged. "That's…good."

I had never loved whiskey, no matter what kind of expensive bottles Matt had gotten me to try. But I absolutely recognized a good one when I tasted it. This was one of them.

"A celebrity of London, are ye?" I said, mimicking his accent as best I could. "To have the owner send ye a wee taste of this."

He tossed his head back in laughter before he put a hand on my knee beneath the table. "I love when ye try and do that."

"Do what?" I asked, taunting him.

"Talk like you're from Norn Iron," he said. He took another sip, his eyes not leaving mine. I loved when he looked at me like that.

"Who do you usually come here with?" I asked. "Since they know you so well."

He looked at me and replied simply, "Myself."

"Liar," I said, even though I saw he was earnest.

"I mean it," he said, laughing. "It's a good place, so it is."

"Mmmhm," I said, sipping my gin martini with a raised brow. "Sure."

He sat back in his chair, his rugged demeanor returning as he ran a hand through his thick, red hair that was nearly as dark as the bottles of Cabernet on the bar behind him. I wondered if he knew how sexy it was when he did that, but I guessed not. I remembered from the night I met him that I thought he was relatively unaware of how good-looking he actually was. His unassuming humility had always been charming to me.

"I don't have other lovers, if that's what you're getting at," he said seriously. "And even if I did in the past, no one matters anymore besides ye. I hope ye know that's been the case since the day I met ye, Jasmine."

"I know," I said, shrugging. I did.

"Do ye?" he asked, leaning back in toward me, his jawline severe beneath the candlelight as a dark shadow was cast across his freckled cheeks. "Even here, in this setting, do ye believe me when I tell ye I'd bleed for ye?"

I remembered his blood-soaked face in Spain. When he emerged from Hell to come back to me.

"Yes."

"Good," he said simply.

We ordered our dinner, and I was relieved to go through yet another one of the motions of normality.

"This isn't bad for a first date," I said playfully. "I think I'll say yes to a second."

"And hopefully many more after that," he replied with a smirk.

I smiled back as I thought of how strange it would be to go back in time and be traditionally courted by Seamus. If I had lived in a different world where he'd asked me on a date and I'd nervously accepted, not knowing what to expect.

I couldn't imagine it, and I was glad I didn't know a world like that. This one was just fine.

Our food came, and of course it tasted like nothingness. Neither of us cared.

After we ate, we were out in the cold street once more and decided to take a scenic walk rather than head to the tube straight away. I knew we were going to see what else London nightlife had to offer before we headed home, but first I wanted to see Buckingham Palace at night.

"Have ye been here before?" Seamus asked, hands in his pockets as I peered through the tall gates in awe.

"Yes," I said wistfully. "With Matt. And Raj. At separate times."

He fell silent, allowing me to relive the memories for a moment by myself if I desired. I thought I'd want to recall them like I always did, but I didn't. Not tonight. I wanted to experience a new one as it happened.

"You know I used to dream as a girl," I said. "That one day I'd marry Prince Harry, become a princess, spend the holidays at Balmoral…all of that."

He let out a loud bark of laughter. "Christ, ye'd give the royals a run for their money with that mouth of yours."

"What?" I said, laughing. "You think I'd be worse than Meghan?"

"I think ye'd be a lot more formidable," he replied. "Ye'd play the game of thrones better than her, I think."

I took it as a compliment.

"I have a thing for redheads, I guess," I said, turning to face him. When he looked the way he did, his dark crimson waves lining his handsome face, how could I not?

"Is that right?" he laughed, picking me up off the ground and spinning me around. "Ye know it's an insult ye'd ever compare me to a Brit, Jasmine. One of the *Crown,* no less."

"Speaking of," I said suddenly. "Are you going to…"

I couldn't finish the sentence, but he knew what I meant. I wanted to know if he'd stage a reunion with James and the others the way I had done with Kristen and Marissa. If he'd find his British best friend, and explain his mysterious nearly three-month absence to him.

"Aye, I will," he sighed. "Tomorrow. But just James."

He looked into the distance and I touched his cheek softly, his faint freckles shuddering beneath my fingertips in the cold.

"I still have to decide what to tell them," he said quietly. "Explain why I didn't come back sooner. And explain how you're even *here*."

Yes, we would have to explain that despite the County Clare police department recovering my clothes and other belongings that had been smashed against the side of the Cliffs of Moher, I was actually not dead. I wondered for a moment what Kristen and Marissa had done–if anything–since I had seen them in Tampa. Had they told people I was alive? Did anyone care?

I repeated what I had said back in Atlântida. "We've been in Spain and Portugal."

Seamus inhaled sharply and looked at me, his green eyes peering into my very soul.

"Aye, I *could* say that," he said, his hand falling into mine as we lazily wandered by the gates. The other remained in his pocket. "But I thought of something else."

"Have you, then?" I asked, this time harnessing my British accent. "*Do* tell, mate."

He smirked at my attempt, but kept walking straight ahead.

"That's right," he said, then turning to me. "Something that would explain it all away. Something I knew I wanted from ye since the day I met ye, anyway."

I had no idea what he meant, but as my eyes met his, I saw something like shyness behind his smile. Or was it nervousness?

"What's that?" I asked earnestly.

His piercing stare reflected every single thing–human or supernatural–that we had been through together.

He knelt for me.

"I want ye to be mine, in every way possible," he said. "I've seen what it is to live without ye, and I don't want to see it again. I'd rather die."

Oh, *that's* what he meant.

My breath caught in my chest as I looked down.

Seamus extended a hand that held an elegant platinum ring adorned with a massive, emerald-shaped jewel that I recognized instantly. It was not from the collection of Atargatis, but I knew this stone.

It was pale, yet somehow brilliant at the same time. Cornflower in color that was nearly white under direct light, it was unmistakably a blue diamond.

Found exclusively in South Africa, India, or Australia, the blue diamond was one of nature's most beautiful anomalies–forged by the chance presence of boron within the stone's carbon structure during its formation deep within the earth's core. I knew all about them, because Marie Antoinette had had one–The Queen's Heart, it was called. And because of my father's interest in all things relating to scientific discovery, I remember my jaw dropping to the floor when I read that The Oppenheimer Blue had sold at auction for over fifty million dollars back in 2016.

This was one of the most sought-after gems in the world, and it was for me.

Whatever I had expected Seamus' explanation for our disappearance to be, it wasn't this—that we ran away and got married. But he wasn't doing this for the sake of an alibi. I knew him better than that. Seamus wanted me forever.

"Jasmine, I know it's soon, and I hope ye'll forgive me for asking something so bold when I don't deserve it," he continued. "But will ye do me the honor of being my wife?"

I didn't even think. It was almost silly to view our union as something so simple as *marriage* when we were bound to one another in so many other, deeper ways.

There was nothing to decide. From the moment Seamus entered my life, he owned my entire soul.

"Yes. Yes."

He smiled widely as he slipped the ring around my finger. As I looked at the gem that was equally impossible to find as it was to buy, I knew immediately that Artur had something to do with procuring it. *This* was the treasure he had been researching, and in the morning hours they had been preparing for our journey to Norway, he and Seamus had been secretly vanishing through Green Windows to dig for this relic somewhere at the bottom of the sea.

This was a diamond that Seamus had gone to the ends of the earth to find. There was nowhere he wouldn't go for me.

He stood, wrapping his hand around the back of my neck as he kissed me deeply, his lips curving into a smile against mine. I had melted when he called me his *girlfriend* for the first time only hours earlier, and now I was going home as his *fiancée*.

I hoped, despite what my dreams made me believe, that Matt would be happy for me.

CHAPTER 33

EXECUTIVE DECISIONS

I woke up like I was still dreaming, looking out the window of the beautiful townhouse and wishing I could stay here forever. I never thought I'd love a perpetually gray sky as much as I did at that moment, knowing it was enabling me to live in my perfect existence for a few more days.

It was hard to imagine that the fate of the oceans was in my hands when I was living a milestone that so many other, ordinary people lived. The morning after I got engaged.

I never thought I'd be experiencing that morning here–with this man, in this life, but I was certainly happy I was.

Seamus placed his arm on top of me and inhaled my hair from behind.

"My fiancée," he said into my ear. "Even that doesn't sound like enough."

"Wife?" I offered.

"There's not a word grand enough for ye, a stór."

I knew what he meant. I turned to face him and marveled at the ring, taking it off to hold between us in the light of the morning.

"It's beautiful," I said. "Thank you."

"I'm glad ye like it," he said.

I slipped it back on my finger and pulled him in for a kiss. I couldn't help but remember the faint embarrassment I had felt when Elias' smug face had beheld my bare finger back in Atlântida, smirking as if Seamus' lack of marking his territory meant he could have me if he wanted me. A smirk that would be wiped off his face instantly when he saw this rock.

But then I remembered he had betrayed us and I'd never see him again if I could help it. His crude jokes, once mildly funny, now seemed like such an obvious ploy to disarm me. To weaken my senses. And it worked. I felt a surge of annoyance for my stupidity, as well as the fact I was thinking about him at all.

"I've got to go see James today," Seamus said, bringing me back to the present.

I sighed. "Yes, you should."

"But first," he said, pulling me on top of him.

We surprisingly still hadn't been together since our arrival the day before, because last night I had been so happily exhausted. And maybe a little drunk. We had, of course, gone to celebrate our engagement at three (four?) more establishments in the lively city after the ring was on my finger. I rubbed my head now, hoping mermaids didn't get hangovers.

I smiled and lifted the Chelsea t-shirt of his I had slept in over my head, throwing it off to the side as I bent down to kiss him.

"*Fuck*," he sighed softly, staring up at me in awe. I felt a wave of satisfaction ripple through me at his admiration of my figure, knowing I felt the same about his own.

He held my hips for a moment before running his hand up my back and into my hair, pressing me closer to him. I absently ran my thumb across the diamond on my finger and smiled to myself. I always knew what I was to Seamus, but still. It felt nice to see it, even if it was horribly old-fashioned to admit it.

He rolled me onto my back and grazed his lips along the side of my neck, his hand slipping between my legs. I gasped as his fingers entered me, and I felt him smirk against my skin.

"I love when ye do that," he said into my ear. "When ye let me know I'm pleasing ye."

"Of course you are," I said back. He always did.

"Aye, well I live to serve the goddess of the sea, even on land," he replied.

He ran his thumb across the most sensitive skin between my legs before removing his fingers from within me and wrapping his hand behind my neck, the other on the headboard. He pushed himself inside me, sighing as he closed his eyes and I did the same.

This time I swore, letting the familiar waves wash over me as he slowly made love to me. He spoke to me here and there in the way he always did, calling me '*cailín álainn*' like he had when I first met him. The Irish translation for *lovely girl* took on a much different meaning when I was under him.

I reached up and brought his face to mine, my ring glinting as it ran beneath his rich, auburn waves.

"I want more of you," I breathed.

His green eyes looked at me with the faintest hint of darkness. "Then ye'll have it."

He knew what I meant. He was gentle when I wanted him to be, but powerful when I was craving that, too. It was the type of chemistry that I had never thought could be real until the first time we were together; when he had taken me so assertively that it surprised me how much I liked it. He did it again now, turning me around and bringing me up to my knees with one arm, the other still tightly gripping the headboard. I sank my hands into the pillow in front of me, moving my hair across one shoulder as he kissed the other from behind me. I sighed as he gave me everything he had.

As I felt the current starting to pull at me, I thought that my mild, yet unrelenting guilt might soon cease now that we were engaged. Now that this wasn't just a fling from my trip to Ireland–even though we both knew it had always been more than that. I hadn't had a horrible dream since my nights alone in Atlântida, but I still remembered what Matt had said to me in them.

I felt a fleeting twinge of sorrow that Seamus was now more to me than Matt had ever been; at least on paper. Several years with Matt, erased by three months with someone else. Someone else who had proposed to me without asking when I had made Matt wait years to do the same. And because of the timeline I had imposed upon him, he had never gotten to do it at all.

But Seamus didn't ask for permission. Not for anything. He would take what was his, and because I loved him so fervently, I wanted him to.

I let him take me under.

* * *

IT WAS A FRIDAY, so Seamus knew that James and the others would be at work. As I had rendered the cell phone errand unnecessary, we knew our best bet was attempting to literally run into him on the streets of London near their office. Seamus hoped it would just be James that we'd see, not wanting to cause a scene with the whole gang. I privately agreed with the desire, primarily because I hardly remembered the others at all. I didn't know *what* they had thought of me back then, but they surely wouldn't have a high opinion of the American tourist that Seamus had abandoned his entire life for now. I hoped James would go easier on me, even though I didn't deserve it.

We got off the tube at Monument and stepped into the financial district where the cold November air whipped against my face. The collection of tall buildings created a brutal wind tunnel that I was eager to get away from, but no matter how quickly we walked, we couldn't escape it. I ignored the moderate pain that was running down my legs as we made our way along the street—the sun wasn't bright by any means, but it was peeking through the clouds today.

"It'll be fine," Seamus muttered as he resumed his familiar morning commute. I think he was talking to himself rather than me.

We rounded the corner just past Leadenhall Market and a few moments later, Seamus came to a halt directly in front of a massive silver building with countless tube-shaped windows running up the sides. It wasn't exactly as famous as The Gherkin, but it was still somewhat of a historical landmark so I knew what it was. It was Lloyd's of London.

"Insurance?" I questioned, thinking he had grossly downplayed what he did for a living.

I looked straight up at the modern building that housed what was the original birthplace of the entire global industry. Because I had done an architectural tour of the city with Raj as a kid, I knew that what had started in the 17th century as a modest hub for marine risk management was now the most powerful insurance marketplace in the world.

Seamus grinned. "Aye, I'd love to show you my office, but I think I've been sacked by now."

I couldn't help but laugh. Whatever his colleagues had thought his fate had been for the past three months, we could guarantee that he was no longer employed. Seamus glanced down at his watch. It was nearly nine in the morning, so it wouldn't be long.

I saw him before Seamus did.

James was approaching from the south, wearing a clean, black suit and tie with a cup of coffee in one hand and a backpack hanging off one shoulder. He looked so incredibly normal, and I tried to imagine Seamus dressed the same and doing the same. I couldn't. Even when completely alone, he had a jovial, welcoming smile on his face. I hoped it would stay that way once he saw us.

Seamus turned as he saw me staring. That's when his friend spotted us both.

Just as Marissa had done, he dropped his drink. The dark coffee splattered all over the sidewalk and directly onto his clean shoes. My questions regarding whether or not my own friends had told him they'd seen us were answered. Apparently not.

"What the *bloody* hell–" James whispered as he stared in shock.

His eyes scanned us from head to toe, and I could see the confusion beneath his gaze–not just for our general existence, but for the attributes of our physical appearances. Seamus and I were undoubtedly different from the way he remembered, even if he couldn't put his finger on exactly what had changed.

"All right, mate?" Seamus asked tentatively.

Without responding, James reached out for Seamus and pulled him into a crushing embrace. I thought he might shed a tear, so I looked down at my shoes to give them a moment. James was Seamus' best friend of nearly a decade, and they'd never gone more than a few days without speaking. To have experienced radio silence from Seamus for almost three months was more than cause for concern.

"You gave me a right good scare, I'll tell you that," was all James said.

He then looked at me, his eyes widening as he shook his head in disbelief.

"And *you*," he said, reaching for me and gently shaking my shoulders as if to ensure I was really there. "Jasmine, we thought– I mean, everyone thought…"

"I know, but I'm not," I said, not knowing if I should smile or look apologetic. Whatever he thought of our disappearance, he was receiving us much better than my own friends had.

"I owe ye an explanation," Seamus said seriously.

"I'd say so," James acknowledged, taking a step back and looking between us with the same incredulous stare. "Let's… come on, let's go–"

He started to motion for the doors of the massive building in front of us, then stopped.

"Ah…yeah, I suppose you don't want to be going up there right now, do you?" he said, surveying Seamus with a grin. "Bet ye'd be *up to feckin' ninety* with all the work you've missed, aye?"

Seamus laughed at his friends' attempt at Irish slang and shook his head.

"Come on then," James continued. "This way."

We walked about a block before ducking into a coffee shop where we sat in a secluded corner away from the noisy street and other customers. James' eyes darted to my ring almost immediately.

"Oh, I see," he said, nodding his head and grinning. "Ran away to get married, did you?"

Excellent. He'd already gotten to the point, so we didn't have to.

"That's right," Seamus said. He lifted my hand to show him the ring more closely. The blue diamond was magnificent, even in the fluorescent light.

"Blimey, that's nice," James said, peering into the stone with intrigue. He then looked between us and said awkwardly, "Is it because you're–"

He caught himself, clearly not wanting to suggest that we had only gotten married out of obligation rather than passionate, sudden love. I already guessed what he was going to ask. Even before we left the house that morning, I knew he'd assume. Everyone would.

"No, I'm not pregnant," I said flatly. Seamus squeezed my hand.

James nodded and grinned.

"Sorry, I had to ask," he said. "Then…what happened?"

He stared at us expectantly, and I inhaled sharply. Seamus told him a very brief–and extremely vague–story of us deciding to elope in Portugal and going on a quick trip to Spain for our honeymoon. He said how we would have called, but we just wanted to enjoy some time alone. We were so wildly distracted and in love that we simply didn't think of anyone's concern., and we were deeply sorry we had let everyone worry about us.

James didn't buy a damn word of it. I knew he wouldn't.

"Now I know that's rubbish," he said seriously, his smile fading. "Come on, Seamus. Why didn't you call?"

Seamus looked at me, and I bit my lip apprehensively. I didn't know what to do.

"Jasmine," James said, turning to me.

I gulped.

"You know they found your clothes," he said in barely a whisper. "You were all over the news in Ireland…and in America. And even here, for a while. They declared you *dead.*"

"I know," was all I could say. It sounded like a pathetic squeak–nothing at all like my real voice. As he said it, the hair on the back of my neck prickled.

James pressed on. "And Seamus…mate, you ran away from your life and career without a word. I'd never have thought you'd do something that thick."

I squeezed Seamus' hand as I looked up at him.

'Should we just tell him?' my eyes said. I hoped he could hear me like he sometimes could, but I didn't think Atargatis and her stones would get involved in a matter like this. It wasn't her business. It was our own decision to make.

Seamus seemed to be having an excruciating internal debate that was not lost on James.

"What?" James pressed, and I saw the hurt behind his eyes. "What is it you're not telling me?"

I made the decision for us, for no reason other than I couldn't bear it any longer. James deserved the truth. He was Seamus' best friend. Additionally, we had never been explicitly *instructed* that we weren't allowed to tell our human friends what we were…but as supernatural creatures from fairy tales do, we sort of just *knew* it was against the "rules".

But James would be the only person that would know the truth. I didn't count Aidan if and when we reunited with him, because he already knew about the legends to some degree…and of course the same went for Kiana. If and when I'd ever see her again, only Manannán knew.

"We have to show you," I said with a sigh. I felt Seamus tense beneath my hand, but he didn't stop me. "But not now. Will you meet us tonight?"

Undoubtedly perturbed by our demeanor but intrigued enough to agree, James nodded his head in dismay.

"Yeah, alright," he said. "Name the time and place."

CHAPTER 34

THE WHOLE TRUTH

Seamus and I returned to the townhouse and he was quiet, contemplating what had just happened and what we were about to do.

"Was it a mistake, coming back?" he asked me, rubbing his nose as he leaned against the doorframe.

"I don't think it was," I said from across the kitchen, holding up my hand to display my ring.

Even aside from my new jewelry, I had been having a wonderful time in London, and I knew he had, too. We would deal with what happened next, like we always did.

He looked up at me with a smirk.

"I could've given ye that in the ocean," he said. "Would've been a lot easier than hiding it in there." He pointed to the golden cuff from Artur that was sitting on the kitchen island.

So *that* was the stone he taught him to hide. I recalled our conversation from the previous night when he had asked me if I wanted the Thulite exposed or concealed on my own bracelet.

"No, I'm glad you asked me here," I said, meeting him on the other side of the island and wrapping my hands around his neck. He picked me up and placed me on the countertop where we were eye-level with one another. "As much as I'd love a loose stone from the bottom of the ocean, I think it was best that you had it put on a ring…so I won't lose it."

He laughed.

"Aye, it made for a challenge, finding a reputable jeweler in London who would cut and set a blue diamond with no trace of its origins in one day," he said, shaking his head. "The peelers are out looking for me already, I suspect."

I reached for his hand, knowing he was avoiding the topic of James on purpose. I brought him back to it.

"He won't tell anyone," I said in a quiet voice. "He's your best friend."

"I'm not worried about that so much," Seamus said with a sigh. "I just dunno how he'll react when he sees…"

"I know," I said. It was the same reason I didn't want to show Kristen and Marissa what I was.

"We both *became* this," Seamus said, gesturing between us. "That's a hell of a lot different than watching someone else turn into one, so it is."

"Yes," I acknowledged. "But this is much better than him thinking you're lying to him."

I thought of Kiana again as I spoke. Surely Marissa and Kristen would have told her they saw me by now, and she would've figured out that she and Seamus had been right all along. I hoped that if I ever got the chance to show her what I was, she wouldn't shriek in terror while watching my legs turn into a tail.

* * *

WE SET OUT AFTER DARK, both of us silent as we emerged from the underground at Tower Hill. Seamus took my hand and we swept beneath the beautifully illuminated Tower Bridge, slipping into the darkness that fell just on the other side. I could see he still wasn't sure that we were making the right decision, but there was no turning back now.

After a brisk ten minute walk, we reached the spot where we'd agreed to meet–right where a small drawbridge separated the marina from the River Thames. I looked out at the black water, watching the moon dance across the surface.

St. Katherine's Docks wasn't exactly an inconspicuous place, but it was certainly quieter than the rest of Central London during the winter months. And of course, the main reason I had thought of it was that it provided the one thing we needed to show James what we were. Water.

"What's the craic?" came a voice from behind us.

I turned around and saw James laughing, amused by his own attempt at Seamus' accent again, and I smiled.

"Going to throw me in, are you?" James asked, pointing to the river behind me.

"There's some rubbish even the Thames won't tolerate," Seamus quipped back.

James grinned and smacked his friend on the back. "Good to see you're still the *wee skitter* I remember."

I smiled and then cleared my throat. I didn't know how to properly introduce what was about to happen, so I settled on the only thing that made sense.

"Don't be alarmed," I said to him. "When you see."

Before James could reply, Seamus hoisted himself up and over the drawbridge in one swift motion, dropping into the tiny inlet of water below with a loud splash. I followed right behind him.

"Are you *mad?*" James yelled, rushing to lean over the ledge.

We tumbled in the black water of the filthy river that slowly began to clear for us as we became creatures that were capable of dwelling in places like it. I opened my eyes and the lamplight returned, lighting my way through the murkiness where Seamus' hand was reaching for mine. We emerged on the surface in the darkness of the London night, flicking our tails above the water so James could see them.

He took one look at us and turned frighteningly pale. I thought he was about to faint.

Instead, he threw up.

"Up ye go," Seamus said, reaching a hand of assistance down to the sputtering James.

Seamus' tail had already melted back into the dark green pants he had been wearing, and his friend was rubbing his eyes in disbelief.

"How did you–but you just–" he looked at Seamus' legs and back at me, still lingering in the water with my elbows propping me up on the dock. I nearly laughed, but I refrained because I knew he was probably afraid.

Seamus then helped me out of the water, scooping me up while still on his knees. Since my transformation took longer, we waited on the dock and James' eyes went wide as he marveled at my iridescent tail in the moonlight. I felt self-conscious, but not in the way I had been under Elias' gaze. This time, I felt like I was an animal in a museum. One that was incredibly rare and border-line frightening. I didn't know whether to make eye contact with him or not, so I looked at Seamus instead. He was smiling.

"Bloody hell," James said quietly, reaching for my scales with curiosity. "Can I–"

"Sure," Seamus nodded, and I raised an eyebrow of amusement that he thought James was asking *him* permission to touch *me*.

"Yes, you can," I said pointedly, looking at Seamus who smirked back.

"Possessive asshole," I thought. He winked at me.

"This is unbelievable," James said, running his hand along my scales.

His voice was riddled with amazement as my lower half slowly began to fade into the night, signaling my transformation was beginning. After a moment, my legs reappeared in my jeans, the denim materializing and falling into place as if it had been there all along. I imagined my hair the same way I had in the oasis room, and it fluttered once in the wind before drying instantly.

While James was certainly dumbstruck, I was relieved to see that he didn't run away in fear. In fact, he looked fascinated. I glanced up at Seamus and saw his shoulders had relaxed in the wake of his friend's reaction as well.

Once I was fully changed, we all stood and stared at one another on the dock. The sound of the gentle, black waves lapping against the wood was all that existed between us for a long moment.

"How did this happen?" James asked. His voice was barely more than a whisper.

Seamus put his hands in his pockets and rocked back on his heels as he let out a deep breath. "It's a long story, so it is."

"I've got time, mate," James replied. "Shall we grab a pint?"

I smiled. "Let's do it."

We began the walk back toward civilization, leaving the freezing cold water of the Thames–and his shock–behind us. The wave of relief had washed over all three of us now that the truth had been revealed, and I knew that from this point forward, nothing we told him would be too burdensome to share.

The mention of a pub reminded me that Seamus and I hadn't actually eaten what we needed in several days. We had gone through the last of our stores of seaweed that Artur had given us, but it was definitely time for more. I knew the Thames would have the plant we needed, but I imagined it would taste similar to the less-than-preferable lagoon seaweed we'd had back in Porto. Seamus turned on his heel and took one more dive to the bottom of the marina, emerging with a blackish brown clump that looked positively disgusting.

"Don't tell me you're going to eat that," James said, his nose wrinkled in disgust.

But we did, and it actually wasn't as bad as it looked.

We made our way to a pub called The Dickens and sat at a table near the window, James still shaking his head in awe as he undoubtedly replayed the scene of us in his head.

"I *thought* you looked different," he said, taking a swig of his beer and pointing at me. "Your eyes were brown before, weren't they? They're still brown…but there's this bright green some-where in there now, too."

I nodded, remembering the electric rim around my irises.

"They flicker a bit, too," he said to both of us. "Like a fish. It's bloody eerie, to be honest. Back there in the water, it looked like they were glowing in the dark."

Seamus laughed and I looked at him sideways, seeing nothing but the beautiful emeralds that had made me fall in love with him. I knew we looked different to others, but I was glad we still looked the same to each other.

We told him more about what we had been through, and James was fascinated by it all, particularly our time in Atlântida and the fact that Seamus' mother had been a mermaid as well. I didn't know how much James knew about Seamus' upbringing, but he seemed familiar with the story of Saoirse's traumatic death to some degree. I noticed that Seamus skipped over the part about his dealings with The Santa Compaña entirely, and I didn't blame him. There were some things–disturbing things–that his friend simply didn't need to know.

But we did tell him about the stones. The Amalgams, and our race to find the gems before them. And of course, because it was impossible to explain *why* we were so strongly obligated to do such a thing without mentioning it, we told him who I was.

"Atargatis," James said, rolling the name around on his tongue as he didn't–*couldn't*–understand what it really meant.

But as he heard of the stone leading Seamus to the mystical

island to find me, he understood that it made what existed between us so much more significant than the average relationship. He understood why we were engaged after knowing each other for a total of three months, and he understood why it meant we had to go back under the sea.

"It's your duty, innit?" he said. "To find the stones before the others do."

"It is," we said at the same time.

James told us all about what we had missed, carefully glossing over the anger that most of them had felt during Seamus' radio silence. Apparently Seamus had been granted a sabbatical at work despite not asking for one or even acknowledging that he was gone, but James had pushed for it on his behalf. I felt Seamus tense with guilt.

"So since you're going back," James said, his eyes dropping to his lap. "When will I...when will I see you two again?"

He was hopeful. I saw it in his eyes. He didn't want this to be goodbye forever.

"We'll be back when this is over," Seamus said. "Ye have my word."

"Don't break it, mate," James said, his eyes twinkling.

We wouldn't.

* * *

THE NEXT FEW days were pure bliss. With our most difficult obligation out of the way, we now felt like we could truly relax and enjoy the city. James arranged for us to meet up with the others in his and Seamus' friend group, and because *they* weren't Seamus' best friends for nearly a decade, they didn't seem suspicious at all when we explained that we'd wildly eloped on a whim.

"He was a pathetic bloke for you from the beginning," Harry

said to me with a shrug. "I'm not surprised. I actually said I thought he'd run off with her, didn't I?"

Jack and Benjamin murmured in agreement, and Seamus winked at me from across the bar. I blushed.

We did all of the London tourist must-dos for my sake, while Seamus took me to all of his favorite places around the city. The days of exploration included both the well-known spots in Westminster, Covent Garden, and Kensington, as well as areas with which I was much less familiar like Battersea, Marylebone, and Camden Market. There was only one single day where the sunlight bothered me at all, and we opted to duck inside the British Museum to pass the time.

"I'm glad we did this," I said to him, wandering along the rows of artifacts from Japan on one of the upper floors. I knew we'd be going there next, so I scanned the glass cases for any hints regarding mermaid treasure. There were none, considering a museum was a place of facts rather than fantasy.

"Aye, me too," Seamus replied, kissing the ring on my hand. He stood next to me, surveying the samurai armor I'd been admiring. "Where do ye think it is?"

He meant the stone of Japan—or *Yamato* as Duarte had referred to it—and I had no idea. One of the smaller, outer islands, I assumed. I shook my head in dismay, moving on to observe a case of Jōmon ceramics. I settled on a pair of beautifully ornate white and orange elephants, realizing that the thirty-thousand years during which the Japanese islands had been inhabited was certainly ample time for someone—indeed, *many* someones—to hide a stone of Atargatis and subsequently move it around. The odds of us finding it now...

No, I couldn't think that way. We'd found the others, after all. We could do it again.

"I can't say," I said, turning to Seamus with a sigh. "I'll have to just feel it."

"Ye will," he said confidently.

We perused the remaining relics in the next room, the remnants of the Shoguns taking up the majority of the floor. I thought of the constant struggle for power that existed across the world, seeing now that endless conflict was an entirely seamless theme from land to sea.

I hoped that history would remember our side of the cause as the righteous one.

CHAPTER 35

BACK TO THE SEA

The morning of our decided departure arrived, and I sighed as I woke up in the beautiful townhouse for the last time in who knew how long. The week had been an absolute dream of feigned regularity and romance in light of our engagement, and I was relieved to find that being with Seamus in the normal world was just as incredible as it was in the fantasy realm.

Although we didn't sleep much, we spent a lot of time in bed, which was something I knew I'd miss dearly once my tail returned. I was sad to go, but I had gotten the rest and relief that I needed.

Seamus was already downstairs, rummaging around for something.

"What are you looking for?" I asked.

We couldn't bring anything with us, after all. Artur's cuffs could fit about a single credit card and maybe some cash. Each of us only had one, and Seamus still insisted on carrying his dagger in his, which took up a good amount of space.

"The wee box for the ring," he replied. "I thought ye might want it."

I shrugged. "It's not like I'll ever take it off."

He smiled and brought my hand to his lips, kissing the blue diamond as his eyes met mine.

"I hope not."

We decided it was best to get as close to the coast of Ireland as possible from the other side of the water in order to save ourselves time and energy for the journey. The Thames seaweed certainly did nothing for our strength which was noticeably fading, and I didn't think I could endure an entire swim around the English Channel and back up to Belfast.

I had initially suggested flying, but we both quickly shut down the idea since I had no form of identification–a realization that hit me in the gut. I hadn't thought of it once until that moment, and then I broke out in a nervous sweat as the reminder of my ghostly disappearance descended upon me again. Would I ever be Jasmine Atarga again? Or would I remain dead to the world, and take the new name of Jasmine McCarthy, used only when I needed a passport or other ID? *Would* I ever need those things again, now that I could navigate the seas? Where could a plane go that I couldn't get to faster?

We arrived at Euston Station and boarded our train to Liverpool. During the journey that was just under two and a half hours, I fell in and out of sleep, lazy daydreams coming to me in spurts that were all jumbled with one another. As I drifted, I saw scenes of the news, labeling my death as both a tragic accident as well as a suicide–as if the reporters couldn't decide which made for a better story.

While the countryside flew by me, I was reminded of Matt again. On our own trip to England, we had made a last minute decision to go to a Manchester United match, taking the train from London and planning to take it back in the same day. It was an ambitious itinerary that resulted in us missing the train entirely and sitting on a bench at the same station that Seamus and I had just left.

.   .   .

"Sʜɪᴛ," Matt said, looking up at the departure screen. "I got the time wrong."

I was irritated, but I didn't want to show it. After all, I hardly cared about soccer. Or *football,* as I supposed it was called here.

"It's fine," I shrugged lazily, suppressing a yawn. "European clocks are stupid, anyway."

It always took my brain an extra minute to decipher the time once I passed 13:00, no matter how embarrassing it was to admit.

Matt let out a hollow laugh.

"No, I have no excuse," he said as he shook his head. Of course reading a twenty-four hour clock was customary for him considering he was a medical professional. "I'm really sorry, Jazz."

"It's fine," I repeated.

He looked at me with his hands in his pockets as we contemplated what our alternative plan for the evening would be. It was still early afternoon, and we had plenty of time to figure something else out. He paused his pacing to look down at me.

"You didn't want to go, did you?"

I shrugged.

"Not really," I said, and then I remembered how ridiculously expensive our tickets had been and I felt apologetic. I looked up at him and bit my lip. "Sorry."

"We didn't have to, Jazz!" Matt exclaimed earnestly. "I don't care."

"Please," I said. "You were dying to go. And that's why I wanted to."

"I appreciate that," he said, taking my hand. "But it's no big deal."

It was a small memory, but a significant one that reminded me of so many others.

I loved seeing Matt happy. In the many years that I knew him, I had never seen his joy dimmed by anything. Of course, everyone had bad days, but there was nothing but pure goodness inside him—and anyone within his orbit knew him to be a special kind of person. Nothing was ever the end of the world to him; not even a complete loss on expensive tickets to a game he had wanted to see.

To watch Matt get excited about anything was a gift to me. So I did a lot of things with him that I didn't truthfully care to do. Just to see his light.

I CAME BACK to the present, looking at Seamus' strong side profile as he stared out the window. I pictured him drinking the blood of a demon, his lips covered in liquid onyx. Him holding a dagger at Elias' throat and only refraining from slicing it because I asked him to. Him pressing me into the ground while he made urgent, nearly forceful love to me.

Seamus was not light. He had darkness in him.

He must have sensed my gaze upon him, because he then turned and began to study me from across the aisle, his green eyes scanning me from my face down to my hands, all the way to the blue diamond that marked me as his.

"What is it?" I asked, sensing something was on his mind. I spoke first, because I didn't want him to ask what was on *mine.*

He sighed and leaned forward, hands on his knees. "I've been thinking about something ye said," he began. "To James."

I didn't reply, silently urging him to continue.

"When he asked where we'd been and ye said you're not... pregnant," he said, his gaze returning to the passing countryside of England out the window.

I stared at him blankly, unsure why it mattered.

"But I'm not."

"I know," he said slowly. "But the way ye said it so fast...like it would be terrible if ye were."

"It would be," I said with a disbelieving laugh, recalling my conversation with Artur back in Tampa. The conversation that scared me enough to ingest an emergency contraceptive from inside of an oyster shell. "Right now, anyway."

"Right now, maybe," he agreed. "But I hope ye don't always feel that way."

The pause that followed was loaded with unspoken thoughts I didn't dare to say.

I *had* wondered what his thoughts on the matter of children were, and now I knew. I hadn't wanted to even hope, fearing the disappointment I'd feel if we disagreed on something so integral when I had already fallen in love with him. I was relieved to know we didn't, even if it wasn't a possibility right now.

"Of course I won't," I whispered.

I looked at him, abstract scenes of him as a father rushing through my head. Scenes that I wanted to see in real life. Scenes that were lovely.

"So ye would want a child?" he asked me tentatively. "One day?"

I nodded. "Would you?"

"I would," he said, reaching for my hand. He ran his thumb along my palm where the scar that had started it all was etched for life. I felt a faint tingle at his touch; a softer version of the electric shock I'd experienced when he touched it for the first time back in Ireland. "I can't imagine anything I'd love more than to see ye as the mother of my children."

I beamed at his words, but I was embarrassed.

"I'd be lousy at it," I said, thinking of the fact that I had never had a mother of my own.

There had been no one to show me the ropes for my own eventual attempt at motherhood. I'd meet Aine soon, but I was nearly thirty now. It was too late to experience the same things that would have been so precious in my formative years.

I didn't know what it was like, to be held by your mother after a tough day at school, a fight with a friend, or when you cried over a boy. I was raised by Raj alone, and I never wanted to talk to him about any of those things. I'd dealt with those raw emotions primarily on my own, which was likely why I was terrible at expressing anything of the sort to the man across from me.

"No," Seamus said seriously. "I know ye'd be grand at it."

I kissed his hand, rubbing it appreciatively.

"And you would be a wonderful father," I said. "I know it."

"I dunno about that," he said.

His eyes flickered this time with sadness, undoubtedly because he was thinking along similar lines as I was. His father had been horrible. There had been no one for him to look up to besides Aidan, and his older brother was troubled in his own ways.

"You would," I assured him.

I squeezed his hand before laying my head against the window, daydreaming about what it would be like to have a child with Seamus.

He would be a wonderful *girl* dad, I was sure of that. But then again…my heart would explode to see a miniature version of him. A little redheaded trouble-maker with natural athleticism and a smile that would melt your heart. Yes, I thought we'd love to have a son. I looked at his handsome Irish features and hoped our child would have more of him than me. More adorable freckles, rich red hair, and his green eyes. Oh, his eyes…

"What did he do for a living?" Seamus asked, shaking me from my thoughts.

I looked up, knowing he meant Matt, but I didn't know why he was asking. Perhaps because he was wondering if my late fiancé and I had ever had the same discussion about kids and what my answer had been back then.

"Matt was a doctor," I said quietly.

Seamus grinned and rolled his eyes.

"Oh, Christ, of course he was," he laughed. "The man saved

lives for a living, did he? Does he have to be better than me in every way?"

I smiled and looked down at my feet. Matt was better than *everyone*. It wasn't a fair comparison. But I didn't say that out loud.

"There weren't too many emergencies in pediatrics, but yes, every now and then," I said.

Seamus' eyes widened and I couldn't help but laugh this time.

"A *children's* doctor no less," he said. "Well, feck me, I know who would've been a better father of the two of us."

I clucked my tongue and attempted my best Norn Iron accent. "*Catch yerself on.*"

He laughed, but I knew there was a tiny bit of truth to what he said. I didn't know how to respond, knowing that while it was *technically* true–Matt would certainly know more about the ailments of our children should they have any–it wasn't the only factor that was relevant. Not even close.

I hated the constant comparison that my mind seemed to force me to draw between the two of them, but I didn't blame Seamus for asking questions here and there. He'd be naturally curious. He had no idea, after all, what truly went on in my dreams. I'd certainly never tell him.

He spared me from spiraling too deeply into my own thoughts as he changed the subject.

"London was so nice with ye," he said. "When it's done, would ye want to live like that all the time?"

"What–never return to the sea?" I asked.

"Would we need to?" he asked, shrugging. "Would we *want* to, when our job's done?"

Our job. Harnessing the power of the seas by finding all of the remaining stones and stealing back those that were already in the enemy's hands, and then somehow ensuring their safekeeping for the rest of eternity. Simple.

"I don't know," I said truthfully.

The absurdity of us sitting here, two lovers deciding upon our main dwelling being the land or sea was a notion that would have made me laugh had it not been my own choice to make. "I think I'd like a mixture of both. What about you?"

"Aye, I agree," he said, eyes glinting with humor. "I can't eat human food anymore, so we'd have to at least find a way to grow our own seaweed at home."

The rest of the train ride was quiet. When we arrived in Liverpool, I felt the wind slapping my face with the brutal cruelty of winter in the United Kingdom. I was exceedingly grateful for my internal heater as we shivered near the river's edge. The River Mersey was just as vile as the Thames, but I didn't care. The sun was peeking through the clouds, and my legs were starting to hurt.

Saddened as I was to leave the life I had enjoyed with Seamus over the past week, I was inexplicably excited to meet my mother. I couldn't stand the anticipation of finally seeing the woman that I had thought never cared to know me, but I had been wrong. She'd wanted to know me so desperately that she'd escaped the Pools to come and find me.

"Back to the Emerald Isle," Seamus said, squeezing my hand.

I had felt weakened by the betrayal in Norway, but now I was refreshed and revitalized.

I was ready for whatever was coming.

PART VI

LISTENER

CHAPTER 36

ANNIE

It took no time at all to cross the sea to Belfast, and I smiled as I saw the turrets of Carrickfergus Castle calling us home.

I was looking forward to my reunion with my mother, not only because I was dying to meet her, but because I also had my suspicions that she knew more about the stones than anyone else. After all, she had led us to the hiding place of the Iberian Iridescent Ammonite, and I had no idea how she knew where it was. I had so many questions for her, both about the stones and the story of where she had been for the entirety of my life.

There was, unfortunately, no way of telling if Cearbhall and Camila had gotten to any of the gems first, but Aisling had mentioned that Niamh, her mother, was going to do some recon on Hy-Brasil for us once she found Aine. My heart leapt at the thought of my tiny family coming together, when just a few months ago I hadn't had one at all.

"As expected," Seamus said with an upward glance. "No sun to worry about here."

Belfast truthfully looked wholly depressing against the gray November sky, and I wondered why Aisling and Fintan even wanted to meet here, now that Oisin was gone. I thought it might sadden my cousin to return to the same place where she had watched her great grandfather die not long ago, but I sensed she wanted to carry on the legacy of the tiny Belfast clan herself. I still thought she and Fintan would take up permanent residence on Hy-Brasil eventually, but given his recent reunion with his father, maybe they'd choose Atlântida instead.

As we approached Oisin's old castle, I realized with a jolt that the great selkie leader was actually *my* relative, too.

There were lights coming from the bottom of the castle's dungeons, and we wound through the labyrinth that seemed haunted to me the last time I saw it. The slimy passages admittedly looked friendlier now that I knew I belonged here.

The tunnels flew by us on either side and we ended up in the wide, stone room that was surrounded by mirrors. It was within the very same room where the mighty Oisin had fallen, and the Ollphéist had spared me, simply because I was Atargatis' Heir. Even if I had known back then that I could command it, I still don't think I would have reached for its scales. He was by far the most frightening of the serpents I had seen.

"Took ye long enough," Aisling said, floating from beyond one of the arches. Her red hair was flowing in the gentle breeze of the underwater dungeon, and she had a bright smile for us. "Did ye enjoy your time in London?"

I said nothing, but held up my left hand. Her eyes went wide and she flew to me, squealing in a way that was extremely uncharacteristic of her. I grinned broadly as we embraced.

"Oh, Seamus, that's a *special* stone," she said with admiration, holding the gem to the beam of light that was streaming in from the ceiling of the hall. "Artur helped ye find it, I imagine?"

Seamus nodded as his cheeks turned the tiniest bit pink. Fintan emerged from behind Aisling, his mouth full of seaweed. He tossed us each a few strands which I gratefully swallowed immediately, feeling the nutritious snack of Northern Ireland bring me back to life.

"Man, stop making me look bad," he said to Seamus as he examined the ring.

Aisling's own engagement ring was a beautifully ornate, classic, bright green emerald. I thought it was equally as beautiful, and the fact that both of our men had actually gone to *find* the uncut gems somewhere at the bottom of the ocean made the stones more precious than anything they could have picked out for us on land.

"There's someone here that's excited to meet ye," Aisling then said, reaching for my hands with bright, excited eyes. She lowered her voice and asked, "Are ye ready?"

I froze. It was happening. I was going to meet my mother, Aine. Or as Raj had referred to his elusive, lost love for my whole life...*Annie*.

I took a deep breath.

But before I could answer, I heard someone else say my name. "Jasmine?"

I knew her voice. Like I had heard it in a dream long ago.

I turned to my left and saw her. My breath caught in my chest because I had pictured her so many times, but I couldn't have known how it would feel to really see her. She had always been blurry in my imagination, like my mind was afraid to sharpen her outline out of fear of allowing myself to believe her to be real.

But she was. I looked directly into my mother's eyes.

She had cascading garnet hair—even darker than Seamus'— and beautiful, bright eyes that I recognized as mirror images of my own. Even with the lamplight sheen they exhibited in the murky water, I knew they were brown, not green. Her complexion was a fair honey with faint, nearly undetectable stamps of freckles on her cheeks and arms rather than my even olive tone. I had clearly gotten the majority of my darker features from Raj, but we had the same sharp jawline and nose–one look at the shared traits of our facial structures told me that we were undoubtedly of the same blood.

She rushed to me and pulled me into a crushing hug that I welcomed whole-heartedly, too overwhelmed to speak. I thought I would have cried, but now that it was happening, I couldn't even do that. I hadn't known what to expect, but it was the most natural feeling I'd ever experienced in my life—like she had pulled me into this exact embrace a thousand times before.

I closed my eyes as my mom stroked my hair for the first time I could remember.

"I have a lifetime to make up for," she said, her voice musically gentle with just a whisper of a British accent that softened the ends of her words while her Irish accent attempted to sharpen them. I knew she and Raj had met at Cambridge, but the rest of her life before and after that was a mystery to me. I wanted to know it all. She locked eyes with me and didn't let go. "I hope you'll forgive me."

"I already have," I stammered, hardly believing she could think otherwise. "I know you did it for me. For Raj."

Her eyes welled with silver tears. "I love you both, very much."

My heart felt like it was going to burst with insurmountable happiness for myself, but an equal amount of grief that she would never get to see my father again. I imagined what it would be like, leaving Seamus without a trace and then seeing our child nearly three decades later. It made me ache with sadness that I couldn't express, so I hugged her again.

"You didn't know it, but I watched you grow up," she whispered to me. "It wasn't always consistent, but sometimes...sometimes she let me see you."

She...meaning Atargatis. I knew without asking.

I wondered if my mother thought of her as the benevolent goddess to be revered, or a terrible tyrant whose pools had imprisoned her for what would have been eternity had she not found a way out. And how had she? How had she found the ammonite–the stone that was now on my chest–and led me to it? I had so many questions for her, but I couldn't bring myself to ask them now. Not yet. I wanted to just enjoy her presence.

"You're beautiful," she said, touching my cheek. "You look just like your father."

"And you, I think," I said, suddenly feeling shy. "The nose."

She wrinkled hers in laughter and placed her arm around me, turning to the others who had attempted to give us our private moment. But as I turned, I saw they all had been watching intently, just as plagued with suspense as I had been for this reunion. Seamus was beaming at me.

"And *you're* Seamus," my mother said, meeting my fiancé's gaze. "Thank you for keeping her safe."

Seamus grinned and welcomed her embrace as well.

"I'm sorry I didn't ask your permission," he said, motioning to the stone on my hand. "I couldn't wait."

"I've heard everything I need to know about you," she said, winking at Aisling. "Permission granted."

I couldn't help but reflect on how I had been led down such a twisting path that I never could have predicted. I had lived one life where Raj was clinking whiskey glasses with my boyfriend of several years after being asked for my hand in marriage, and now I was living another where my mother that I had met five minutes ago embraced my fiancé without even knowing him. Without caring that *I* technically barely knew him.

I suppose it was because we had all learned—the hard way—that time was too precious to waste.

* * *

As HEARTWARMING as our exchange had been, Aisling and Fintan's glances at one another told me we needed to get to business.

My cousin called a meeting to order in which we learned of what Seamus and I had missed during our week spent in London.

Her mother, Niamh, was still in Hy-Brasil and had sent word that there was trouble on the island.

"The Amalgams have dropped all pretenses regarding the nature of their mission," she said. "My mam's said they've completely secluded themselves from the regular selkies of the island, blocking off their half with a barrier somehow conjured by the power of one of the stones they already have."

"Have they found any others?" Seamus asked. "Other stones?"

"No," Aisling shook her head confidently, and I let out a slight breath of relief. "But they're growing in number."

Seamus glanced sideways at me and I gulped. Considering they were unable to procreate the natural way, I knew there was only one way *that* was possible. I looked down at my own scar, the silvery streak reminding me that I had once been cursed by them as well. My blood boiled for the innocent victims they were undoubtedly dragging into the sea as we spoke.

We ran through the roster of stones while my mother sat contemplatively, listening to the brief recount on how we had secured them all. I showed her the Thulite that was still embedded in the cuff on my wrist, the Ammonite she had led me to around my neck, and Seamus showed the Citrine around his own. She looked upon it knowingly, as if she wanted to say something about it, but thought of a more important question first.

"And you know the number of the stones to be absolute?" she asked. "How?"

I looked at Seamus who shifted uneasily in the water. I didn't know how he'd feel about telling his future mother-in-law the first day he met her that he had sucked the blood of a Spanish demon.

"Seamus went to Duarte of the Santa Compaña," Aisling told her before either of us could decide if we would. I looked at my mother, wondering if she was familiar with the legend. Her eyes went wide. Evidently, she was.

"Blimey," she said under her breath, studying Seamus intently. "In the pools, we heard legends of Duarte and Nabia..."

I started at the mention of Atargatis' pools, burning with questions, but she gave me a knowing look that seemed to say, *'In time. It's not important now.'*

"He told me the locations of them, but it's broad," Seamus said. "Japan, The Middle East, and Norway. Actually, he said some other words like Yamato and Nóregr, but Jasmine knew what he meant."

"Your father's brilliance," my mother said simply, tucking a strand of hair behind my ear. "Doesn't surprise me at all."

I blushed furiously.

"I'm impressed you convinced him to give up the locations at all," Aine continued, eyes back on Seamus.

"Japan's a big place," interjected Fintan, who was busying himself trying to catch a small turtle that had been lurking in the shadows of the dungeons. "The Middle East is even more broad. I mean how many countries are there? There's Iraq, Iran, Syria, and then–"

"Atargatis spoke to me many times during the years I was imprisoned in her pools," my mother said, cutting him off. "If those are the areas we know for certain, I think I can narrow it down."

My heart leapt. I had hoped she'd say that.

We all agreed that we'd need to return to Atlântida to get to Japan, knowing that there was no possibility of accomplishing the swim without using the Room of Windows buried beneath Artur's castle. The great leader had promised to answer our call for aid, and I was looking forward to enlisting his help once more. I wanted to return to Hy-Brasil to do some recon on my own before we left, but Seamus and my mother shut that idea down immediately.

"There's a high price on your head, Jasmine," Seamus said. "That's swimming right into a trap, so it is."

He was right, unfortunately, so we would have to trust that Aisling's mother had accurate information. She planned to return to Belfast within the next day or so, and I counted the number of attendees planning to embark on the mission in my head before privately voicing to Seamus that it was too many. We needed to cut our numbers down.

"Aye, I agree," he said quietly as the meeting adjourned. "We go on our own to Japan, and I think your mam and Artur take the others to start on the rest of the stones."

We decided we'd both think separately about how best to break the news to everyone, and come up with a united plan by the time Niamh returned.

Later that evening, Seamus busied himself with Fintan and Aisling in order to give my mother and I some privacy.

She floated to the archway in what would have been called a guest room, had there been walls or doors in the castle's magical dungeons. We both wanted to learn more about each other, so I welcomed her questions about Seamus and everything else in my life. I wondered if there would be any lingering awkwardness between us, considering we didn't actually *know* one another at all...but there wasn't.

"I can tell he's a good man," she said to me. "Seamus."

"He is," I said softly. I liked how his name sounded when spoken in her voice; like she already loved him as her own. I knew she would.

Then her eyes glinted mischievously as she slid onto the marble column beside me. "And not bad to look at either, hmm?"

I grinned broadly, unable to suppress a giggle. I realized I hadn't had anyone to whisper with regarding Seamus and his *charms* since the first time I saw him in Dublin with my friends. Back when Kiana had gaped at his unusual accent and Kristen had swooned over his height. It was all a lifetime ago, with friends I no longer had. I did miss it, every now and then, when I thought of how unserious matters were back then. But now, to talk *boys* with my mom, at the bottom of the ocean. It was just as nice.

"You got that right," I smiled, looking down at my ring.

She took my hand in hers and placed the other over her heart.

"It's blinding me," she said, laughing. Her blended accent was charming and perfect, just like her personality. "It's beautiful."

"Thanks," I said.

Her smile flickered and she bit her lip, as if debating telling me something. I hoped she would, whatever it was.

"I saw glimpses of you growing up," she said. "I was always proud of you, every time Atargatis granted me a small window to your life."

"And how did she–"

My mother patted my hand and closed her eyes. "I know you have questions," she said. "And I'll tell you everything now. We have time."

I beamed with gratitude and waited expectantly.

"You best go get Seamus," she said. "He'll want to hear this as well."

I nodded and rushed to retrieve him from the main hall. I didn't even need to say a word; he looked at me knowingly. It was time to learn the full truth.

As intrigued as I had been hearing about mermaids from around the world during my time in Atlântida, I was practically breathless with anticipation as my mother divulged the lore of her own life.

CHAPTER 37

ANSWERS

"Not long after I met your father, I learned what I was," she began, taking a deep breath. "Niamh had just changed, and she warned me that I would, too. I didn't believe her. I was already pregnant with you, so I adamantly avoided the water, just in case. I hoped you wouldn't have to carry the burden as well, but Niamh assured me that selkies could live very normal, happy lives. I clung to that belief as I imagined you growing up with a fish tail."

I laughed briefly and she returned a smile.

"Either way, I thought I'd tell Raj some day. I knew he'd still love me, despite it," she said.

My heart fluttered. I was sure he would have. Being the scholar that he was, I knew he would have found it *fascinating*.

"I had no idea, however, who *he* was," she said. "I had no clue that Raj's bloodline would reignite the line of Atargatis. I learned that when I began having The Dreams. The Dreams where Atargatis herself would visit me to tell me that I was forbidden to have his child. She reignited my fear that your existence as a mermaid would be one of severe hardship. She told me she wanted to prevent anyone from ever making the same mistakes she had made, including you."

"Accidentally killing her human lover," I said, recalling the story of Semiramis–the mortal descendent of Atargatis' fated union that resulted in a dead man and the goddess turning into the mermaid that she was. Semiramis, the queen from whom my Syrian father was descended. My mother nodded.

"But since her warning was too late, I begged that you would be spared from the curse, selkie or otherwise," she said, biting her lip. "I was so terrified she would take you from me in her rage, but…she showed me mercy. She visited me in another Dream, telling me you would be spared, if I promised to pay a debt if and whenever she called. I answered without hesitation that I would."

I watched as she swam back and forth. Pacing like a human.

"When you were born, there were no signs of selkie or any other mermaid blood in you, so I knew Atargatis had honored her promise. We were in Florida for your birth–Raj thought it very important that you were born in America–and I was visited by the Amalgams one night when I snuck away to the beach to transform. It was my first time doing so, and I felt immediately relieved as soon as I hit the water. Like my entire life I had been called to the Sea, and I was finally answering it. I'm sure you know the feeling."

"I do," I said quietly.

"The Hy-Brasil Amalgams had already started gathering followers, and the leader at the time, Eamon, came to see me. He told me that I had broken the laws of nature, and that Atargatis had *wanted* to reignite the line of royal blood. He said I was mistaken in my interpretation of her wishes. The Amalgams threatened to take you from me, to turn you into one of them."

"No matter how many times I begged and pleaded with them, telling them they were wrong, they didn't believe me," she said. "They had already become obsessed with the idea of an Heir that they could use to harness the full power of the seas."

"With the stones," I said.

"Correct," she nodded. "They had been discovered and lost many times in the past, but this group was already proving more formidable than any other. It was the cult that Cearbhall and Camila would eventually take over as they rose to power. They were disguising themselves as Atargatis' messengers; her prophets who had come to tell the world that she *wanted* the stones discovered. But I knew better."

I shuddered, recalling how I myself had almost once believed them.

"Needless to say, I refused to hand you over. Raj and I lived in Cambridge, so we were safe from the Amalgams while land-locked. But Eamon knew I would go to Belfast to see my sister eventually, so his crew waited for me to return," she said. "They ambushed me when I was approaching Carrickfergus, where Niamh had already begun to pay visits to our great great grand-father Oisin who had a clan here. When I could see they wouldn't take no for an answer, I told them that I would go in your place. But of course *I* wasn't Atargatis' Heir, so I had to be valuable to them in another way."

I knew what she was going to say.

"I told them that I knew where the stones were. I said that Atargatis had told me in My Dreams while I was pregnant because she was telling *you.* I made them promise that as long as I went with them, they would spare you. They wouldn't let me go back to say goodbye to you or Raj. They took me right there."

She saw the horror on my face, but pressed on.

"The stones are volatile in the wrong hands," she said. "Only you—because you are the true Heir of Atargatis—could ever harness them for their full power. But the Amalgams can certainly use them for evil even without you."

She paused, biting her lip.

"Eamon took me to Atargatis' Pools in Cyprus, a cave that had once been a holy, healing place of worship, but the Amalgams had turned into a prison. I knew no one would be able to come and search for me, because of a barrier they had laid upon it that made it invisible to anyone they didn't permit. For a few years, I fed them information intentionally designed to result in long, drawn out searches for the stones. Even when they returned without success, they still believed I knew."

"I started trying to communicate with Atargatis again while in her Pools, and even though she didn't directly answer me for a long time, she planted seeds of information in my head. I'm sure of it. I guessed that one of the stones would be in Manza Bay, near Tanzania…and I was *right*. It came to me so suddenly that there was no explanation other than Atargatis had given it to me as a gift to keep me alive. A young Amalgam, Cearbhall, ended up being the one to retrieve the green Tsavorite, and he became the new clan leader. It gave me credibility with him, even though he already thought Eamon had kept me alive too long."

This was the part of her story that began rounding out to become the history that I knew. I recalled Elias' tale of his fight with Cearbhall in Manza Bay. The showdown that had gotten him scarred for life. The asshole deserved it, in my opinion.

"I thanked Atargatis, and it opened up our line of communication once more. She began to show me glimpses of your life, knowing little gifts such as that were keeping my spirit alive. One day, a woman came to the pools with a stone trying to strike a bargain with the Amalgams, whom she falsely believed had powers that they did not. She had been tricked by them, of course, and it was easy to see how. They had become so widely accepted as benevolent creatures among us that no one suspected they had anything but respect for Atargatis' true wishes. Those of us who believed she wanted the stones to remain hidden were slowly becoming the minority."

"The gem the woman wore was a beautiful, bright Citrine,

and I knew instantly that it was a real stone of Atargatis. It did not react to anyone's touch, of course, like it would for you. But when present near the pools, it glowed radiantly in contrast to all the others that had been discovered as ordinary."

The hair on the back of my neck prickled. I already knew the woman of whom she spoke.

"The woman said she had come to beg for her sons to be spared from our curse. They were already born, and were starting to show signs of the selkie blood she so deeply resented in herself. I pitied her, because I knew the Amalgams had tricked her into believing they could grant such a request, had they even had the motivation to do so."

I felt Seamus' hand go limp in mine. I wondered if he'd ask questions, but he patiently waited for my mother to finish.

"I heard she was from Ireland as well, and we bonded over that, even in our misery. The woman, despite having been fooled by the Amalgams, was a fighter. She told me one day that the stone actually originated *from* Cyprus, and she had stolen it right out from under their noses. The reason they never forcibly took it from her in the caves was because there seemed to be a protective curse that Atargatis–or someone else–had put on it. It couldn't be removed from her body unless she chose to do it herself."

I started at this, wondering if the same magic existed with my stone. Would Camila be *incapable* of taking it from me, even if she or Cearbhall tried?

"And then I heard Atargatis again, but she wasn't there to see me. She visited the woman the following night–I assume because she had the stone–telling her that one of her sons could be spared, but the other's fate she wouldn't touch. She would only delay the curse as long as possible. She wouldn't say why."

"The next morning, the Amalgams came to torture the woman. Her spirit was broken upon hearing she couldn't save both of her sons, and she agreed to hand the stone over as long as they took her back home to kill her...she knew they wouldn't need her once the stone was in their hands. Cearbhall and his gang dragged her across the world, sending her through The Green Window in Belfast just as it was closing. In their haste, they failed to notice that she had switched the stones. They didn't realize that she had been wearing a fake, and she had left the real one with me. I overheard the Amalgams say later, when they returned, that she ripped it off her neck as she was being suffocated by the whirlpool, cackling that *she* had fooled *them* in the end. I thought it was heroic."

I thought so, too. I hoped Seamus felt the same.

"There was no way of knowing if the protective magic on the stone would transfer to me, and I didn't want to find out the hard way. I knew I had to hide it from the Amalgams before they got back. Ideally I'd be able to place it in the care of someone who would keep it safe, but also have no idea what it truly was," she said. "I couldn't believe my luck when I saw, just outside the cave, someone that I recognized. Someone I had seen in glimpses of *your* life, Jasmine."

"Professor Brennan," I breathed. Seamus had told me where the professor said he found the stone—*while diving off the coast of Cyprus.* To think *this* was how it had ended up in the professor's office at Trinity College...

"I knew he was an academic, and would take interest in something like it if nothing else," my mother continued. "I threw it as hard as I could out into the ocean, praying he'd find it. And he did. I know Atargatis intervened to make it happen. She must have."

I wanted to ask how my mother eventually escaped, but Seamus had to ask his question first. We already knew the answer, but he needed verbal confirmation. I didn't blame him.

He cleared his throat.

"The woman...the one ye were imprisoned with. The one that came to bargain for her sons," he said. "What was her name?"

My mother smiled at Seamus, because she already knew as well.

"Her name was Saoirse. Your mother."

I pressed the small tattoo on his forearm that bore her name. I looked at his side profile, and a single silver tear welled in the corner that I could see, even as he blinked it away. He put his head on my shoulder in an uncharacteristically submissive gesture, and I put my arm around him.

"She was brave, Seamus," my mother said. "Even in the face of death."

He nodded and looked up at my mother, the remnants of tears vanished and replaced by a hard jaw of steely pride. Despite not ever knowing her, I felt it, too.

My mother heaved a sigh as she prepared to conclude her story and connect the final dots for us.

"Even as Atargatis showed me glimpses of Jasmine's life, I didn't see much of Raj's, because I asked her not to show me. I thought that to see him take another lover would hurt too deeply, because I hadn't even gotten to say goodbye," she said.

"He didn't," I interrupted. "He never married anyone."

She laughed. "I said other *lovers,* not *wives.*"

"Fair enough," I muttered.

"Anyway, she kept showing me scenes of some malevolent woman who was too old to be your age, but far too young to be someone in Raj's romantic life," she said, and my face turned to stone because I knew what was coming. "I couldn't imagine why she thought it important, but I watched anyway, knowing she had a reason for showing me."

"I finally understood when I saw her in Raj's classroom, watching him lecture from the back row and..." she trailed off. "I knew they had been together once. But I knew she wanted more from him."

My heart sank. So it *was* true.

"Camila," Seamus said, because I couldn't stand uttering her name.

"Correct," my mother confirmed, her eyes dark.

"When Raj took the job in Portugal, I breathed easy, thinking you were both safe and the Amalgams had lost interest in tracking you for the time being as they worked tirelessly to find the other stones. I tried to push the irritating scenes of Camila away, but I still kept seeing her, lusting after Raj even after he'd left."

I felt ill.

"And then the vile woman appeared to me, not in a dream, but *in person,*" she said. "Camila came with Cearbhall to the cave as a human. I'll never forget her perched up on the rock, studying me in awe while Cearbhall looked over from the clear water just on the other side of my prison."

Her eyes were fixed on the wall behind me as she recalled the memory bitterly, and my blood ran cold.

"Somehow Cearbhall found her; likely with the magic he had harnessed from the Tsavorite. He lured the woman into a trap. He told her that Raj would never love her because he was betrothed to a siren of the seas that had him under a spell," she said.

My eyes rolled.

"Yeah, I know," she said, doing the same.

"Camila then demanded she see me. Apparently Cearbhall had told her that she could actually *steal* my spell from me and put it on Raj herself," she said. "And when I told her it wasn't true, I watched her demand that Cearbhall change her into one of us on the spot. Which was, of course, what he had planned for all along. He was simply growing his numbers for his cause, and he told Camila that she needed the stones to harness the "spell" she supposedly thought existed. If she had them, she'd be able to make Raj–and anyone else for that matter–fall in love with her. I still think she believes that's true to some degree."

My jaw dropped.

"*That's* how she became an Amalgam?"

"Yes," she said. "I tried to stop him, but he marked her right in front of me."

It was pathetic, and I almost pitied the woman.

Almost.

"She took the Tsavorite of Manza Bay from Cearbhall without his knowledge—thinking it would be enough—and then presented herself to Raj in Porto–a vision that Atargatis showed me. Since he already detested her as a human, he was horrified to see her as a sea demon."

I couldn't believe it. I wondered *when* this could have possibly occurred, trying to remember any time when Raj had come home acting shaken or strange. I'd never know.

"She begged to remain in the cult under the guarantee that she'd find the next stone," my mother continued. "But Cearbhall severely punished her for taking the Tsavorite behind his back– I'm sure you've seen the scar across her face."

"That wasn't where he marked her to become an Amalgam?" I asked curiously, remembering how shocking it had been to me the first time I saw the claw mark dragged down her face. Back when I had actually thought she was beautiful. I was disgusted by her now.

"Oh no," she said. "The original mark was small. Right in her palm."

I looked down at my own, and I knew. I think I had for a while now.

"Yes," my mother said, her eyes filled with sadness. "Not long after that, Camila marked you for revenge. Atargatis' promise to spare you or not, the Amalgam curse would still drag you into the sea."

I closed my eyes, cursing all of the forces that brought me to the ocean and those that had kept my parents apart. To think that Aine had been alive this entire time, across the world...I knew

Raj would have gone to find her. Human or not, he would have found a way to bring her home. I was sure of it.

I couldn't bear discussing Camila a moment longer.

"How did you escape? From the Pools?" I asked.

"I escaped once you were called to the sea," Aine said, smiling. "I didn't know when it would happen, but I hoped Atargatis would at least grant you the ability to land-walk when it did. It was all she could do, after all. And something about you returning gave me strength that overcame even the Pools. I can't describe it as anything other than a mother's will that surged through me, telling me I had to get to my daughter."

I beamed with pride.

"Love is a very powerful thing," she said, taking my other hand that wasn't in Seamus'. "Stronger than evil. We all have to remember that."

My head was still spinning, but I smiled.

"Is that how you were able to show me the memory?" I asked. "The one that led me to the ammonite?"

She looked up with a smile.

"I wish I could take credit for that, but that was Atargatis," she said. "I think she knew you'd pay attention if you thought it was me."

I laughed incredulously. "You think she knows I'm afraid of her, then?"

"Probably," my mother shrugged. "Jasmine…I know the curse hurts you when you land-walk, but I promise you, Atargatis is kind. I don't think it's her doing it to you. I think it's the pull of the Amalgam curse Camila inflicted upon you fighting against who you are. Atargatis is *good*."

I wanted to ask her myself, because my head was spinning with conflicting opinions. On one hand, I thought Atargatis wanted me to be a hero, and that was why she kept calling me back to the mission under the sea. On the other hand, I wondered if it *could* be two different ancient lines of magic, battling against one another for which form I would take. Artur had speculated the same.

"Camila told me Raj's death wasn't an accident," I said quietly before I could stop myself. "So in the end, she killed him because he didn't love her back."

My mother nodded. "Atargatis didn't show me, but I think we can assume that's what happened."

Seamus squeezed my hand.

"And she said Matt's death wasn't intentional. He was just collateral damage," I continued, my face hardening.

I looked up at her with a sudden realization. "Did you–did you ever know Matt? Did you see him when you saw me?"

"Of course," my mother replied. "When Atargatis gave me glimpses of your life, she generally focused on the good. I saw a lot of Matt, and how happy he made you."

"He did," I said, looking into my lap and rubbing Seamus' hand. I was here, with him now, but I had loved someone else before. I was glad my mom had gotten to see him, even if she never met him.

"I could feel your love for him," my mother continued. "And I knew how much he loved you. He was so…full of light."

I stared at her in amazement, knowing that she had truly experienced my very own emotions as she saw my life through the eyes of Atargatis. She used the exact words I had to describe him.

I glanced sideways at Seamus whose face was relatively blank in his best attempt to avoid showing the inevitable jealousy that I know he felt, but that he also realized was unnecessary. We had just heard that Atargatis herself had told his mother that his fate was too important to disturb. That he was destined to become a creature like me, to help me do what needed to be done.

I had suspected something of the sort all along, but now I knew that the Heir of Atargatis and the Son of Saoirse–the one who hadn't been spared–had always been destined for one another.

I shed a silent tear as I acknowledged that no matter what, the universe would never have let me have Matt. But maybe now I could let him go.

CHAPTER 38

SEAMUS OF BELFAST

We had one full day before our planned departure, and I spent the morning with my mother. Laughing, telling stories, just…existing.

Seamus eventually came to find us in the main hall and grinned from the archways, observing something he knew I had dreamt about since I had learned of her existence. It was the type of morning that I was sure he wished he could experience, too, which reminded me of something I'd promised we'd do while we were in Belfast. But before I could say anything, Fintan came rushing into the room. He had a bright smile for all of us.

"I have exciting news," he said, eyes flickering to Seamus.

"Hmm?" Seamus said, not taking his eyes off of me.

"Aidan's here," Fintan replied.

Seamus' gaze snapped to him. "What?"

Fintan nodded enthusiastically, zooming around the room like the golden retriever I always thought him to be.

"I didn't want to say anything until I knew it could happen for sure, but I tried my best and waited for him, because I know where he usually waits for ye, and–"

"Thank ye, brother," Seamus said to him, slapping him on the shoulder and silencing what would have likely been a long-winded speech. "Do ye know where exactly?"

Fintan's face fell as he realized that he had forgotten to arrange that part. He hadn't told Aidan about Carrickfergus–Oisin had placed a spell upon the dungeons to hide them, of course, but no humans could ever even *know* what existed beneath the surface of the Belfast landmark. It was a type of magic I didn't understand, but had been told worked similarly to memory loss. Even if word of the secret dwelling was spoken to a human, they'd have no recollection of it moments later.

"I think I know where he'll be," said Seamus.

And given what I had already been thinking moments before Fintan's arrival, I knew, too.

* * *

We flew out of the castle immediately, deciding to alight right across the water from the Titanic tourist attraction despite how busy it would be, because it was the closest point we could get to the side of the city where his mother's grave was. I wondered if now Seamus would feel a sense of pride knowing she had died here as a warrior. It wouldn't overcome the grief, but it was something to hold onto, nonetheless.

I looked up at the sky and noted that the sun was rising on a nearly cloudless winter day. I feared for the pain I would experience once I changed, but I tried to push it from my mind. Seamus had insisted he go without me given the brightness of the day, but I wanted to meet Aidan. I felt that I needed to, considering he had been integral in Seamus' mission to find me.

We waited carefully, lingering in the shadows of an empty marina as there were several people about and we didn't want to be spotted.

"Where did you grow up?" I asked suddenly, realizing we

must be near his childhood home. Belfast wasn't that large. "I'd love to see it, if we have time."

Seamus' smile flickered.

He pulled me out of the water behind him, scooping me up with ease. We waited for my tail to change as he bent over me, forearms on his knees in an attempt to shield me from sight should any onlookers notice us in the tiny marina off River Lagan.

"I warn ye, I didn't have the same upbringing that ye did," he said, and I thought he looked almost embarrassed. "They've built it up a bit now…but back then, it was a shite part of town."

I nearly told him he was being ridiculous until I saw how serious he was. Of course, he wasn't only talking about money. He didn't have the fond childhood memories that I had. His father had been an abusive, alcoholic piece of shit.

"My da moved us out to the countryside when we were still wee ones," he continued as we waited. "I wonder now if it was because he knew what she was. Because he wanted to keep her away from the water."

It was likely, but I didn't know for sure. I thought I remembered Seamus telling me that Aidan said their father was unaware, but I didn't think it was important to ask now. Not when recalling his mother's fate brought him so much pain.

"I'd still like to see it," I said. I didn't know why, but I thought it was important to see where he had come from. To see what had made him into the man he was. "If that's okay with you."

He smiled at me. "Of course it is," he said. "We'll make that our first stop since it's on the way."

At last I transformed and we set off down the street, crossing the main roads and railroad tracks where we likely looked to be lost or otherwise *daft* for not driving instead.

On the opposite side of York Street, there was a small shopping mall and behind it a row of townhouses with dark red brick and white windows. We were both bundled up tightly given the temperature, but the bright sun made me wish I had one less layer. The pain in my legs was moderate, but the aching was definitely there–like I had run a long race yesterday and neglected to stretch afterward.

We walked down a small neighborhood avenue called Henry Street until at last Seamus took a sharp right onto a place called Earl Circle.

"That's the place, so it is," he said, pointing to the building that read "106."

It didn't look so terrible to me. It was modest, and certainly much smaller than where I had grown up. I imagined it being relatively cramped with four people, but there was a small garden out front that looked nice. The windows caught the sunlight in a way that made me think it would be quite bright inside the small home. Given what he had said about the area having changed significantly since his childhood, I wondered how it really had looked when he was young.

I couldn't help but picture him as a small, redheaded boy, doing his homework at the kitchen table through the window in front of me. I didn't know what to say, so I settled on the only thing I could think of.

"Do you want to see if we can go inside?" I asked.

He let out a hollow laugh. "Christ, no, I think from the outside is plenty enough for me, Jasmine."

It was understandable. I also didn't know how the current inhabitants would feel should two strangers come knocking and demand entry to their home at sunrise.

"How do you feel?" I whispered, reaching for his hand.

"Feckin' glad I don't live here anymore," he said. There was humor in his voice, but I knew it was there to cover something else.

I thought of Seamus' life in London, where he had made a name for himself in a distinguished way. Where he lived in an affluent neighborhood and didn't seem to be lacking anything in the way of luxury, should he want it. But his townhouse had been barren to some degree, and he himself was certainly far from flashy. Well, aside from the ostentatious ring he had put on my finger.

"She would be proud of you," I said before I could stop myself. "Your mother would be proud to see the man you've become." Not just because of his success, but because of who he was. How strong, honorable, and humble he had grown to be.

"Ye think she'd be proud of me after what I did in Spain?" he asked, absently running a hand across his lips. I knew he was remembering the demon's blood.

"For the reasons you did it, yes," I said confidently.

We left the tiny brick houses and I took one last glance at the place where he had been born. Born to a selkie mother who would bargain for his fate in the depths of a cave in Cyprus, and a horrible father who didn't deserve any of them—Aidan, Saoirse, or Seamus. I rubbed his arm as we left Earl Circle, knowing it was the first and last time I'd ever see it.

We steadily made our way through the rest of the quiet suburban streets until we rounded a corner directly in front of Antrim Road where sat a relatively rundown building with brightly colored doors and windows.

"And this is where Aidan and I—at different times—got into all sorts of shite," Seamus said, pointing at the building. It read "*St. Patrick's Primary School,*" and I raised an eyebrow.

"*You* went to Catholic school?" I said, trying to picture him in mass, wearing a neat uniform and generally listening to authority at all. I roared with laughter.

"Believe it or not, I did say my prayers as a wee one," he said, flashing me a mischievous grin. "Aidan and I both said the rosary every night until mam…well, ye know."

I stopped laughing and nodded understandingly.

"After that, I didn't want to pray anymore. I know it's not

right, but I couldn't find a reason to. I was angry with God I guess," he finished.

I realized now why he felt so horrible for what he had done inside the church in Santiago de Compostela. He was raised a Christian.

"Maybe one day you'll want to again," I offered. "I'll pray with you, if you'd like."

He stroked my arm affectionately, but he didn't reply.

"We're not far now," he said. We crossed under another major road and I stumbled as a sudden sharp pain shot through my legs. The sun was bright, and he noticed.

"I'll carry ye," he said, reaching for me.

"No!" I shouted, laughing at the absurdity of it. "It's fine."

He looked like he was going to do it anyway, but I shot him a warning look that plainly told him *absolutely not*. He threw his hands up in surrender and we kept going.

"That's where they were married, my mam and my father," Seamus said, pointing up to a church that rose tall against the other surrounding, less impressive buildings.

It was a beautiful cathedral with elegant spires that stretched to the sky, and the front gates were wide open in welcome. There were several people heading inside, and I wondered if there was a service that was about to begin. It was also called St. Patrick's.

"I think in the beginning…I think she did love him," he said, watching the doors open and close absently. "I don't feckin' know how, but I guess that was before she saw the monster he was."

"Would you…do you want to go in?" I asked again, knowing his answer here would be the same.

His grip on my hand tightened. I knew he was imagining the scene of the altar in Spain. The knife he had taken to the woman's throat when he had suspected she was a demon, but wasn't certain. When he knew he'd kill her even if she weren't, because he needed the answers from Duarte and he'd do anything to get them. Anything…even sacrifice his own soul.

"No," he said with a sigh at last, shaking his head as he bit his lip. "I don't think I can."

I didn't press the matter. I hadn't grown up religious, so I couldn't understand. But I knew how it felt to be forced to face something you were ashamed of before you were ready.

"This way," he said, turning another corner.

At last we arrived at the tiny cemetery. It was quite beautiful, despite how morbid I typically found them to be. I never really understood the concept of burial, and I hoped that when my time came, nobody came to visit my grave. Picturing anyone I loved coming to a place like this to mourn my death seemed so…insincere. I had only visited Raj and Matt's graves once in the entire year since they passed, unable to face the fact that the lives of the two most important people I knew were reduced to two slabs of granite.

Then we saw him.

Tall, straight-backed, and shockingly like Seamus in every way–at least from behind–I came to a halt as I looked upon Aidan McCarthy.

CHAPTER 39

SAOIRSE'S SONS

"**A**idan," Seamus said, and the man turned around, beaming at us both.

He didn't look surprised at all that we had found him there. At his feet stood a massive fluffy dog that resembled a bear, with caramel-colored fur and a purple tongue. His tail started wagging excitedly as he saw us approach.

"Ye came back, lamb," Aidan said, and I could have sworn I saw a tear rolling down his cheek as he embraced Seamus. His tender nickname for his younger brother caught me off guard as his appearance did not suggest he'd be so gentle. While he *technically* looked like Seamus, he was entirely different.

Aidan's hair was lighter and brighter red–it was nearly blonde–in contrast to Seamus' darker crimson waves, and he reminded me much more of the wilder, rougher version of Seamus that had returned from Spain. Obviously the elder of the two, Aidan had deep lines and shadows of having lived a tough life painted across his face. Seamus, whom I had always considered to be ruggedly handsome, looked like a pampered movie star next to him.

"And *this* is Jasmine," Aidan said, looking upon me with esteem.

He let out a low whistle that would have been mildly offensive to a woman had I not decided I liked him already. How could I not, considering what I knew about him? I grinned broadly as he embraced me, too.

"I s'pose jumping into the sea like a daft eedjit was worth it," he said, slapping Seamus on the shoulder.

The younger brother acknowledged this with a squeeze of my waist before he bent down to pet the dog that had been waiting for attention from us. It wagged its tail excitedly and let out a friendly *"Ruff."*

"Who's this?" Seamus asked.

Aidan rolled his eyes. "I can't get rid of the wee skitter, so he's mine now, I guess." He tossed him a treat which the dog took gratefully before moving onto me, begging for pets. I obliged.

"His name's Hero," Aidan said.

"Hello, Hero," I said, scratching him behind his ears.

The dog's head nearly flipped upside down as he leaned into my scratches, loving every minute of it. I thought Seamus had told me that his brother lived on a boat, and I wondered how it was to sail with a dog. Hero looked like he could handle it, I supposed. There was no leash in sight, and he was being a very good boy.

Seamus stood and held up my hand to show Aidan my ring. His eyes went wide.

"Ye must still be employed back in London, then?" he said, grinning. "If ye can afford this feckin' rock."

I laughed at Aidan's endearing accent. I would never have imagined it possible, but it was even thicker than his brother's. I almost couldn't understand him if I didn't listen closely enough. I smiled as they exchanged their *Norn Iron* tones that I had learned were somewhat unique to the McCarthy family. To Saoirse's sons.

Seamus shrugged. "I got it at the bottom of the ocean, believe it or not."

"I knew I should've gone with ye to Hy-Brasil," Aidan said, laughing and shaking his head. "Picking up diamonds from the ocean floor to give to a beautiful selkie bride doesn't sound so bad."

I blushed, absently twisting the ring around my finger.

"Well we're here," Seamus said after a moment, gesturing around us. "Shall we?"

We looked down to pay our respects to the stone at our feet.

Saoirse McCarthy had nothing but a simple, elegant black slab of granite with her name. There was no birth year. Just her death. The mystery of her age, still unsolved.

Aidan laid a bouquet of flowers down, and I realized with embarrassment that we had nothing to leave. Looking at my opposite hand, I saw the ring I bought in Galway. I had been wearing it the first time Seamus touched my hand, igniting the ancient line of blood that destined me for him. It was the small, but elegant, triskelion ring that I no longer had a place for on my hand, given my engagement ring now occupied the finger on which I had originally worn it. I had shifted it from finger to finger, but to no avail. It didn't belong anywhere else. It had been my placeholder.

I gently knelt, ignoring the pain in my legs as I set the small ring on her grave. It was all I had, and I wanted her to know that her sacrifice had been worth something. That I was selfishly grateful—and would be every day for the rest of my life—that Seamus had been the one Atargatis chose not to spare.

Seamus placed his hand on my shoulder affectionately. I stood and looked up at both of the brothers, their red hair gleaming in the sun, and hoped that Saoirse felt us here. I hoped she knew how much I loved her son.

* * *

WE LEFT the cemetery with the brothers' arms slung around one another's shoulders while mine were laid across my chest in thoughtful contemplation. I felt a slight pang of guilt for never paying my respects to my own family's graves, and now I didn't know if I would ever get the chance again.

Aidan told us how he had been regularly visiting The Wormhole back on Inishmore since Seamus had left, and eventually Fintan had appeared with his message about us traveling to Portugal. He had finally returned the other day, telling Aidan that we'd be back in Belfast within the week. I laughed as he voiced the same opinion of Fintan that we all had—he was a great person, but damn, he talked too much.

"I thought I'd have a feckin' heart attack when he came out of the water," Aidan said, laughing. "Slipped away just as tourists were coming down…for a minute I wondered if I had imagined it."

We wandered back to the center of the city, and headed toward a coffee shop near The Linen Hall, a library that looked oddly familiar to me. I thought it might have been the one from my dreams of Seamus back when I was still human, but I couldn't imagine how my subconscious would have known what it looked like. I added it to the list of mysteries in my mind, filing it away as one that was relatively unimportant for now.

"Are ye alright?" Seamus asked me. "If your legs are hurting, we can go back to the water."

"I'm fine," I said, rubbing his arm. "I'd tell you, *a stór.*"

Just as we had with James, we sat near the window, the sunshine warming my face. My legs *did* ache, and it was a relief to sit down.

"Have ye talked to the professor?" Seamus asked his brother.

I had nearly forgotten about the significance of Liam Brennan aside from the stone he had provided us and suddenly felt guilty for it, knowing the fundamental role he had played in helping Seamus find me. Had he not been all the way back in Dublin, I would have suggested we go pay him a visit as well. Maybe when this was all over, we would get the chance.

Aidan nodded.

"I did, after I got back, I rang him in Dublin and he was fascinated of course," he said. "When I tell him *this*," he gestured to us. "I can't imagine what he'll say."

"He always thought my scar was strange," I said, taking a deep sip of my flat white coffee. I made a face, having forgotten that I no longer liked human food. It seemed alcohol was the only exception to the rule, which I found highly amusing. Atargatis must have liked a party in ancient Mesopotamia. "He was there when I first got it, as I'm sure he told you."

Aidan nodded and looked at the mark on my hand himself. I noticed that he took extra care not to touch it. Of course he was superstitious, seeing what had happened to Seamus once he had. But he didn't know about his mother's bargain with Atargatis. Not yet.

"Now, are ye gonna tell me where ye've been? And what's happened since I watched ye fall to yer death near the Arans?" he asked Seamus.

We told him an abbreviated version of our story, similarly to how we had filled in James. I waited with bated breath as Seamus mentioned The Santa Compaña, wondering if he'd omit the macabre part of the story from his brother's version.

He didn't.

Aidan didn't react initially beyond the slight widening of his eyes as he heard about demons, dead souls, and illicit potions that turned Seamus into a ghost. After Seamus finished the retelling, he looked out the window, as if he was afraid to see what his older brother's face would reveal. I wasn't as worried, sensing that I had a good read on who Aidan was as a person already.

"Ye did what ye had to do," the older brother said decidedly. "That's what a man does, Seamus."

His seal of approval seemed to do something for Seamus' guilty conscience and I was grateful for it.

"So it hurts ye to walk, Jasmine?" Aidan asked gently, glancing down at my legs. "Right now, are ye in pain?"

"Well…usually just in the direct sunlight, so no," I said, my heart warming as I heard his voice was full of concern. I was his family now, too.

"And ye think it's the ancient sea goddess," he said. "Come to tell ye that yer disobeying her by walking on land?"

I shrugged and laughed. Coming from his mouth–a human's–it sounded ridiculous.

"That reminds me," I said, looking at Seamus. "Do you want to…"

I didn't know if he wanted to spare Aidan the details or if he felt the need to tell him what had really happened to their brave mother, Saoirse. I thought the whole truth was important, but I'd respect Seamus' decision on the matter if he chose not to reveal it. To hear that a centuries-old prophecy damned his brother to a lifelong curse while he walked away a normal man…I didn't know how he'd take it. I didn't want Aidan to feel guilty for something he couldn't have controlled.

But again, Seamus told him everything. His older brother smiled at the conclusion of the story, much to my surprise.

"So she gave the bastards what they had coming in the end, aye?" he said.

Seamus grinned. "She did."

I knew they had both witnessed the many hardships their mother faced at the hands of their father when they were young. I could see the pride in their faces, acknowledging that their mother had been a fighter all her life.

"Well, I'm sorry ye had to be the one to endure this ancient curse when it was an even chance it could've been me," Aidan said, shrugging. "But I think ye fared well, all things considered." He winked at me.

Seamus gazed at my side profile and gently traced his finger along my forearm.

"Aye, I'd say so."

CHAPTER 40

CALM BEFORE THE STORM

I felt like as many loops that could be closed had been as we headed back toward the water.

We promised Aidan we'd see him again after we got back from Japan, and he insisted we get used to the idea of having a cell phone somewhere in London so he didn't have to rely on mysterious sightings at The Wormhole to hear of our whereabouts. I agreed, and we left feeling like it was a casual "see you later" rather than goodbye.

"I want one more evening with ye," Seamus said, taking my hands and coming to a halt in the street. "A normal one. If you're not in too much pain."

I did too. It was well into the late afternoon, and the sky was already darkening with the early sunset of winter in Northern Ireland.

"I'm fine," I said honestly. "Let's do it."

We ducked inside a cozy pub and it was a relief. Although I loved the posh dining scene of London, I felt that the relaxed atmosphere of a casual booth and a Guinness suited the two of us much better. Seamus leaned backward, taking a deep drink of his stout. He offered me a sip and I declined, opting for a glass of wine instead.

"Never liked it," I said, remembering how all three of my friends and I had struggled to keep the thick beers down on our first day in Dublin a few months ago. I thought of what he'd said about Irish whiskey in London and smiled. "Just another tourist thing we had to do."

"That's fair," he said, and then his eyes lit up with remembrance. "Ye know when James ran after your friend, the one with the glasses–"

"Marissa," I said, recalling how James had returned my purse that I had left upstairs at the Guinness Factory. A gesture that had then prompted him to approach us later in the afternoon. I remembered being so jarred by the fact that I had done something so mindless, and it had been because the first signs of my selkie transformation had already begun to appear.

Seamus nodded. "He told me he slipped his number in the pocket."

I tossed my head back and laughed. "I didn't notice. Was it for me?"

"Aye, I'm sure he hoped it would be ye that found it," he said, laughing. "But it was probably for whoever would take the bait, I guess."

"I bet it was for Kristen," I said, remembering the flirtation that had occurred between my tallest friend and Seamus' shortest. But then my face fell. "I wonder if he's said anything to her since he's seen us."

"I hope so," Seamus said seriously. "He might make her see…reason."

Reason, meaning mercy. To forgive me for lying to her and disappearing twice in the same year.

My smile faded, and I knew Seamus wanted to bring it back.

"I'm glad ye didn't find it, in any case," he said. "I would've had no choice but to trade phones with him if ye did."

"Please, like I ever would have texted him," I said, grinning as I teased him. "I actually almost didn't text *you* back, you know."

He raised an amused eyebrow. "Is that right? Wished ye had given me a fake number, did ye?"

"Nah," I said, dropping my pretense. "I was glad you asked."

"Ye know I couldn't read ye at all," he said, his sage eyes meeting mine. "That first night, I had no idea what ye thought of me."

He wanted me to tell him. As much as I *thought* about the intoxicating pull Seamus had on me, I never said much about it to him. I was terrible with my words when it came to expressing emotions, which was why I tried to concentrate on my suspected telepathic connection with him through the stones. I could never bring myself to *say* anything properly, so I hoped Atargatis would tell him for me.

But I saw the curiosity burning in his eyes, and I tried to remember what I *had* thought the first time I noticed him. At Jameson, I thought the obvious. He was extremely attractive. But then when I talked to him later that night, I realized he was so much more.

"I kept smelling you," I said at last. "When you were leaning over me. And I still do that often."

He smiled. *Tell me more.*

So I tried my best. I wanted him to know that he had been on my mind incessantly since the moment I met him. I wished I could find the words to tell him that I had wanted him in every way the very first time he touched my hand.

"I noticed right away that you conversed the way *men* do. Not boys," I began, recalling how he had kept eye contact with me for so long and asked me real, substantive questions about my life. The way Matt had always done, and rarely anyone else. "And you just seemed so interested in what I had to say."

"How could I not be interested?" he said. "Given everything about ye."

I turned red. "No, we're talking about *you*."

He laughed and took another sip of his beer, a combination of amusement and appreciation coloring his face. He knew I wasn't great at this.

I continued. "I remember wanting to know everything about you right away. Your life, your interests, where you grew up," I said. "I still do. With everything that's happened, I still have so much to learn about you, Seamus McCarthy."

"I'll tell ye anything ye'd like," he said, shrugging.

I tapped my chin thoughtfully. "Alright. When's your birthday?"

He roared with laughter. "*That's* what ye want to know?"

"It seems like something I should!" I said seriously, remembering the constellations from Artur's study and how I hadn't had a clue which one was his. "If I'm to be your *wife,* that is."

He bit his lip and shook his head in what I determined was appreciative disbelief, surveying me across the table.

"Christ, I can't believe a woman like ye is marrying me," he said quietly, reaching for my hand as he ran his finger across my ring. "Alright, my birthday is the first of August."

He was a Leo. *That* certainly made sense. Physical, mental, and emotional fortitude. Strength. Bravery. And of course, a healthy twinge of jealousy. All of the traits I saw in him.

"So after I met you...you had just turned..." I began tentatively.

He grinned. "Thirty, a stór."

I breathed a sigh of relief. Of course if he had been younger than me, it truthfully wouldn't have changed anything. But it was nice to know he wasn't. I knew *he* wouldn't have given a shit if there was an age difference of any kind.

"And your birthday is when?" he asked me.

"The seventeenth of January," I said. "I'll be twenty-nine next year."

He sat back in his chair. "Good. So I have some time to think of a grand enough gift for ye," he said. "At least another few months."

"I think you're off the hook for presents for a while," I said, glancing down at my ring.

We were silent for a minute before I spoke again, my bravery for speaking my feelings aloud mounting. There was no reason to be shy around him.

"I feel like even now, our time together seems so…precious," I said quietly, not knowing the next time we'd get to be alone in a pub–talking about nonsense–when we had so much responsibility on our shoulders. "Back then, during those few days in Ireland with you, I felt like it slipped away from us so fast."

"That's why I had to go after ye," he said. "I wasn't done."

"Me either," I said. "If nothing had happened to me, that day at the Cliffs…what would we have done?"

I knew it was pointless to ask, because we couldn't change the past, but I was curious. We'd never known a normal cadence of dating–I met him three months ago and already had an engagement ring on my finger–but I felt like even if we hadn't been catapulted into our supernatural existence, we still would have moved with lightning speed. I had sensed it right away, and I wanted to hear him say he had, too.

"I would've brought ye back to London with me," he said simply, setting his glass down with a shrug. "Whether ye liked it or not."

"Is that right?" I said with a raised eyebrow.

A rush of something I couldn't explain fluttered through my chest. He was moderately joking, of course, but the way he spoke about me, like *having* me was non-negotiable…it was a manner in which I'd never been treated. I was surprised to find that my highly independent self rather liked it.

No, I *loved* it.

"But it sounds like that was never going to happen," I said. "Given Atargatis' prophecy of our union."

"It's not so romantic when ye say it like that, Jasmine," he said with a smirk. "Like an ancient curse is chaining ye to me."

I looked up at him from beneath my eyelashes. "I wouldn't mind if it was."

"Mmm," he said, studying me as he slid a hand under the table and on top of my thigh. "I can't say I would, either."

"Yeah?" I provoked as I leaned toward him across the table, uncrossing my legs. "You'd want to see me chained against my will?"

"I'd do it myself," he said seriously, his hand now between my legs.

I smiled and leaned back in my chair, crossing them again.

He let out an incredulous laugh. "Ye love to tease."

"I do not!" I exclaimed, laughing heartily.

I genuinely couldn't recall a single time I hadn't let him have me, because I always wanted him, too. So I said that aloud, forcing him to provide me with an example.

"That night in Galway," he said, dropping his voice. "I wanted to take ye back to my room so badly, to just–"

He paused, apparently not wanting to say anything vulgar. I thought about that night, remembering the first time I had felt the fire that now constantly blazed between us.

"But...it wasn't right," he finished with a dismissive wave. "Not then."

"Oh," I said.

"I meant because of your loyalty to your fiancé," he clarified. "I could see that ye weren't ready to be with someone else. And I didn't want ye to regret it–to regret being with me."

I softened. I had cried a single tear about Matt that night. I'd tried to cover it up, but he had noticed.

Matt. Seamus never said his name. He always called him by his title, maybe to keep him at a distance.

"I wasn't," I said, acknowledging that I *still* felt guilty at times. Even with a ring on my finger.

"I'm jealous of the man sometimes," Seamus said with a sigh. "Immature as it is."

I coughed and shook my head. "You don't need to be."

"Aye, I know that, but I can't help it when I see your face when he's mentioned," he said. "Like he was the only one ye'll ever really love."

"That's not true," I said lamely, now knowing how to properly tell him that he held my entire soul in his hands. It felt *wrong* to say it out loud, like it was a private thought that needed to remain buried deep within my mind. The sentiment was my own, secret disloyalty to my late fiancé. Once spoken aloud, it would become real.

But Matt was dead, and Seamus was not. He saw my loss for words and rushed to his next sentence, not wanting me to feel obligated to respond.

"But I understand," he said.

"Do you?" I asked, shifting in my seat. I had sort of asked back in London, but now I *had* to know. What if Seamus had been engaged once? Or even married? How would I *know*? I'd certainly never asked. I was sure he'd at least been in love at some point in his life. "I mean, have you ever had...?"

"No," he said in firm dismissal. "I've had girlfriends, but no one serious like what you're asking. My last relationship was over well before I met ye."

I seemed to recall Kiana relaying that information to me in Ireland, but I had too much pride to inquire too thoroughly back then.

"It was not highly romantic, purely physical," he continued. "And over by my choice, I'll add."

Purely physical.

I wished I hadn't asked. Picturing him—*my* Seamus—servicing another woman. Someone else, someone that wasn't *me*, saying his name like it was *hers* to say. And him groaning an Irish curse word into *her* ear as he–

I pushed it from my mind as best I could. There was no use in hurting my own feelings.

"*That* makes *me* jealous," I said finally, shaking my head as I took a sip of wine.

"Does it?" he asked, genuinely surprised. "I didn't expect ye to say that, with your confidence. Sorry, I—"

"No, it's fine. I'm the one who asked," I said, grinning. "But if you're possessive, then I'm...territorial."

"Ye think I'm *possessive?*" he laughed. "Christ, I don't think I like the sound of that."

"Are you not? Because a ring like this would suggest you are." I held up the blue diamond, the massive stone glinting even in the dim light of the pub.

"Well look at ye," he said, gesturing to me. "I can't let ye walk—or swim—around without other men knowing you're claimed."

Claimed. If most modern women heard him say that...shit, if *I* heard someone other than *him* say it, I'd let them have a piece of my mind. But I knew Seamus' intentions, and I knew he respected me. No, he *revered* me. As he'd proven countless times. I clucked my tongue in sarcastic disapproval as a smug grin broke out across his face. I would have thought it to be Elias-adjacent in nature if I didn't love him so much.

"That's the literal definition of being possessive," I said, smiling despite myself.

He shrugged. "Aye, then I guess I am."

"I don't mind it," I whispered.

"Good."

We left not long afterward, taking our time as we made our way back to the shore. It was nearly dark, so I had no worries about being seen while we jumped into a bay that no one in their right minds would consider submerging themselves in at this time of year. Or any other time of year, for that matter. I was also not in any rush.

We decided to walk to Holywood Sea Park, a tiny inlet of sand that was directly across the bay from Carrickfergus. The night was positively freezing, but the selkie blood kept the pain of the biting cold to a minimum.

"Should we go?" I asked.

"Not yet," he said, pulling me into him.

We both fell softly onto the beach–which was a generous term for the patch of sand–not caring how terribly wet and uncomfortable it was. We'd both be submerged in water and become half-fish within the next few minutes, anyway.

"Mmm," he said, sniffing my wrist. "This smell."

"What's it smell like to you?"

"Flowers, I guess," he said. "I remember it from my dreams of ye. Back when I was looking for Hy-Brasil."

I smiled hearing he had dreamt of me. "I had dreams about you, too."

"What were yours like?" he asked, his hand brushing my hair behind my ear.

"A mixture of things," I said vaguely. There was a part of me that liked to keep *those* memories to myself. After all, a good amount of them were speculations regarding how it would be to love him. "And yours?"

"There was one where ye were a sea demon," he said, smiling and kissing my wrist. I shuddered slightly and understood how the vile Demonio could have found his mouth on her own to be sensual in a way, considering how his teeth gently scraped mine now. "And ye kept changing back and forth from that to the version of ye that I know."

"Which version did you like better?" I asked teasingly.

"The one where I can have ye," he said softly.

He pressed me onto my back with one hand, undoing his belt with the other.

PART VII

FIGHTER

CHAPTER 41

AN ACT OF WAR

eeling significantly warmer and more content, I slid into the water and transformed easily, Seamus following behind. We descended below the surface and lazily swam across the bay, the magical veil that covered Carrickfergus seeming to melt away before us as it became a real, breathing dwelling for merfolk rather than the murky dungeons of an ancient landmark.

"There they are," sang Aisling as we approached. She and Fintan were lounging in the center of the grand hall of mirrors, maps strewn about as they made final preparations. My mother was busying herself in the corner with seaweed organization.

"Artur said if we can get to Atlântida by mid-morning, that's fine," Aisling said. "There's a Green Window directly to Tokyo."

I looked at the map she was studying and I shook my head. No, I didn't think the stone would be near there. I tapped the Iridescent Ammonite absently. It would be a small island. I knew it. I ran my finger along the Sea of Japan…no, nothing in there…

I continued off the southern coast instead. Aogashima jumped out at me, but my mother beat me to it.

"Yes," I said in confirmation as her finger landed on the tiny volcanic island. "Near there, at least."

I looked down at the ammonite and it was glowing. The pink Thulite I had embedded into my cuff was doing the same, and I pressed my thumb to it. It popped out and into my hand.

"Here," I said, handing it to Aine. "String this around your neck and keep it."

My mother nodded.

"How do ye know?" Fintan asked, shaking his head in disbelief. "Ye can just feel it?"

"Yes," my mother and I responded at the same time. I smiled at her. I didn't really know how we knew at all, but I just had a gut feeling it would be near there. And I knew now that it was wise to listen to my instincts.

"Tokyo's still the closest we'll get," Aisling said decisively. "We'll leave for Atlântida at dawn in this case. We've got a bit of a swim."

"Well…"I began, and deferred to Seamus who swiftly took the lead. I was grateful for it.

"We'll need to split up," he said firmly. "I go with Jasmine to Japan, and the rest of ye start on the stones in the Middle East. It's the best way to cover more ground."

I thought my mother would protest, but to my surprise, she was nodding in agreement.

"That's for the best," she said. "I have my guesses on the other three, and once we get to Atlântida, we can discuss with Artur on the best way to go about it."

"Sounds good," I said. Aisling and Fintan, whether they agreed with it or not, didn't argue with our plan.

"Where's Niamh?" I asked Aisling, recalling that her mother— my aunt—was supposed to have returned from Hy-Brasil earlier in the afternoon. I thought for sure she'd be here already. "She should have been back by now?"

Aisling frowned. "I dunno, she is running behind…" She

flitted toward the archways as if she planned to go out looking for her and I moved to join, but my mother pulled me aside.

"I don't want you and Seamus apart again," she said seriously. "No matter what, Jasmine, the two of you need to stick together. Given what you know now, I think that's when your connection to Atargatis is strongest. Promise me."

"I know," I said. I looked over at him, talking in low tones with Fintan, and knew we'd never leave each other's sides again if we could help it. The prophecy was—in my opinion—just another reason among many. "I promise."

We all said goodnight to one another in preparation of the early morning, Aisling still worriedly awaiting Niamh. I felt extremely uneasy about it as well, but I couldn't stay awake any longer.

"She'll be here," my mother said reassuringly to Aisling. "Get some rest."

It was impossible for me to sleep. My dreams were riddled with disturbing images of my mother and father being torn away from one another by sea serpents that morphed into images of Cearbhall and Camila, followed by more scenes of Matt bleeding to death. The culmination of the nightmares was a scene of Camila dragging Raj into the ocean with her claws, and I couldn't take it anymore.

I rolled off the marble where Seamus and I had been resting, longing for the soft sheets of Atlântida. *Why* did no merpeople besides Artur understand comfort? I'd have to discuss alternative furniture arrangements for Carrickfergus if we planned to keep a permanent residence here...

"Jasmine, are ye alright?" Seamus asked sleepily. "Ye've been rolling around for hours."

"Sorry," I whispered. "I didn't mean to wake you."

"I can't sleep, either," he said. "Do ye–"

Just then, a loud crashing noise rang through the entire dungeon and we both sat up in alarm.

"What the–" I said, whirling around.

Despite our being tucked away as deeply as possible in the labyrinth of rooms within the sunken dungeons, I could hear that the rest of the castle had been awakened by the noise as well. I heard Fintan's voice talking to someone urgently, and Seamus and I both shot out of the room light lighting and into the main hall.

A woman, who had to be Aisling's mother, Niamh, was in the center of the hall with Fintan, panting heavily. She didn't look physically hurt, but she was wildly distraught.

"Mother!" Aisling cried, flying to her side as she emerged from behind one of the other arches. "What happened?"

She sputtered, Aisling catching her arm as she looked around at us. If my own mother and I looked alike, the similarities between Aisling and hers were positively striking. Had it not been for a faint streak of silver in Niamh's hair, they could have been sisters. The woman looked around at us and was breathing heavily. Her eyes landed on Seamus.

"Are ye Seamus, Aidan's brother?" she cried. "Ye must be."

Seamus' face went white, and my stomach dropped at the mention of Aidan.

"What's happened?" he asked.

The woman choked out a few breaths.

"I–I came back through the window from Hy-Brasil, and I was going to come straight here," she said, steadying herself. "But a great big dog started swimming toward me, right into the middle of the bay, barking its head off in the night…he was out so far in the ocean that I didn't know what it meant. But as I swam toward him, I knew he wanted me to follow him."

Hero, I thought. Aidan's *dog?*

My own mother then emerged into the hall, her eyes wide with alarm as she flew to her sister's side. She didn't interrupt.

"So I followed the dog, and he led me to a boat in the marina just as I saw Cearbhall dragging someone into the water. I couldn't get there fast enough, and the dog went on ahead of me. I heard Cearbhall say Aidan's name as he struggled, and I saw the name of the boat was Saoirse…of course I knew who it had to be." She nodded toward my mother, who clearly had filled her in on the tale of Seamus' heritage.

"Where?" Seamus said urgently. "Where has he taken him?"

"North," she said breathlessly. "The Cave of Dunseverick."

I looked at her blankly, having never heard of such a place. Seamus looked like he was about to speak, but Niamh continued.

"Near Giant's Causeway!" she exclaimed, relaying it in human terms for our sake. "There's a cave, underneath the ruins of Dunseverick Castle. It's another place the Amalgams meet outside of Hy-Brasil, but it's terribly dangerous. The laws of time don't apply within it."

"What do you mean?" I asked shakily.

"I mean ye could be down there for ages…and above the surface, no time would have passed at all," she said. "It's how they keep their prisoners locked away without arousing suspicion. Torturing them for years without anyone knowing."

My heart nearly stopped. Aidan could be down there for years, and somehow we'd never know? I couldn't understand it, and yet, I knew we had no time to waste. I had always known that the cave in Hy-Brasil wasn't the only evil lair of the Amalgams. No, they needed to have another, more secluded meeting place for their doings.

"I need to go right now," Seamus said severely.

We drained the remaining stores of the pink seaweed, and I felt my body charging like a battery the second it slid down my throat. Aisling and Niamh tore off to send word to Artur regarding what had happened. Fintan and Aine were to come with us, but stay out of sight unless we needed them. I knew Cearbhall and Camila wouldn't be willing to negotiate with anyone but Seamus and me.

My mother led us to the late Oisin's massive armory, but we

wasted no time marveling at the impressive selection. Seamus tossed me a dagger that I tucked away into my golden cuff, noting it was much heavier and ancient than those Artur had provided us before our trip to Norway. It seemed to glow at my touch, and I wondered what kind of hidden magical qualities it possessed.

"Jasmine..." Seamus began, but I shook my head curtly. I knew he wanted me to stay out of danger, but I told him what my mother had said about Atargatis helping us when we were together. He didn't like it, but he didn't argue.

Seamus and I flew along the coast ahead of the others, wanting to get the most out of the magical plant that sent us shooting through the bitter cold waters of Northern Ireland. I had discovered that we were faster near the surface than in the depths, so we skimmed just below the waves like iridescent rockets.

The tranquil beauty and rolling, lazy green hills of the Antrim Coast was a stark contrast to the petrifying fear and urgency that pounded in my chest. Seamus' face was white the entire way, him barely saying a word. I couldn't imagine the guilt he felt. I couldn't let myself picture anything other than a successful rescue.

We passed what Seamus told me were the ruins of Kinbane Castle, and he glanced ahead.

"We're close," he said.

I nodded and watched as the inlet that humans knew as Dunseverick Castle rose in front of us. Just past the site of Cearbhall and Camila's evil lair was Giant's Causeway, and I shuddered to think of all the innocent, oblivious tourists snapping photos at the landmark. They were all entirely unaware of the horrors taking place in the ocean just below...

The inlet of two towering cliffs topped in the signature green grass of the beautiful country was entirely empty, and the sky above us was turning gray in the light of early morning. I heard a distant crack of thunder, and knew there would be no sun today. The rock formation rose like a trap on either side of us, and I wondered where the entrance would be.

Seamus reached for my hand and pulled me beneath the water before I could ask, as if he instinctively knew where to go. As if he could sense his brother's heart pounding in fear.

We descended to the floor and immediately I saw a mist that was similar to both the veil of Hy-Brasil and the mysterious isle in Norway. It shimmered in the black water where the sand should have sloped upward toward the shore, instead indicating a severe drop off that I knew was invisible to the human eye.

I touched my stone on my chest, asking Atargatis for protection, prompting Seamus to tap his own. We reached toward the mist and both of our hands went through the barrier, sending a shockwave of freezing cold water down our arms. This was it.

"Let's go," Seamus said, dragging me behind him as we shot straight down into the lair of the Amalgams.

CHAPTER 42

IRREVERSIBLE DAMAGE

"Ah, the arrival of the brother at last," Cearbhall said from the darkness.

He turned to face us, his wicked grin revealing his sharp teeth that looked more like fangs every time I saw him.

The cave was much smaller than the one on Hy-Brasil, and to my relief, Cearbhall seemed to be alone. The rock walls rose around us like an exact replica of those above the surface, and I glanced above our heads to find there was what looked like a dark blue, ominous skylight that extended to a galaxy beyond our own—as if the hole in the ocean floor through which we had descended didn't exist at all.

Silver streaks of what I knew to be selkie blood coated the walls, and behind Cearbhall was a dark black, iron throne. He wore one of the stones of Atargatis on his chest–the green Tsavorite of Manza Bay. The first one I had ever seen.

"The Iridescent Ammonite of Iberia," he whispered, slinking toward me and marveling at the gem on my chest. "How disappointed I was to find that it had been taken right out from under me. I must say, wearing stolen jewelry does not become you, Jasmine."

He reached a finger toward me, but Seamus swept in front of me. I thought he'd go right for Cearbhall's throat, but he restrained himself. He wouldn't use force just yet. Not when Aidan's life was at stake.

"Where's my brother?"

Cearbhall's gaze flickered to him, and he snapped his fingers.

A bright, sapphire light shot down from the skylight opening above and directly upon a floating cage that had the same magical mist surrounding it that appeared to be keeping the prisoner dry. The sleeping (or knocked out) figure of Aidan was slack against the bars while sharks circled around it menacingly, waiting for permission to descend. Seamus made a move toward Aidan, but as he did so, the bars of the cage holding him lit up a bright, violent red.

"I would be patient, if I were you," Cearbhall said. "Until you hear the terms of the deal I'll make with you."

I looked at Aidan's chest and saw it rising and falling. He was asleep, and under some sort of spell, but he *was* alive. Cearbhall swam back and forth, enjoying playing with us.

"You know, I was so intrigued, when I finally awoke in the cave… after you knocked me out, that is," he continued, clucking his tongue disapprovingly at Seamus. "I had heard rumors about the human man that descended into the sea for the Heir…and I was admittedly very impressed."

Seamus said nothing, his face turned to stone. I could see his fingers itching to reach for the blade that was tucked into his cuff.

"I knew you were *hers*," Cearbhall continued, pointing to me. "But *I* wanted to know more about *you*."

The way his eyes raked Seamus disgusted me. I had to speak.

"Let Aidan go," I said. "He has nothing to do with this."

"But he has everything to do with it," Cearbhall said softly.

I shifted uneasily. What did he mean by that?

"Do you remember when I told you it would be a terrible

waste to change for a man?" he said to me. I recalled him making the comment in the cave when I had begged him to show me the way back to my old life. A request I had been a *fool* to think he could grant. "Now that I see him, I think I may have been wrong."

"Enough," Seamus said before I could express the same. "Name your price for Aidan's life."

Cearbhall cackled. "You know my price," he said. "The stones."

"Never," we replied at the same time.

"Then you take his place," Cearbhall said to Seamus. "With the power of the stones, *I* can decide which of the sons is to be spared and which is to suffer the curse."

I froze. He knew about Saoirse's bargain with Atargatis.

"You're lying," I said quickly. "You don't have the power to do that. Atargatis *chose* Seamus."

But even as I said it, I doubted my own words regarding the specifics of the prophecy. *Had* my mother ever explicitly said that it was destined to be Seamus? Did it truly matter—to anyone besides me—which brother suffered the curse?

Neither of us spoke as Cearbhall tapped the Tsavorite on his chest and nodded to my own gem. "You can die in Aidan's place while *he* lives under the sea. To exchange one brother for the other...it does nothing to violate the agreement your poor mother made with the goddess."

But it would destroy me, and that was his goal.

I glanced at Seamus. His face was as lifeless as it had been under the influence of the Nuvem Morte. I was terrified, because I knew it meant he was considering the deal.

"Seamus," I hissed.

He finally turned to look at me, his beautiful green eyes full of resignation that I couldn't accept. I shook my head gravely.

There has to be another way, I thought as loudly as I could. I know he heard me.

"Too much of a coward? Too selfish?" Cearbhall questioned. "I expected more from you."

Before either of us could respond, another person entered the cave.

"Maybe we can arrange another deal," came a voice from behind us. It was the voice that filled my very soul with hatred. "You don't know all of your options yet, after all."

I didn't need to turn to know it was Camila, the evil sea demon returned to torture us both. Her red lips were grinning with satisfaction, and the bright blue Larimar of the Antilles glinted on her chest. She spotted Seamus, and ran a disgustingly long fingernail down his black scar from the demon as she passed us.

"I only got a quick glance at you in Portugal," she said, eyes shining wickedly in the sapphire light. "I owe you a thank you… for *saving* me."

I made a move to lunge at her, but Seamus caught my arm. Had it not been for Aidan, I would have gone for her throat once more.

"She has a temper," Camila said to Seamus. "Are you sure you'd want to spend the rest of your life with a woman like that?"

Her eyes fell on my ring finger.

"A blue diamond," she said, circling behind me. My entire body went rigid as it took all of my self control to refrain from lashing out. "Incredibly rare. It's a shame to see it on someone so…ordinary."

Seamus gripped my waist and pulled me closer to him, the dagger now in his other hand.

"Name your terms," he said.

"As you wish," she replied.

Camila grinned cruelly at me and snapped her fingers, revealing another beam of sapphire light on the opposite side of the throne where a second prisoner lay, sleeping in the same type of cage as Aidan. My heart thundered and Seamus' arm went slack against mine as we realized who it was.

Kiana.

Just as my mind was attempting to process *how* she could have known about her, *how* Camila of all people could have tracked down my best friend that lived across the world, my question was answered.

Elias slithered out from behind the cages, his onyx tail gleaming in the light.

Of course. I had told him. Back in Atlântida, I had been stupid enough to tell him all about her.

"AND ANYWAY, my best friend wasn't even there. She lives in Washington D.C., not Tampa. And she's the one that I owe the strongest apology to."

And then I had said her name, telling him how we had gotten into a fight on the Cliffs and it was my biggest regret.

It was my fault. I had led him right to her.

"YOU," I whispered venomously. "After we let you go."

Seamus closed his eyes and I felt him seething. He had Elias' life in his hands and spared him back in Norway. If only he had dragged the blade across his throat, we could have prevented this.

Elias didn't meet my gaze, but swept to Camila's side as she ran her fingers through his hair. She kissed him deeply on the mouth and I cringed. To my dismay, Cearbhall then did the exact same thing. Of course, Elias was working with them—or *for* them as some sort of pet, I couldn't tell. Either way, I had no one to blame but myself for what I had enabled the traitor to do. I cursed my stupidity.

"I'm so glad you chose to confide in Elias," Camila said to me as she watched Cearbhall rub Elias' shoulders. "Telling him all of your *secrets* really made this easier for us."

She must have seen something flash in Seamus' eyes, because she cackled maliciously and narrowed in on him.

"Oh, you didn't know about their relationship while you were away?" Camila asked, now circling Seamus with her eyebrows raised in amusement. The scar across her face gleamed in the darkness. "How she cried to him because she missed her friends and her old life–"

"I did *not*," I spat.

Camila ignored me, and spoke directly into Seamus' ear.

"Elias told me how her blood pounded for him when they were alone," she whispered. "And how if you had been gone any longer, she would have *begged* Elias to take her to his bed."

I didn't need to look to know Seamus was seeing red. He would have reached for her throat, but we were outnumbered, and Aidan and Kiana's lives were in our hands. I was sure he saw through her lies, but I also knew he had been taken aback by the familiarity in which Elias had spoken to me before his betrayal. I stared at Elias with daggers now, but his expression was blank. He wouldn't look at me.

"Enough," I said. "We came to make a deal."

"We've already offered you our deal. Two of them actually," Camila said. "The stones for your friends…or you take their places."

I looked at Seamus, but he didn't turn to me.

"Just me," he said to them. "Not her."

"Seamus," I warned.

Camila chuckled.

"How admirable," she said, surveying Seamus with interest. "But unfortunately, you're not very valuable to us on your own. We need The Heir."

I touched the stone on my throat, praying my mother could feel our urgent need for backup. But even if she came…I glanced at the prisoners' cages, having no idea what kind of magic they contained.

There was a crack of thunder overhead that seemed to reverberate all the way to the ocean floor.

"Well?" Cearbhall said lazily from behind Elias. "We have other matters to attend to."

Another crack of thunder. A pounding noise.

Someone trying to break through something. A barrier.

All of us looked upward to find the source of the noise, and I watched Camila's eyes go wide in fear.

"What the—"

There was a thunderous boom and the nebulous ceiling above us suddenly shattered, sending a shower of blue sparks throughout the chamber. We all covered our heads as we were thrust backward against the walls of the cave, Camila shrieking as she went. The bars on Kiana and Aidan's cages quivered and seared bright white before returning to their menacing red glow.

Seamus and I took advantage of the momentary distraction and fled to our respective prisoners, but as soon as we got to them, we froze. One mistake could flood their cages and cut off their oxygen supply, and we could never get to the surface in time. I tentatively pressed my hand to the barrier, reaching for Kiana beyond.

"Don't even bother," Cearbhall shouted across the cave as he regained his balance, clutching his chest. "It's–"

I never found out what *it* was, because at that moment, the source of the noise was finally revealed. From the now broken barrier above us descended a monstrous beast of dark blue scales and bright, pink eyes that pierced the cave with a nearly blinding light. It opened its mouth and breathed violet fire, and I realized that it hadn't been thunder I'd heard in the sky.

It was Otima.

Seamus, of course, did not realize what this meant for us having never met the creature down in Atlântida, but he saw my relief as the massive tail whipped across the room, sending Camila and Elias flat against the wall. Camila hit the rock and a small, silver stream began to emit from the back of her head which made her hiss and lunge for the monster's eye.

"Is this like the others?" Seamus yelled, having seen how Selma had yielded to me.

"She's even better," I called back.

Cearbhall made a move toward us, but the monster saw him, too. Otima turned her head and breathed her fiery substance–that I now realized was similar to volcanic lava–which thrust him back against the wall. At the same time, the beast's claw had a firm grip on Camila's throat and she was sputtering in pain. Once he regained his strength, Cearbhall flew to her aid, attempting to pull her free from Otima's grasp.

But where was–

I turned and saw Elias was coming up behind Seamus, who was again bent over Aidan's cage as he tried to test the limitations of the fragile barrier by reaching inside of it. I yelled to warn him and he turned, drawing his blade, but Elias dodged it. He swept in front of Seamus and brought his own blade down swiftly, cutting through the red iron bars like it was nothing more than a stalk of bamboo. The mist around the cages vibrated and buzzed like a cloud of angry bees, but Aidan still appeared dry within the center.

Seamus and I looked at Elias incredulously and back at each other before another blast of lava from the monster shot directly past us. I turned around to find Camila and Cearbhall now both clawing at the monster's eyes, unconcerned with us for the time being.

"Go!" Elias hissed at Seamus, who now held Aidan's limp body in his arms. "The mist lingers for only a few moments after the cage is broken, and then he'll be out of air!"

Seamus looked at me, but Elias had already done the same for Kiana, and she was free. The cloudy mist around her face looked like a cracking fishbowl, and I prayed that Elias' definition of "a few moments" was longer than mine.

We took off toward the exit, flying through the shattered ceiling of the cave and dodging the sparks that were still raining down from above. They were like tiny stars from a broken sky; searing my skin each time one of them caught me. I glanced back down at Otima who seemed to have been stabbed in one of her eyes by Camila. I cringed slightly, but I knew the serpent would beat them. Seamus reached for my hand as we sped straight up, desperately searching for the way out.

Through the sparks, I saw the faint outline of the opening to the world–the human world–directly above me. Seamus shot through it, one arm clutching Aidan's body, and his other hand firmly on my wrist.

"I don't think so," said Camila from below.

I gasped in surprise as I realized she had me by the tail. She pulled me back downward, my wrist slipping right from Seamus' grasp. She snapped her fingers, and I heard a faint rumble that I knew signaled her ordering the closure of the cave once more. The opening was narrowing–I wouldn't be able to get through.

"*Jasmine!*" shouted Seamus, turning back for me.

But it was too late.

The exit closed with a sharp snap of force that sent Kiana and I both backwards as she slipped out of my hands. Elias rushed to grab her, looking at me in alarm.

"NO!" I shouted as the barrier separated me from Seamus. From our escape. From my friend's only possibility of living.

Kiana's eyes flew open, and the bubble of oxygen vanished immediately. She let out what would have been a scream of terror if she could produce such a noise underwater as she took in the scene around her, her wild brown hair tangled around her face. Water flooded her lungs and she began to choke.

"Watch her die first," Camila said from behind me. "And then your lover is next."

Elias held onto her as Kiana thrashed about, her eyes wide with the helpless fear of someone who knows they're going to die.

"Jasmine–" Elias said severely.

"I'm sorry," I sobbed to Kiana, desperation descending upon me as I realized there was nothing I could do. "I'm so sorry!"

Kiana's face was white as she met my eyes–perhaps she already thought she was dead. After all, she was staring at me, the sea demon version of her friend that had fallen to her death from the Cliffs of Moher. She looked at me in dismay, her body jolting madly.

"Jasmine–she's out of air," Elias warned, his voice cracking. I didn't have time to contemplate his double agent status; I just hoped his charity would last a single moment longer. I hoped he knew of another exit.

"Please, Elias!" I begged him. "Get her out!"

Kiana started convulsing as her lungs reached their limit.

I was watching her organs shut down before my eyes. I had to save her. I'd do anything.

Elias looked around wildly, and I knew without him saying so that there was no other way out. Camila cackled behind me maniacally, her own endeavors to kill me momentarily on hold as she gleefully witnessed my agony.

Kiana's body shook in what looked like its final surge of life, and my breath caught in my chest. *I* had been the one that dragged her to this fate, and I could do nothing to save her. After all the wrong I had already done to her during my human life, I had now killed her in my next life, too.

"I–I'm going to do it," Elias said shakily as he looked upon my dying friend he held in his arms, her eyes pleading with him to help her. "Jasmine…tell me it's okay if I do it."

"What?" I shouted. And my eyes went wide as I understood what he meant. "NO!"

Before I could stop him, Elias took one of his fingers and dragged a nail down Kiana's arm, leaving a streak of silver that looked exactly like my own. It dripped ruby red human blood for a moment.

Just one moment.

And then it seared silver, a blinding light emitting from the mark as it sealed, marking her as an Amalgam forever.

"Elias," I cried, but I had no time to fight with him. Camila was upon me within seconds.

"Enough!" she screeched, lunging for me. I dodged her, but only just. I looked at Elias.

He was frozen, apparently dumbfounded at what he had done, staring at Kiana's limp body that he still cradled. As I had been forcibly yanked out of the water when I was marked by an Amalgam, I had no idea what would happen to someone that stayed in the water. Would her change be instantaneous? Painful? What was going to *happen?*

Camila then took a swipe at me, and I dodged her clawed fingers. My shock vanished and was replaced by the reminder that she was the more pressing of the two matters. I'd deal with Kiana in a minute.

I grabbed Camila by the hair with ferocity that I knew surprised her and started to wrestle, knowing my best bet was to get her against the wall. Otima was battling with Cearbhall below who had struck her in the neck. My stomach flipped when I saw she had a deep wound that was oozing into the water, dying it violet.

I successfully pinned Camila against the wall, but she had her hands around my throat. Her grip was like iron, and I felt myself losing the ability to breathe. Stars were in front of my eyes. I heard a roar from below and I prayed it was one of victory and not defeat from the sea serpent.

"You could have worked with us," she said. "I told Cearbhall you were too stupid, too vain, but he would have let you."

I dug my nails into her forearms and she loosened slightly in pain, a silver stream running from her left arm.

"I'd never work with you," I spat, slipping from her grasp.

"You think this is about good and evil," she said, dodging me as I lunged for her again. "But you don't realize what the power of the stones could give *you*."

"I don't want the power of the stones," I said. "I'm not like you."

I knew it was risky, but I went for it, even as she caught me by the throat again. I reached out my hand and in one swift motion, ripped the Larimar of the Antilles right off her neck as she held me against the wall. Her eyes went red with fury and I knew she wanted to reciprocate by taking mine, but she never got the chance.

Otima roared once more and shot up toward me, a burst of lava from her throat sending Camila directly into a sharp, jagged rock against the cave's wall where she hit her head with a sickening crunch. I watched as the evil woman's body fluttered to the ocean floor, landing next to Cearbhall who was already knocked out cold.

I latched onto the water serpent's tail as she blasted the cave open with another flaming blow, revealing the hole in the ocean floor above once more.

Elias was right behind us, dragging Kiana to the surface like a rag doll.

CHAPTER 43

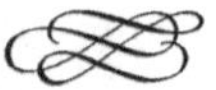

REDEMPTION

*B*ecause of the laws of timelessness within the cave, Seamus was right there on the other side of the opening. I gasped as I saw him, reaching for him like my life depended on it.

He dragged me out and pulled me up by the waist with one arm, immediately shooting up to the surface. Elias had a firm grip on Kiana and pulled her up with him, her scar now healed and looking exactly like my own. In Seamus' other arm was a motionless Aidan.

"I got ye," Seamus said, kissing the side of my head as he sped through the water. "I got ye." He continuously repeated it for his own reassurance more than my own, I was sure of it. His grip on me was iron.

"Aidan," I said shakily, eyeing what looked eerily like a corpse.

Seamus shook his head.

"I dunno," he said, and then his eyes went blank with mindless fear. "How *long* were ye down there, Jasmine?" His voice shook as he was undoubtedly terrified to hear the answer.

"Don't worry," I promised. "No more than minutes."

His shoulders sank with relief as he realized I hadn't been fighting Cearbhall and Camila for an eternity.

"Thank Christ," he said.

We reached the shore of the tiny inlet and I let Seamus go ahead of me, dragging Aidan up onto the sand. Elias transformed but remained in the shallows with Kiana, hovering above her as he stared at her with a grave face. I waited anxiously, uncertain of how—or if—I could help either of them.

Otima lurked in the shadows like a watchful protector, presumably monitoring our wellbeing before she descended back into the depths of the sea. Her wound had healed itself, and aside from a few minor scratches, the great beast seemed to be fine. I nodded at her gratefully, and she understood me.

Kiana was almost entirely still, aside from a faint fluttering of her chest that indicated she was alive, but barely. Seamus glanced between her and Elias before his eyes went wide with realization as he saw the silver streak that now ran the length of her arm.

"Ye fucking bastard!" he shouted. Had it not been for Aidan, he would have knocked Elias out on the spot. "What the *hell* were ye—"

"No, no!" I shouted. "Seamus, it was the only way. She was dying."

He looked at me wildly, but saw the sincerity in my eyes and nodded, trusting my judgment. He turned back to his brother, knowing there were more important matters to attend to. In addition to having been underwater far longer than a human could possibly hold their breath, Aidan had a deep gash on his neck that was bleeding heavily. Seamus was covering it with his palm, but all three of us knew it was fruitless. The wound looked fatal.

"Seamus..." I said, reaching for his hand. He looked down at his brother's face and his shoulders began to shake with fear.

"No, no," he whispered, bending over Aidan's body. "We haven't had enough *time*."

I had never seen Seamus break. He was the strongest person I'd ever met. But now, as he watched his brother who had gone to the ends of the earth with him take his final breaths...I thought he'd shatter in front of me.

Elias looked up.

"Jasmine, you remember the Nova Vida?" he called to me urgently.

"Yes," I said, knowing what he was getting at, but it was useless. "We'll never make it there in time. And Aidan's a human. He can't go through the Green Windows."

"No no no," Elias continued, shooting to his feet. "Duberdicus grants these healing waters to select locations all over the world and there's one here! In Belfast, I swear."

Seamus' gaze snapped up to Elias like a hawk, regarding him with anything besides hatred since the day he met him.

"LoughLeagh, Lake of Healing," Seamus said quickly. "Are ye saying that's-"

"Yes, it's Lough *Neagh*," Elias said. "The *eedjit*-as your people would call him-got the name of the lake wrong when he wrote the original story. Made it seem like a fairytale. But I promise, Lake Neagh is the one."

I had no idea what they were talking about, but I sensed the hopeful urgency. My tail had melted away at last, so I stood and faced Elias while Seamus looked up at him from the ground, deciding whether or not to give him one last chance with his trust. He didn't deserve it...but Aidan was dying either way.

"Man, that's a thirty minute drive at least," Seamus said at last, shaking his head as he stared into the distance and then back down at Aidan's bloodied neck. "He won't make it."

Otima let out a loud screech from behind us, and we all turned to face her.

I looked at Seamus.

"Do ye think she can...?" he said. I didn't dare hope.

But apparently she could. Otima lumbered out of the water,

her massive frame pounding large prints into the shore as she bowed to us, inviting us to join her. She stretched out her wings that I had admired under the sea, showing us that she was well equipped to assist.

She was going to fly us there.

"Go," urged Elias. "I have to wait for her to change. It's better for her if we stay in the water until it's done."

I could see my best friend's chest heaving now, but her eyes remained shut and she shivered like she was fighting a severe illness. I, too, remembered being slightly cold when I had been marked as a child…but the blood of Atargatis ran through my veins. I bit my lip as I wondered what kind of pain *she* was in.

"I've got her," Elias promised, looking directly at me with the aquamarine eyes that had lied to me so many times already. I tried my best to determine if the trace of sincerity I saw now was worth believing. But I didn't have a choice. Aidan's clock was ticking.

Seamus hoisted me and his brother up on top of the beast and I put pressure on Aidan's wound. Otima took a running start and in no time, we were in flight.

We shot over Belfast and past the highways that spiraled out of the city, buildings flashing past us in blurs of colors that were reminiscent of the Green Windows. Aidan let out a loud groan that made Seamus tense, but I took it as a good sign. It meant he was still alive. He was fighting.

It was now midday. Artur had told me that Otima was invisible to humans, and I had to believe it, considering not a single person in Northern Ireland seemed at all puzzled by the sapphire dragon streaking across the sky. The wind whipped my face as we shot across the country, the green and gray flying below us.

"What are we *doing?*" I asked Seamus finally once we were well in the air. "The lake of healing?"

He sighed as neither of us much felt like telling stories, but we also knew there was nothing we could do besides trust that Otima was flying as fast as she could.

"Don't tell me there's a bit of Irish mythology that *ye* don't know?" he said humorlessly. I met his gaze with the same lack of amusement.

"According to the legend, LoughLeagh was situated in County Meath, Ireland–" he began.

"We're in County Antrim," I interjected before I could stop myself. I was anxious, and I often interrupted people when I was nervous–something Raj had told me not to do at least a thousand times.

"*Christ*, woman, it's not the time for your smarts," Seamus said, shaking his head. "I know that, but that's what I'm getting at. Elias says that the actual lake is here. Lough *Neagh.*"

I nodded. "Go on."

"It was believed that the waters of the lake had magical abilities to heal those who bathed in them," he said. "People would travel from around the world seeking relief from illnesses by immersing themselves in the lake."

"Like the Nova Vida," I said, beginning to believe it.

"Right," he said. "It's retold a hundred different ways, of course, but ye get the idea. So Elias is saying Duberdicus granted this lake as one of the locations where he feeds the healing waters."

"Why here?" I asked curiously.

"I dunno," he said. "All that matters is it works, aye?"

I saw the lake emerge below us. It was a grayish black, plain massive body of water that simply did not look magical at all. Seamus nudged Otima's side, and she began to descend. We touched down upon the shore and I leapt off the dragon, prepared to rush into the water. Seamus lifted Aidan quickly and put his foot out in front of me to stop me.

"In the tales, the man becomes a healer because he outsmarts the guardian of the lake. He completes the trials given to him," he said seriously. "I have to go alone, a stór."

I wanted to question him, but I didn't. There was no time for this to be done incorrectly or not according to legend.

Seamus kissed me fiercely one time before descending into the lake with his motionless brother in his arms. He transformed instantly and melted beneath the surface as I stood on the shore, praying that they'd come out victorious.

I had to believe he would. He always did.

CHAPTER 44

THE LAKE OF HEALING

"Hold your breath, brother," Seamus said to Aidan's unresponsive frame.

Christ, this better work.

The water was feckin' freezing and he shivered, even with the warmth of his selkie blood pulsing through his veins.

He opened his eyes below the surface to find there was near nothingness, just as he remembered it from childhood. He had been to the lake many times, and in fact, this was where Aidan himself had taught him to swim. He had done so by way of throwing Seamus headfirst into the depths. At the time he had been livid, but he was grateful for it now. He knew these waters, and they knew him.

"Aidan," Seamus said absently, speaking to himself more than his brother. "Hang on, I got ye."

He knew instinctively that he'd have to go to the very center, just like Jasmine had done in Norway. He'd have to go down to the bottom where the black, healing mud would be, assuming the legends were true. He sped as quickly as he could, praying Aidan could hold his breath just a bit longer.

"What have we *here*?" came a slick voice from the darkness.

418

Seamus' lamplight eyes adjusted immediately.

He whirled around, his brother's limp body now floating at his side. He reached quickly to cover the gaping wound, but it seemed the bleeding had subsided already with the healing properties of the water. Or at least that's what he hoped. He was grateful the guardian of the lake revealed himself so quickly. He needed to get this over as fast as possible.

"I've come for the healing mud," Seamus said. "It's urgent."

The voice then appeared at his side in the form of a strange water nymph. A pointed nose, and an eye for trickery.

"Are you here to *become* the healer of the lake?" it asked.

"Yes."

He smirked. "Well, you must answer my riddle–"

Seamus had reached the end of his patience for the feckin' riddles.

"I don't have time for games!" he shouted into the mist. He was so damn tired of this. Exhausted with the legends and mythology that haunted him at every turn. He would choke this melter out before he would waste another second of Aidan's time.

"A temper, I see," said the nymph, swimming around Seamus' head. "If you agree to pay me a debt, if and when I should call, I will show you to the healing mud."

"No," Seamus replied immediately. He knew anyone who agreed to a deal like that never fared well. Jasmine might have learned her legends through books, but *he* had grown up in a country where the fairytales *happened*, for Christ's sake.

Seamus had tried to count the seconds he was underwater in the back of his mind to keep track of Aidan's breath, but it was useless. He felt his brother starting to choke.

The wily being didn't like his response, and it clucked his tongue at Seamus.

"Pity," it said. "How I–"

The nymph then glanced down at Seamus' scar on his arm

and reeled backwards at the sight of the mark. The black streak of Demonio glinted in the dark water with a horrific, metallic glare.

"The mark of a *demon*," he hissed, meeting Seamus' eyes. "You bring curses to my blessed waters!"

Seamus glanced at his scar. He saw his opportunity and swam with it.

"Aye, and I'll drag ye with me into the pits of Hell unless you show me where the healing mud is," he replied.

The nymph trembled, pointing to a small circle at the bottom of the lake. It was surrounded by a whirling pool that would surely send anyone flying backwards should they try to break through it, but the nymph snapped its fingers and brought the tornado to a halt.

Seamus wasted no time, darting straight to it while clutching Aidan's arm. He took the largest handful he could grab and flew to the surface, not looking back at the nymph as it called after him.

"Leave my waters and never return, Devil!"

Seamus couldn't help but laugh with bitter irony that the scar of the demon that almost killed him was likely going to save his brother's life.

But he needed to hurry. There was no use in healing a man who couldn't breathe.

He broke through the surface of the lake, taking care to hold onto as much of the mud as possible as he took it out of the water. Dragging Aidan to the surface, he sped back to the shore and thrust his brother upon the sand where Jasmine was waiting for them, anxious tears streaming down her face.

"Oh, Aidan," she whispered, cradling his head as Seamus smeared the black mud over every inch of his brother's wounds. The one on his neck first, then the arm...the chest. He hadn't noticed the number of gashes from Cearbhall's claws before, and he realized Aidan must have put up a hell of a fight. Of course he had.

Seamus prayed to every god he could think of, begging for forgiveness for everything he had ever done. He and Aidan had wasted so much time. They had spent so many years harboring resentment toward one another for things that didn't matter at all. For things that Aidan had done for Seamus' own sake. He had just barely reconciled with his older brother during their search for Hy-Brasil, and since then, had still thought of all the things he needed to say to him.

Seamus needed him to live.

"Ye tossed me in this lake once, and I swam...I swam out," Seamus said, willing himself to stay calm as the magic worked. "I need ye to do the same for me. Can ye do that, Aidan?"

He waited and looked up at Jasmine. Her face had gone white as she shook her head ever so slightly in the way one does when they think an outcome is inevitable. Seamus watched the hope drain from her beautiful, tragic gaze as she reached for his hand.

Aidan was motionless. He wasn't breathing.

"No," Seamus whispered. "No..."

He would not accept it. He couldn't have failed. This was the simplest of tasks he'd had to complete.

How could *this* be what finally beat him? His failure to move quickly enough? *Time?*

"Seamus..." Jasmine whispered, but her voice was far away.

He could still taste the blood of Demonio...he remembered the Virgin Mary, looking down upon him with shame as he slit the throat of what he had been told was an innocent human. Was this his reckoning? Was this how he was to pay for his sins?

And then something was happening.

As if a light were emerging from the gray clouds that hung over Belfast, there was hope again.

Aidan was stirring. He was coughing. He was–

Jasmine laughed incredulously, gripping Seamus' hand and

running the other down Aidan's muddied face with disbelief. She looked up, tears of a different kind now falling down her face. Seamus stared down at the gasping figure of his brother, back from the dead.

It seemed God had forgiven him. At least for now.

"What the FECK just happened!" Aidan exclaimed, sitting up suddenly while rubbing the mud out of his eyes. "Why am I covered in this shite?"

He looked at Jasmine and Seamus, their eyes both shining, and Seamus pulled him into a crushing embrace.

"You–you were captured by the Amalgams," Jasmine said, her voice cracking. "We thought you were dead, but the healing lake…it worked."

Aidan seemed to be gathering his senses as he recalled his memory from the past few hours since his imprisonment. He looked at Seamus, the shadow of remembrance crossing his face as he spoke.

"The bastard with the shiny eyes got me in the middle of the night," he said faintly. "Hero bit the man, but it wasn't enough."

"Aye well, the wee skitter still led us to ye," Seamus said, thinking gratefully of the fluffy dog's valiant effort in getting Niamh's attention. "He swam out to the damn near middle of the ocean for ye."

Aidan laughed. "That's my boy."

"Can you walk?" Jasmine asked, her eyes on his legs. "We should get back. Kiana–"

"Kiana?" Aidan asked, remembering the name from their days of seeking Hy-Brasil and tracking down legends. He tried to connect the dots. "Yer friend? What's she doing here?"

Jasmine looked at Seamus and bit her lip.

"She's…hopefully alright," Jasmine said, her cryptic response doing nothing to answer his question, and she knew it. "But we don't really know."

Aidan fell backward into the sand on his elbows.

"I appreciate ye saving me," he said earnestly, patting his brother's arm.

And then he said something that both Jasmine and Seamus could hardly disagree with, given the events of the past few months.

"But being associated with ye two is a feckin' curse, so it is."

CHAPTER 45

RECONCILIATION

Otima woke up from her patient nap on the shore of the lake to fly us back to Dunseverick, but we all agreed it was best to travel further down the coast. We had no idea when Cearbhall and Camila would come to, and where they'd go once they did. Would they emerge on the surface right near where we had? Or was there another exit through which they would flee?

"Look," I said, pointing to the water below as I nudged Seamus.

Elias clearly had the same idea as us, because we could see his black tail whipping across the coastline from the sky as we approached. My heart skipped a beat as I saw another shiny black tail next to him. *Kiana's.*

We followed them from above as they streaked past Giant's Causeway and Dunluce Castle's ruins. They finally slowed down at a small inlet with striking cliffs and rocks that Seamus told me was called The Wishing Arch. We swept down and found that thanks to the bitter weather, there was no one there but us.

Seamus helped me down from Otima's back and I stroked the dragon-serpent's neck gratefully. She touched her snout affectionately to the stone on my chest, and I connected the dots that my pressing of the Iridescent Ammonite down in the cave had been what summoned her aid. I laughed incredulously at the beautiful magic, hoping it would work again should I need her in the future.

Despite her punishment of me on land in the sunlight, I truly believed Otima's aid was a gift from Atargatis. My mother's words rang in my ear:

'*She is* good, *Jasmine.*'

The dragon smiled and returned to lounging in the corner of the inlet. I wondered if she would descend into the sea or take flight back to the coast of Iberia before returning to Atlântida, but she waited as if she knew her job wasn't over. I supposed–glancing at Aidan who had no way of getting home–it probably wasn't.

Kiana saw me from the water, and my breath caught in my chest as we locked eyes.

I dropped Seamus' hand and sprinted as fast as I could, my legs vanishing and turning to my silvery green tail once more as I crashed across the cold waves.

And then she was in my arms, my best friend since childhood, sobbing into my shoulder. She was cursed, and damned to be the worst version of the creature she could be, but she was *alive.*

"Jasmine," she cried. "I'm so sorry I stopped looking for you, I knew all along, I–"

"It's okay," I said, backing away to look at her.

She was even more stunning as a mermaid; her dark skin and hair were gleaming even in the cloudy gray skies of Northern Ireland. Her tail was like Elias'–a fearsome onyx with flecks of pink and orange, and her eyes were already starting to develop the signature hue of the seas that lurked below the surface of her familiar brown irises. Again, in true Scandinavian mermaid fashion, hers had undertones of blue rather than the green that was present in mine. I thought for a moment about Elias and Kiana being *connected* in any way and felt horribly guilty, but there was nothing to be done about it now. I was just grateful to be speaking to her. Her bracelets that she never took off were clanking as she shook my shoulders with relief.

"It's me who's sorry," I said, finally choking out my words. "I never got to apologize to you, for what I said–"

She waved her hand dismissively.

"Shit, I don't care about that at all," she said. "I forgave you right after you said it."

"I love you," I said, crying again as I pulled her in for another embrace. To hear her say those words–words I didn't deserve–allowed me to exhale the deepest breath of relief I had in months.

Everything was going to be different from now on, but Kiana forgave me. It was going to be alright.

"Is that what I think it is?" she then gasped, pulling away as she reached for my left hand. Her eyes went wide as she laid them upon the rare diamond that sat on my fourth finger. It looked even more beautiful as the waves gently washed over it.

"It is," I smiled.

"My God..." she said, marveling at the gem. "Tell me everything."

I never divulged the intimate details of my romantic life to my friends. It had been something I'd always been so afraid to do in the past, but now I knew that time was precious. Here she was, my best friend, caring about *me* after everything that had happened. I didn't deserve it.

"There will be time later," I said. I paused briefly before deciding to add one detail. "You wouldn't believe the things he's done for me. I really love him."

She looked up at me, and, knowing how rare it was for me to speak in this way, had more tears brimming in the corners of her eyes. They were silver, as I knew they would be, but it still took me by surprise to see them on her face.

"Oh, Jasmine, I'm so happy for you," she said sincerely. I knew what else she wanted to say before she even spoke the words. "And…Matt. He's happy for you, too."

"I know."

I had to believe he was.

We towed our way toward the shore together, and I wondered how much Elias had already told her on their way here.

"Do you know–" I began awkwardly as the others were all now standing on the sand. I hated to be the one to tell her, but it needed to be done.

She nodded.

"Yeah, he told me that I can't change back into a *land-walker*," she said, her eyes flickering momentarily with sadness. "But I'm *alive*, Jasmine, and that's all that matters."

She propped herself up on one of the low rocks and the others gathered around us. I laughed as she marveled at her newfound upper body strength in the same way I had after I had first transformed.

I caught Seamus' eye and he winked, knowing how badly I had wanted this moment of reconciliation with my friend. I would never have guessed it would happen this way, but I was endlessly grateful for it. He hugged Kiana in the water and she looked at him with bright, excited eyes.

"We were right," she whispered. "*You* were right."

"Good to see ye again," Aidan grinned, looking down at Kiana and undoubtedly admiring her now supernatural beauty.

Kiana smiled back and reached her arms up for him. Aidan met her on his knees, his muddied clothes dropping into the water as he embraced her tightly. Elias glanced between them and me, plainly wondering what the nature of their relationship was. As the two of them pulled away from one another, I realized I didn't quite know. I glanced up at Seamus and he shrugged as Aidan's hand lingered on Kiana's back a bit longer than either of us had expected.

Aidan and Seamus then launched into a retelling of what had

happened at the lake while Kiana's eyes went wide in shock. I studied her side profile, still not believing what had happened.

Despite being relieved that she was breathing, I felt so much guilt, so much regret...I didn't want this life for her.

Elias saw me and crouched down on the rock next to me, now in his land-walker form.

"She was happy, you know," he said quietly. "When she woke up and realized what she had become."

I looked at him and remembered feeling similarly when I changed, but only after I had realized my physical strengths. And as soon as I remembered what I had left behind, I was miserable once more. All of the nights I had cried for my old life, wishing I could be with Seamus...what would I have felt if he *hadn't* come to find me? If I had truly said goodbye to him forever? Kiana didn't have a romantic interest back home as far as I knew, but it didn't mean she wasn't leaving other precious things behind. Friends, her family...her career. She had worked so hard in law school. I hung my head.

"Do you think it'll last?" I asked him quietly.

Elias sighed. "There's no way to tell, but when I told her you were alive and well, and happy with *him*," he nodded toward Seamus. "She was thrilled, Jasmine. She really was."

I watched my friend talk to the two brothers. As she laughed and clapped her hand to her mouth at the surprising parts of their story with her tail hanging lazily off the rock, it looked like she was already comfortable in her new skin. She always had been that way. She was a confident, resilient individual. It was one of the things I admired most about her, and why I had always wanted to be her friend. She inspired me to be strong.

"You owe me a lot of answers," I said to Elias, surveying him intently. I was still furious with him, but I realized there might be more to his betrayal than I thought. "But for now...thank you."

He laughed and nodded, eyes still on the others. "Oh, I know I'm no one's favorite in this camp," he said. "But I am sorry for what I did. I didn't ever want to hurt you. And I hope one day you'll believe me...when I have time to tell you everything."

I didn't know if I would. But looking at Kiana breathing and alive, with Cearbhall and Camila nowhere in sight, I thought I could one day.

"How'd you know that Lough Neagh was one of the healing lakes?" I asked him. "I didn't think you knew Irish mythology like that."

"I don't. But it was an ancient alliance between Duberdicus and Oisin," he said. "The lake is dangerous, and has plenty of tricks beneath it, but one who can master the guardian will emerge a victorious healer."

I thought of how Seamus had told me he handled the guardian of the lake and wondered how it was *supposed* to be done, had he not been marked with a demonic scar that terrified the water nymph.

"Of course, I had hoped he *wouldn't* be successful," Elias continued, gesturing to Seamus again, who had his arm around Aidan and was laughing with relief. "I was hoping the guardian would kill him instead, and you'd be left helpless and alone, with no choice but to cry in my arms."

"You're an ass."

Elias grinned.

"Nah, I knew he'd come back out," he said. "I had no doubt in my mind."

"Really?" I asked, surprised to hear him say something so flattering about the man he resented. "How'd you know?"

He smirked. "The main character in the original tale of LoughLeagh...the man's name was *Shemus*. Look it up next time you're near a library."

I laughed. Of course it was.

"Where will you go now?" I asked. "I mean, since Cearbhall and Camila realized you were a double agent."

He shook his head in dismay.

"I'll beg for Artur's forgiveness and ask him to return to Atlântida," he said. "But who knows what he'll say."

I smiled softly and nearly said, *'I'll put in a good word,'* but decided against it. I was still pissed at him.

Elias returned a smile that had the tiniest, almost untraceable hint of humility within it. Something I had never seen in his countenance, and probably never would again.

Seamus then came over to me, sweeping me up in his arms with his familiar, effortless strength. My tail remained intact, but I wanted it to. I didn't want Kiana to feel alone. He cradled me and kissed me deeply, my tail dripping sparks of silver into the water below. I reached up to touch his face that was streaked with the mud from the healing lake, his freckles curving into a smile of relief.

"I love you," I said.

"And I love ye back," he said, his bright green eyes staring directly into my soul as they always did. He kissed me once more before setting me down gently on the other rock next to Kiana. He finally turned and acknowledged Elias.

"Ye have sins to atone for, ye bastard," he said, looking down at him.

Kiana gripped my arm and I also tensed. I wasn't sure where this exchange would go.

Elias cocked his head toward Kiana and said, "I think I'm off to a good start," he replied.

"Ye brought Kiana into this danger and we won't forgive ye for that," Seamus said decisively, speaking for all of us. "But she is still alive because of ye–whatever change of heart ye had. And that's worth something."

Elias nodded in grave acknowledgement.

"Thank you," he said seriously. "For sparing me in Norway."

Seamus searched him, and I wondered what was going through his mind. I'd find out from Kiana eventually *who* had actually dragged her into the sea, but I knew that Elias had been the one to give up her location, either way. Even though he had saved her in the end, it was still his fault.

"Aye, well I did that for Jasmine, not ye," Seamus said carefully. "And I still don't feckin' like ye."

"Good," Elias said, his smug grin returning. "Because I don't like you, either."

Seamus let out a sigh of frustration and extended his hand toward Elias who took it, rising from the rock.

* * *

VICTORIOUS AS WE FELT, we also knew there were significant messes to clean up.

For one thing, Kiana was entering our company in the midst of war, and I had to explain everything to her. It would take hours, maybe even days, to bring her up to speed on the Amalgams and the stones. It actually hurt my head to think about it. She promised that she would be patient, learning as much as she could whenever we had the time to tell her.

Additionally, we had no idea how much the others back at Carrickfergus knew of what had happened. When no backup came to our rescue or even to inquire after what was taking us so long, I suspected something was wrong. Aine and Fintan had been nowhere to be found upon our emergence from the cave— something none of us had noticed in the wake of Aidan's injury. I was anxious to return.

But the first thing we needed to do was see Aidan safely home. Otima had so kindly stayed with us during our reunion, and I could see she was more than willing to do us one last favor.

"How about along the water?" I asked, but then glanced at Aidan nervously. "Unless it's too cold for you?"

I forgot that just because *we* were always comfortably warm didn't necessarily mean a human would be. After all, we were in Northern Ireland in the middle of the winter. I looked up at the sky, grateful for the gloom that had protected me from pain for most of the time I'd been above the waves.

"The healing mud's got some warming qualities to it, it seems," Aidan said, shrugging. "I'll come along."

So we took off across the coast once more, Aidan on the back of the giant beast that he couldn't see. I wondered what kind of a terrifying experience *that* would be, but he seemed enthralled. Even without a trace of the selkie blood within him, it seemed he was a true man of the sea. He laughed incredulously as the dark water flew below him, the invisible wings of Otima coasting along the wind.

We reached Belfast again where Elias parted ways with us.

"Is there a window to Portugal here?" I asked curiously.

"No," he said, aquamarine eyes on the horizon. "I'll be taking the long way. I need some time to think about what I'm going to say to Artur, you know?"

"I wish I could overhear *that* conversation," I muttered to Seamus as the Norwegian merman dove into the depths of the ocean.

Seamus clucked his tongue and shook his head.

A loud *ruff* resounded across the waves, and we saw a massive dog paddling furiously toward us. He swam right up to Aidan and Otima, where the two creatures licked and sniffed, apparently able to see one another quite clearly.

"Hero!" shouted Aidan, scratching him behind the ears. "That's a good boy!"

"That's a good dog," I agreed, grinning widely as he licked Aidan's filthy face, grateful that his owner–and primary food source–had returned.

Otima saw Aidan and Hero safely back to the marina while we followed, and Aidan climbed onto the boat that had the name *Saoirse* painted in bright navy letters on the back.

"Don't disappear forever, aye?" Aidan said to Seamus as he leaned over the boat to shake his hand.

"I'll be in Asia and the Middle East for a bit," Seamus replied. "But I'll be back. I'll send Fintan for ye again if ye'd like."

"Christ, I'd prefer ye didn't," Aidan said under his breath, and turned to me. "Keep my brother safe, and bring him back to land for a wedding, aye?"

"No promises," I said, winking.

He looked at Kiana, breaking into a wide grin.

"And ye," he said, gesturing to her tail that was peeking out of the water behind her. "If I had slim chances with ye before, I guess there's none now, is there?"

Her cheeks turned bright red.

The three of us then descended below the surface, taking off across the bay and weaving our way through the depths of Carrickfergus.

Nervousness began to return to our pounding chests as all of us feared what we would find in the castle. I knew something had gone wrong, I just prayed it wasn't as bad as my heart was telling me it was. I had just met my mother. To lose her again so soon… no, I couldn't think that way.

We approached the gate to find it had been blown open, and there were signs of battle all around us. I looked at Seamus in alarm. He pulled my hand through the entrance and we shot across the labyrinth of tunnels, winding and weaving until we reached the grand hall of mirrors where Fintan, Aisling, Niamh, and my mother were huddled, looking like they had just battled to defend the castle after being severely outnumbered. Silver streaks of blood littered the hall, but as far as I could tell, no one was seriously injured.

"Oh, thank *Manannán*," my mother exclaimed, flying to me and pulling me into a crushing embrace.

"What happened?" I asked, looking around at all of them.

They launched into a detailed retelling of the past few hours while we had been in the cave, and I didn't know whose story— ours or theirs—was worse.

The Amalgams, as we knew, had been growing their army in Hy-Brasil. They had been marking humans and dragging them into the sea to serve their cause, and apparently they now vastly outnumbered the regular selkies on the once peaceful island. Just after we left for Dunseverick, a regiment of them had come to take Carrickfergus, knowing that even if Seamus and I weren't there, there was a group of us mounting in number and seeking an alliance with Atlântida. The very first thing I looked for after realizing my mother was okay was—

"It's safe," she said, patting the pink stone on her chest. "They tried to take it but—"

"But she's a damn warrior," said Aisling proudly. "She wouldn't let them have it, no matter what."

I looked at her proudly, scanning her for serious wounds. A few scratches here and there, but she looked alright.

"How did ye get rid of them?" Seamus asked.

Aisling grinned. "Jasmine, ye remember the Ollphéist?"

How could I forget the terrifying sea monster that had spared me in this very hall only a few months ago? The sea serpent that was gifted to Oisin by Manannán mac Lir himself. The one that bowed to me, because I was Atargatis' Heir.

"But how?" I asked. "Who did it answer to?"

Aisling shrugged. "It must've recognized she was your blood, or maybe that my mam and I are Oisin's...either way, the beast scared them all off."

I beamed with appreciation for the river monster. I'd have to thank him with a touch of the claw the next time I saw him, which I hoped, come to think of it, wouldn't be soon. He seemed to only appear in times of severe danger.

"Mom," I said, moving aside to reveal Kiana, who had been nervously floating behind me, clearly not sure of her place in our world yet. "This is my best friend—"

"Kiana," my mother said, hugging her. "I've seen glimpses of you throughout Jasmine's life. Of course I know you."

Kiana smiled with radiant warmth as my mother kept her arm around her shoulders and looked upon her like she was already part of our family.

"How–?" she asked, gesturing to Kiana's tail.

I shook my head quickly. "Later."

Given the retelling of the Amalgam's attack on Carrickfergus, I didn't feel like drawing attention to Kiana's true nature immediately. I wanted her to meet Artur first, so she could see that some of the hybrid merpeople were good. I glanced down at my own scar, remembering I was one of them. Atargatis' Heir or not, I was marked. There had been a time, albeit brief, when I had been nothing more than a member of Cearbhall's cult.

"Oh, one more thing," I said brightly, and I turned the cuff on my wrist over to reveal the Larimar that was now deeply embedded into the golden bracelet.

"No way," Fintan whispered excitedly and everyone marveled around the discovery of the stone I had ripped from Camila's neck. I hadn't even had the chance to show Seamus in all of the chaos, and he grinned broadly before putting his hands on my shoulders and kissing me.

"There's nothing ye can't do," he said, shaking his head in admiration. "You're amazing, ye are."

We all agreed that the next course of action was to get to Atlântida as soon as possible. Artur would likely have a clue as to something that had happened, despite Niamh's inability to get to him during the siege of the castle. Surely the call of the Otima had not been lost on him. We were to set out first thing in the morning, after everyone had rested.

That night, I slept well. Until I didn't.

I WAS in another one of my familiar nightmares. I was in a dark cave, begging for Camila to spare someone.

"Please," I said desperately. "Open the exit!"

I assumed I was reliving the scene with Kiana before I realized with a jolt of horror that it wasn't her that was locked up in the cage ahead of me.

It was Matt.

Camila wrenched the bars open, dispersing the mist that had been held at bay. The cloud lingered around his face for a single moment before disappearing entirely, leaving him choking on the water that now filled his human lungs with poison. Elias looked at me, holding Matt from behind the way he had held Kiana.

"Jasmine…" he said nervously, his eyes darting between me and the love of my life. "Do I–"

I knew what he was asking me.

Camila rounded on me, her eyes bright with pure evil on either side of the massive scar that marked her face.

"Let him go!" I screeched.

She looked at me. "Should Elias change him?"

"What?" I cried desperately. "No!"

I didn't want him cursed. I couldn't bear the thought of subjecting someone so pure to this life of hardship. This life of darkness.

"You wouldn't change him, because you don't *want* him here with you," Camila said in a severe whisper. "It would ruin your new life with Seamus if he returned to your world…so you'd rather see him die."

"No I wouldn't!" I cried, the impossibility of two terrible choices weighing on my heart.

But Matt was dying…I couldn't bear it.

"JASMINE! Tell me now!" Elias cried as we both watched Matt's body convulse. "Do you want me to do it?"

"What if there were another choice?" Camila whispered, her voice laced with poison.

She snapped her fingers, and Matt and Elias stopped moving. Time was paused.

I froze. "What do you mean?"

She cackled, knowing she had my attention. But then Seamus appeared at my side, tugging on my arm.

"We have to go, a stór," he said. "Don't listen to her lies."

Camila stroked his cheek, tracing his freckles. Seamus looked at me but he didn't move. He wasn't quite frozen like Matt and Elias, but I felt very far away from him. Like Camila and I were watching him through a window.

"Oh, he's *terrified* you'll let Elias change Matt," Camila said, savoring his distress. "Because once they have to compete for you, he knows he won't win."

"Please," I said. I had refused to beg in real life, but now I couldn't help it. "Just let Matt go."

"When you let Seamus make love to you," she said softly. "Don't you feel guilty?"

I did. She knew I did.

"When it comes to their looks, it's certainly a tie," she said as she ran her hand through Seamus' auburn hair and down his sharp jawline. She then glanced at Matt's frozen, beautifully elegant features. "I see why you're so torn."

I let out a sob, having nothing else left within me. I had no resolve, no fight. Not here; in this torturous nightmare.

"They're so different from one another though, aren't they?" Camila continued, swimming behind Matt and placing her hands on his shoulders as she looked up at me. "It's as if you aren't quite sure what your type is."

"Stop," I whimpered pathetically.

"One, the valiant warrior of darkness who would do even worse than *die* for you," she said, nodding toward Seamus. "And the other…the golden lover boy whose heart is simply too big for someone as broken as you and your curses." She rubbed Matt's shoulders.

She spoke aloud my deepest insecurities. It was true.

My memories of Matt placed him on a pedestal for a reason.

Because it was *warranted.* He had been a shining light of positivity, and I had *always* questioned whether or not I deserved him. On my most honest days, I knew that he was better than me, because he was kind. He was *good.* Even before the trauma I had endured and the darkness it thrust upon me, I was neither of those things. Not really.

The sun didn't set around Matt, and I wondered how he never saw that I was the storm cloud in his sky.

And then there was Seamus who lit my very soul on fire. I'd seen him with knives to people's throats, blood dripping down his chest that was either his or someone else's, and had heard the sincerity in his voice as he said he'd kill for me. Matt had never shown these qualities, because he'd never *needed* to. There were no trials and tribulations in my life with him. It wasn't a fair comparison, and I knew it. But I couldn't silence the tiny voice in my head that told me I *needed* Seamus in a way I had never needed anyone.

He was the only person who really saw me for everything I was.

"You think you're the hero," Camila whispered to me. "But you have no honor. Not when it matters."

She then snapped her fingers and time resumed, Matt taking his final gulp of water before falling limp in Elias' arms.

And because of my indecision, he was dead.

CHAPTER 46

AN OLD FRIEND

I awoke the next morning much earlier than everyone else. I wandered to the great room, tracing my fingers along the mirrors while I looked at the reflection of myself within them. My nightmare still haunted me, and I thought it was the worst one I had had since becoming what I was. I wondered if they'd ever cease.

Kiana swam up behind me. It took me by surprise to see her metallic, black tail glinting in the faint light of the sun that streamed through the skylight above the dungeons.

"You alright?" she asked, speaking to my reflection.

I turned, smiling.

"I'm fine," I said. "I should be asking *you.*"

"I'm *great,*" she said, shrugging. "I mean, the seaweed actually tastes good."

"Surprising, right?" I said, taking a bite of the snack as she offered it to me. The Irish variety was still my favorite, despite all of the other strands I now knew were out there. I wondered what Japanese seaweed would taste like. Probably quite delicious, considering humans already ate it regularly.

"I'm sor–"

"Don't say it," she warned. "I mean it. Never apologize again."

I knew she was serious, because Kiana never said anything she didn't mean.

"I'm actually excited about looking for the stones," she said. "Aisling filled me in a bit last night. And it sounds like we're already a step ahead."

"That's true," I sighed. "But we'll still have to steal back the others, even when we find the last four."

"What do you think the Japanese stone will be?" she asked. "Jade?"

I shook my head.

"No, that's too obvious," I said quietly as I speculated while speaking, realizing I had no clue at all. "But then again, the Thulite *is* the national stone of Norway…"

"Ready?" came Fintan's voice from the archway that led to the other rooms. "I've got some extra seaweed if you'd like. Kiana, I think you're really going to like the purple kind. But also, wait until you try the one from Atlân–"

"Ready," Kiana interrupted loudly, speeding off to join him. I saw she had already learned how to hold a conversation with the most excitable member of the gang.

Niamh led the way to the best Green Window for our departure. She had lived in Belfast the longest, and knew more about the network than any of us.

"Beneath Strangford Lough," she said as we sped out of the castle's gates. "There's a Green Window to the Azores…from there we can find Atlântida relatively easily."

"Much better than the way we found it, aye?" Seamus said, elbowing me.

We reached the large inlet just around the bend that wound its way south of Belfast. I had never seen the body of water in person, but I knew it to be the Ollphéist's home, and said a quick thank you to him–wherever he was–before we descended to the bottom, finding a swirling whirlpool that looked just like The Wormhole had it been underwater. It was a bright, perfectly rectangular pool on the bottom of the green lake, and none of us hesitated to dive into it.

Whipping through the sea, we were spit out directly below the collection of Portuguese islands. Niamh then led us to the much more direct entrance to the underwater kingdom of Atlântida. It was the proper guest's entrance, I assumed, considering it didn't send us right into the basement that housed Artur's Room of Windows.

And *this* entrance was the one that ignited the stories everyone knew.

The spell Artur had placed around the city created a mirage of underwater pyramids that humans could surely see. They would not see, however, the vast network of towers that were hidden behind the magic, and I grinned broadly as we descended through the thin, blue mist and the world of color popped into sight below us. We were on top of the gleaming, ivory towered city, and I felt a wave of relief wash over me.

"Welcome," Artur said as we entered.

He pulled his son into an embrace and told him he was proud of his bravery while defending Carrickfergus, a statement that made the humble Fintan blush madly.

Then he turned to me and beamed.

"Jasmine," he said. "Otima came for you."

"She did," I smiled, tapping the stone on my chest. "Thank you."

I then showed him the stone I had taken from Camila. He led us inside the grand, gleaming halls of the palace and I smelled the familiar bright, floral scents of life that teemed in the place. Despite how lonely I had been during most of the time I spent in the city, I still loved it.

As we reached the main table where so much business had been discussed, I saw the backs of two people to us, one of them with gleaming, white blonde hair and the other with a long, dark brown ponytail.

My jaw nearly dropped as I realized who they were.

"Hello, Jasmine, long time no see."

It was Sorcha and Lachlan, and they both had wide grins for me.

Sorcha. I was so relieved to finally lay eyes upon her again. I hadn't seen her since I had been unknowingly kidnapped from Hy-Brasil by the Amalgams, and though I knew messages of my safety had been relayed to her, I found myself nearing tears as she looked upon me with pride. I embraced her tightly before introducing her to my mother who thanked her endlessly for taking care of me.

"And this must be Seamus," Sorcha said with a smirk, looking him up and down as she floated into his line of sight. "My son has told me of your bravery, and how ye went to the ends of the earth to find yer woman. It is admirable, to say the least."

Seamus grinned and put his arm around me.

"Aye, well she's a treasure worth finding," he said.

Sorcha winked at me as she glanced at my ring.

"I'm glad I was wrong," she whispered, and I knew what she meant. She had told me I wouldn't desire him the way I once had–physically or emotionally–once I became a selkie. But that was before either of us knew that Seamus was one of us. I squeezed his hand.

As was customary for him, Lachlan was quieter, but he expressed that he was proud of me in his own cautious manner. I had suspected back when I first met them that he and Sorcha told me the shallows were dangerous simply because they wanted to discourage me from going close to the shore and risking exposure, but Cearbhall had also once told me they were highly superstitious. I sensed, given Sorcha's wisdom, that perhaps it was Lachlan who feared the shallows. Perhaps he was much older than he looked.

I looked at Artur whose eyes were on Sorcha's side profile as she conversed with Niamh, who she obviously knew quite well. I knew about Artur's past with Sorcha, and I wondered what kind of conversation had led to this sudden, renewed alliance. It was a sign that war was here, that was certain.

"To business?" Artur said at last.

We gathered around the grand table, discussing what was to come. I sat on Seamus' lap, and Kiana across from us.

"The ningyo will empathize with our cause," Artur said. "The Japanese mermaids have always been on the side of preserving the stones' secrecy. Once you reveal who you are to them, they'll be willing to help."

I lit up at this positive news.

"But getting them to believe you could be challenging."

I raised an eyebrow.

"Can't she just touch one of the wee stones and they'll see it glow?" Seamus asked. "Is there any other proof aside from that?"

Artur shifted in his seat. "It's rumored that they already believe the Heir of Atargatis to be one of *them*," he said. "Amabie—there used to be many of them, but now he is the only one left."

"Who is he?" I asked.

"Amabie is somewhat of a prophet. The creature is similar to the ningyo, but looks more like a bird with a fish tail rather than half human-half fish. According to legend, he was seen as a glowing object in the water near Higo Province for many nights before he revealed himself and predicted a bountiful harvest for the small town. He emerges every now and then to make predictions, either good or bad, and he's never been wrong. Over the centuries, most of Asia has come to accept him as the Heir to the goddess of the sea."

"So we go find the melter and tell him who the real Heir is," Seamus said, shrugging.

"They might put you through some trials," Artur said to me. "But nothing you can't handle."

"*Christ*, it's always the trials," Seamus muttered under his breath and I let out a sigh.

I wondered if they would ever end, and I was highly insecure about what was to come. I knew a *ton* about European folklore thanks to Raj. But Asia...I knew almost nothing about Japanese legends. I could very easily see myself being outwitted by Amabie. I would need to prepare before we went.

I voiced this to everyone, having no shame in admitting there were things I simply didn't know.

"Not to worry," he assured me. "I have allies over there that will assist. Ambassadors on your behalf, let's say."

I didn't question him any further, knowing if he were confident in them, I would be too.

"So, we'll go after the Japanese stone, first, as discussed," Artur said, casting the map floating in front of us at the table. "And then onto the Middle East."

I repeated my plan that I had told the others back at Carrickfergus, mentioning that we needed to split up for the sake of covering more ground.

Artur raised an eyebrow at me. "Do you think that's wise?"

He wasn't challenging me, he was genuinely asking. The great leader was really looking to *me* for my opinion. I had always appreciated the trust he put in me, but now I felt that it was deserved. I had successfully stolen back one of the stones as well as summoned Otima, proving that I was harnessing my powers.

"Yes," I said firmly. "I say the rest of you set out for the Middle East since there are more to find there. I'll go alone with Seamus. At least to start. Once we get the Japanese stone, we'll come meet you."

Artur still looked uneasy.

"We have these," I reminded him, tapping the Iridescent Ammonite on my chest. "I'll leave the Larimar with you. I believe we *can* communicate through them. If we have faith, it works."

"Alright," he said at last. "But we need to prepare. Jasmine, I want you to study everything you can gather from my library here."

"How much time do we have?" I asked, now deferring to his judgment rather than my own.

Artur tapped his chin thoughtfully. "Let's take two full weeks."

I sank with relief. Preparation sounded nice. We hadn't given ourselves time for *that* in a while.

"But before we go, we need to procure more of the pink seaweed," he continued. "We'll have several long days of journeying ahead of us, even with The Green Windows."

I looked up in surprise. "The pink strand doesn't come from Atlântida?"

Fintan grinned, suppressing a laugh. "No, it's from a disgusting place."

"The Great Pacific Garbage Patch," said Aisling, her nose wrinkled in disgust. "In the North Pacific Ocean."

I looked around at everyone who wore matching expressions of horror at the mention of it. Mildly embarrassed that of course the most filthy part of the oceans was in *America*, I wondered if they thought I'd be the one to go get it. I hoped not.

"But, that should arrive by tomorrow," Artur said. "We have a shipment coming from someone very special."

"Who's that?" asked Niamh.

"Well, I had to find a way for him to prove his loyalty to the right side and see the error of his ways," Artur said. "So I sent Elias."

Seamus howled with laughter and I couldn't help but do the same.

CHAPTER 47

DREAMS REMEMBERED

*L*ater that night, Seamus came to find me in the courtyard where I was looking up at the moon. I could see it, even through the misty barrier that encompassed the beautiful palace. Otima was snoozing beneath the statue as always, and I watched her peacefully as her huge body rose and fell with the ocean's gentle breeze.

"A stór," Seamus said, settling in the sand in front of me and kissing the ring on my hand. "I was wondering where ye went."

"I just like it here," I said, gesturing to the general area.

He glanced at the sleeping dragon and laughed. "I wouldn't find this all too peaceful myself, but she answers to ye, not me," he said.

He sat next to me, and I put my head on his shoulder while he took my hands in his lap.

"I want to show ye something," he said. "To see if ye see what I see."

I knew where we were going, but my heart still pounded in my chest as we floated through the empty, quiet halls of the lower parts of the castle.

We entered the room, the small oasis we had come to love. He pulled me through the cloud of purple shimmer and I gripped his arm with both hands. There were no harsh memories in my way this time. Not even a semblance of them. The oasis must have known I was exhausted.

This time, the galaxy melted away and into a surprising scene. It was a small inlet, with a similar look to Nohoval Cove back in Southern Ireland, but on a much smaller scale. There were cows grazing lazily in the grass atop the cliffs that gently sloped down with a neat path that led right to the shore.

We made our way to land, Seamus picking me up as my tail took its time transforming. He looked down at me as he carried me, running a finger along my scales.

"Beautiful," he said, shaking his head in admiration. "Human or selkie."

I touched his cheek, examining every freckle on his handsome face. He was beautiful, too.

Once we reached the top of the path, there was a small cottage that had a piping fireplace and smelled like warm bread and stew. I knew we saw the same thing–I didn't need to ask.

"I loved London with ye," he said. "But I want something like this every now and then."

"Me too," I said truthfully. It was peaceful, serene, and entirely private. Knowing the possibilities that accompanied our magical existence, I didn't doubt that we could have both.

He led me inside the cabin and it was dark, but in a cozy rather than ominous way. He set me down as my tail vanished at last. That was when I realized that I recognized the small space.

"Seamus," I said suddenly. "I've been here before. In a dream."

He raised an eyebrow at me. "Ye have?"

I nodded. "Right when I transformed, and I didn't know what you were…" I said. "We were sitting here, right in front of this fireplace."

"I hope ye like the place as much as ye did then," he said, laughing. "If it was a good dream, at least."

I remembered what had happened in that dream. It was one where I had awoken feeling hollow, lonely, and positively on fire for him. We sat in front of the hearth now in the way I had back then, and I leaned into him.

"Are ye hungry?" he asked, gesturing vaguely toward the kitchen.

"Not really," I said. "Are you?"

His eyes twinkled with a look I knew well, and he leaned into me, taking my face in both of his hands.

"Starving," he said, and he kissed me like he was.

I kissed him back, my hands snaking up his stomach and onto his firm chest, feeling the familiar fire ignite inside me. It was the one that bound me to him; the one that made me crave him every second I was awake.

I rose up and unhooked my flimsy top, tossing it into a corner while he looked up at me. He ran one hand down my neck, breasts, and eventually settled on my waist.

"Christ," he said under his breath. "It never gets old."

"What?"

"Looking at ye."

I smirked and bent down to kiss him. He lifted me with ease and then lowered me back down as he pressed himself inside me, sending a shiver down my spine while I said his name into his ear. He sighed deeply, closing his eyes in ecstasy as I kissed his neck. Then he sat up, holding me with one arm as the other stroked my cheek.

As our lovemaking was often urgent and passionate, I found it a nice change of pace to move slowly and intentionally in front of the roaring fireplace just like we had that night before he left for Spain. It made me feel like we had more time than we had, and showed me a glimpse of what our life would be like for us once we had accomplished our mission….what it would be like on the other side of the dark storm. He kissed me tenderly, brushing his hands down my back as I shuddered into his shoulder, my hands in his hair.

Because he knew my mind, body, and soul like it was his own, Seamus sensed what I wanted next without me having to ask. He overpowered me and turned me on my back, giving himself to me as I sank into the rug beneath us. I saw the glinting black scar down his arm and touched it lightly, for no reason other than to remind him how much I appreciated what he had done for me. That it hadn't been in vain.

I let him own me against the floor, speaking directly into my ear with his seductive words laced with what would have been forbidden poison had we not been what we were to one another. I had never craved the sound of a man's voice like his.

I tried to push Camila's words from my dream out of my mind.
Don't you feel guilty? When you let Seamus make love to you?
I did, but…

"Do ye belong to me?" Seamus said into my hair, his familiar darkness rising to the surface. One of his hands was on my throat. It was gentle–not gripping in any way–but it was there.

"Yes," I said through a soft gasp. "I'm yours."

The current was dragging me out to sea as he kissed me behind my ear. I knew it was doing the same for him upon hearing my words. He wanted to hear me admit that I was gladly his own and no one else's. I felt him approaching the same wave as me, and we both let it pull us under at the same time.

"*Jasmine,*" he groaned, ensuring me that while I belonged to him, he was also mine.

* * *

I came down from the euphoria and let out a deep sigh. I rolled on my side and traced my finger along his chest as the warmth he radiated made me sleepy. We were quiet for a long time.

Seamus spoke first over the crackling embers.

"I know what's coming next won't be easy," he said. "But we'll be fine, a stór."

I smiled, closing my eyes as he played absently with my hair.

"But do you think it'll ever *really* end?" I asked. "Even after we find all the stones, and steal the others back…will that end the war?"

"It will," he said firmly. "And ye'll be the one to finish it…when the time comes."

"I don't know if I can," I said quietly.

I thought of the army of Amalgams, growing stronger in number every day. Would *I* be able to mobilize others across the world like they had?

Seamus smiled down at me, one hand cradling my head while the other traced my stomach.

"Ye don't have to do this alone," he said. "Ye forget how many of us you've already enlisted in the cause."

I thought of my family, Artur, and now Sorcha and Lachlan… maybe we did have a chance.

And of course, there was Seamus himself, who counted for at least ten warriors.

"I know," I said, the black scar reminding us both of the battles already fought. Then I grinned and teased, "But are you really going to slay our enemies one by one?"

He stared straight ahead this time, eyes blazing like the fire in front of us.

"Aye. I'll end them all."

ABOUT THE AUTHOR

A.G. Whitt is the author of the award-winning novel, *The Heir of Atargatis* and its sequel, *I Dream of Iberia.* She lives in Tampa, Florida, with her husband, Ryan, and their rescue Chow Chow, Hiroki. Follow her on social media for more updates on what's to come in the *Atargatis* series!